ALEX MARWOOD

AUTHOR OF THE EDGAR AWARD–WINNING
THE WICKED GIRLS

THE
DARKEST
SECRET

"THE DARKEST SECRET IS
ALEX MARWOOD'S BEST BOOK YET."
—LAURA LIPPMAN

A NOVEL

Alex Marwood is the pseudonym of a journalist who has worked extensively across the British press. Marwood lives in South London.

Praise for *The Darkest Secret*

"*The Darkest Secret* is Alex Marwood's best book yet—no small thing when one considers that her first two crime novels were both award winners. Her plots are always top-notch—deft, twisty—but it's the humanity she grants all her characters that makes her one of our best. This story will grip you to the final page, but Milly and her troubled family may never leave you."
—Laura Lippman, *New York Times* bestselling author of
The Most Dangerous Thing

"With the psychological acuity of Kate Atkinson and a dark wit all her own, Alex Marwood draws us into *The Darkest Secret* with utter narrative cunning, then surprises with its emotional wallop, its deeper resonances. In so doing, she demonstrates, without a doubt, that she is one of crime fiction's brightest stars. Not to be missed."
—Megan Abbott, author of *The Fever*

"At turns suspenseful, chilling and deeply, unexpectedly moving, *The Darkest Secret* is a true tour de force. Alex Marwood's richly detailed, heartbreakingly human characters will stay with you long after the book's shocking conclusion. I loved it."
—Alison Gaylin, bestselling author of *What Remains of Me*

"With *The Darkest Secret*, Alex Marwood has become one of my must-read crime writers. It's an amazingly gripping book, and the structure is a thing of beauty." —Sophie Hannah, *New York Times* bestselling author of *The Wrong Mother*

"Simply tremendous, so tense and packed with pathos. I loved every page of it." —Sarah Hilary, author of *Someone Else's Skin*

Praise for *The Killer Next Door*

"If you read Alex Marwood's *The Wicked Girls*, her new one—*The Killer Next Door*—is even better. Scary as hell. Great characters."
—Stephen King

"Chilling, suspenseful, and darkly comic, *The Killer Next Door* is not only a terrific crime novel, but also a fascinating exploration of memorable characters, each individually lonely and secretive, and yet inextricably tied to one another by circumstance."
—Alafair Burke, author of *All Day and a Night*

"This tightly plotted story that grabs you from the opening paragraphs and will keep you up far too late at night is highly recommended for fans of Laura Lippman, Tana French, and Gillian Flynn."

—*Library Journal* (starred review)

"Taut, assured and reminiscent of Ruth Rendell's psychological novels, Marwood's second book more than lives up to the promise shown in her splendid debut, *The Wicked Girls*." —*The Guardian*

Praise for *The Wicked Girls*

"The suspense keeps the pages flying, but what sets this one apart is the palpable sense of onrushing doom."

—Stephen King, "The Best Books I Read This Year," *Entertainment Weekly*

"Harrowing... while the received wisdom on violence committed by children seems to be that 'some people just are born evil,' Marwood makes a strong case that these crimes are more likely rooted in poverty, abuse and parental abandonment."

—Marilyn Stasio, *The New York Times Book Review*

"In addition to being an excellent intelligent dark thriller in the vein of Gillian Flynn, *The Wicked Girls* presents an intriguing insider's account of salacious British tabloid journalism." —BoingBoing

"The swirling mass of perceptions and happenings behind the main drama of Kirsty and Amber's past crime is what makes *The Wicked Girls* more than a plot-driven mystery novel. (Not that it isn't also that; Marwood sacrifices no speed, no engaging details or cliffhangers for the sake of the book's spiky undercurrent)." —*The Rumpus*

"[Alex] Marwood is equally at home with terrifying, potentially violent scenes and quieter ones revealing the tensions of work and family life. She is also adept at depicting the subtle and not so subtle ways differences in class shape the lives of the girls and the women they've become."

—*Columbus Dispatch*

"*The Wicked Girls* is utterly compelling. It's psychologically rich, complex and masterfully plotted. I couldn't put it down, even when I sensed it was taking me somewhere very dark indeed. I can't wait to see what Alex Marwood comes up with next."

—Jojo Moyes, *New York Times* bestselling author of *Me Before You*

THE
DARKEST
SECRET

ALEX
MARWOOD

PENGUIN BOOKS

For Sally and Bunny Frankland
With love

PENGUIN BOOKS
An imprint of Penguin Random House LLC
375 Hudson Street
New York, New York 10014
penguin.com

First published in Great Britain by Sphere,
an imprint of Little, Brown Book Group 2016
Published in Penguin Books 2016

LIBRARY OF CONGRESS CATALOGING-IN-PUBLICATION DATA
Names: Marwood, Alex, author.
Title: The darkest secret : a novel / Alex Marwood.
Description: New York : Penguin Books, 2016.
Identifiers: LCCN 2016014748 (print) | LCCN 2016022511 (ebook) | ISBN 9780143110514
(paperback) | ISBN 9781101992685 (e-book)
Subjects: | BISAC: FICTION / Suspense. | FICTION / Literary. | FICTION / Mystery &
Detective / General. | GSAFD: Suspense fiction.
Classification: LCC PR6063.A2438 D37 2016 (print) | LCC PR6063.A2438 (ebook) | DDC
823/.914—dc23

Printed in the United States of America
1   3   5   7   9   10   8   6   4   2

Set in Sabon LT Std

Acknowledgements

Ooh, this one's been a hard one to write, so I not only owe a lot of people for the contributions they've made, which, as always with a book, are far greater than most people realise, but for the patience, thoughtfulness and emotional generosity with which they've put up with the moaning and the groaning. I feel hugely blessed, both by the brilliant team of brains and creativity on both sides of the pond that have brought this book to pass, and the amazing team of friends and family who keep the lights on in my life.

First up, as always, Laetitia Rutherford, agent of my dreams. God, you're amazing.

In the UK, at Sphere: Cath Burke, whose talent for cat-herding and clever adjustments is unsurpassed, Thalia Proctor, Hannah Wood, Emma Williams, Kirsteen Astor. And also Linda McQueen. This probably isn't something that's often said by writers, but I've never had copy edits that actually made me laugh out loud before.

In the US, at Penguin: Emily Murdock Baker and Angie Messina, who have not only made an art form of guiding and supporting a foreigner through the mystical realm (and the things Americans would notice that Brits just wouldn't), but who are also splendid, talented and thoroughly stand-up individuals.

Erin Mitchell, worker of quiet miracles, source of much laughter and a brilliant friend.

Mum and Bunny, Will, Cathy, Ali, David, Elinor, Tora, Archie and Geordie, who are the light of my life.

There's someone out there who has cause to thank Robert and Maria Gavila for helping them through the winter with their generous donation to Authors for Nepal. I also have to thank them for donating their names to me. Names are surprisingly hard to come by, and theirs are just glorious.

Enid Shelmerdine, Valerie Laws and Angela Collings for the illuminating discussions on you-know-what. I hope you like what eventually came out at the other end!

Patricia Mackesy, who is one brave woman and a fine example of grace under fire.

My FLs; god how I love you. Thank you for proving my point.

The Board. I know we're not there all that much these days, but you carried me through and are always in my heart.

My friends (in no particular order) John Lyttle, Brian Donaghey, Jane Meakin, Charlie Standing, Nickie Schrager, Joce Buxton, Joe and Janet Camilleri, Antonia Willis for the Dingli cliffs and so much more. And oh dear, I'm going to forget someone, but Merri Cheyne, John Amaechi, Paul Burston, Alex Hopkins, Jo Johnston Stewart, Venetia Phillips, Diana Pepper, Ariel Lagunas, Helen Smith, Linda Innes (oh, yes!), Marie Causey, Rowan Coleman, Jayne Rogers, Sarah Hilary, Claudia Clare, Chris Manby, Jenny Colgan, Lisa Jewell, Jojo Moyes, James O'Brien, Lucy MacDonald, Jules Burke . . . if you're not on this list, don't think it's because I don't love you.

Stephen King, who has always been a huge inspiration, but has made a personal difference to my life that is incalculable. What a mensch.

Baloo Mackesy for being a little sod and the most entertaining of muses.

And finally, my lovely father, Piers Mackesy, who I will miss forever.

I pray you, in your letters,
When you shall these unlucky deeds relate,
Speak of me as I am; nothing extenuate,
Nor set down aught in malice. Then must you speak
Of one that lov'd not wisely but too well.

William Shakespeare, *Othello*

When a man marries his mistress, he creates a vacancy.

James Goldsmith

TO: Client, Media, Contacts
SUBJECT: URGENT, MISSING CHILD, PLEASE SHARE
DATE: 31 August 2004
ATT: Coco.jpg, bracelet.jpg

Dear all –
Apologies for the general email, but I desperately need
your help.

My goddaughter, Coco Jackson, disappeared from her
family's holiday home in Bournemouth on the night of
Sunday/Monday August 29th/30th, the bank holiday
weekend just gone. Coco is three years old.

All police experience suggests that the first forty-eight
hours are crucial in cases of child abduction, so time is of
the essence. If you would please, please forward this email
to everyone you think might respond and pass it on, we
can raise awareness of Coco's plight and increase the
chances of her being brought safely home.

Coco is three feet tall and has blonde hair cut just above
shoulder length with a fringe. She has pale colouring,
though after the summer she has a light tan and a marked
line of freckles across her nose. She has blue eyes and
darker, clearly defined eyebrows. She was wearing
SpongeBob pyjamas when she disappeared.

Vitally, she was also wearing a christening bracelet
which Robert and I gave her, which was designed to be
hard to get off, so her abductor might not yet have done

1

so. It's made in 22-carat gold, hallmarked, and has a pattern of hearts etched around the outer surface and her name and date of birth (11.07.01) etched on the inside.

I attach a photo of Coco taken this weekend on her family holiday, and of the matching bracelet worn by her twin sister.

Please, please forward this to as many people as you can. I cannot stress how important this is, or how grateful we will be. Coco's parents are distraught and we are all desperately worried.

If you read this email and think you may have seen her, even if it's only a suspicion, please call Sgt Nathalie Morrow of the Bournemouth CID on 555-6724, or contact me directly. We are all desperate. Please help us.

Love, *namaste*

Maria

P1 WITNESS STATEMENT
Emilia Pereira
Family nanny
17 September 2004

I want to start by saying that Mrs Jackson fired me the Wednesday before they went away and I wasn't even there. She fired me because she was mad about her husband. She thought every woman who came near him was going to try to take him, but I was not. I thought he was creepy. Always standing too near, asking things like did I have a boyfriend, looking for reasons to touch me. I am not surprised she was suspicious, but it should not have been me she was suspicious of.

I went to stay with my friend Lisa Mendes in Stevenage after she sacked me, because she didn't give me any notice, just my wages in cash and an order to pack my bags, and I had nowhere to go. I was sleeping on Lisa's floor and waiting for a flight back to Lisbon, when Coco disappeared and you arrested me as though I was a criminal. I have not been near the Sandbanks house in the six months since Mr Jackson bought it. I think they did spend one weekend there, before the builders moved in, but they came back early, in very bad moods, so I was surprised when he chose to have his birthday there. I would have expected Dubai or somewhere like that, if you understand what I mean.

What I know is that Mr Jackson's fiftieth birthday was happening that weekend and he had been planning a big party down at the beach house for months. Then he changed his mind about a month before – I think maybe he realised people did not want to come all that way – and planned the big party for London and a smaller one on the weekend itself. In a way it was a relief when Mrs Jackson sacked me, as I know what their parties are like and I would have been working twenty-four-hour days over the long weekend. They had their friends coming, and these are not people who like their children to interfere with their fun. In fact, if she had not sacked me, I had been planning to leave anyway as these are not good people.

I have worked for them for three years, since soon after the twins were born, but, as I said, they are not good people. I stayed because they paid well, but I never liked Mrs Jackson. She is lazy and vain and unfriendly. After three years she still did not know when my birthday was, or anything about me, really. She never talked to me, or asked questions, just criticised and gave orders. She didn't do anything all day with the time she had free because of me apart from go to salons and shops and get ready to go out with him in the evening. They were always out, when he was in London. They lived in restaurants, but she never seemed grateful for everything she had because of him. And when he was away she was always in a temper, constantly texting him and shutting herself away in her room. I think she did love the little girls, but in the end she always chose to do whatever he wanted to do, and never spent much time with them. I don't know. Maybe that's how rich people are, but I don't understand why you would have children and not want to be with them.

I would not have stayed as long as I did, but I was very fond of the little girls. That anybody would even think that

4

I did Coco any harm makes me red with anger. I did not even get a chance to say goodbye to them when she sacked me, and now I feel terrible as it was the last time I would ever see Coco.

I went to Stevenage on Wednesday afternoon and stayed there until Tuesday when the police turned up on my friend's doorstep. I was in the company of other people most of the time – I have some friends in the area and I wanted to spend time with them before I went back to Portugal – and was never alone for long enough that I could have gone to Bournemouth and back without someone noticing. I have no idea what took place at the Jackson house over the weekend, and have no idea what has happened to Coco Jackson.

P1 WITNESS STATEMENT
Janusz Bieda
Builder
Taken by Krakow police
Translated 15 September 2004

I did not know the Jackson family. I only met Mr Jackson three times. I was working, with Karol Niemiec, Tomasz Zdanowicz and my brother Gabriel Bieda, installing a swimming pool at Seawings, the house next door to Harbour View. We had been working there for a week and the project was running over as the pool was custom-made with a portrait of the owner as a merman and had to be installed in one piece by crane and digging the hole to fit it had turned out to be more difficult than had been thought as it went below the water table. We had had to source and hire pumping equipment, and the job was spilling over into the weekend.

Mr Jackson and his friends arrived on Thursday afternoon, and by Friday he was already around complaining about the noise. We thought it was funny, as we know that he had builders in all summer at Harbour View and did not care about the neighbours one bit. On Saturday morning he came again and asked how long we would be working and, when we told him that the work would probably run into the evening, he explained that he was having a party for his birthday and offered us a significant sum of money to suspend work until the following afternoon. As the crane could not be returned until Tuesday once work ran over on Friday, because of the bank holiday, we agreed, and split the money between us. My brother and I were due to return to Poland for a month with our families as soon as the job was finished, and Karol and Tomasz were happy to stay the extra couple of days to finish off the sealing and paving and oversee the return of the crane equipment before they followed us. We spent Saturday shopping for presents for our families and came back before lunch on Sunday. The Jacksons' house was quiet, but this did not surprise us as Mr Jackson had indicated that they intended to stay up late at his party.

He came back on Sunday afternoon, soon after we started work, and gave me a bottle of whisky to thank me for delaying the works. He had Coco with him. Her sister had been sick in the night and was not with them. They both looked happy and relaxed, and he was much friendlier than he had been before. She was a lovely little girl, dressed in pink, and, though she was a little shy, she warmed up and seemed happy.

The work went smoothly, and Gabriel and I made the 11.30 ferry from Portsmouth on Sunday night, leaving Bournemouth around 8 p.m. We have the tickets still, and I am sure CCTV will confirm that we were on board. It was not until the following evening that Karol telephoned and told us what had happened. They were putting the pointing between the paving stones around the pool on Monday morning when the commotion began next door, and, as they had started work around 6 a.m. in order to catch up, he estimated that this will have been some time around 10.30 a.m. I am sorry that I cannot be of more help, but, as you see, I had left the country when the child went missing. We are all shocked that you would even think that we might be involved.

The last time I saw Coco Jackson was on Sunday afternoon. From a distance, the girls looked well cared for and healthy, though I only actually spoke to Coco. But I saw the other one and she too seemed fine. Mr Jackson was clearly a devoted father, and held Coco constantly by the hand as he talked to us.

P3 WITNESS STATEMENT
Charles Clutterbuck
Guest
Taken by Metropolitan Police
3 September 2004

. . . Imogen and I went to bed sometime around three, and when we got up again at eleven on the Sunday we found that there had been another altercation between Claire and Sean and she had departed for London. Neither of us was particularly concerned. The marriage has always been a fiery one and this is hardly the first time she has swept off in high dudgeon. The truth is that, strictly *entre nous*, we felt that he had made a mistake in divorcing his first wife, who was at least not offensive, and marrying her. She's not an educated woman, if you get my drift, and has a terrific talent for taking offence. I know my wife is godmother to Ruby, but Imogen and I have for some time been thinking that we might be wise to back off a bit from them. I know it sounds harsh, but one's political career can be damaged by the people whose company one keeps, and I have a responsibility to my party not to bring it into disrepute.

Sean was clearly chastened when the twins and the Orizio children got up, and we all spent the day quietly. In the afternoon we packed the children off to the Neptune's Kingdom water park with the mothers who had seen fit to stay around, my wife, Imogen, and the Gavilas' teenage

9

daughter, and parked Ruby, who was a little under the weather, in front of the DVD player with a box set of something: *Dora the Explorer*, I think. It never occurred to any of us that there was anything odd about the fact that the twins' mother hadn't bothered to take them to London with her: frankly it seemed par for the course. As I said, she's a flouncer, and probably believed she was teaching him some kind of lesson. And I suppose we were all more or less hung over and not thinking particularly clearly. We spent most of the afternoon in the drawing room, eating leftovers and reading the weekend papers. There had been a threat that some scandal might erupt in the party, and I was relieved to see no sign of it.

The other children returned around five o'clock. They were somewhat fractious, not surprisingly, as it had been a long weekend, and we barely survived tea, bath and bedtime. They were all in bed by eight, and, clearly tired out, slept right through, all of them. The Orizio children were sleeping on air mattresses in their parents' bedroom, and the Gavilas' had been out in the annexe over the weekend, though they left to return to London by boat that evening. Coco and Ruby were sharing the single bed in the maid's room on the ground floor. They have both taken up night-wandering recently, and we all felt it was safer to keep them away from the open stairs, which are really not designed with toddlers in mind. Sean had a wireless baby alarm in the room with him, but he heard nothing in the night and, when the fact that Coco was missing was discovered, it transpired that it had been switched off at some point over the weekend without his noticing.

My driver came and collected Imogen and me at 8.30 on Bank Holiday Monday, and we were back at the London house by 10.30. We got up and breakfasted and left before anyone else was up. It never occurred to us to look in the twins' room; we were busy and running late as it was. I was in my Westminster office catching up on preparation for the new parliamentary term when you called, soon before the first bulletins made the early evening news . . .

WITNESS STATEMENT
Maria Gavila
Guest
12 September 2004

. . . it was a lovely weekend. Glorious weather and great company, the children getting on like a house on fire and enjoying themselves hugely on the beach and at Neptune's Kingdom on Sunday afternoon. I can't believe that such a beautiful weekend has ended so badly; I think I'm still in shock. My husband, Robert, has been friends with Sean Jackson for decades, since they met at university, and Charles Clutterbuck is a friend of a similar vintage. Linda Innes is a more recent friend; she has been acting as an interior designer for Jackson Enterprises for a couple of years and a firm friendship has grown up between them. This weekend was the first time I'd met her partner, Dr James Orizio, but I gather he is well known and well respected and has a practice in Harley Street that a number of my clients recommend highly. (I work as a media advisor and my husband is a lawyer, and we have considerable contact with the world of showbusiness.)

We left on the Sunday evening, after we got back from taking all the children apart from Ruby to the water park. Robert had stayed home in order to be fit to pilot our boat, the *Gin O'Clock*, up to Brighton. We keep her at St Katharine Docks in London and it's too long a trip for a single day. We had our son, Joaquin, and Robert's daughter, Simone, with us, and spent the night at the marina in Brighton, having a late dinner at a restaurant there, and set off for London in the morning. Sean called us at three o'clock on Monday, as we were entering the Thames Estuary. When we docked I went straight to my office in Soho by cab and Robert took our luggage and the children home and joined me later.

The Find Coco campaign started as quickly as I could get it up and running. I am well practised at getting media campaigns afoot at extremely short notice, be it helping clients capitalise on a fortunate turn of events or having to put my hand to rapid damage limitation, and I am aware of the speed at which one needs to act in cases of child abduction. I had composed an email to send to my entire address book by the Monday night, but held off from sending it until first thing on Tuesday, so that it would be at the top of people's inboxes when they logged in . . .

P4 WITNESS STATEMENT
Camilla Jackson
Half-sister to Coco Jackson
2 September 2004

I don't know what I can say that's any help. Me and my sister India were down at Harbour View on Thursday, but we left on Friday and went back to London. We don't get on with my stepmother. It's no big deal, not, you know, abusive or anything, but she's never made much effort to get on with us so we don't see much point in trying to get on with her. We were pissed off because Dad had forgotten we were coming even though it was his birthday and had been in the diary forever, so when we realised that Claire had got into some sort of snit with the nanny and we were going to be unpaid babysitters all weekend we left again.

Yes, I said, we don't get on with our stepmother. Why are you asking? You don't seriously think that would make us kidnap our own sister, do you? Look, Claire's a cow. She stole our dad off our mum and broke up our family. D'you think it would be normal for me to like her? It's not like she's ever made any effort to get us to. But I honestly don't have any strong feelings either way about Coco and Ruby – well, didn't until this happened. It's awful. This is the worst thing that's ever happened to our family. I keep waking up in the night because I've been dreaming she's dead.

We caught the train to Waterloo and went home. Our

mother was in Scotland because she thought we were gone for the weekend, so we asked some friends for a sleepover. They were there until Monday. We were mostly playing computer games and watching DVDs. So yes, if you want the names of people who can give us an alibi . . .

Chapter One

2004 | Sunday | 4.45 a.m. | Sean

He waits while she pulls up her dress, then helps with the zip. In the grey dawn light she looks washed out, her blonde hair brassy rather than rich, her forehead shiny from too many preservative treatments. But still: better than the woman almost ten years her junior who's stormed off across the lawns ahead of them. Sean suddenly feels every year of his five decades. I'm going to have the hangover from hell in a few hours, he thinks. And I bet Claire won't give me a hall pass just because it's my birthday.

'Shit,' says Linda. 'Shit, shit, shit, shit, shit.'

Absently, he reaches out and kneads the muscles at the back of her neck. They're tense, like granite. He's sure they weren't like that when he had his hand there ten minutes ago. Claire spoils everything.

'It'll be okay,' he says.

She rounds on him, her eyes narrowed, but still not a line to be seen on the shiny, shiny skin above. '*How* will it be okay, Sean? Go on. Tell me. What, you think she's going to keep this to herself? Think she's going to just meekly ignore this? She'll be on to her lawyers before they've even opened. You'd better check out your pre-nup, because you're going to need it to be water-tight.'

Sean sits down on the nearest sun-lounger. 'Maybe it's for the best,' he says ruminatively.

'Best for who?' she snaps.

'For . . . well, it's not as if we stood a hope in hell. I can't even remember why I married her. I'm just sorry about the kids, that's all. They deserve better than this. And, you know, if it all comes out, you and I . . . '

She starts back, her mouth open in surprise. 'You and I *what*?'

He gapes back. 'I thought . . . '

'What? That this was some sort of . . . middle-aged *Romeo and Juliet* thing? You didn't think that, did you?'

'Well, no.' He lets out a short, nasty laugh, salving his dignity. 'Hardly *Romeo and Juliet*, but . . . '

'Oh, Christ,' she says. 'I'm married, Sean.'

'Not exactly,' he says, and tries his naughty-little-boy smile on her. 'And so am I.'

The disgust in the look she gives back is more eloquent than any words.

'Okay,' he says. 'Well, at least I know where I stand.'

'Oh, don't come the wounded soldier with me. It won't work. Come on. We'd better get back. I need to get to my *common-law* husband and father of my children before *she* does.'

She bends to retrieve her strappy gold sandal, lost in the heat of the moment and lying on its side beneath a stone urn that weeps lobelia. It's an exact colour match for the lace from which her dress is made. Sean is constantly amazed by the time and concentration the women he lives among put into these things, trawling from shop to shop, twisting and turning themselves in full-length mirrors and frowning as though on their decision rests the very secret of the universe. Some part of him admires it – he wouldn't be drawn to these high-maintenance women if he didn't – but as he ages he is beginning to long for simplicity; for an artless creature who holds these fol-de-rols in lower regard and him as a man in higher. 'Shit, it's broken,' she says, and stares mournfully at a piece of gilted leather that flaps uselessly in the damp air. 'Five hundred quid, for God's sake.'

'Happy birthday, Seanie,' he says, contemplatively.

'Oh, lord,' she says. 'Honestly, you men.'

She pulls off her other shoe and sets off ahead of him across the lawn, stepping where Claire has stepped only minutes before. Sean sighs and falls into step behind her. 'Don't just follow me,' she hisses over her shoulder. 'Go for a walk or something. We don't want to be walking back in together. Maybe I can head her off, if it's just me.'

I very much doubt that, he thinks. 'D'you think there's any point?'

'Yes! Look, your marriage might be fucked, but that doesn't mean mine has to go down with it. Go on!'

She gestures to her right, to the slope down to the front gate and the ferry road. Sean shrugs and peels off.

It probably is a good thing, in the end, he thinks as he trudges in his dew-damp shirt, a lock of the thick sandy hair of which he is so proud broken loose from its gel coating and flopping into one eye. It's not something I'm proud of, but I'd rather be the bad guy than drop her because she's nasty. And she is. I can't think how I didn't see it before it was too late.

'Got to stop thinking with your todger, Seanie, old boy,' he says out loud into the silent air. It's not as though it's ever a rewarding way to go. Women like that can only keep up the performance for so long. Once they've got the legal papers, the blow-jobs dry up and the headaches begin. My God, he thinks,

I didn't even get a birthday treat this year, and it's a Big Birthday. You'd have thought at the very least she could have put in a bit of effort today. No wonder I'm forced to look elsewhere.

The gazebo is filled with party detritus. Discarded champagne glasses lie on their sides on the table and three empty bottles of Bolly sit in a row down the side of the sofa. There's a half-smoked Cohiba in the ashtray from earlier and he picks it up and lights it as he passes, to keep him company as he walks. It makes him feel a bit sleazy, doing that, but sleazy suits his current mood quite well.

He decides to go and investigate the works in progress at Seawings. Even when he finds himself in a Situation, Sean can never resist a good building site, and his dealings with the Poles who are working this one haven't been cordial enough so far to allow him a good poke around. He slips out through the gates of Harbour View and hurries into the shadow of the digger parked on the shared driveway. Though he's not doing anything much wrong, just a little light trespassing, he doesn't really want to be seen doing it at five in the morning, for there will be little he can say to explain it away.

A small crane sits on the house side of the digger, the long chain with its spider arms already unwound and draped up the slope ready to be attached to the holes in the lip of the pool liner. The liner has been inverted like a dome to keep out the rain that hasn't come. He clambers up in his formal shoes, leather soles slippy in the sandy mud, and inspects it. It's a good solid thing, though the blue Perspex it's made of is far thicker and heavier than is really necessary to get the job done. Typical amateur developer, he thinks, in the spirit of self-congratulation that makes inspecting other people's works such a pleasure. The liner to the pool at Harbour View is half the thickness and cost half as much, and didn't need all this costly equipment to manoeuvre it into place, just eight burly builders and a lot of swearing. He pats it as he passes and it lets out a pleasing hollow boom.

The chaos up above is of a familiar sort. Builders' bits: ladders and buckets and slabs piled high ready for laying, a concrete mixer standing by to prepare for sealing the pool's rim once it's in place, a pile of roughcast and assorted rubble awaiting disposal from where a patio of 1970s crazy paving was broken up to make room for the hole. Spades and pickaxes and smoothing tools lie in a pile by the front door, an invitation to passing thieves – something that would earn his own contractors an educational fine if he saw it on one of his own developments. A new diving board lies on its side on the lawn, its back jutting into a flowerbed and crushing the hydrangeas. He drags it out as he passes, tutting that anyone would treat something so beautiful, so delicate, with such careless contempt. Some stems have snapped almost clean off.

The garden, inside the fence, is bordered with Leylandii. Troublesome weeds, in a general context, but the poor soil here is keeping them in check, at least for the time being, and it will be some time before they get big enough to blight Harbour View's garden, which by then will be long-sold. Beech trees. He loves a stately beech, himself. In a few weeks their green will turn to gold and light up the landscape like beacons while these things remain blackish green all year round. It all passes so quickly, he thinks. These last ten years: it only seems like yesterday that I turned forty, and I haven't done half the things I swore I'd do that year alone. Still haven't drunk an icy cocktail at the foot of Ayer's Rock, still haven't flown my own helicopter, still haven't swum with sharks, other than the ones in the business world. I thought it was Heather holding me back, squashing my dreams, but then it was Claire doing the same thing, and I'm as much on the hamster wheel as I ever was. Maybe I need

to face the fact that it's me, not them, at all. I'm not the bucca-
neer I always fantasised, just a middle-aged man who's hoping
he won't lose his life savings in his next divorce. Thank God I
did get a pre-nup this time.

He reaches the edge of the hole they've dug for the pool. It's
disconcertingly deep, but then so is the liner, at its deep end. But
he doubts the liner will reach the bottom. Perhaps they're planning to fill it up to the water line with the piles of rubble. It
would certainly be the thrifty way of disposing of it, rather than
paying for the dump.

The builders have been true to their word and have even
switched off the pumping equipment during their absence. The
bottom of the hole has filled with water: black, brackish, with
saline scum floating on the top. If the average homeowner only
knew, he thinks, how many of their smooth, expensive walls
were just wire cages filled with rubble and covered with plaster-
board, they wouldn't be throwing their money about as though
they would stand forever.

Out on the drive, he hears the beep and clunk of a car door,
and, seconds later, an engine revs and a vehicle starts to back
out. Hopefully that's Claire, he thinks, running off again the
way she does. Good. It's too late and I'm too tired to go into
Round Two tonight.

He starts to cheer up and heads back to the house. He often
finds that, once decisions have been made for him as they were
tonight, his first feeling is actually one of rushing relief. It's not
been easy, keeping up a mistress and a nag. If the mistress has
really dispensed with him, it's a clean sweep. No one harbouring
any illusions about him, no more dreams to shatter. I'll miss the
kids, he thinks. But, once I'm done with her, there's no question
that she'll have full custody. If there's one thing a pet lawyer like
Robert can do, it's find another lawyer to do one a good divorce.

22

And then I'm free. No more sulking, no more accusations, no more we-can't-because-of-the-kids, no more going to restaurants to give us something to distract us from our enmity. She can have the London house. I don't need more than a mansion flat myself anyway. I can start slowing down. Buy a big house in the countryside, have a few house parties, start working my way through my wine cellar. I've done well for myself. Even after paying Claire off, I've still got enough to live well for a long, long time.

As he nears the house, he begins to pick up the sound of raised voices. His house-guests: Robert and Maria, Linda, Charlie and Imogen: all awake, all calling out, shouting, the women hysterical. Oh, Christ, it's kicked off already, he thinks, and slows down. You'd've thought she'd have the dignity not to involve the rest of them. Bloody Claire. Never content with a crisis when she can make a drama out of it. Maybe I'll just . . .

And then the words begin to separate themselves from the hubbub. 'Christ, Jimmy! Oh, my God, do something! Jimmy!'

Sean begins to run.

Chapter Two

I heard it often as a child, but I am still shocked when I hear my mother crying.

I sit up. An old, faded tartan boy-duvet, pillows so thin they must be cast-offs, as no one would have bought them like that. Dim grey winter daylight filtering round the edges of mean rental-house curtains, a collection of cardboard boxes and an exercise bike that's doubling as a clothes horse. I could be anywhere. I don't remember much about last night. I mean, where even *am* I?

'Mum? What's wrong?' I ask.

'I'm sorry, darling,' she sobs down the phone. 'I didn't mean to cry. I mean, I don't even really know why I'm doing it. It's the waste, I suppose. All the things that could have been but weren't. I thought I was way past caring.'

Coming to the point. Not her greatest skill. She rambles around subjects with all the abstruseness of a metaphysical poet. 'What's wrong, Mum? Are you okay?'

The body in the bed beside me starts to stir. He's pulled one of his sad little pillows over his head to block out the light, so I have no idea what he looks like. I have some vague memory of long dark hair and a Jesus beard, of hair getting in my mouth and giving me the giggles, but it could be a race memory from another night, another hangover. I don't even remember his name. It could be somebody I know. I sort of hope it is. It has been known to happen. But this room of Xboxes and bare magnolia walls gives nothing away beyond the fact that the owner is probably male, and probably in his twenties.

She sighs, and her voice steadies. 'I'm sorry, darling. I'm useless, I know. I have bad news, I'm afraid. Maria Gavila rang. She's been trying to track you down since yesterday, but she couldn't find you, so she rang me.'

Maria Gavila? What the hell? I know she's stayed in touch with Mum all these years but it somehow still feels odd to hear her name. 'Uh-huh,' I say, non-committally. I know at least that it's not Mum or India that the bad news is about, and the rush of fear I felt when I heard her weeping is receding. Now I'm sitting up, I feel giddy. Dry-mouthed and nauseated. Too many mornings like this, Mila. You need to take stock, get a grip on your life. Was it just drink last night? I know it started with bitter brown cocktails in a members' bar in Shoreditch, and that's always a bad start. No food. Certainly no food. So there must have been drugs or I would have got hungry at some point. That's why booze makes you fat, far more than its own calorie content. I don't want to be here. I want to be magically home. 'What did she want?'

'Milly,' she says, 'I don't know how to say this, so I'm just going to say it. Your father. I'm afraid your father died the night before last.'

A thud, somewhere in my chest. 'Oh,' I say. I'm not sure how I should be feeling, but right now I feel nothing but a weird curiosity. So this is what it's like when your father dies, I think. Nothing at all.

She's waiting for a response. I can feel it through the ether. But I don't know what response to give. They've not been married for the best part of twenty years, so I don't suppose telling her I'm sorry is the thing I'm meant to do. 'Does India know?' I ask, eventually. My voice sounds strangely dull, and far away.

'No. I'm going to call her next,' she says.

'What happened?'

'I don't know the full story,' she says, and I know from her tone that she's lying. My mother was always a terrible liar. She always clears her throat, as though the untruth is stuck down there somehow, and needs help to get out. 'He was in a hotel. The Dorchester. Have they given up the London house, or something? I knew they'd gone to Devon, but he spends so much time in London . . . anyway, that's where he was. They've taken him to the Chelsea and Westminster, apparently. A heart attack sometime in the night, they think. The housekeeper found him yesterday morning.'

There's a bottle of water in my handbag. I flip the top and take a suck. Give myself a bit of thinking time. Stare at the blank wall and wonder what I'm meant to do. I could do with a cigarette right now, but if this is a rental house then there will be smoke alarms going off in seconds. Sean Jackson, my absentee father, his famous charm and his Savile Row suits no use to him now.

'Darling?'

'Sorry,' I say. Then, 'Shit.'

'I know,' she says. 'It's a shock.'

'Yes,' I say vaguely.

'You can call Maria,' she says. 'She says she'll be in the office all day. They're going to have to have a post-mortem and an inquest because he was by himself. Or at least . . . ' She trails off. She's clearly changed her mind about however she had been planning to finish the sentence. 'Anyway, there are no witnesses, so that's how it's done, apparently. You should call her. I'm afraid you might need to ID the body.'

Now I'm bolt upright. 'No!'

'Um,' she says.

'Why me?'

'Someone has to do it, Milly. And I think . . . maybe Maria or Robert could do it. I don't know. Does it have to be family? Maybe it does. I'm sure Maria will know by now. She seems to be able to find out anything in minutes.'

'But why can't . . . why can't *she* do it?'

I can't bring myself to say her name, even now. Not to my ma. Even after all these years, naming the latter wives feels a bit like slapping her in the face.

'Darling,' she says, apparently feeling no such queasiness herself, 'Simone is in Devon with a small child, and I should think she's in a state of collapse. Robert's on his way down there now and Maria's going tonight. You don't really want to make her come up to some London morgue to look at her dead husband on a slab, do you?'

No, I think. Much better that I go and look at my father on a slab, obviously. She's a grown-up. She chose to marry him. She must be more grown up than me. I can't imagine ever being adult enough to want to be married, let alone have a child. 'No,' I say, reluctantly, because it's the right thing to say. Form matters, in my family. At least the surface bit of doing the right thing, the things that people can see. 'But I don't know what to do.'

'I think Maria will be able to tell you,' she says. 'She's probably got her PA finding everything out right now. We're lucky to have her, really. The resources of the Gavila empire.'

'Okay,' I say.

'I'm sorry, darling,' she says. 'I'd better call India now. Are you going to be okay?'

'Sure,' I say, though I'm not certain I'm telling the truth.

'I'll call you later, just to see how you are.'

'Okay.'

'And darling?'

'Yes?'

'I love you. Very much.'

'I know,' I say, automatically. 'I love you too.'

I hang up, drop the phone back into my bag. My companion, seizing his moment, peels the pillow away and looks at me out of one eye. That's right, I remember now. It wasn't just the drink; my mother's news must have been more of a shock than I'd thought it was. Dark hair and a Jesus beard and lovely smooth brown skin. Tom. Works in a gallery next to the Shoreditch club where I gatecrashed a private view last night, lives in Kentish Town. Damn, I'm in Kentish Town. A million stops on the black line before I can get home. I wish I had a teleporter. Why can't they hurry up and invent them, for God's sake?

'All right?' he asks. He's probably hoping he's going to get to make use of that morning glory, being as how I'm still here.

'Yeah,' I say, brightly. 'My dad died.'

He looks at me with an open mouth and I see the whites of panic in his eyes. He has no idea what to do, what to say. He's not even sure, from the tone of my voice, that this isn't some sort of crazy-person prank. This is not a good situation to find yourself in with a naked stranger. Still. It'll make a good story once you've got over the fear, I think. Don't worry about it.

'Christ,' he ventures. 'I'm sorry. Are you okay?'

'Sure,' I say. 'He was a fucker. I hadn't seen him in years.'

Chapter Three

2004 | Thursday | Claire and Sean

A whooping gasp from the back seat and the telltale plash of liquid.

'They didn't,' says Sean. 'Oh, God, tell me they didn't.'

Claire pushes her sunglasses to the top of her head and cranes to look behind her. Coco, strapped into her car seat, holds her hands up splayed and stiff: Wile E. Coyote contemplating the ever-shortening fuse on the dynamite. The cardboard cup is upside-down in her lap, lid and straw off, ice sliding down her thighs, diet Sprite pooling on the Range Rover's cream leather seat. Ruby leans out of her booster seat to look, her face a strangely triumphant blank.

'I told you it was a bad idea,' says Claire. She can't stop herself. Because she did, and, as always, he ignored her. 'I said we should use the sippy cups. That's never going to come out.'

Sean's grip on the steering wheel tightens. 'Of course,' he says in his carefully measured in-front-of-the-children voice, 'the original plan was to send them in the Prius, with *Emilia*.'

'Yes, well,' Claire snaps, 'if some people could be *trusted* around *Emilia* that would have been dandy.'

'How many times do I have to . . . ' he starts, then sighs, like a patient teacher dealing with a toddler, and reins himself in. 'You're paranoid.'

Claire shoots him a look.

'Christ,' snaps Sean, and swings off on to the hard shoulder. The traffic is nose-to-tail on the M3 – the whole country going somewhere other than their own house for the last bank holiday of the summer, and God knows how they've all managed to get off on a Thursday – and it will probably take ten minutes for someone to let them back out into the flow again. He's noticed that, about the provinces. London drivers let each other in all the time – the whole city would grind to a halt if they didn't – but get outside the M25 and people behave as though you're trying to steal their road. So weird, he thinks. And people are always claiming that Londoners are rude.

He sits behind the wheel and waits for his wife to show some signs of movement. No, thinks Claire. It's your mess. You were the one who insisted on buying them a great big drink and not waiting to decant it. It's your mess. Your turn to clean it up. She carries on sitting, hands in her lap, dark glasses back on and staring ahead at the rubbish scattered on the grass bank.

'Well?'

She turns her head slowly. 'What?' Waits two beats. 'They're your children too, Sean.'

Sean feels a small surge of rage, but unbuckles his seatbelt and gets out. Takes five deep breaths among the ragweed and the fast-food bags before continuing. I must keep my temper under control, he thinks. It's not her fault. She's a three-year-old. This is what three-year-olds do. You can't blame her for her mother.

Beyond the glass, he sees Coco's mouth go square and hears the beginnings of a wail, like a police siren in the distance. 'It's okay, baby,' he calls through the hot August air, 'hold on. I'm coming.'

He walks around to the back of the Range Rover and throws open the boot. His brain clunks into neutral as he surveys the devastation within. Claire has no talent for organisation at all. He remembers finding it charming when they were starting up – ditzy, classic bohemian, carefree – but now he just finds himself enraged. It's not as though she's got anything else to do all day, he thinks. How did it get like this? What happened to my life? At least with Heather the huge quantities of Stuff – the clothes, toys, medicines, books, essential teddy bears, mysterious electronic gizmos, nappy wipes, sun cream, shady little hats, bibs and sippy cups that seem to follow every child around these days – were organised. I used to sneer behind her back at her collection of Cath Kidston carry-alls, her love of pockets and dividers and ziploc baggies, but any-thing – anything – would be better than this.

'Where's the cleaning stuff?'

Claire holds one hand out in front of her face and gazes at her nails. She's had them done dark blue, and he hates that. It's as though she chooses it to spite me, he thinks, because she resents the fact that I like a woman to have a decent manicure. Those dark colours: you never know what's lurking on the underside. When we were going out, when she was still the competition, she listened to what I said; took up pinks and golds and silvers so that her nails flashed like jewels in the candlelight. She'd do anything to make me happy, when she was doing it to spite Heather. Now she's got me, it's a different game.

'In the bag,' she says, that 'tchuh, *men*' edge to her voice.

He surveys the high-piled chaos, twitches hopelessly at the yawning lip of a Harrods carrier. The only thing he recognises is Claire's leather vanity case, which he gave her the first time he took her to Paris, to give her a little chic. The same chaos will reign inside, colours and unguents and eyelashes thrown in without thought, but at least the cover is glamorous. A metaphor for our lives, he thinks, and feels clever for a moment. He rummages. A black bin liner reveals bundled children's clothes, un-ironed. What do these staff I pay for *do* all day, he thinks, that my kids run about like scarecrows?

He plunges a hand in among them and draws out a corduroy pinafore with an OshKosh label. It must have cost more than his mother's entire clothes budget for a year, and it's been shoved in like an old rag. He flaps it to get rid of the worst of the creases, rummages until he turns up a pack of wet wipes, its adhesive closure open and flapping, and returns to the back seat.

Coco is wailing now, and Ruby has her fingers in her ears. 'It's okay,' he says, brimming with his own parental virtue, 'it's all right, Coco, my love. Can't be helped. These things happen. Come on.' He unbuckles her seatbelt, gets his hands under her armpits and lifts her out with an 'oopsadaisy'. Despite the aircon in the car, she's hot, her golden curls plastered to her forehead and her cheeks flushed livid red. He feels her forehead. Prays silently that she's not going down with something. Not this weekend, of all weekends.

He throws the wet wipes at Ruby. 'Come on,' he says. 'Make yourself useful. Mop that lot up.'

Ruby stares at him. 'She's three years old, Sean,' says Claire. But she picks up the wipes and starts dabbing at the pool of sticky drink herself. She flicks the empty cup out through the door, where it lands in a polluted hawthorn. It'll be there forever, thinks Sean, then forgets about it as he puts his daughter down on to the hard dry mud and starts to unbutton her dress.

*

A suspicious smell starts to rise from one or other of their nappies outside Southampton. Claire looks at them in the rear-view. It's Ruby, she thinks. Her cheeks are getting that chapped look. God help me, how can identical twins be so different? Coco's almost done with nappies, though of course he claims that they should have been done with yonks ago, that India and Milly were totally on the potty by the time they could speak or something, and she talks twice as much as Ruby, and she's always laughing while Ruby just stares, half the time. It would be hard to believe that those two came out of the same womb at the same time, if I hadn't pushed them. I hope she's learned to poo on her own by the time she starts school. I'm sure it's not normal. It's like she does it to spite us.

Her husband drums his fingers on the steering wheel. He drums his fingers all the time when he's sitting still, and it drives her frantic. How can you go from love to irritated indifference in less than six years? she wonders. I don't understand. Though at the same time I do. I really, really do. You do it by marrying someone who was pretending to be someone else. Someone whose first wife's lack of interest in him had made him miserable because he was only interested in himself. I married what I thought was a man damaged by lovelessness, and discovered that lovelessness starts at home.

The aircon is cranked right down to tundra, but she can still feel the heat from outside beat against the tinted windows. A fantastic weekend for a birthday party. Just a shame she's got to spend it with all his friends. Not that she has any of her own any more. One by one by one they have dropped away. Sean never made an effort to welcome them in, of course. She hadn't thought it odd that he would never agree to meet them when they were an affair: discretion, secrecy, the necessity to keep things under wraps – there were so many reasons. It hadn't occurred to her that the real one was that he wasn't interested.

She sighs. Four days. Four long days with people who barely bother to speak to her, who all remember Heather and, though they never say it, all clearly see her as someone who's passing through. But I must be nice, she thinks. If this marriage is to survive, I must be nice.

On Saturday, thinks Sean, I shall be fifty years old. It's natural to question your life when you turn fifty. I look at my life, and I should be pleased. Every goal the western world holds dear, I have achieved. I'm rich by standards my parents wouldn't even have dreamed of. My children are healthy, and just about speak to me. I am the king of a thriving business, and those who don't respect me are, by and large, still afraid of me. I am sitting in a new, expensive car, going to my multi-million-pound property in one of the country's most sought-after locations. In a few weeks I'll be another million better off. My friends are influential, well known and wealthy. My wife is thirty-three and a beauty by anybody's standards, even if she has been letting herself go. I have a swimming pool. My life is a resounding success. So why am I so unhappy?

Chapter Four

India calls when I'm on my way down Clapham High Street. It
must be going on work-time in Auckland, I guess. High summer,
so she'll be wearing a sleeveless top under her conservative lawyer
suit, her hair pulled back into a stern nanny bun, as I shiver my
way through the freezing drizzle, shrugged deep into my leather
jacket with a scarf pulled over my head like a *dupatta*. We couldn't
be more different, my sister and I. She's reacted to the chaos of our
upbringing by imposing order on every corner of her life while I've
embraced it, refuse to make plans, can barely remember to take
my keys out with me, have no idea where the documents are stored
that say I own my flat. She loves the law, loves its rigid boundaries,
the minute detail to which each inch can be nailed down. She used
our grandmother's legacy to get herself out of the country, set
herself up in a waterside apartment lined with pale wood floors
and full-wall windows where she starts each day with sunrise
yoga, and drinks a single glass of sauvignon blanc on her balcony
each evening. Me, I got my act together enough to buy a couple of
rooms on the same road as the house-share I was in at the time,

and I'll probably get carried out of there one day, if they ever find my body beneath the sea of paper.

'Hey,' I say.

'Hi,' she says. 'How are you doing?'

'Okay,' I say. 'You know. Life goes on, eh?'

'Right,' she says. She doesn't sound particularly upset either. What would he feel, I wonder, if he knew that the only person who's shed a tear for him so far is the first of the wives who weren't good enough? Knowing Dad, he wouldn't even notice. Out of sight, out of mind was always his policy. He always sounded surprised to hear from me back in the days when I *did* ring for a duty chat.

'I'm going to identify the body tomorrow.'

'Blimey. How do you feel about that?'

'Freaky. Can't decide whether I should go before lunch, or after.'

'I'd go before, if I were you. Better to be put off your lunch than throw it up. So what's the scoop on inquests and funerals and that?'

'They're going to do the PM after I've done my bit. Apparently if they can work out the cause of death the body can get released before the inquest.'

'Even with the . . . other stuff?'

'Yeah,' I say. 'Even with that. If he had a heart attack or something, the handcuffs and that don't make a lot of difference. It's still natural causes.'

'Okay,' she says doubtfully.

'Though there were poppers on the bedside table, apparently, so that's nice.'

'Oh, God,' she says. 'Oh, God, oh, God, could he *be* any more embarrassing?'

'Farmyard animals?'

'Okay. Stop.'

'When are you coming over?'

A pause. 'Milly, I'm not.'

'You're not?'

She sighs. 'What's the point? He's dead already. He's not going to notice. There aren't going to be any affecting deathbed reconciliations. It would just be . . . no. I'm not going to fly right across the world to pat the Constant Nymph and make like I'm sorry. I know he was my father, but I barely knew the guy.'

A memory flits through my mind. The four of us in a swimming pool somewhere hot, Indy and I little enough to still be in rubber rings, Mum laughing, laughing, Dad throwing us up, up, up into the air, our delighted shrieks as we plummeted into the water, sunlight shattered on blue. He loved us once, I think. He did. Or he did a good job of looking like it.

'I . . . ' I say.

'I'll send flowers,' she says. 'But I'm not a hypocrite.'

But what about me? How about how I feel about it, India? I'll have to go for both of us, and, if that's the case, you're making me a double hypocrite. A double hypocrite who has to do everything alone.

'Okay,' I say. Wonder what we'll do about each other's funerals, when the time comes. Will we even know each other then?

'You'll come back for Mum's, though, won't you?'

'Don't be stupid,' she says. 'It's completely different. Listen, I've got to run. I've got a deposition at nine-thirty.'

'Okay,' I say. There's no point in arguing about it. India is one of those people who decide and, once the decision is made, there's no going back on it. And she decided to move as far away in the world as she could manage without having to share her space with actual icebergs.

'I suppose you're on your way out, are you?'

I laugh. 'It's Tuesday. What else would I be doing?'

'Milly,' she says, 'have you ever thought about getting a job?'

I laugh. 'Please. What on earth is the point of a trust fund if you're going to do that?'

I hang up and push open the door of the Handful of Dust.

I am my father's daughter. He loved a party, and so do I, especially *in extremis*. He was good at parties, too. No one could work a room like Sean Jackson, be noticed by all, make everyone feel special. You would literally see faces light up when he entered a room. The glad-hander, the joke-teller, the man of influence, the charmer of the ladies. He had many, many people who called him a friend, my father Sean. And he never forgot a name.

The bar is buzzing, as it buzzes every night. The good Trustafarians of Clapham Common: not as rich as the Chelsea lot, not as desperate for attention as the ones in Notting Hill, not as driven by hipster rage as everyone east of the Old Street roundabout. But as reliable and predictable as a clockwork doll: clothes whose cut (ragged hemlines, overlong sleeves) and colour (black with just the one touch of something else) declare their membership of the counterculture, but which never have a tear or a burn or a stain that might suggest that they've bought them at a charity shop. People who say they're artists, people who say they're writers, people who call themselves journalists and people who have given their days spent clicking through the internet names like 'viral visioneering'. My tribe, the one I'm part of. The staff here despise us. You can see it in the way their shoulders move up towards their ears every time someone puts in an order. But we don't care. We spend too much money for them to ever do anything about it. And besides, anyone who works in a place that sells Indonesian-Peruvian fusion dumplings as bar snacks is sort of asking for it.

I weave my way through the crowd and order a vodka, lime

and soda from a woman whose lip-ring looks as though it might be getting infected, change my mind and order two. The dieting drunk's favourite drink: barely any calories and the bubbles get you drunk faster. And I need to get drunk tonight. If I can do one thing to mark my father's life, it's that. I lean against the bar and scan the room as I suck the first one down through a straw as quickly as it will go, look around to see if there's anyone I know, or at least want to know, here yet. Someone will turn up soon. The people I know don't *do* staying in. And besides, I know a *lot* of people, just as my father did.

While I wait I amuse myself with my favourite game: Spot the Personality Disorder. It's a good game, this, especially when you're alone in a crowd. When there's two of you, you can play 'yours', but this is lovely for those quiet moments before the fun begins. I keep a copy of the *Diagnostic and Statistical Manual of Mental Disorders* beside my bed and refer to it often. I wish I'd gone to university and read psychology. I still think about going. I've even got the application forms a couple of times, but somehow time flows past with them sitting on the counter in the kitchen and suddenly another year has passed and I'm still propping up the bar, wondering what to do with my evening. I can't be an Avoidant, can I? No, I'm out all the time, and you almost never see Avoidants out in crowds. Though I do see them tucked into corners of dark restaurants, having monosyllabic tête-à-têtes with Dependents, or resentfully listening to Borderlines' tales of being hard done by.

No, a bar like the Handful of Dust is Narcissist Central. The walls are lined with cream leather pouffes and every one of the stripped-back walls bears at least three mirrors. You can look at yourself from every direction in here. I'm surrounded by women glancing sideways while sucking in their stomachs, by people pressing their heads together like space robots exchanging data as they pose for selfies to put on Instagram, by people nakedly checking their phones in case they could be somewhere better. People so busy checking in that their brains have checked out. I'm sure there's the odd psychopath among them, but they're harder to spot unless there's some drama going down. They'll be easy to single out then: they'll be the only people still smiling.

I know, or have known, a few of the people here, but none that I want to speak to. Over there, Anne-Marie, dyed dark brown hair like a mountain of seaweed left on a rock after a storm, pouts up at a man in Armani who clearly hasn't yet seen the crazy glint in her eye. I put up with her narcissism for a couple of years because it was so extreme it amused me, but when she added orthorexia into the mix and started talking about nothing but her bowel movements it stopped being entertaining. Propping up the bar, eyes going slowly up and down the women's bodies like a scanning machine, Anthony, too old to be in here but too vain to recognise it, mane of silver-grey swept up and back into two loose wings the better to emphasise its glory. I've never fucked him. I've never got *that* drunk.

I finish my drink and take the other on a wander. A young couple are gazing at each other as though they're looking in mirrors, discussing their eyebrows. 'Do you get them waxed?' she asks, admiringly. 'No, threaded,' he says. 'It looks so much more natural.' I don't understand eyebrows these days. His look like plastic stick-ons, the skin between and around bald like chemotherapy, the ends squared off with geometrical precision. 'They look amazing,' she says, and she seems to mean it. 'You should try some of that clear mascara on yours,' he says. 'It'll tidy them up.'

I can't resist drifting up behind Anne-Marie. 'Oh, no, I never go there,' she is saying, 'and I tell my clients not to, too. I said to him: bad mistake, pissing off a celebrity publicist and a high-end events organiser.' 'Oh, right,' says her prey. 'I thought it was pretty good. The food's amazing.' 'That's as may be,' says Anne-Marie, 'but they know nothing about service.' 'And how did the shoot go, yesterday?' 'Oh, God,' she says, 'total nightmare. I had a photographer all lined up to be outside the restaurant and he pulled out at the last minute. Said his son had been run over.' 'Oh, my God,' says the man, 'how awful!' 'I know,' she says, 'do you know how hard it is finding a papp at no notice?'

I see a tiny flinch. Ah, London, I think. I love you so. And then I see Sophie and Vickie in the garden, then, sitting at the table with them, Jono and Luke and Sam, and I push my way through the crowd to join.

They cheer when they see me coming. In my world, if you don't get a cheer when you turn up, you're nobody.

'I'm here,' I say. 'You can start having fun now.' They all laugh. They laugh every time I say it. It's the joke that never gets old. I slip into a space on a bench and put my drink down. I feel weird tonight. There, but not there; glad of the company but despising them all. There's a joint going round, and I take a puff. I feel sorry for the people who live next door to pubs since the world got *laissez faire* about cannabis and judgey about smoke. It's not a lovely smell, is it? There's a reason they call it skunk. And now even the winter won't keep the shouty drunks indoors. I'm wearing a black halter dress, fifty-denier tights and cowboy boots with my leather jacket. The halogen heaters should keep the worst of the cold at bay.

'What's been going on today?' I ask. 'Any scandal? Anyone been arrested?'

They all look at me slightly oddly. Oh, don't say they know, I think. But you know, it made the Sidebar of Shame at some point this afternoon, some bastard at the hotel topping up their minimum wage, and though these people never read a newspaper they pretty much have the *Mail* on alert on their phones.

It helps fill the silences, when you don't want to talk about your own stuff, if you can have gleeful discussions of the pratfalls of people you've never met.

'It's Vickie's birthday,' says Luke.

'Oh, no!' I say. 'I didn't know! Happy birthday!'

Vickie beams. She's quite a poppet, Vickie; thick as slurry and good-natured, makes her living from doing people's colour mood boards. I think of her as Thicktoria in my head. If I think of her at all. She's definitely not a narcissist. Narcissists enjoy their birthdays in anticipation, their heads filled with thoughts of how this time, *this time*, they will be the centre of attention all day and everyone will give them all the presents they want. On the day itself, they always look like a slapped arse, disappointment in other people's performance seeping from every pore, grudges building against the ones who've gone down with flu or late work days. I feel around my wrist and select a silver bangle. I buy them by the dozen from a jewellery designer that has warehouse sales every season down in Southfields. They make good presents; people always think they cost more than they did.

'Here.' I take it off. 'I'm sorry. If I'd known I would have wrapped something properly.'

She looks stunned. It's a nice little bangle, plain and shiny. I think it cost a fiver. 'Oh, no,' she says, 'I couldn't.'

'No, please,' I say. 'I'm just embarrassed it's not something proper.'

'But . . . ' She looks up at my face with big brown eyes. 'This *is* proper. It's *yours*.'

'And now it's yours,' I say, firmly, and close her hand around it. She beams again and slips it on her wrist. Turns her hand this way and that so it catches the light. I get my cigarettes out and light one. The ashtray is already full. I lean over to the next-door table and swap it with the empty one that lies there. Vickie smiles at me as though she's seeing me for the first time. Amazing how easy it is to make a new BFF with a bit of cheap jewellery.

The conversation moves on. Hangovers, launches, holidays. Sam tries to tease me about the Jesus figure I shagged last night. 'Didn't he have a topknot?' he asks. 'No,' I say, 'I would never shag a topknot. Where do you think I'm from, Shoreditch?' And everybody laughs. Luke's been backpacking in Thailand. He says they have great beaches and the Full Moon parties were still rocking. 'Oh, you should go to Mozambique,' says a fierce-looking Australian woman called something like Gaia or Euphrosyne or some other name she's picked out of a hat, 'they've got a great party scene there.' She has a Bedouin scarf wrapped round her head like a turban and a dozen piercings. She looks like she's fallen through a hole in the space–time continuum from the 1990s. 'Wasn't there a war there or something?' someone asks. 'Yeah, well, that's over now and all they want to do is party,' she says. 'It's amazing how much joy the simple people can feel when they've got nothing at all. I slept on the beach. You have to show the landmines you're not afraid.'

Schizotypal. No doubt. Probably protected herself from malaria with homeopathy, too. I finish my drink, put in an order for two more when Sam says he's going to the bar. Give him £20, because that's what two drinks cost in a bar like this, even in the tail end of a raging recession.

Sophie turns to me and lowers her voice. 'I saw about your dad,' she says. 'I'm sorry. Are you okay?'

'Fine,' I say.

'Because, you know . . . I know how I'd feel . . . '

'Yeah, well, you're not me,' I snap, and then I think: gawd, that was nasty of you, Mila. But I never know. People are always wanting to know about my family, and most of the time it's so they can gossip about it. Okay, so maybe I'm a Paranoid. But at least I'm not an Obsessive-Compulsive, like my sister. 'Sorry,' I add. 'I just don't want to talk about it, okay?'

'Okay,' she says. 'But if you need to . . . you know. I'm around.'

Oh, lord, a Caretaker. God preserve me from them, working out their own issues by taking on everybody else's. Narcissist parents, of course. Narcissists always produce at least one Caretaker if anyone is fooled into breeding with them.

'Thanks,' I say, and turn away to put an end to the conversation. I don't want to talk about it. I don't. Don't want to think about it. What's the point? It's going to be nothing but thinking about it, over the next few weeks. I just want to get obliterated and forget about it, tonight. Isn't that the point of spending time around other people? To forget about yourself?

'So are you seeing him again?' asks Jono.

'Who?'

'Jesus-boy.'

Ah, Tom. Not exactly likely. We couldn't get away from each other quickly enough, though manners made him give me a mug of instant coffee, no milk because the milk was off, and manners made me drink it while wishing that there was milk because then I could have drunk it faster.

'Naah,' I say. 'What do you think this is, a Richard Curtis film?'

They all laugh again. We all hate Richard Curtis because our mothers love him. 'Well, he certainly wasn't Hugh Grant,' says Jono.

'I – I – I – I say – fuckitty fuck,' Vickie puts on an accent that no one British has spoken in outside the movies in thirty years, and we all laugh again. Sam comes back with my drinks and I sink half of the first one in one go. I feel empty and distant, as though a glass wall has fallen down between me and these people I call my friends. But then, I feel like that a lot of the time, so nothing's new.

Chapter Five

'God almighty,' says India. 'I could be at a festival right now.'

Milly raises an eyebrow. 'What festival would that be?'

India frowns. 'The . . . um . . . '

'Creamfields? Glasto? Reading? T in the Park?'

Her sister's eyes narrow. 'Oh, shut up,' she says. 'Just because I've got better things to do with my time than read the *NME* all day.'

Milly considers jacking up the wind-up by asking what those things might be. She loves winding India up, puncturing her self-regard, but they're alone on this doorstep and she knows that, despite her family reputation as the Good Girl, her sister's temper can be explosive, and erupt with little warning. 'Well, look,' she says, 'there's no point hanging around here. How about we go over the chain ferry and get a drink at the café? No point just sitting here all afternoon.'

India picks up her overnight bag. 'What are you doing *now*?' asks Milly.

'I don't want it getting stolen.'

Milly sneers. The brickwork of the driveway is soaking up the heat and it's like sitting on a barbecue. I can't believe you're the elder sister, she thinks. You're scared of *everything*. 'Who's going to steal *that*? We're in Poole, not Peckham.'

'There are people,' says India, 'all over the place. Tourists. And, you know – builders.'

Milly bursts out laughing. The builders working on the house next door have come and gone through the gate as they've been sitting there, bellowing to each other in some language she doesn't recognise. Six feet tall and generously muscled, half of them with moustaches, only distinguishable from gay porn by the loose fit of their jeans. 'Yeah. I can see that. They'll be after your polka-dot sundress to wear down the pub.'

India throws the bag on to the drive. 'Oh, shut up! Just *shut up!*'

She considers baiting her sister for a little longer, but it's too hot and the fight isn't in her. She picks up India's bag and her own – canvas, matching flower patterns, one red, one blue; their mother is scrupulous even in her division of luggage – and carries them over to the rhododendrons that line the fence. 'We can hide them here, look.'

'Has it ever occurred to you that they might have girlfriends?' India can never leave an argument alone.

'Yeah,' she replies over her shoulder, 'and I'm sure they're just *longing* for a second-hand dress from What She Wants.'

She ducks beneath the low branches, looking for a space that will take the bags. Spots something and turns back to her sister. 'Hey, Indy, come and look at this!'

India shuffles sulkily over. 'What?'

Milly holds a branch back so she can see. 'Look!'

There's a hole in the fence. One that has been used several

times before, by the looks of it. The leaf drop from the bush has been swept off to either side, making a clean run of sandy earth.

'Ooh!' says India.

'Right?'

'Do you think we should?'

'It's our *house*, eejit!'

'Well, sort of. But what if he's got security? Cameras, that sort of thing?'

'Come on, when was the last time he had cameras on a house he was turning? Anyway, I've got my student travel card. It's not like we can't prove we're family. Come on!'

India still hesitates.

'Oh, what*ever*, India. I'm not sitting out here looking like a pillock. There's a pool in there, and sun-loungers. I'm going for a swim.'

She crawls into the dark cave beneath the shrub. She doesn't have to force her way through the hole. Use has made it comfortably body-sized already. A couple of wriggles, pulling herself along by her forearms, and she's in the flowerbed on the other side. It's planted with roses and azaleas: the easy-colour low-maintenance plants her father always dresses his properties' gardens with when they go on the market. Tough enough to survive the skimping he always does on topsoil at least until the house is sold. She shimmies past them and stands up on the newly laid turf on the other side.

India follows a few seconds later, pushing the bags ahead of her. Crawls red-faced on to the grass and drops back on to her buttocks. 'Cor!' she says.

The house is totally Sean and totally not. Totally Sean because it's what he makes his money from, and totally not because he would never be seen dead living in a place like this. The homes they have lived in through their childhoods have always been period houses, filled with antiques and tulips in vases like Dutch still lifes, always dressed for sale even when they were staying a while. But Sean has never let personal taste get in the way of profits. There has always been a collection of modern buildings on his books, nice easy modern buildings with no listing issues, waiting to be demolished or given the Deco treatment to hide their antecedents. And for these he has a warehouse of furniture: things with no handles, things with no frills; the sorts of characterless expensive things the newly minted, still unsure of their taste, like to buy in shops they know are safe. Sometimes he even sells the houses furnished, and turns a tidy profit on the contents in doing so. This house on Sandbanks, gold-rush destination of the seagoing stockbroker and the digital millionaire, is very much one of his turnaround jobs: picked for its location rather than its looks and filled with mod cons to tempt the yuppies.

'Oh, hurrah!' says India. 'It's a jacuzzi house!'

They set off to explore, both of them feeling instantly cooler at the prospect of what they are likely to find. The house itself is of little interest to them. A three-storey box of white-painted concrete, balconies and sliding doors dotted here and there. They know that the doors and windows will be alarmed. Their father might not think it worth installing cameras, but he's certainly not going to leave the place wide open to squatters, or burglars with a taste for the Conran catalogue. Plenty of time for that later, when the grown-ups arrive. Meanwhile, there is a garden in which the only thing that's old is a monkey puzzle tree, with three sets of patio furniture, a croquet set and, oh, the joy of it, over there behind a white picket fence, a pool.

'Why do you think it's called Harbour View?' asks Milly, looking at the back of a small apartment building that stands between the house and the water. It, too, is covered in scaffolding; it's as though the whole of Sandbanks is being developed to cash in on its voguishness.

'Maybe it had one once.'

'Doesn't any more. You could probably get done under the Trades Descriptions Act.'

'Naah. They'd probably just claim it was an ironic name. Or historic or something. There's a house on the King's Road called Sea View Cottage. I don't think anyone expects to actually be able to see the sea from there.'

Milly is fifteen, India seventeen. They have their mother's tall, dark-Celt colouring and their father's patrician nose and heavy brows. People sometimes assume that they're from a more exotic parentage than the bog-standard British-with-a-dash-of-Jewish they are, and they're happy to play along with that. Last summer in Tuscany, Milly convinced some boy from Haberdashers' Aske's school that she was an Arab princess. His Islington parents were all over her until her mother came to collect her from a pool party and they learned that her name was Heather Jackson.

It's the end of summer and both of them are brown as caramel, their black hair cut into mops about their faces, toenails painted neon orange. They duck and shriek and dive-bomb each other from the pool's fixed board for a bit, then settle on sun-loungers and rub themselves with low-factor, tan-encouraging Soltan from India's bag. That's Indy all over: ever cautious, ever equipped, always trailing along behind her foolhardy younger sister with sting remedy and sticking plasters. 'Is there any noise from Dad?' she asks.

'No, but there's a bloody lot of noise from those builders next door,' says Milly. 'Claire's head's going to spin round on her neck if they're still at it when she gets here.'

She tries her phone again. No voicemails, no returned calls.

Their father, it seems, has entered a long dark tunnel without a signal. 'Should we call Mummy, do you think?'

India glares at her. 'And what's *she* going to do? She's on a plane. And besides, she'll be furious.'

Milly stares at her for a moment. This is the difference between us, she thinks. Indy will do just about anything to avoid awkwardness, and she's constantly on the edge of rage as a result. And it's not like it even gets her anything. Everyone's so scared of her, she's barely got a single friend.

'Well, what *are* we going to do?' she asks. 'We don't actually know if he's even coming down today, do we?'

'*I* don't know, do I?' snaps India.

Milly sighs. 'I'll try him again,' she says.

She dials her father's number and is diverted straight to voicemail. 'Maybe he's driving,' she says, ever the optimist. 'Maybe it's a good sign if he can't pick up.'

India has a bottle of Ribena in her bag, and Milly, after some rummaging, turns up a bag of M&Ms. They share them in sisterly silence, basking beneath the azure sky in their heart-shaped Primark sunglasses.

'So who's coming this weekend, anyway?' asks Milly.

'Not sure. The usual suspects, I suppose. I know the Clutterbucks are coming.'

'When aren't they? Anything for a freebie.'

'I know. Sometimes I think Dad loves Charlie Clutterbuck more than he loves his family.'

'Well, school, you know,' says Milly. 'Boys can develop lifelong attachments at public school. All those cold baths and rugby scrums.' She thinks for a moment. 'Rugby scrums are clusterfucks, really. Charlie Clusterfuck.'

India sniggers. 'Charlie Clusterfuck. Love it.'

'Imogen Clusterfuck,' says Milly, and they both crease up.

'Okay, so the Clusterfucks. Who else?'

'I guess probably the Gavilas.'

India groans, 'Oh, God, not Soppy Simone? Tell me they're not bringing her.'

'I don't know. Are they all bringing the kids? I hadn't even thought.'

'Well, Maria won't go anywhere without Joaquin,' says India. 'Remember when she insisted on bringing him when Dad married Claire?'

'Screaming!'

'And throwing up in the register office! Priceless!'

'To be fair,' says Milly, 'he was only acting out what we all thought.'

'The look on Claire's face!'

'You could tell the difference? She always looks like a slapped arse to me.' Milly fiddles with her phone, gives their father another fruitless go. 'Is that it? Not much of a fiftieth birthday, is it?'

'I don't suppose you've got much energy for partying when you're that ancient. God, it's going to be boring, though. I think there might be more people, but they're work bods. Some woman who's taking over his interior design or something. And her kids.'

'Gawd. It's all just fun, fun, fun in Sean Jackson's world, isn't it? How many kids?'

'Three, I think. Tiggy, Fred and Inigo.'

They do the gagging mime again.

'Yes,' says India, 'well, I suppose you do need to work quite a lot when you've got an expensive wife.'

They fall into silence, ruminate on their father's choices. It's not much fun, living with an angry mother.

'It's funny, isn't it?' says Milly. 'I actually look forward to going back to school these days. It's so much easier there, isn't it? You know the rules.'

India turns on to her front. 'Mmm. And no brats you're expected to be nice to because they're your sister. Ugh. I still can't believe he's breeding at his age. It's just – *wrong*.'

'Ugh,' echoes Milly, 'I know. Some sort of man thing, isn't it? Wants to show it all still works?'

'Well, I wish he wouldn't. It's disgusting.'

Milly finishes off the chocolates and washes them down with a swig of Ribena. 'We should probably make a plan, you know. In case they don't turn up.'

'Oh, shush, Milly,' says India. 'Of course they're going to turn up. It's just *her*, isn't it? She's never been on time for anything, ever. I'd be surprised if they got out of the house before ten.'

Milly checks her watch. 'Well, it's gone lunchtime now.'

'Oh, honestly.' India reaches out and pinches the skin on her hip. 'It's not like you're going to die of starvation if you miss a meal, is it?'

'Ooh, you *bitch*!' squeals Milly, and only half of her is joking. She developed a habit of eating as much as she could during the silent meals that characterised the end of her parents' marriage, because fullness somehow dulled the ache, and now she's no longer forced on to a sports field every schoolday the food is catching up with her, and she knows it. Doesn't like it, doesn't seem to be able to stop, but she knows it. She flicks some drink out of the top of the open bottle she still holds on to her sister's bare back. India shrieks and leaps to her feet. And then they're off, filled with one of those sudden surges of teenage energy, India chasing Milly through the garden, in the sunlight, until Milly flings herself back into the water to get away. India throws herself in after, ducks her, and they retreat to opposite sides, sweeping armfuls of water into each other's faces, laughing, with an edge of desperation, because this might be the last fun time they have this weekend.

They're making so much noise, and are so intent on acting out their pleasure, that they don't notice that they are no longer alone until a shadow falls across Milly's shoulder and their father's voice breaks into their shouts. 'What on earth are you two doing here?' he asks.

Chapter Six

Someone's been training the staff at the morgue. It's not wall-to-wall counsellors or anything, but the receptionist walked me to the waiting room rather than waving me to a seat and the room itself has a relatively comfortable sofa rather than the usual rock-hard NHS benches. The table is scattered with helpful leaflets. I half expect them to have titles like *So You've Lost Your Dad*, but the patronising touchy-feelyness of the People's Princess era has passed and we're on to Plain Speaking for Hard-Working Families now. I leaf through a *Guide to Services for the Bereaved* as I wait. It's divided into sections like 'What Is Probate?' and 'Choosing a Funeral Provider'. I'm sort of glad it'll be a few more years before I need to know about this stuff. Robert, as Dad's solicitor and Simone's father, has been named as executor. All I have to do is say whether the man on the slab is really my father.

And all the time, I'm watching myself; studying Mila in Mourning and wondering at my emotions, because as far as I can see there aren't any. Just curiosity. Fascination at doing something I've never done before, that no one I know has ever done. All I feel is the occasional faint surge of anger. Here's the thing I know so far about death. All those things you've put to the back of your mind, the things you've decided it's best to just ignore because protest has got you nowhere, they come creeping back around your barriers when someone dies. All my resentments at his failures and his neglect and his selfish choices that I'll never be able to call him on now: my brain seems to be cycling through them like a couple in a traffic jam, going 'and another thing, and another thing'. But missing him? No. You know why? Because there's nothing to miss. It's one of those things that people don't get about the children of divorce. I did most of my mourning when I was nine years old.

The door opens and a woman in a white coat appears. I assume she's a doctor.

'Camilla Jackson?' she asks.

I nod. Put down *Post-Mortems Explained* and look at her.

'I'm Dr Badawi, the duty pathologist here. He's ready for you now,' she says, and gives me a neat little smile that must have taken years of practice to get right. I don't know if they have bedside-manner lessons in med school these days, but this smile is familiar to me. Not too jolly, not too mournful, sympathy denoted by a tiny head tilt but never a stray into overfamiliarity. Keep the rellies calm, it says, and we can keep the interruptions to our working day, these irritating hold-ups in the important business of chopping and slicing and sawing the tops off skulls, as brief as is humanly possible. But it feels weird, the way she calls him a 'he', as though there's a human being waiting beyond that door on the other side of the corridor, rather than a quietly decaying corpse.

She leads me to the viewing room, talks as she goes. 'We've just left his face visible,' she says. 'It's standard practice. I'm afraid it's all rather clinical in there. But don't be afraid. It's not the way it is in the movies. There's only him. But I'm afraid quite a lot of people find the whole procedure distressing anyway. You'll let me know if you feel faint or . . . anything, won't you? We have chairs in there, if you need. I'll come in with you and let you have a look, and then I'll ask if it's him by his full name and all I need you to do is give me a yes or a no. Is that okay?'

'Yes,' I say.

The room's not the way I'd expected. *Silent Witness* and all those movies are big fat lies. It's a normal hospital consulting room, two wide doors to let trolleys and fat people through, walls as plain and white as a chapel of rest, not a single distinguishing feature apart from the body on the trolley that sits in the centre of the floor. He's covered in a sheet, which has been turned back to reveal his face before we entered. None of that your-dinner-is-served theatre you see on the TV. Just . . . my father, dead.

For a moment I don't recognise him. Death slackens the face, shows up the bones beneath. His jaw has travelled backwards with the help of gravity so he looks as though he has no teeth. But then I see that it's him, five years older, hair a little longer as if to compensate for the fact that it's further up the crown of his head, what looks like a little network of broken veins on the upper parts of his cheeks. I stare. And stare and stare. My mind is blank.

'What did he die of?' I ask.

'We can't say yet, I'm afraid,' she says. 'We'll be doing the PM once you've identified him.'

'Hazard a guess?'

'Sorry. Can't do that. Procedures and legal stuff. Can I ask you, is this the body of Sean George Jackson?'

I nod. 'Yes.'

I feel a sudden lurch of sorrow somewhere deep inside. Ah, there you are, I think. I was beginning to wonder if you were ever going to come. Sean George Jackson. No longer here. I wonder what you were thinking, when you died? Did you know that this was it? Did you think of us, at all?

'You can stay as long as you like,' she says, kindly. 'Some people find it helpful.'

'No,' I tell her. 'No, I'm done. Thank you.'

Chapter Seven

2004 | Thursday | Sean

He texts his ex-wife when he gets an opportunity to be by himself in the annexe under the pretext of checking that all is well. The inflatable mattresses are still in their boxes, all five of them; he'll be having a word with the staff about ticking things off on lists when he gets back to the office. As he closes the door and cuts off the sound of the pneumatic drill they're using at Seawings next door, he realises that he's in relative quiet for the first time since he got out of the car. Another thing I'll have to have a word about, he thinks. Once I've done this.

'When did we agree I was having the girls this weekend?'

The reply comes in in less than a minute. She's clearly been waiting for him. Which means that she's done this on purpose.

'Do I really have to keep your diary for you still, Sean? This is the standard schedule.'

He inhales sharply through his nose. Bloody women. It's just typical of her to sabotage his plans like this. She's bitter still, six years on, and she can't resist just having the odd go when she gets the chance.

'As the keeper of my diary you know perfectly well that this is my birthday weekend.'

'Yes! The girls are really looking forward to celebrating with you!'

'But I . . . '

He stops, deletes, starts again. Must not give her any ammunition.

'I'm delighted to see them, of course. But I thought we'd moved the weekend.'

'No, we didn't.'

'Yes, we did.'

'I'm sorry you don't want your daughters interrupting your birthday, Sean. It's a terrible inconvenience, having leftover children, I know. Sadly, the court thinks you should have access. If you didn't want to step up and do your bit you shouldn't have asked for it.'

He gasps out loud. 'I don't – God, you bloody – ugh!'

He shoves the phone back in his pocket. She's done this on purpose, he knows she has. Heather is beyond anal about dates and times and places; always has been. Used to strike people off invite lists for being late more than once. The odds on her forgetting a date she made a big deal of every year for twelve years are so minuscule a bookie would refuse to offer them. He goes back to the kitchen to face the music.

India and Milly are perched on chrome bar stools at the kitchen island, eating toast. They're still wearing their bikinis, Milly's a size too small, the breasts she seems to have suddenly sprouted in the month since he last saw her threatening to spill out into the butter. 'Girls,' he says, 'can you get a bit more decent before the guests arrive?'

They turn and gawp at him. 'What are you saying?' asks Milly. 'That you're hanging around with kiddy-fiddlers?'

He refuses to rise. Milly and her mouth. She likes to provoke and provoke, and always feigns amazement when someone eventually reacts. 'I'm just saying that bikinis are for beaches and swimming pools,' he says. 'You need to cover up when you come into the house.'

'Frankly,' says Claire, coming into the room, 'I don't think those bikinis are fit for public display at all. We should get Milly a one-piece, really. There's a bit of an abundance of flesh going on there these days.'

Milly's jaw drops open and her eyes fill with tears. Oh, God, the sensitivities of teenage girls. But really, if she doesn't want people to comment on her weight, she should try eating less. Now he looks, he sees that there's a roll of fat coming on to the small of her back. Sean doesn't approve of women who don't look after themselves. It's the least they can do, frankly. Claire's gone up a dress size herself since she had the twins, and he's not happy about that, either. Milly will be a size fourteen soon if she doesn't watch out, and then no one will ever look at her apart from the chubby-chasers.

Milly bites into her toast and stares at them both like they've sprouted extra heads.

'Maybe a bit less toast and a bit more exercise,' he says. 'That'll probably do it.'

'Yeah, fuck you,' says Milly. 'Maybe you could do with a hair transplant.'

'And crowns,' says India. She always backs her sister up when it comes down to it. It's a horrible little nation of two they've got going there. He sometimes feels that they've formed a consortium against him. Oh, well. You can't help it if your kids get bitter after a divorce. They're so self-centred it would never occur to them that their parents have a right to happiness. 'You can totally see those cigars on your teeth these days.'

60

Claire purses her lips. You shouldn't let them talk to you like that, the look says. They're guests in my house.

'Just do it,' he says. 'I'm requesting it, so I expect you to do it.'

'That's not really the meaning of requesting,' says Milly.

'Okay,' he says. 'Well, I'm telling you.'

He sets the girls on to taking the mattresses up to the bedrooms and inflating them. Might as well make themselves useful. He can hear them padding about over his head, giggling and pulling things about. Outside, someone revs the engine of the digger at the building site next door. A crash, then a chorus of Polish expletives. I must find out how to get some Poles of my own, he thinks. I hear they cost a stack less than your average British brickie, and they don't seem to be stopping for tea breaks every ten minutes. Hurrah for the Common Market. Country's going to be full of Eastern Europeans before the decade's up. Marvellous to have the outsourcing bringing itself to Mohammed rather than having to go and find it. It's been irritating watching all those call-centre savings in action and not having the sort of company that could benefit from the cheaper labour available elsewhere in the world.

'Well, this is nice,' says Claire. 'Where are they going to sleep? The maid's room's full of boxes. Not that anybody's going to be getting much sleep with that lot crashing about outside.'

'Weekend starts tomorrow,' he says. 'They'll be in the pub by three o'clock. They'll just have to share with Simone, out in the annexe.'

'Lovely. Yes, *that'll* work.' Her voice drips sarcasm.

'They'll enjoy it. It'll be like a sleepover.'

'I doubt Simone will think so.'

'Well, what else am I meant to do?' he snaps. 'Any suggestions, given you know best about everything?'

61

Claire gets the look again. 'I'm just *saying*, Sean,' she says, in that nasal voice he's learned to dread. 'I'm going to unpack. Perhaps you'd like to go and check on the twins, if that's not too much to ask? Your *other* daughters?'

She stalks away. He follows her like a smacked puppy and watches as she climbs the stairs. A brand-new staircase, sourced by Linda, the treads made of toughened glass, abraded at the edges to look as though they have been hewn whole from living crystal. Thirty thousand pounds' worth of stairs that will have added a good hundred-k to the asking price. Even though he can't see her face, her very backside radiates offence. How a pair of buttocks can look offended he doesn't know, but there they are, right there, going up the stairs in high dudgeon. Sean flicks a finger at them and pulls a face.

She has settled the twins on a white combed-sheepskin rug in front of the shiny gas firebowl that sits proudly in the open chimney breast. They've knocked the rooms together to create a large open-plan space from two poky ones, but left the fireplace as a focal feature. A spend of ten thousand pounds that will reap another hundred and fifty thousand when the house goes on the market on Thursday. Sean is no longer able to think of houses as places. To him they're bank statements, expenses sheets, 3-D illustrations of investment-to-profit ratios.

He's killing several birds with one stone this weekend: saving a few thou on a rental property and testing out the house's impact value on a tame audience. It's the first time he's used Linda Innes for her design skills, and he suspects it won't be the last. His building team are standing by to make speedy adjustments if anyone notices something they really, really hate, but to his well-trained eye it looks as though every choice she's made has been perfect for the market. She's even picked out the perfect yuppie dream furniture from the warehouse without any guidance at all: the white leather cubic sofas, the fluffy rugs, the coffee table with the glass top and the display boxes beneath, where she's placed souvenirs from seasides thousands of miles from this one: a giant conch, a dried-out rainbow starfish, a lump of coral the size of an ostrich egg. The firebowl is polished copper, the cupboard doors have no handles, the floor is quarry tiles of Aberdonian granite. In a dark and useless corner, a giant Ali Baba pot filled with Brobdingnagian bamboo feathers. Not a place to fall over in, but perfect for impressing your sales director.

The children, however, are not impressed. In fact, they're making a start on redecorating. They've begun with the rug and a set of crayons. Ignoring the A3 sketch-pad that sits on the floor beside them, they sit face to face in their OshKosh pinafores, colouring each strand in by holding it up and pulling a crayon along its surface.

Oh, God. Sean squats down and asks them what they're doing. They look up and beam. 'Claire?' he shouts. Then, louder, 'Claire? Who gave the twins a box of crayons?'

That's another three hundred, right there.

Chapter Eight

The papers love it. They are all over it. It's like being fifteen again, ducking and wincing as my family is laid bare once more, except now nobody's sending me to the shops to buy hard copies. Now we have the internet, and Facebook is recommending that I read all about it in the *Mail Online*.

I sit in bed with the laptop and wonder what time counts as too early for a drink. I slept until ten, but then the phone started ringing and it's not stopped long enough to let me get back to sleep. The web is abuzz with my father's demise. People are tagging my friends to URLs as though they don't know that I can see what they're saying. Victoria, is this your friend's father? OMG, Toby, he was handcuffed to a bed at the Dorchester how embarrassing is that LOL! I always thought there was something dodgy about him, Sophie. What do you think really happened to that kid?

Eventually I succumb and click through. Might as well see what the *Mail* has to say. Let's face it: no one's going to be more vitriolic, or dwell with greater pleasure on the detail. Might as well get the worst out of the way.

It would be an inside feature if it were in an actual paper. In this connected world it's a click-through from the Sidebar of Shame.

LONELY DEATH OF SANDBANKS MILLIONAIRE
Dorchester chambermaids find body of tragic Coco's dad in mysterious circumstances

Sean Jackson, 62, father of missing toddler Coco Jackson, was found dead on Sunday morning in Mayfair's swanky Dorchester hotel. Jackson, in London on business from his palatial home on the north Devon coast, had failed to check out at the given time and, after attempts to rouse him had failed, hotel staff let themselves in with a room key and discovered his body.

'He was handcuffed to the bed,' said a source, 'and had clearly been dead for some hours.'

A source. Some chambermaid or security bloke or person who hangs about behind the reception desk pretending not to notice you but taking copious notes. Hotels are leakier than brothels. The wages they pay, you can hardly blame them for supplementing them via the newsdesks. I read on.

According to the family's solicitor Robert Gavila, husband of celebrity publicist Maria Gavila, property developer Jackson had been in London since Thursday night, attending planning meetings and tying up legal documentation related to a conversion he was planning on Cheyne Walk, Chelsea. 'We are all devastated,' he said. 'I have known Sean all my adult life. We grew up together in business and have always been close. His loss is a terrible shock. Our thoughts are with his family.'

'Yes, he had been staying here since Thursday,' said a source in the hotel. 'He was a charming man, friendly to all the staff, and quite a regular here, even though we think he kept a flat somewhere in Knightsbridge. I guess he didn't want the trouble of catering for himself and his associates when his wife wasn't with him. He had guests to dinner in our restaurant on Thursday and Friday nights, and ordered room service on Saturday as he said he was making an early start back to Devon the next day. He ordered chateaubriand and two bottles of Dom Perignon champagne. I don't know if he had a guest, but chateaubriand is usually a dish for two people.'

Jackson leaves behind a wife and an infant daughter. He remarried for the fourth time in 2011, after the death of his third wife, Linda. Friends from cabinet ministers to retail billionaires describe him as 'inspiring', 'larger than life', 'a man of boundless energy', 'charming', 'a huge loss'. He lived big, spent money like water, was open-handed to his friends, lending houses, dispensing loans, jetting entire parties off to foreign locales, and was a generous donor to Conservative Party coffers.

To the public at large, though, he is best known for the tragedy that overtook his second marriage in 2004, when his three-year-old daughter Coco disappeared from the family's newly renovated holiday home in the Millionaires' Row at the Sandbanks Peninsula, Bournemouth. The family were there celebrating Jackson's 50th birthday, when Coco vanished from the ground-floor bedroom she was sharing with her twin sister, Ruby, in the middle of the night. A hole was discovered in the fence that separated the property from the road outside, and the latch on a sliding window leading to the house's main reception room was found to be broken. None of the many people in the house admitted to hearing a thing in the night, and Ruby slept through the entire incident. Not a trace has been seen of Coco again.

Ruby. Oh, God. She must be – what? Fourteen? Fifteen? Same age I was when Coco disappeared. I've not thought about her at all. I can't believe I've not thought about her.

I get up and go to put the kettle on. Realise there's no milk and make a gin and tonic instead. I don't care. I don't care what anybody says, not that there's anyone to say it. I'm not leaving the house today. I have to think. About Dad, about what to do now. I make some toast to soak it up with. Spread it with peanut butter and get back into bed. My flat feels small, today. Small and safe.

The case quickly became a national event. Jackson's then wife, Coco's mother Claire, a former secretary, harnessed a newly discovered talent for publicity to galvanise the Find Coco campaign, appealing repeatedly for members of the public to search for her missing daughter. With its mix of glamorous wealth and celebrity house-guests – present at the house that weekend, as well as the Gavilas, were Shadow Health Minister Charles Clutterbuck and a Harley Street doctor with links to many household names of show-biz – the story became one of the biggest of its era. Maria Gavila, a well-known broker of tabloid tales, started an email chain letter among her rich seam of contacts that quickly proliferated and is thought to be the first ever to have reached over a billion people worldwide. Repeated television appeals, email chains and poster campaigns meant that pretty Coco briefly became one of the best-known faces on the planet.

Public sympathy quickly ebbed away, however, as stories of Claire Jackson's behaviour around the time when her daughter vanished leaked out. It transpired that she had dumped the twins on her husband and house-guests when she returned early to London, and had been seen spending lavishly in designer shops while her daughters awaited her return uncared-for. Former employees and neighbours and former friends described her variously as 'a harpy', 'unstable' and 'a terrible, selfish mother'.

The Jackson marriage did not survive the tragedy. The Jacksons divorced in 2006, and soon after Sean married his 'dear friend' Linda Innes, who had also been part of the ill-fated weekend party. Innes had been working as a designer for Jackson's construction company, and continued to decorate the interiors of his developments. 'She comforted me, which was more than my wife was able to do,' he said at the time. 'I hope that this will be the beginning of a new era of happiness for me.'

Despite his former wife's soured reputation, Jackson surprised the public when he did not apply for custody of Ruby. Not long before the divorce, Claire dropped off the radar. Increasingly unhappy at the negative press she had received, she left London with Ruby, and seemed to vanish from view like her daughter before her. It was widely believed that she had left the country and was living in an ex-pat community where she was not known. The *Mail* can now reveal that she is in fact renting a smallholding in rural Sussex, and has been living quietly in the three-bedroom house with her surviving daughter, largely unnoticed by those around them. When our reporters called to seek a reaction to her former husband's death, she refused to answer the door and Ruby was nowhere to be seen. A statement relayed via Maria Gavila read: 'I am deeply saddened by the death of my former husband. We had not been in contact for some time, but we shared a devotion to our two daughters that never waned for either of us. My surviving daughter is devastated by the loss of her father, and both she and I would be grateful to be left in peace to digest this sad development.'

Neighbours were unwilling to discuss her. 'I don't know her,' said Norman Colbeck, whose farm borders on to the two fields in which she keeps a ragged collection of pigs, chickens and goats. 'She doesn't mix. I don't think you'll find anyone much around here who'll have anything to say to you.' In the nearby village of Mills Barton, residents were equally unforthcoming. 'Yes, they come to the church from time to time,' said vicar Ruth Miller. 'Nice people, but quiet. They don't mix a huge amount, but they are always willing to contribute to church events and fundraising efforts.' No one at the school would comment. 'She isn't a pupil here,' said head teacher Daniel Bevan. 'We don't know them. Though obviously our thoughts are with them both.'

So the mystery of Claire Jackson's vanishing act is finally solved, but the mystery of Coco lives on. Many people believed at the time that Claire knew more about her daughter's disappearance than she was admitting. Cross-questioning would bring about a robotic shutting-down and a repetition of stock phrases and stories, as though she didn't trust herself to go off-message even for a moment. As the *Mail* columnist Dawn Hamblett said just before she dropped out of the limelight, 'It was as though Coco Jackson was an escapee from Stepford rather than a much-loved child.'

The death of Sean Jackson is far from the only disaster to strike the lives of the Jackson Associates, as the guests at the kidnap house were quickly dubbed in the days after the event. Jackson faced more heartbreak when his third wife, Linda, was found at the bottom of a flight of marble stairs in a house whose interior she was designing in Leyton, Essex, in 2010. She had suffered a fractured skull and died soon afterwards.

Her former partner, Dr James Orizio, was found guilty of malpractice and struck off in the summer of 2008 after one Miranda Chace, singer with hip-hop band Ton Ton Macoutes, died as a result of painkilling drugs he had prescribed on tour earlier that year without carrying out necessary health checks. The subsequent police investigation revealed a raft of prescriptions for painkillers such as Vicodin and the 'Hillbilly heroin', OxyContin, plus a number of other metabolism-enhancing drugs which had been, at the very least, handed out too casually. He was jailed in 2009 and released in 2012.

Charles Clutterbuck, once a rising Tory star, found himself sidelined to the back benches after the party came to power in 2010. After an early career in which he had been tipped for stardom and a Cabinet position at the very least, it wasn't hard to infer that his involvement in the ill-fated weekend might have had some influence over this exclusion. Clutterbuck himself blamed it on having attended 'the wrong school', a swipe at David Cameron's preference for surrounding himself with his fellow Etonians. In 2013 he gave up his safe Tory seat and defected to the newly formed Britain Together, an anti-immigration, Eurosceptic party, and failed to win it back at the ensuing by-election. His LinkedIn profile currently lists him as a 'consultant', although the *Mail* was unable to trace any companies using his services. Clutterbuck and his wife, Imogen, currently live on the Dalmatian coast, where the parliamentary pension, as a waggish former colleague put it, 'goes a lot further if you don't mind drinking local'.

As his reappearance on our televisions on the 10th anniversary of his daughter's disappearance made clear, Sean Jackson never lost hope that one day his daughter might be found. With his death, and with his second wife reluctant to engage with the outside world, the possibility of a solution to the mystery of what happened to Coco recedes that little bit further. Yesterday, gates leading to the Jacksons' Queen Anne manor house near Bideford remained closed, Robert and Maria Gavila the only visitors given access. No funeral is planned as yet, as the body awaits release by the coroner. But, with another gravestone soon to join the others in a green English graveyard, now perhaps might be the time to consider adding a further memorial to its carved granite surface.

The piece is illustrated by half a dozen pictures of Dad, three of them with the twins, one from twenty years ago, when India and I were still part of the picture. I look at it long and slow. We're at a table somewhere shady, a bright sunlit beach outside, red wine on the table, Indy and me hooked, one on each side, into the crooks of his arms, the three of us tanned and smiling broadly at what presumably is Mum taking the photo. He was a good-looking man, I can see that now. I thought he was handsome when I was a kid, but all girls think their fathers are handsome, don't they? But now that I'm little more than a decade off being the same age I can see that a man of forty could be handsome without me projecting it on to him. Thick sandy hair touched with grey at the sides, his body still hard and shiny, three-day stubble on a jaw that had yet to show signs of slackening.

I have no memory of this being taken. I don't know where it is. We did a lot of holidays when I was a kid, and some of them were happy.

I feel a sudden contraction somewhere deep in my bones. My joints ache, as though I've developed a fever. My God, I think, there *is* something there. I *do* miss him. I put the laptop aside and roll on to my side. Wrap my arms round my body and squeeze. Daddy. We loved you, when we were little. We thought the sun shone from your eyes.

I remember what it felt like to be wrapped in those big strong arms, before he stopped touching us. When was that? Sometime around the divorce, I guess. I remember the day he finally left, another day of bright sunshine, watching him walk down the path to his BMW without once looking back. We stood in the window of India's bedroom and watched him go, and Mum clattered things in the kitchen as if to signal that she wasn't bothered. He was wearing aviator sunglasses. I've never been able to like a man who's wearing them since.

And then I'm crying. I'm not sure what for. The fact that he's gone, or the fact that he went? I don't even know who I'm crying for. Nine-year-old me, or the mess I am at twenty-seven? But the sadness tears at my chest like a trapped animal trying to get out, and my face seems to have taken on a life of its own. I grit my teeth and feel my lips pull back to expose them, feel the wet flood over the side of my nose and soak the pillow.

'Oh,' I say, out loud. Then, 'Oh, oh, oh, *oh.*'

I'm alone. I have no one to comfort me. Everyone I know is elsewhere, going on with their lives, and I've ensured over the years that there is no one I can call on. I grab a pillow and wrap it in my arms, and somehow find it comforting. Oh, Dad. What a sod you were, and yet here I am mourning you anyway.

The phone begins to vibrate on the bedside cabinet. I swipe my sleeve over my eyes and sit up. A withheld number. Someone calling from an office, presumably. I consider for a moment not answering. It's not beyond the realms of possibility that someone from the press has got hold of my number. But then I think: it could be anyone. It could be India, or Maria, or Robert, looking to give me information, someone from the morgue or the police or something. I hit Answer and put it to my ear.

'Hello?'

Silence. For one second, two. I'm beginning to think that it's a wrong number, or an Indian call centre taking its time to connect me to the salesman waiting to ask if I've ever had PPI, when a voice I've not heard in years speaks and the back of my neck prickles.

'Milly? It's Claire.'

'Claire who?'

'Claire Jackson,' she says.

Chapter Nine

2004 | Thursday | Maria

Maria Gavila feels a bit weary as they sail past the chain ferry. Time on the *Gin O'Clock* is precious, because it's the only time when they don't have to be on parade. And even though Harbour View has fences and, according to Robert, gates like prison bars, they'll be back on show again once they get there and she'll be back to giving people what they need, or at least what they think they need. Robert is at the helm in his comical captain's hat and he's as happy as a pig in shit. This weekend will be exhausting. Sean and Charlie's appetite for partying is almost inexhaustible, and of course they'll be leaving it up to the women to work through the hangovers and keep the kids out of their hair in the daytime.

Her vodka, lime and soda is almost finished, and there's not enough time before they put in at the marina berth they've booked to make it worthwhile getting another. Simone is in a swing chair reading *Harry Potter and the Order of the Phoenix*. Whether she's reading or rereading is anybody's guess. It's such a long book, and Simone is such an idle reader, that it could well have taken her a year to get halfway through. Linda and Jimmy are nursing bottled beers at the aft table, still playing Beggar-my-Neighbour with the kids, though the fun must have worn thin by Southampton. It's partly to avoid talking to each other, she thinks. I'd have got fed up with Jimmy's 'rock'n'roll medic' act years ago, too. The only thing that keeps them together is the fact that he's off on tour prescribing pharmaceuticals to overpaid musicians half the time. I would probably have backed off from being friends with them years ago myself, if it weren't for the stream of gossip that pours out of him after every tour, and God bless the Hippocratic oath.

She uncurls herself from her chair and makes her way forward to find her husband. The *Gin O'Clock* is their largest boat yet – four compact berths below deck, white leather upholstery and drop-down walls that turn the canopy into a makeshift saloon in inclement weather – but it still takes her less than thirty seconds to reach him, hanging on to the guard rail as she walks. She comes up behind him and encircles him with her arms, leans her chin on his shoulder. There's more of him than there was when they met; he's filled out, become more substantial as his status has grown. She doesn't mind. Maria has kept her figure despite the almost nightly stream of events she attends, sticking to a single glass of champagne and waving away the canapés in order to compete with her actress-model-singer clients, all twenty years younger than her and thin as whippets and all wanting shots with their Alpha Rep in front of the sponsor boards; but weight feels better on a middle-aged man, as long as it doesn't wobble. He's her power husband, the other half of her power couple, and she likes him as he is.

'It's not too late to say we've sprung a leak at the Isle of Wight,' she says.

Robert shakes his head. 'You know we can't, Maria. They'll just tell us to come over on the ferry.'

'It's all right for you,' she says. 'No one's going to be expecting you to spend the weekend playing house with the laydeez.'

Robert sighs. 'It's just a weekend. And I'll make it up to you, I promise.'

The boat reaches the pontoon and Robert starts to manoeuvre. Maria lets him go and goes to lean on the railing to look at sunny Poole. It's hardly a Visit England brochure. But then, old people need a lot of ramps and guard rails in their retirement communities.

'Simone!' shouts Robert. 'Stand by to tie up, will you?'

Simone drops her book on to the deck and uncurls herself slowly from her chair. Like a cat, thinks Maria, or a marmoset. My goodness, where did those legs come from? And the bosom? I could swear she was a child when we set out on this trip, but now look at her.

Simone is wearing white hotpants and a gingham shirt that she's knotted beneath her breasts to show a little brown midriff and emphasise her neat little cleavage. Her poker-straight – no need for these ceramic straighteners they're all carrying in their make-up bags these days – waist-length hair shines chestnut with glints of gold, as though someone's come in and dipped it in glitter varnish. Maria stares, mesmerised, at her stepdaughter. My God, she's a woman, she thinks. Then an awful thought rushes through her head – *I must watch her around Charlie Clutterbuck* – and she squashes it down before it can take root. Charlie has known Simone since she was a toddler. He would no more . . . he's no Woody Allen even if he *does* like to play the lusty *monseigneur*. Good God, he's spent enough of his career watching his parliamentary colleagues fall one by one to the *News of the World* to never want to go anywhere near a teenager as long as he lives.

76

Simone sashays along the deck in her pink flowered mules towards the little gate in the guard rail. She's wearing make-up. All the way around the coast, marina-to-marina from St Katharine Docks, she's been as bare of face as a ten-year-old, and has stuck to a uniform of smocks and leggings when she's not been spreadeagled on the prow soaking up the sun in her bikini. Now she's as brown as nutmeg and her skin, usually freckled and scattered with evidence of her hormonal age, is smooth as marble, her eyes lined black like a cat's and – good God! Are those false eyelashes? What's going on? Is there some boy I didn't know was coming?

A thunder of footsteps and the smaller kids barrel up behind her in their flotation vests, push her out of the way before she reaches the gate. 'Me!' shouts Joaquin, her son with Robert, seven years old and loud as a foghorn. Simone presses herself back against the cabin wall and treats them to a look of teenage contempt. She studies her nails, and Maria sees that they're painted. A subtle shade of pink, thank God, but painted. 'Me! Me!' shout the Orizio kids at Joaquin's heels, three and four and six and caught up in the web of hero worship. It's all monkey see, monkey do at that age.

'You look nice,' she says, experimentally, and Simone silently tells her to back off through her curtain of shiny hair.

'Look,' says Robert as they walk up the road through Poole, their dependants trailing along behind, the young ones poking things with sticks and the two of them savouring their last few moments before the world kicks in again. 'I'll tell you what. You just get through this weekend and I promise we won't have to do it again. He's only fifty once, and I can guarantee you that she won't be around by the time he's sixty.'

'Really?' she asks, brightening.

'I doubt she'll be around by the time he's fifty-one, actually,' he says. 'The bloom is most definitely off the rose.'

'Thank God for that,' she says.

'She'll be toast come Christmas. It'd have happened years ago if it weren't for the twins. As it goes, I think there's someone else on the horizon.'

'Oh, really? Who?' She glances around and notices that Simone is walking a few feet behind them, fiddling with her phone. '*Attends! Pas devant les enfants,*' she says.

Simone looks up and says the first words she's shared all day. 'I do speak French, you know,' she says. 'Actually, I probably speak more than you do. That's what you get for sending me to private school.'

The queue for the chain ferry seems to run all the way back off the Sandbanks peninsula and into the suburbs behind. They walk past car after car full of red-faced children staring hopelessly out in search of the sea. Adults stand on the tarmac, lean on roofs, smoking, and she's painfully aware of how many eyes follow her stepdaughter's barely covered buttocks as she sways along the road. It's an endless worry, parenthood, she thinks. No sooner do you stop worrying about them eating bleach than you're yelling at them to LOOK before they cross the road, and now it's oh, darling, you don't know about the nasty men in the world, please take care. I was no better. I used to walk around in a rugby shirt and fishnet stockings and it never occurred to me that I was doing anything other than dress-up.

Jimmy jogs up beside them. 'So tell me about this Charlie Clutterbuck?'

'What do you want to know?'

'He's a bit of an arch Toryboy, isn't he?'

'A slavish free-marketeer,' says Robert. 'I can tell you that.

Always was, even at university when the rest of us were huffing and puffing and supporting the miners. He's tipped for Cabinet if they ever get back in again, especially now he's got such a safe seat. He'd have gone straight into politics with the Thatcherites if he'd had a private income. Had to go into the City for fifteen years first, to save up.'

'Yeah, what I'm wondering,' says Jimmy, 'is how much we're going to have to mind our Ps and Qs. Am I going to get MI5 banging on my door?'

'Oh, I wouldn't worry about that,' says Robert. 'Dobbing people into MI5 is far more of a New Labour thing. Besides, our Charlie had the busiest of noses the moment he had the income to support it. He's never done things by halves, be it entertainment or fascism. I should think he's gone underground a bit, but you know Tories. I don't suppose he'll manage to keep it under wraps for long. As it were. If anything he'll be beating you to it.'

'Okay,' says Jimmy. 'Well, I'll play it by ear.'

'There'll be lots of drink,' says Maria, reassuringly. 'Gallons and gallons of excellent wines.'

'Yeah,' says Jimmy, 'good old drink. How old-school.'

She's just starting to wonder if they might have missed the house when she sees Sean, standing on the pavement with his hand on his hips, talking to a man in a hard hat. Beside him, on the ground, is a slate nameboard with the legend 'Seawings' painted on it in gold cursive lettering, obviously awaiting reattachment to one of the ugly red-brick pillars that have been recently built to take heavy gates.

'Christ,' she says, and peers at the building site behind the pair of them. A man with four-day stubble sits high up on the seat of a JCB, looking down. Suddenly conscious of how her neat little sundress must look from above, she pulls her cardi tight over her bosom and glares back. 'This isn't it, is it? I thought he said it was finished.'

The driveway beyond the digger is a chaos of mud and scaffolding. Up a bank, she can see half a dozen men heaving paving slabs into place. A patio? Swimming-pool surround? Either way, it's clearly not done. It looks like it might be for the pool. A pre-cast resin shell, twenty feet by ten, sky-blue and still cloaked in protective tape, leans against the devastated turf. She guesses that the crane that looms over the wall is there to lower it into place once the hole's been dug. Everything's smoke and mirrors, even the most expensive houses. Pull the wattle-and-daub off a palace wall and you'll find that it's all made of rubble. Behind the swarming workers, a man leans from a window and paints its metal frame in a garish tone of seaside blue. Seriously? Men with muddy boots still in the bedrooms? You've brought us to stay here? 'What is he thinking?' she asks.

'Maybe the contractors have been fibbing,' says Robert. 'It wouldn't be the first time.'

They approach the two men. The builder glances over Sean's shoulder and gives them an 'I'll be with you in a minute' nod. Turns back to Sean.

'I am sorry,' he says, in perfect English whose lack of elisions betrays it as his second language. 'We are only doing our work. Your own house was full of builders itself until yesterday, you must remember. We have taken longer than we thought, because your own builders were here until yesterday, I am sure you know that. And they were not – there was no co-operation. Until today they were blocking the drive and we could not get the digger in. So now we have to make up the time.'

He heaves a shrug that takes both arms in their entirety to complete. All this, it says, we could have shared. The famous Polish influx, she thinks. Bane of the British builder. Amazing how they've all forgotten the dosh they made on the Costas last decade. Europe should only work one way, the way most of our people see it.

'So . . . how long?' asks Sean. 'I've got little kids, and guests coming any minute.'

Another expansive shrug. 'Our contract says end of Saturday. But, you know . . . the sooner we carry on, the sooner we are done, hey?'

He nods over Sean's shoulder at her little party. Jimmy and Linda have caught up now, the kids gathered around their knees and Joaquin inspecting the digger's caterpillar tracks as though they're made of real caterpillars. 'I think maybe these people want to talk to you?'

Sean turns. He's pink-faced and sweaty, the heat and the unaccustomed failure to get his point across raising his body temperature. 'Oh,' he says. Comes over and kisses the women, leaving damp patches on their cheeks, shakes the hands of the men. 'Sorry about this. Good to see you.'

'Builders behind?' asks Robert. They've known each other for thirty years, shared a flat in Sheffield, barely bother with verbs and pronouns when communicating with each other.

'Not mine, fortunately,' says Sean. He turns back to the Polish builder, who has taken his hard hat off and is polishing the per-spiration off its interior with a grubby handkerchief. He's tall and wiry. They all are, as far as she can see. A far cry from the lardy backsides she's got used to seeing over the years around British work sites. 'So can you try to keep it down a bit?'

The shrug, again. 'You are a builder yourself, I think? It is not much longer. I promise. These guys are all . . . gagging to get back to Krakow.'

'There's a guy turning up,' says Sean. 'Big car. Probably a Mercedes, I should think. Can you move the guys out of the way to let him in so he can park on our drive? And not damage it?'

'*Benz!* Sure! We will treat it as though it is our own!'

'Come up to the house. Simone, you're sharing with Milly and India. I hope that's okay?'

Maria sees her daughter roll her eyes as Sean picks up Linda's bag and leads the way between a pair of giant electronic gates, newly painted in shiny black, a plaque on each one that will presumably one day hold the initials of whoever buys the place. Russian money is starting to flood into Sandbanks, a suburb of Bournemouth which has mysteriously become Britain's most expensive real estate, as it is into any bit of London within a limo's drive of Harrods, and the Russians love a gold-highlighted monogram. I'll bet there are gold-plated bath taps, too, thinks Maria. And rainforest showers. Looks as if they're doing the same at Seawings. You couldn't get people to buy these places forty years ago, when we were preparing for an Ice Age and the whole of Poole Harbour was going to be a glacier.

'Oh, very Jackson Associates,' mutters Robert under his breath.

'I did the interior on this one, you know,' says Linda, proudly.

'I know,' replies Maria. She's beginning to guess who Sean's Someone on the Horizon might be.

Chapter Ten

The Stepwitch.

I actually don't recognise her voice. It's been over a decade. And something has changed in it in that time. She sounds tentative, sure; nervous, even. But it's not that. Her voice has dropped. It no longer has that shrieky edge that made you feel nagged the moment she opened her mouth.

'Claire,' I say. Think for a moment and add the appropriate pleasantry. 'How are you?'

'I'm – fine,' she replies. 'More to the point, how are *you*?'

My nose is blocked but I'm desperate not to do anything to clear it. I don't want anyone to know I've been crying. I gave up crying over my father when I gave up contact with him, and I'm damned if I'm going to let anyone know that that has changed. Especially not Claire. I don't remember crying over anything other than the normal childhood things before she came on to the scene.

'I'm fine, thanks,' I say carefully.

She pauses again. Then, 'I'm so sorry about your father, Milly. It must have been a terrible shock.'

'I'm sure you know we weren't close,' I say, and let all the accusations that go with that statement echo down the line.

She doesn't take the bait. 'No. But still. I'm sure there are . . . emotions involved.'

'Sure,' I say. 'Thanks.'

She can't just be calling me with condolences, can she? 'How's Ruby doing?' I ask.

Another little silence. And then, 'Not good, I'm afraid. She's in bits.'

Oh. I have another weird little surge of emotion, and it takes me a moment before I identify it as jealousy. And then I'm disgusted with myself. I had no idea that I still had that in me: that I still think of Ruby and Coco as usurpers, as though I am the only one allowed feelings in the matter.

I think about my half-sister, this stranger devastated by our common bereavement. Fifteen years old. I don't even know what she looks like now. Like little lost Coco, she is set in amber in my mind: three years old forever. I've honestly never thought about her growing up. Going through the horrors of adolescence, living with a loss so huge it's hard to comprehend. She and Coco have been no more than bit-players in my own misery. Not people in their own right at all.

'I'm so sorry to hear that.'

Claire sighs. 'It's not that surprising, I suppose. They hadn't seen much of each other lately, but she did love him.'

Another twinge of self-pity. So did I, once. 'I'm so sorry.'

'She doesn't seem to be able to stop crying,' says Claire. 'She's in her room right now. I've tried to talk to her. But I . . . I sort of don't know what to say. It's hard. We . . . your father and I . . . she knows there was no love lost between us, and . . .'

Not my problem. *Not* my problem. You drove a wedge between my parents and took him away, and suddenly he was saying my mother was mad and he'd never been happy, and you want me to sympathise because you couldn't make it work? I'm not responsible for the world you've created, Claire. I have enough difficulty staying above the surface in my own.

'Claire—' I begin.

'No, look, I'm sorry. I know you don't want to hear about this. But I have to ask you a favour and I know it's a big ask, but I *can't* go to his funeral. I just can't. I can't. I *can't*.'

There's an edge of hysteria to the last few words. Claire is panicking. She must have been thinking about this for hours before she worked up the guts to ring me, and now she's started she's desperate to get her request across before she loses her nerve. But I'm not going to make it easy for her. She never made it easy for me. She wants me to tell her that no one would expect her to, that I understand, but I'm not going to do that. Each time we went to stay with them, she was more sulky, more standoffish, sniping at Dad in a passive-aggressive way that made it very clear that we weren't welcome, that there was no room for us. I know he was weak to go along with it, but I'll never forget how she wanted to edit his life so none of the stuff that happened before he met her mattered.

'So I . . . ' she continues. 'I don't know what to do, Milly. I'm sorry to ask, I really am, but she's desperate to go . . . '

'You want me to take Ruby to the funeral?'

Another pause. She hasn't realised that she hasn't asked. 'Yes.'

'Oh,' I say.

'I'm sorry,' she says. 'I just don't know who else to ask. And you *are* her sister.'

'Half-sister,' I say, coldly.

'Yes,' she says. 'But she doesn't have anyone else now.' And Coco hovers between us, daring us to mention her name.

I don't answer. My brain is buzzing.

'Do you know when it is yet?' she asks. 'We're out of the loop a bit.'

'Not yet. The coroner has to release the body.'

'So not till after the inquest?'

'No, it'll be before then if they find a medical cause. But I think he has to be buried, not burned, so they can dig him up again if they need to. But that's okay. He always wanted a big flashy gravestone near his mother's in the village he grew up in. No revenge like success, eh?'

Claire gulps at the bald facts and the way I tell them. I don't add that they won't be able to embalm him either. Little Ruby won't be having any final bonding sessions with the open coffin.

'Will you think about it?' she asks.

'I hadn't decided whether to go myself,' I say, reluctantly.

'Oh,' she says, and I hear her throat fill with tears. 'That's sad, Milly. I'm sorry. I thought maybe you'd . . . I don't know. None of his kids at his funeral? I can . . . I don't know. Maybe I could bring her down to Devon and ask someone to pick her up? I just. I can't. I really can't.'

She sounds so different from the woman I knew. There doesn't seem to be any anger left, just fear.

'I'll think about it, Claire,' I say. 'I can't say more than that.'

She sucks in a heavy breath, steadies her crying. 'Thank you,' she says. 'Thank you. I just don't know what to do, that's all. She's been crying and crying and I'm afraid she'll never . . . '

She trails off.

'I'll let you know when it is.'

'Thank you. Do you have my number?'

'Why don't you text it to me?'

'Oh, yes,' she says. 'You are clever . . .'

I hang up before she can go on. Sit under the duvet and let my eyes wander over my bedroom. I've not given it a lot of love since I moved in. I didn't even bother to cover over the old owners' paintwork, just moved Granny's hand-me-downs in against the walls and bunged her pictures up with nails. Apart from my clothes, there's very little in this place that came here through my own choices. Perhaps that's why I spend so much time on my wardrobe, why I cherish my tattoos, why I like to stand out each time I pass through the front door. Even the pots and pans in the kitchen are Granny's. India was on her way across the Pacific by that point and didn't want the cargo, and Mum was in her fifties and had adult versions of most of the things you need in a house, so I was basically able to take my pick. It's a bit like living in a furnished apartment. A nice one, where the kitchenware is Le Creuset, but still a furnished apartment, like the ready-for-sale houses we grew up in. Only, I've covered every surface with books and unread mail and discarded food wrappers, as if I'm trying to disguise it. How odd that I've never noticed that before.

My tears have passed. As is often the way with bouts of emotion, I feel tired but also weirdly calm. And almost unable to fathom that such strong feelings can ever have existed, or ever could again.

I think about Ruby. I'm not so far from fifteen that I don't remember what it felt like, that horrible, confusing time suspended between childhood and adulthood, longing for and terrified by independence in equal measure. The world was a scary, exciting place, back then, and home was a place we longed to leave. Mum struggling to find her post-marital personality, Dad spawning offspring at what felt like a repellent rate in one so old, and boys sprouting extra pairs of hands. We didn't fit in anywhere much, never having had the sort of home you brought people back to. And when I was fifteen the Coco thing happened and we went from anonymous misery to total, public isolation.

My tea has gone lukewarm. I drain it and get up to make another. God, what a family. There will be a large turnout at Dad's funeral when it happens, I have no doubt of that. He's a rich man, and rich men are powerful, and people like rich men because, although trickle-down doesn't work as a society-wide principle, it sure as hell does work if you can get yourself next to the people with the money. He was a charming man, one who married four women and could probably have had half a dozen more if he'd had the time. His parties were the best parties, with the best champagne and the highest-quality canapés, and the funeral will have more of the same, and people will go a long way, and say a lot of nice things, for a sniff of vintage Bolly and some truffled foie gras.

Will they even notice that his family aren't there? That, of the four wives and five children, there's only the last one and the toddler who can't get away? Does it matter? We weren't the important thing about Sean Jackson's life. He barely even paused for breath after his third daughter vanished, before he was diving into another marriage, another set of condos on the seafront in Dubai, chewing on fat Havana cigars and slapping the shoulders of smiling politicians. Of course there will be people at his funeral. And I can't leave Ruby to brave it by herself. Standing all alone in that sea of social mourners. I can't do it.

Chapter Eleven

Myocardial infarction. I've always found it a comical-sounding phrase for something so serious, but then my British ear is trained to hear the breaking of wind at a thousand paces, and the fact that it's the cause of my father's death doesn't cancel out the Pavlovian smirk. I read it several times after I got the email from Maria, and the actual meaning didn't sink in until the fourth or fifth. *Myocardial infarction.* I need to just refer to it as a heart attack. It's the only way to make it real.

I scan the email each time I stop for queues and lights and mini-roundabouts on the dreary haul through Croydon towards the M23 and Claire's 'run-down smallholding'. If Maria's sent me the details she'll probably have sent them to Claire as well, but I need to have it all straight in my head, in case I end up being the one who has to explain it all to Ruby. The best part of five days, we'll be together, and it's not all going to be small talk.

They live in Sussex. On the edge of the Downs, outside one of those villages that have remained cute by dint of belonging in its entirety to an aristocratic estate. I'm impressed by its beauty as I pass through: front gardens neat even in winter, not a wheelie-bin or a caravan to be seen. The shop, with its cute little multi-paned window that makes it look like a Thomas Kincaid painting in a Kentucky trailer park, sells pesto and 'locally sourced produce'. You can tell what the tenants are like.

I buy a goat's cheese and tomato tartlet and eat it sitting on the war memorial; I never feel well enough for breakfast and I'm starving now, unsure what will be coming my way for the rest of the day. Goat's cheese and tomato tartlet. Whatever happened to Cornish pasties? At least they haven't gone the whole hog and called it a *tartelette*, I suppose.

I get the print-out of the email out once more as I sit on the steps, smooth it out on my knee and read as I eat. I wonder idly if the polite woman who showed me through to the viewing room is the same person who sawed open my father's breastbone and pulled off the top of his skull. Probably. No one's got the budget to keep a show-pathologist around for the visitors. Maria's cut the name off, has just said that they're satisfied that the cause of death was the heart attack, that it was so huge that even if whoever was with him had called an ambulance it would have made no difference, and that this is enough to release the body for burial.

The inquest will be later. They don't need the body around for it. But the handcuffs, and the poppers on the bedside table, and the traces of cocaine in the blood . . . it's pretty obvious what happened. I wonder what the woman – I'm pretty sure, at least, that it will have been a woman – felt like, backing off as he writhed on those Egyptian cotton sheets, if she even paused to think about unlocking him before she fled. What a way to go. What a horrible, lonely way to die.

A man approaches slowly up the main street. From the holes at the elbows of his Tattersall check Viyella shirt and the fact that his trousers seem to be held up with string, I guess that this is the proprietor of the great house at the bottom of the drive. He confirms it when he opens his mouth and a tumble of vowels barely held together by consonants falls out.

'Are you lost?'

'Nope,' I say pleasantly. 'I'm eating a delicious goat's cheese and tomato tartlet.'

He regards me with an assaying eye. I suspect my paisley ra-ra skirt, animal-print boots and shearling jacket are not the sorts of clothes you see often on this high street. 'As long as you're not lost. Visiting people, are you?'

'Nearby. I'm a bit early so I thought I'd take a break. This is a nice village you have here.'

'Thank you,' he says, and thrashes at a patch of gnarly nettles growing out of the bottom of a signpost with his walking cane. 'Who are you visiting?'

'Do I need permission?'

'Just asking.'

'My ex-stepmother and my half-sister,' I say.

'Name?'

I raise my eyebrows at him. 'No need to take that attitude,' he says. 'I'm just curious.'

'The Jacksons. A place called Downside.'

'Thought so,' he says. 'We really don't like journalists around here, you know. Why can't you leave those poor people alone?'

'Um – because they asked me to come?'

'I've not seen you before.'

'No,' I say. 'It's my first time.'

He gives me another of those country-people looks. You're down from That London, it says, but I've got your measure. 'Well, enjoy your tartlet,' he says.

'Thank you,' I reply, and take another bite.

*

The village road leads on down to the gates of the big house, then veers off to the right into some woods and starts to climb the hill. It's one of those little trickling roads that people pay extra for with their holiday cottages. Even with the leaves off the trees, the wood is dark and enveloping. I'm surprised to find a place like this here, a place that feels this ancient. Sussex *is* ancient, of course; but I had thought that the witchy, druidic feel had long since been overrun by the onward creep of suburbia.

I emerge on to the lower grasslands that edge the Downs and the road turns to run parallel with the headland. On the other side of the hill is the sea, vast panoramas looking out to France, but here it feels as though we are sunk deep in the centre of the country. A farm passes by on the right. Must be the Colbeck farm they mentioned in the *Mail*. Not neat and chichi and gloss-painted on every window frame like the properties bought up by fleeing Londoners, but a proper farm with a stack of giant straw-rolls wrapped in black plastic towering over its chimney pots and bits of several vehicles scattered along the verge and a splendid smell of cowpat. Three hundred yards further on, the road comes to an end at a gate. Beyond, an unmetalled track dips back down into the treeline. DOWNSIDE, says a pokerwork notice on the fence. PRIVATE ROAD.

I stop and think. Get out of the car and lean on the gate. I decide to have a cigarette to calm my nerves. I never gave her an exact arrival time, and there's still plenty of daylight left, and if I can't procrastinate on a day like this I don't know when I can.

To my right is a mailbox – literally, a box, big enough to take a case or two of wine. The lid is open and nothing sits within. I lean against the gatepost and roll my fag. Light it and look at the sky.

I'm still not convinced that this is a good idea. My mother has told me that it is, India has told me it is, Maria has said that I will 'earn my place in heaven' by doing it, but that's easy for them to say. They don't have to do it, after all. I dread the next five days, but I dread tonight most of all. She says we should get to know each other before we set off on a road trip together, and I see the logic, but oh, God, that means spending my first night with Claire in twelve years.

There are fungi by the ton growing on the trunks of the beech trees, among the moss. I think they might be Chicken of the Woods, but I wouldn't want to hazard my life on it. The cigarette tastes great in the cold damp air, as all cigarettes do when you know it's going to be a while before your next one. If I know Claire at all, the entire property will be a smoke-free zone. Daddy used to deliberately light up his cigars within feet of the windows at home, just to annoy her. As a result I've always rather liked the smell of cigars; they smell to me like the fight for personal liberty.

'Ah, there you are,' says a voice, and I whirl round. A woman stands twenty feet away on the drive. Small and skinny, middle-aged and dressed in a fleece and wellingtons and heavy-duty jeans. If I saw her in London I would think lesbian, God bless me for my stereotyping, what with the greying cropped hair and the zippered weather gear. It takes me several seconds to recognise my stepmother.

'Claire?'

'I was expecting you a bit sooner,' she says. 'Tiberius rang to say you were on your way – well, to warn me about some journalist lurking in the village – twenty minutes ago. I was beginning to think you must have got lost, or I'd forgotten to take the chain off the gate or something.'

'No, sorry,' I say. 'I was just—' I gesture shamefacedly at my cigarette, a teenager once more.

'Oh, you never grew out of that, then?' She advances, and gives me a smile. Then she's at the gate and I can't dither over how to greet her any more. We kiss, awkwardly, one cheek only, over the top bar to avoid having to work out what to do with our bodies. Her skin feels rough against my cheek. Claire Jackson's days of Crème de la Mer and weekly facials are clearly long since passed.

'You look great,' she says, looking my clothes over. 'Ruby will love you. You always were inventive with your clothes, though. You nearly gave Tiberius an aneurysm.'

'Is he really called Tiberius?'

'The Strangs have been calling their eldest sons after emperors since the 1680s,' she says. 'His father was a Julius and his elder son is a Darius. Rumour has it he had to be talked out of calling him Khosrow.'

She unhooks the gate and swings it open. It's old but well maintained, the hinges well oiled and firmly set in the post so that it doesn't need dragging even when it reaches the verge.

'Come on in,' she says.

I drive us back down to their house. Soon after it enters the trees, the track swings back uphill again; the kink is there for extra privacy, she says. And then we're out in the field and I'm stunned. It's all so . . . un-Claire. Well, not the Claire I remember. But of course, she was living in my father's houses back then. There's a big shelter where I can see a stack of hay bales and several dustbins and, beyond the fence, two paddocks. In one, a donkey and two goats stare at us from the dark interior of the field shelter. In the other, two smiling Tamworth pigs loll around in the mud outside a mini Nissen hut. A flock of chickens flaps away squawking as I creep through them, bolting into a large vegetable garden that has little at the moment to show for itself other than kale, early-sprouting broccoli and a few last heads of cabbage.

'This is so good of you,' says Claire. 'I really do appreciate it.'

I try to work out how to reply. Convention would demand that I dismiss the whole enterprise as nothing, as a pleasure, but I'm really not feeling myself there yet. 'That's okay,' I say.

'She's calmed down quite a lot since you said you'd do it. Just your saying yes has been a real help.'

'Good.' I can't think why. I can think of few prospects less enticing than going to a funeral with a stranger, but there you go. It takes all sorts.

'She remembers you, you know.'

I blush. Oh, God, we were so horrible to them. 'Oh, dear.'

'No, it's good. Don't worry. It's one of the few memories she has of Coco, too. Down on the Studland beach, I think. She says she went there in a boat, which I guess must have been the chain ferry. It's a bit of a weird memory, actually.' She laughs. 'Actually, now I think about it, it might not be a memory at all.'

'What?'

'She says you found a jellyfish and cut a slice out of it like it was a cake.'

I remember it suddenly and with great clarity. The day before that dreadful row with Dad, when we went back up to London and had a party at home while Mum was up in Scotland at Granny's. If it hadn't been for Coco we probably would never have got busted, either; it's not like they ever compared notes with each other. As it was, we ended up phoneless and cashless and under curfew for an entire month while the search parties were scouring the Purbeck coast and flotillas of boats out of the Isle of Wight were scanning the sea. The last time I ever saw Coco. Another thing I'd forgotten. Indy found some boys on the beach and we ended up on a houseboat tripping off our tits. I got off with some boy called Josh that India had her eye on, but

I was so wasted that I can't remember if I fucked him or not. Jesus, I got away with murder when I was a teenager.

'Oh, yes!' I say. 'I remember! That was a fun afternoon.'

'Yuh,' says Claire. 'I'm sorry you never really got to know each other.'

And whose fault is that? I think, and shut up.

We round several ranks of naked bean canes and the house comes into view. Another surprise. Again not what I would have thought of as a Claire sort of house. Squat and red-brick, it looks as though it's been knocked together from a pair of farm workers' cottages. Outside, a rusty Datsun and a mini tractor, an array of things you can hook up to the back of a mini tractor, and several sheds. An oil tank the size of my bedroom desultorily camouflaged by some trellis and what looks like a leafless grapevine. A patch of rough lawn dotted with early crocuses, tubs of winter pansies either side of the front door and a handful of withered hanging baskets. 'Here we are,' she says. 'You're not seeing it at the best time of year, I'm afraid.'

'No worries,' I say. 'After Clapham North everything looks glamorous.'

The Claire I knew never let any living thing more chaotic than a single white orchid clutter up her space. She was a hundred per cent natural stone and feng shui ringing bowls. Then again, you'd never recognise my mother's cosy Persian-rug-and-cushioned-window-seat set-up with Barney in Sutherland as belonging to the same woman who was married to my father.

There's a dog. A big, bouncy black Lab who tumbles from the front door as though he's not seen her in days. He dances around her wellingtons, wagging and panting, then walks over, looks up at me and simply leans against my leg. 'That's Roughage,' she says. 'He likes to lean.'

Roughage gives me a big grin, which widens when I chuck him behind the ear. 'Hello, Roughage,' I say.

'I got him for burglars and journalists,' says Claire, and elbows him with a knee. 'Always important to have someone around to welcome them in and offer them a nice cup of tea, I think. Come in.'

The lintel is weathered and the light inside is dim. Despite the greyness of the day, Claire walks past the light switch as though it doesn't exist, and winds her way up the passageway. She has to wind her way, because the hall is full of boxes. But not like Tom's cardboard box collection; not Xbox packaging she's forgotten to throw away: boxes that are neatly stacked and sealed with parcel tape. The hallway is quite wide, I see, but the route along the length of its flagstone floor is no more than a couple of feet wide, and it bends in the middle. Boxes are piled up on either side. Boxes and those plastic crates you buy in pound shops, and somewhere beneath them some tables and a couple of chairs, a couple of rugs rolled up and stacked against the wall, dog bowls, a collection of wellington boots so large it's as though they're breeding down there, and, thrown down seemingly at random on top of the boxes, piles of coats and scarves. Enough to clothe the population of a homeless shelter, and none of them suitable to be worn even in a public space like the village.

'Excuse the clutter,' says Claire, casually as though she's referring to a few coffee cups and a pair of shoes. 'We're having a bit of a sort-out.'

No, you're not, I think. That's what I say every time I can't avoid having a visitor round at mine. *I'm in the middle of a clearout. It's at the worse-before-it-gets-better stage. I'm going to take these books, boots, belts, bags, to the charity shop.* And everyone knows it isn't true; everyone plays along with it because they know I will never change.

I play along too. 'Don't worry about it,' I say. 'You should see my flat.' Because that's what everyone says to me as they skirt around the empty wine bottle collection and gather up my bath towels to make a space on the sofa.

I glimpse a sitting room and a dining room as we pass, spaces left between the boxes to allow access to the doorways. The dining-room walls are lined with shelves and the shelves are filled with jars. Great big Kilner jars all the way down to little tiny ones that must have once held fish eggs, each jar neatly labelled and each label written on with black Sharpie. Ranks and ranks of them: 'tomatoes' 'peppers' 'green beans' 'cannellini' 'butter beans' 'sauerkraut' 'chutney' 'rhubarb' 'gooseberry' 'red-currant jelly' – there must be at least twenty of these – 'stewed apple' 'mushrooms' corner to corner, floor to ceiling. I catch a glimpse of the interior of one of the cardboard boxes where the lid has been left open and see that it, too, is replete with jar lids. Claire, it seems, is preparing for the zombie apocalypse. But in an organised way, at least.

'Sorry,' she says. 'I can't bear to waste all that spare produce. We thought we'd sell them at a farmers' market or something, but . . . well. I thought maybe I'd give the land a rest this year. You know, Jethro Tull style. I try not to use too many chemical fertilisers, so it could probably do with a rest. I collect the don-keys' droppings and the sweepings from the chicken coop, and compost everything, but . . . you know . . . it's probably not enough, in the end.'

'How about the pigs?'

'Oh, no, not for vegetables. Parasites.'

'Looks like you've easily got enough to last you out a year,' I say, generously.

Claire turns round and looks at her hallway as though with

newly opened eyes. 'I guess so. Oh, dear. Come and have a cup of tea. Or a drink. Would you prefer a drink? After your drive?'

I would love a drink. Love one. But I think I'd better pace myself. It's going to be a long few days. 'Tea will be fine,' I say.

'I've got a lot of gooseberry wine to use up,' she says. 'And rhubarb and blackberry and elderflower.'

A proper little liver-off-the-land. I can't believe that this is the same woman. The one I knew got in a state if she broke a fingernail. Now her hands are rough and red and the nails are clipped to the quick.

'Do you buy anything at all?' I ask.

'Not if I can help it,' she says. 'There are so many chemicals, you know. And additives. Colours. Even the stuff you think is really simple. Shop bread's full of other stuff, did you know? I'd grow my own wheat, really, but it's just not practicable. I get organic flour delivered and we make our own. I won't have Ruby exposed to that stuff.'

She stops at the bottom of the stairs, calls up. 'Ruby! Milly's here!'

'Mila,' I say. 'I go by Mila these days.'

'Oh!' she says. 'When did that happen?'

'University,' I say. Not the entire truth. I changed it just before I went up, but never got round to the going-up part. Too many mentions of 'Coco's sister Milly' in the press over the years for my liking. And besides: Millys are chirpy. They have things like jewellery rolls and they colour-code their underwear. They work in Human Resources and aspire to living in Tunbridge Wells. With a name like Milly you either change it or you abandon all hope.

A sound of movement far away in the house. A faint 'Coming!' drifting along the landing. 'I'll make the tea,' says Claire. 'Why don't you go and sit in the living room and I'll bring it through?'

'Sure,' I say.

'It's mint,' she says. 'Is that okay? I've got ginger in the freezer if you'd rather.'

I wonder if it's too late to change my request to coffee. Think about the additives and decide that there's no hope she'll have it. 'Mint's great,' I say, and start wondering how quickly I can claim to need to top up my petrol and stop at a garage in the morning.

I go into the living room. Low ceilings, a faded carpet that was once patterned with flowers, two low chintz sofas and an armchair. Roughage leaps on to the nicer-looking sofa, the one near the fire, which is lit and provides the only heat I can feel in the house. Flops down among the cushions and sighs.

No food stores in here, but the room, away from the seating area, is full to the brim. More shelves, this time stuffed with knick-knacks and souvenirs. A shell, a feather, a piece of salt-bleached wood. A teddy bear, a pair of tiny pink shoes, a christening cup, a My Little Pony. And more, odder things. A sippy cup. A spoon and pusher, made for tiny hands, with red plastic handles. A hair bobble with small plastic pandas. Some alphabet building blocks. Some Lego. Baby sunglasses. A tiny floppy hat. I know what it is. On a table in front of the shelves, a church candle, one of those six-inch-thick ones that lasts for weeks, burns in a saucer, surrounded by framed photos. Of Coco.

The walls are covered in them, too. Coco smiling, Coco on a white rug on a cold stone floor surrounded by Christmas wrapping paper, Coco on a beach, Coco and Ruby, identical in the sorts of gauzy dresses she would take any opportunity to dress them in back then, Coco in an inflatable rubber ring by a paddling pool, Coco at the top of a slide in a pom-pom hat, Coco and Ruby as tiny babies, wrapped around each other in a cot, an echo of how they were in the womb. Scrawled childish drawings – a wobbly flower, a scribble, a stick person – framed up in gold and glass as though they were precious art.

The room is a shrine.

I hear someone walk along the landing above my head and thunder down the stairs. I feel strangely guilty, staring at this evidence of Claire's loss, the plastic tat that should long ago have been thrown away. I move over to the fireplace and squat down to talk to the dog while I wait for my sister to appear.

Chapter Twelve

2004 | Thursday | Simone and Milly

She had her first dream of Sean when she was seven, and the memory still makes her shiver. It wasn't much of a dream by the standards of what has followed, as hormones and knowledge have shaped her brain. But the first time – that shiver of surrender and the feel of his imaginary arms encircling her – will always stay there at the back of her mind.

And he doesn't even know I'm alive, she thinks. I got all dressed up and he barely even glanced at me. I hate my age. He can't see me because of it. Can't see that I would do anything for him. Anything. And the Anything I've been given is taking the children to the beach so his spoiled sour wife can take time off.

She glances up the sand. Milly and India have the twins and Joaquin, and they've gathered around something that lies in the sand. Tiggy and Inigo Orizio wobble hand in hand at the water's edge, jumping back in shock each time a tiny wave – more wake from passing boats than actual waves; Poole Harbour in high summer is more like lake than sea – breaks over their plastic-sandalled toes. Tiggy sports an inflatable doughnut around her waist and Inigo wears a pair of waterwings. They're fine. It would take them so long to get out of their depth that there would be time to launch the coastguard long before they did. Fred sits nearby, studiously burying his legs in sand with a tin shovel.

Simone settles down on her back with *Harry Potter*. She's not reading. She rarely reads, but looking as though she is doing so makes her look less lonely. She longs to take a swim, but she's too conscientious about her job and doesn't want to leave the three kids she's somehow ended up watching while the other two just stick to their own siblings. This bikini, pink gingham with a pair of shiny buttons between her breasts, picked with such scrupulous care when she had found out she was coming down here, has never got wet. I'm such a fool, she thinks. All those daydreams, and he just thinks that I'm a kid. I need to stop. He's got a new wife now. A man like that was never going to wait.

But oh, if I had his children . . . I would never be casting around for people to take them off my hands. They would be the most precious things in my world, not an inconvenience to be dealt with by employing staff. Not every woman is made for a career, like Maria. I don't want suits and BlackBerries and expense accounts. I want a home. A home I can call mine for my love to grow in.

She thinks about Claire. The streaked highlights and the perfect manicures and the suspiciously still forehead though she's only thirty-three years old. I hate her, she thinks. Not only because she has what should be mine, but because I just hate her. She has my life. She has the life I should have grown up to have, and she doesn't even appreciate it.

'Have you seen what she's wearing?' asks India. Joaquin has run off to the sand dunes in one of those explosions of boy energy that come in very useful when you want to do a bit of bitching.

'Can't exactly miss it,' says Milly.

'She's not gone off Dad, then.'

Milly laughs, nastily. 'God almighty. It's like – how sad can you be?'

'It's disgusting. It's like she doesn't realise how old he is.' Fifty, to both of them, seems as far away as the moon. The twins seem to them unnatural phenomena enough, evidence as they are that he and Claire have been having creaky old-man sex. The thought that anyone of their own spectacular generation could see him as anything other than an object of pity makes them shudder.

'She's weird, though,' says Milly. 'She always has been. Daddy's little duckling. You don't think she really . . . you know . . . do you?'

'Soppy Simone? Oh, please. I know she's creepy, but she's not *that* creepy.'

'No. You're right. Besides. She's not exactly, you know, sexy, is she?'

'String bean.'

'And all that stringy hair all down her back like seaweed.'

'Do you think she's even *snogged* anyone?'

'She's saving herself for Daddy,' says Milly, and they both roll over in the sand and make gagging gestures.

Coco pokes at the jellyfish with a stick. Ruby, always the follower, sits and watches. Claire has dressed them all matchy-matchy again, like dollies, in little elasticated skirts over their ruched swimsuits and pink cotton sun-bonnets, their soft baby skin white with factor 50. They're nice little things, thinks Milly. It's not their fault who their mother is.

Coco looks up at her enquiringly. 'What that?' she asks.

They're a bit thick, though, she adds to herself. I'm sure they should be reading or something by now. 'Jellyfish,' she says. 'It's called a jellyfish. Cause it's like jelly, look.'

She pokes the dead animal with a toe and thinks actually, it's not like jelly at all. There's no wobble to it; it's more like rubber.

'Fish!' cries Ruby, and splays her hands in the air.

'Fish!' says India.

'What time are we meant to go back?' asks Milly.

'Oh, who cares? If they want free babysitters they get free service.'

'Pay peanuts, get monkeys?'

'Yeah, as if anyone's going to pay us. I'm so pissed off. It's quite obvious he wasn't expecting us, the gnarly old sod. So now he's just going to use us as staff so he and Claire can get pissed. He can bugger off, quite frankly.'

Milly grunts in response.

'I've a good mind to go back to London,' says India.

'Oh, come on, it's not that bad.'

'Whatever. It's not exactly going to be a barrel of laughs, is it? All those blustering old blokes drinking brandy. If Charlie Clutterbuck tries flirting with me again I think I'm going to throw up.'

'Oh, he's harmless,' says Milly. 'It's that new guy, Jimmy. Not sure about him *at all*.'

'Junkie,' says India, authoritatively. 'Pupils like pinpricks.'

'No!'

'And as for his missus, I mean. What's all that about?'

'She's quite pretty,' says Milly.

'Well, if you like that sort of thing,' says India. 'She's all a bit too Daddy's Little Girl for my liking. I bet she does baby-talk in the sack.'

'You're obsessed with sex,' says Milly.

'Said the kettle. Not that I'm going to get any of *that* this weekend,' says India glumly. Then she spots three lanky figures moseying up the beach and brightens up. 'Ay-ay! Maybe I spoke too soon!'

Simone hears laughter and looks up from her book. The Jacksons have attracted a small knot of boys. Three of them, sun-browned skin and salt-bleached curls falling into their eyes as they look at whatever it is they've got over there on the sand. One, the tallest one, digs in the pocket of his long-line surf shorts – as much use on this piece of sea-line as a shark net – and hands over an object that proves, when Milly flips out a blade, to be a Swiss army knife. The twins sit complacently side by side, straight legs in Vs and toes pointed at the sky. Her half-brother dances on the balls of his feet, doing jazz hands with excitement in that stupid way he does.

Curious, she leaves Fred and saunters over. Milly sees her coming and pulls a face, then pretends that she's unaware of her presence. They don't like me, thinks Simone for the millionth time. They never have. It's as though they're suspicious of me. It doesn't matter what I do, they just turn their backs when they see me coming. Even when we were kids, the same. I wonder if they know that I know the names they call me. Soppy Simone. The Limpet. The Little Mermaid. And, this year, Slimeoan. They probably don't. It probably never occurs to them that just because they can't see someone, it doesn't mean they're not there.

She reaches the group and sees the focus of their attention. It's a jellyfish the size of a dinner plate, a deep-water animal washed up from God knows where. Beautiful, in its way: translucent white with an inner circle of palest pink. And India has sliced it open with the knife. As though it were a cake. 'Look,' she's saying. 'It has air bubbles. I guess that's how it floats. How on earth do they get air in there?'

'I guess they're born like that,' says one of the boys.

'Yes, but they must get more as they get bigger. Don't you see? Where do they get it from?'

'Are you sure it's dead?' she asks.

One of the boys looks up, looks her over and finds her unfascinating. 'It is now,' he says, and looks at Milly with a yearning sort of greed. 'Besides, it can't feel anything. Jellyfish don't have brains. They are the only animals that don't.'

'Well, not the *only* ones,' says Milly, pointedly looking at Simone, and the whole group bursts out laughing. Simone feels her cheeks burning.

'This is Simone,' says India, and again she hears the sound of a joke in the tone: a joke that, as ever, she's not allowed in on.

'Hi, Simone,' says the youngest of the boys, and once again she feels a ripple of mirth run between them all.

She sends her charges to join the others, and takes her swim. Pounds along against the current twenty yards out and repeats and repeats her daily mantras. It's not for long. Not for long. I don't need friends. I don't need their approval. I don't need friends. All I need is Sean. Time, time, time. All I need is for time to pass. One day, all this will be behind me.

No one believes in love the way I do. If I told them, they would laugh. They think that at fifteen you don't know your own mind, let alone seven, but I always have. I just knew. In the way I knew how to eat, or knew how to breathe. I knew it again and I know it now. And if I wait, wait, wait, one day he will know it too.

When she gets out, panting from the exertion, she takes her time about dressing, gives attention to every detail, because soon it'll be time to get back to the house. She has brought a big beach bag with everything she needs. She hops and jumps, skin sticky

107

with damp and salt, back into her white shorts and ties her top back up above her midriff. Smooths lavender – she heard him exclaim how he loved the smell in the South of France when she was ten – body lotion on every limb, checks that her toenail varnish remains unmarked by the eroding sand. Lets down her hair from its swimmer's topknot and combs it out slowly, slowly, with a little serum so that it ripples, sleek and fluid, over her shoulders and down her back. She pulls out her mirror and checks the waterproofness of her mascara. Slicks a touch of pale tan colour on to her lips. It's only when she's finished and is packing her stuff away that she registers that the laughter she hears from up the beach is aimed at her.

'Gawd, look at her. She'll be dabbing perfume on her fanny in a minute.'

The boys laugh awkwardly. They're quite unsophisticated compared with the lads Milly and India meet around Camden Town: the difference, she supposes, between London and Salisbury, where they're from. But they're boys, and Josh, the eldest of them at nineteen, is quite lush in a gangly sort of way.

India stretches in her bikini, shows off her breasts with a look of knowing insouciance. Beside her, Milly feels quite young and gauche. India's moved to Camden for the sixth form, and she's soared ahead in the year she's been there. I'm not sure I'm ready for grown-up yet, she thinks. All those new people, and they've probably been going to nightclubs and that for years. I suppose I should get some practice in, but – boys. I don't really know what to do with them. They don't seem to be interesting the way girls are. It's all football and showing off, with them. She's had a few encounters at parties, because it's pretty much a hiding to Coventry not to be seen to have a snog and a feel, but she's found them clumsy and unsexy, their skin rough and their fingers poky. It'll be okay, she thinks, when I meet someone I fancy. I'm just choosier than India. She really doesn't seem to be fussy about anything much. So funny. It's usually me who wants to push things, kick over the traces and see where an adventure will lead me, but when it comes to boys it's like there's ten years between us.

'So what is there to do around here at night?' she asks, and gazes at Josh over the top of her sunglasses.

Chapter Thirteen

People often use animal metaphors when they're describing teenage girls. It's not that surprising: with the long legs and the big eyes, you can't help thinking of deer and fawns and cats when you see them. A group of Year 12s who'd found their way into a gallery show I was at recently, swaying on giddy heels in micro shift dresses, looked to me exactly like a small herd of giraffe gazing over the Serengeti.

Ruby looks like a yearling foal. A Clydesdale yearling. She clops into the room on momentous platform wedges, reels to a halt, snorts and tosses her mane. Okay, so I made up the bit about snorting, but the rest is accurate. When she sees that I am alone she panics for a second, backs off a couple of paces and does a clumsy gavotte.

'Oh,' she says, 'hello.'

I unfurl myself and get to my feet. She towers over me. In those shoes she's a good couple of inches over the six-foot mark. 'Hi,' I say.

She gives me an uncertain attempt at a smile, reveals heavy braces on both sets of teeth. Exactly the same ones both Indy and I had to suffer through, though hers are a disconcerting shade of swimming-pool blue. 'You're Milly.'

'I am.'

'You look . . . different.'

'So do you.'

And then some. Last time I saw Ruby she barely came up to my hip. They were stunted little pixie creatures then, all Cupid's bow lips and soft blonde hair that fell constantly into their big blue eyes. Really, Coco was the ideal kidnap victim for the tabloid press. She personified all the fantasies white people no longer admit to about what their children might look like. I would never, in a million years, have predicted that one of those eerie little doppelgängers would grow up to look like this. Nor, it seems, would the age-progression artists who did the poster of a thirteen-year-old Coco for the tenth anniversary.

Ruby is what they call strapping. Nearly six feet tall, with shoulders that could carry a beam across a building site and hands and feet that suggest that there's more growing to come. They may have taken after their mother when they were little, but there's no question who she takes after now. And her hair is black. Synthetic black, obviously, with a hard-cut fringe and pink – bright pink, the sort of pink you find on gynaecological doodads – tips draped over her shoulders. Her skin is pale – not snow-pale but the pale of risen dough – and caked in a layer of clumsily applied foundation, and her cheeks are round with puppy fat. Her mouth is still the same, though: a perfect Cupid's bow, strikingly rich in colour in contrast with her face. Above the platforms, she wears black leggings and a black jersey dress, and a cardi that must have cost a fair few quid on Etsy, so covered is it in small crêpe appliqué roses. And she rattles as she moves. There must be ten, fifteen bracelets strung up her arms, a couple of ankle bracelets, four or five necklaces, half a dozen earrings and a nose ring. Her eyes, still blue, have been outlined in wobbly black eyeliner. She looks a sight. And I love her immediately.

She hovers in the doorway. Eventually, she says, 'Thank you for coming.'

'That's okay,' I reply. 'I guess in the end we're the only ones who really understand, aren't we?'

Ruby's chin wobbles and I see that she's very much not okay. That the make-up has been put on for my benefit, to hide the fact that the eyes are red-rimmed and the skin on the upper parts of her cheeks is roughened by salt. Oh, poor kid, I think, and feel a sudden urge to cry myself. Don't, Mila, I think. You're the grown-up here.

'How did you hear about it?' I ask.

'Godmother Maria rang,' she says.

'I'm so sorry, Ruby.'

A patch of red appears on her throat, beneath the necklaces. She squirms in the doorway, wrings her hands.

'I need to feed the chickens before it gets dark,' she announces, and flees.

The tea is a brackish minty swill in a pot that doesn't seem to strain. Bits of half-hydrated herb float at the top of my mug, surrounded by little oily halos. I take a taste and it's acrid like nail varnish remover. 'I don't suppose you've got any sugar, have you?' I ask.

Claire looks surprised that I should ask such a question. 'Um, no, sorry,' she says. 'I've got honey, if you like? I keep a hive. Still can't guarantee they're not getting to GM plants, of course, but it's better than nothing.'

Ah. So the control issues haven't gone away; just transformed. No more trailing round Knightsbridge looking for a suitable manicurist; now it's sugar-is-the-devil and is-that-phosphate-free? Typical Paranoid/Histrionic. Clearly has an OCD in there, to boot. She goes back to the kitchen and returns with a jam jar half filled with honey. HONEY, proclaims the label on the outside. I wonder if she has a label on her toothbrush reading TOOTHBRUSH.

'Would you like a slice of toast?' she asks. 'We don't have biscuits, I'm afraid.'

Of course you don't. Some things never change. I well remember those long, hungry afternoons after a salad lunch. I bet you don't make butter from that goat, either. God knows what you use for fats. The toast will be dry, most likely. There will be no more biscuits after the zombie apocalypse.

'No, thanks,' I say, and silently regret having bought only one of those tartlets.

Ruby comes back in after dark, face flushed with the cold, unwinding a scarf from around her neck. 'I've done the hens and the pigs and the donkeys,' she says.

'Oh, thank you, darling,' says Claire.

Ruby goggles at me as though she'd been hoping I would have disappeared while she was out. 'Tea?' asks Claire.

She pulls a face. 'No, thanks.'

'Come and talk to us.'

A micro-expression that looks like fear, then she comes over to Roughage's sofa and plonks herself down. The dog lets out a little squeak, then leans his chin on Ruby's thigh. Gazes at me.

'So what are you doing with yourself now, Milly?' asks Claire.

'Mila,' I say. 'I'm a designer.' I always say I'm a designer. You say you're an artist and everyone immediately thinks 'Trustafarian'.

113

Say you don't do anything much and they look as if their heads are about to come off with the effort of trying to think of the next question. And besides, I *have* done a few logos for my friends' various businesses. Mostly importing knick-knacks and sustainable clothing from places they think of as spiritual, like Indonesia, or things to do with hemp. God, I despise my friends.

'A designer!' she says. 'What sort of design?'

'Oh, you know,' I say airily. 'Corporate branding, logos and the like, mostly. And labels. I'm good at labels.'

I could do you a few labels, I think. You certainly use them enough.

'Oh, great,' she says. 'You always were creative. Are you with a company?'

'Self-employed,' I tell her. See the 'ah' cross her face. Oh, well. I never really wanted to impress you anyway, Claire. You're just a secretary who shagged my father.

'Ruby wants to go to art school,' she says.

Ruby blushes.

'Art's your thing, is it?' I ask.

'I like it,' she says. 'I don't know if I'm any good or not.'

'Oh, pooh,' says Claire. 'She got an A at GCSE last year. And English, and French.'

'Wow.' Where did *those* brains come from? 'Where's school?'

'Oh, I don't go to school,' she says.

'I home-school her.'

'*Home* school? I thought that was for Christians and stuff? Have you gone Christian? How do you square it with the council?'

I realise once it's out of my mouth that I've been blurting. Claire looks slightly annoyed. 'Quite easily,' she says. 'I'd have thought that three GCSEs at fourteen wasn't a *bad* reflection of whether it works, wouldn't you?'

'And I go to tutors for the things she doesn't do,' says Ruby. 'I do maths and physics in Lewes and philosophy in Hove.'

'Yes,' says Claire, and raises an eyebrow.

But don't you worry, I want to ask, that she's going to end up completely handicapped, stuck up this hill with you going on about additives and nobody else to talk to? Because trust me – she's not going to make friends talking about Wittgenstein until she's at least seventeen, and then only in a six-month window.

'She goes to the youth club in the village,' says Claire, as though she's heard my thoughts. 'And people have her over all the time. And we go out, a *lot*. To galleries and the theatre and the cinema and such.'

Ruby's eyes flick between me and her mother repeatedly. But she doesn't say anything. I decide to change the subject. 'So when did you move here?'

Claire breathes, goes with the change. 'When Ruby was five. We went to Spain for a year, but . . . you know. It was lovely and sunny, and people left us alone, but it felt like being in exile.'

You *are* in exile, I think. You're still hidden away where no one can find you, sticking to a tiny village where the big house clearly rules the roost. 'And then Tiberius saved us. Literally,' she continues. 'I knew him when we were young, and he tracked me down at my lowest point. It was a complete lifeline, this place. I don't know what I'd have done without it. He said he was having trouble letting it because of its position. I'd been thinking about Wales at that point. Somewhere in Snowdonia or something. Where it's cheap. But here is better. I don't want Ruby growing up with no access to the world, even if I *don't* send her to school.'

There's an edge to this last remark. I guess I know what she means, really. My last three years at school were fairly much a living hell, after the Coco thing; every experimentation with the

115

way I looked resulting in a trip to the counsellor, people's parents shying away from having me over because – I don't know what? Scared I'd steal their younger children? Or scared I'd find their copies of the *Sunday Times* lying around, with its lengthy editorials about me and my family?

'Anyway,' she says, 'I must get on with supper. We eat early around here. Go to bed early, get up early. It's the healthy way to live. Are you sure I can't tempt you to a glass of rhubarb wine?'

Me and Ruby alone again. She scratches the back of Roughage's neck and Roughage grunts approvingly.

'She just wants to keep me safe,' she says. 'The Coco thing – she's scared, you know? She doesn't want to lose me too.'

I take my time about answering and my eyes drift over to the Coco wall. A lock of blonde hair tied up in a ribbon. A battered Barbie that looks as though she's had her face chewed off. A christening shawl, framed and hanging on the wall beside the shelves. Handprints in a lump of plaster of Paris. She's not got over it, not at all. How could one?

'Modern food is full of nasty stuff,' says Ruby, as though she's reciting a mantra. 'People get cancer from it all the time. She's just looking out for us.'

It's a modern disease, this neurosis about being poisoned by your food. We've never had a diet this healthy, food so readily available, medicines so effective, and people are giving their kids rickets by deciding they're lactose intolerant. Has Ruby been deprived of all the vaccinations too?

'It's fine,' I say. 'As long as you're happy.'

She doesn't reply, just bends down and kisses Roughage's snout repeatedly. Jesus. I wouldn't let my face anywhere near those teeth if I were her.

'How are you feeling about this weekend?' I ask.

She sits up and looks at me again. 'I don't know.'

'It's going to be tough.'

'I know that. But I want to do it.'

'I've got to do the eulogy,' I tell her. 'Can you help me with that?'

She brightens. 'Of course!'

'Some – an anecdote or two, maybe? Something a bit poetic about how you felt about him?'

'Feel,' she corrects, and her face starts to crumple again. Oh, Ruby, I think. What am I meant to do? You so clearly need a cuddle, need someone to put their arms round you and tell you it'll be okay, and I'm so not the person to do that for you. And nor is your mother.

'Are you packed?' I ask. 'We should get off at a decent hour. It'll take five hours or so, plus finding the place.'

'Finding the place? Don't you know where it is?'

'I know the *address*,' I say.

'Haven't you been?'

'No. I – Simone, you know . . . '

She look surprised, then relieved. 'Oh. I thought it was just me,' she says, and looks away.

'No,' I tell her, 'not just you.'

Supper is pork chops with kale and quinoa. 'I didn't ask if you still ate meat,' says Claire, and places a glass of rhubarb wine firmly by my tablemat. The table is long and sturdy, a big lump of roughly hewn something that would be quite beautiful if you could see it. But it's piled high with stuff. Papers and unopened envelopes and tools and folded clothes and shopping bags full of empty jars and a couple of dozen schoolbooks. She's cleared an extra space for me by shifting some things up, put a couple of

117

candles on saucers in between us all in an attempt to make it look pretty. The kitchen surfaces are cluttered too. There's a space a foot square by the stove where I guess she crams in a chopping board. When she opens a cupboard to get me the salt I see her automatically put a hand up into it to stop the contents cascading on to her face. On the fridge, more childish drawings, held on with magnets, yellow with age and curled at the edges.

'Thank you,' I say, 'I love meat.'

'This one was Blossom,' says Ruby, with a gloomy glee.

'I told you not to give them names,' says Claire. 'Haven't I always told you not to?'

'She was a particularly nice pig,' says Ruby, ignoring her. 'She liked apple cores and a good hard scratching behind the ear.'

I cut off a slice of Blossom and put it in my mouth. It's quite dry, grilled without fat, but beautifully tender. 'She clearly had a happy life,' I say. 'It shows in the meat.'

Claire goes to the sink to fill the water jug and I surreptitiously scatter salt over my plate. The kale is steamed, naked, and the quinoa is boiled, unbuttered. How has Ruby put on so much weight, I wonder, when they live on a diet that's entirely devoid of pleasure? Ruby puts a finger to her lips and reaches for the salt pot. 'No, Ruby,' says Claire, her back still turned to us. She must have been watching our reflections in the window. 'Salt's just for guests, remember?'

Ruby subsides and goes back to poking her kale.

'There's plenty of salt in veggies as it is,' declares Claire. 'No need to fur up our arteries.'

I wonder if I should tell her that only ten per cent of the population is actually responsive to salt, but I decide to let it lie. I learned a long time ago that once someone's adopted a belief there's little point in trying to argue them out of it. And besides, I'm trying to train myself not to be a pedant.

She comes back to the table and fills our water glasses. I half expect it to be some exquisite peaty well water, but it's just plain old tap. She sits. Takes a mouthful of quinoa on her fork and chews it for about twenty minutes.

'Gosh, it's nice to see you,' she says.

'And you,' I reply politely. I've never unlearned the family training. I lie reflexively when manners are at stake, but I can never keep the lack of enthusiasm out of my voice.

We go to bed at ten o'clock and I'm already dropping. The strain of trying to keep up conversation with someone you've hated all your life sucks the strength from you. My bedroom is at the end of the landing, next to a tiny bathroom with fixtures that look as though they were put in in the 1940s. There's a single bed and a tea-chest covered with a piece of batik that clashes with the floral wallpaper, a lamp on top, a stand for a suitcase and a couple score more boxes piled three deep against the walls. I'm tempted to look inside and see what it is she's keeping up here, but they're sealed up with masking tape and I don't trust myself to reseal them well enough that she wouldn't be able to tell I'd been in there. No labels up here. Just blank cardboard and a layer of dust on the windowsill. I content myself with quietly opening the wardrobe door and looking inside. It's ram-full of rolled-up clothes, stuffed like a mattress. They bulge at me, threatening to explode out into the room never to return, and I hastily latch the door shut before they can escape.

I brush my teeth in the bathroom, give myself a speed wash in my nightie, because it's absolutely freezing up here. I can't imagine that anyone ever has a long bath in that tub with the shower hose draped over the back of the taps, at least not in winter.

How has this happened? Dad muttered several times over the years about how she'd taken him to the cleaners, so how come

119

they're living so poor now? Mind you, I remember him saying the same thing about my own mother, when she wanted a share of a fortune that had been seeded with her own inheritance. Sean was always a bit 'what's mine is mine', I guess. And what's yours really wants to be mine, too. That's how the rich get rich, and why they're so suspicious of benefits claimants.

There are radiators in every room, but each one is turned down to the anti-frost setting, no more. Dominated by an ancient Aga, the kitchen was warm, and the scented heat of the sitting room wood fire at least kept the chill from the downstairs rooms, but up here I can imagine that I'll wake tomorrow to find frost on the insides of my windows. The bed itself feels slightly damp, but that could just be the long-term cold leaching itself from the springs into my body. I put a jumper on over my nightie and retain my socks, and huddle under the duvet, wondering how many other people have slept in this room during Claire's tenancy, if any. I don't even know if she has any family, apart from Ruby. Certainly there was no sign of them during the Coco era. It's a cheerless sort of room, not designed to encourage guests to linger. The lining paper is beginning to peel in a high-up corner and the carpet is threadbare.

I know it's hardly an underfilled space, but what happened to all the *stuff*? I remember her as the Constant Shopper, filling her houses with bits of formless 'modern art' in chrome and glass and fol-de-rols for tables, lining up pair after pair of unworn stilettos in her walk-in wardrobe as though they were precious evidence of her very success at life. 'It's for your father,' she would say, fingering a piece of embroidered satin, a swatch of pleated Lycra, a sheath dress with some long-retired Italian's name emblazoned on the neckline. In a way it was a form of hoarding, I suppose. Just . . . one approved by society, where accruing a collection of rusty car parts or feral cats is not. There was far more in that walk-in than she could ever hope to wear in a year, but she added to it constantly with near-religious zeal and had the staff swap everything in and out of a storage unit in Battersea with each change of season. The hoard here is just as regimented, kept hidden from prying eyes by its obsessive use of containers, but I know from looking in that cupboard that inside those cardboard boxes is a wormhole to a world of chaos.

That was what she was always like, I suppose. Rigid control on the surface and the howling void beneath. That's why so many people cling so fiercely to their semblances of discipline: their habits, schedules, routines, diets, personal trainers, personal grooming, theories of morality. It's all about the fear of the chaos beneath.

It's certainly true of India. Nothing in her life is real unless it's been ticked off on a list. For us, the recognition of the void came so early that we were always going to go one of two ways: spend our lives fighting valiantly to hold back the tide the way she does or, like me, accept the truth and let the chaos reign.

Chapter Fourteen

2004 | Thursday | Charlie

'Why can't we get the girls to do it?'

Claire Jackson rolls her eyes. 'Which girls? Because if you mean my husband's, good luck finding them.'

'Oh,' says Charlie, his heart sinking. 'Gone off-piste, have they?'

'You could say that. Linda saw them heading for the chain ferry half an hour ago. In mini-skirts.'

She's cutting up vegetables. Halving cherry tomatoes, julienning carrots and celery and steaming cauliflower. Supermarket packs of anaemic cooked organic chicken, ham the colour of a bridesmaid's dress and wholemeal pitta breads sit on the counter next to the chopping board. Imogen is laying the table with miniature cutlery and plastic plates, filling sippy cups with juice diluted with water and gathering what seems like an endless stream of toddlers to strap into chairs. Do all of these even *belong* to us? he wonders. There seems like such a lot of them. Did Imogen collect a couple on the way down without my noticing, just to keep up with the general fecundity? That Linda woman can't possibly have produced three, can she? Her stomach's as flat as the Norfolk Broads.

'They can't have got far, surely?' he asks, hopefully.

'Don't kid yourself,' says Claire. 'If I know anything about the sort of mini-skirts those two were wearing, they'll have had no trouble thumbing a lift. They could be anywhere on the peninsula by now.'

'Aren't you worried?' asks Imogen.

Claire shrugs. She's never made any great secret of her distaste for Sean's first family. 'It's Purbeck, not Peckham. And they're Sean's children, not mine,' she says, simply. 'Besides, they've got phones.'

Wow, thinks Charlie. You really are a piece of work, aren't you? No wonder he's getting tired of you.

'Well, what'll we do?'

Claire pulls a face. 'I daresay *we* won't do anything,' she says. 'I should think *you* will take your cue from my husband and go and drink champagne in the garden while the women feed the children and put them to bed.'

He draws breath to reply, but catches Imogen's eye before he does so. Don't, says her look. Don't even think about it. Charlie has been with Imogen for enough years, has looked to check her expression at enough parliamentary cocktail parties, to ignore her judgement on all matters social. He looks at the children. *En masse*, with their staring eyes and their open mouths, the snail trails running from nose to upper lip, he finds children quite frightening, like a herd of tiny zombies. He's secretly quite glad they never had any themselves, though Imogen's liking for involving herself with them suggests that she might be more conflicted. He takes the prompt to leave.

*

Beneath the gazebo by the pool, Sean has gathered his party on the Indonesian teak benches. The strange doctor, Jimmy, is already skinning up a joint; Robert and Maria Gavila are holding hands; Linda the interior designer is curled up like a Siamese cat, somehow both decorous and faintly obscene in a tight little dress that shows off every hour she's put in at the gym. Strange little Simone, having changed out of the frankly terrifying hot pants she was wearing when he arrived into a turquoise maxi-dress, gazes at Sean the way a rabbit gazes at a snake. Or is it the way a snake gazes at a rabbit? Either way, Sean at least gives the impression of being unaware. She's been staring at him like that since she was ten, thinks Charlie. That monumental crush she's got would be embarrassing if he gave it even the slightest moment of acknowledgement.

Sean has lit a cigar. He sits back against the cushions like a pasha in a harem. 'Ah, Clutterbuck!' he cries. 'About time! Glass of fizz, old boy?'

'I should say so!' he says, and flings himself into a seat. This weekend has taken far longer to get started than he would have liked. It's the last weekend of the parliamentary recess, and he'll be back at his desk on Wednesday. And with an election next year it'll be all hands to the pumps. He feels a bit end-of-school-holidays-ish and wants to make the most of the time he's got left.

Maria pours him a glass of Veuve and he downs half of it in one, lets out a hearty sigh of contentment. Sean and Robert are his oldest friends. It's rare for him to get the chance to be this much at his ease. 'Ah, that's more like it,' he says. He really fancies a line of his namesake pick-me-up, but with Simone there he supposes he'll have to wait.

'All well in the house?' asks Robert.

'Teatime,' he says, and waggles his head.

'Ah,' says Maria. 'Are they okay? Is Joaquin up there?'

'Yes, he's up there. He's discovered the bongos in the corner of the living room.'

Linda shifts from one elbow to the other. 'Those are real zebra skin,' she says, proudly. 'They marry the disconnect between the white floor tiles and the black marble in the fireplace.'

Five pairs of eyes flick over to look at her, then back to Charlie. 'Maybe I should go and help,' says Maria, reluctantly. She looks happy where she is, lounging against a kilim-covered bolster.

'I'll go,' offers Simone in her little-girl voice.

'Ah, there's a good girl,' says Sean. She beams as if someone's turned a super trouper on to her face. God, it's almost pathetic, thinks Charlie. She's like a spaniel puppy, begging for attention.

Simone gets slowly to her feet, pulls her tummy in hard as she stands up. Stretches and sticks out her tiny bosom. The adults all watch her and say nothing as she sashays away across the lawn.

'She's growing up,' he says, once she's inside the door.

'Don't,' says Maria. 'I'm going to have to lock her in a darkened room or something.'

'Heh,' says Charlie, 'I wouldn't worry too much. She's only got eyes for one man.'

'Watch it,' says Sean. 'She'll grow out of it.'

'I bloody hope so,' says Robert. 'If you think I'm going to give her away at your wedding, you can think again, matey.'

Maria shudders melodramatically. Linda shifts again, pulls in her own stomach and pushes her breasts forward. No sign that she intends to join the feeding frenzy; an admirable belief that other people will take over if she just leaves it. The breasts are disproportionately large on her slender frame. Enhanced, thinks Charlie. They're going to have to change standard sizing to deal with it, the way all these ambitious girls are hurling themselves in to get double Ds clamped on to their size eight bodies. He's not much of a one for fake tits himself. He likes his women to fly under the radar. But then, you don't want your wife to look like a hooker if you're aiming for Cabinet.

'What's all this about the nanny?' he asks.

Sean takes a long suck on his cigar and exhales a long stream of smoke into the evening air. On the other side of the coffee table, Jimmy lights his joint and holds his breath like a deep-sea diver. 'Yes, sorry,' says Sean. 'Polly Paranoia got it into her head to sack her, this weekend of all weekends.'

'Why?'

Sean reaches for the champagne bottle. There are three empties sitting on the side table already. It's quite clear no one's planning to do anything by halves. 'Frankly, if I were fucking as many women as she thinks I'm fucking I'd have had a coronary by now.'

'God,' says Charlie, 'women,' as though every woman's suspicions were naturally the product of mental health issues. Imogen has never once complained about the high turnover of parliamentary researchers that pass through his office.

'I suppose it's inevitable, to a degree,' says Robert, 'given the way your own relationship got started.'

Charlie lets out a thunderclap of laughter. 'On the nail, Robbo! On the nail!'

'Oh, you bugger,' says Sean, but he doesn't show much sign of being offended. Jimmy holds the joint out to Linda, who takes a short toke and passes it to Sean. Their fingers brush as they pass it, too slowly for it to be an accident. Oy oy, thinks Charlie. Doesn't look like the competition was from the nanny.

'So that's it?' he asks. 'No childcare all weekend? Couldn't you find a temp or something?'

Sean shakes his head. 'God,' he says, 'you can tell *you* never had children.'

'Thought I'd bequeath my quota to you, old boy,' says Charlie. 'Looks like you need it.'

Sean sucks down a lungful of smoke and looks, for a moment, as though he's going to cough it straight back up again. It smells vile to Charlie. Not the way dope smelled when they were at university. He remembers it as fragrant, back then, not this acrid, chemical-scented stuff that hangs around London's bus stops like melted tar for millennia after the user has departed.

'Have you ever tried getting staff at no notice on August bank holiday weekend? No go, my brother. We're on our own.'

'Well, at least we've got the girls,' says Maria. 'They can help out.'

'I wouldn't rely on mine,' says Sean. 'They're already in a snit because I forgot they were coming. Apparently they've taken off into the fleshpots of Purbeck already.'

'You forgot they were coming?'

'Well, or Heather wanted to spoil my birthday. Which I think is probably more likely, don't you?'

'Nice way to talk about your offspring,' says Robert.

'Hell hath no fury,' says Jimmy, and Charlie notes that he has one of those cracked drawls, slightly higher than it should be, slightly slurred, slightly Cockneyfied. A junkie voice. I need to make sure we never get photographed together, he thinks. I bet there's going to be a licence-loss scandal attached to *him* before the decade's out. Still. At least he knows now that the strangers in the group won't be rushing off to tell tales to the tabloids.

He feels in the breast pocket of his polo shirt for his wrap. Linda has thoughtfully picked a coffee table topped with glass for the middle of the gazebo.

'Well,' he says, bending forward, 'no point in letting it ruin the weekend, is there?' and starts chopping.

127

Chapter Fifteen

2004 | Thursday | Claire

'I can't sleep.'

Joaquin stands at the top of the stairs, rubbing his eyes.

Claire glances at the clock. It's gone ten. The men look up for a moment and go back to shouting at each other. Linda doesn't shift on her perch on the kitchen island in among them, like a little pixie statue, smoking a Vogue and flicking the ash into the sink.

Maria clicks across the marble floor. 'Hello, darling,' she says. 'Why aren't you in bed?'

'You're making such a racket,' he says, 'I can't sleep.'

Maria trots up the stairs. Scoops him up and carries him out of sight. The third downstairs visit tonight. Joaquin's been once already and the twins, together, hand-holding on the brink of disaster at the top of the stairs until she swooped up there and grabbed them. Claire doesn't doubt for a second that they'll be back soon enough.

'Maybe we should move through,' she says, vaguely. 'We *are* making a lot of noise.'

'Through to where?' asks Charlie, crushingly. He's always been crushing to her, Charlie Clutterbuck. No man so short of stature should have been able to master looking down his nose at women the way he does. She doesn't know if his dislike is related to some residual loyalty to Heather, whether he simply despises her on a personal level or if it's a simple gender thing, but she has no desire to find out. His pupils are like pencil tips and the smile is frozen back from his teeth, no humour in it, though he probably thinks he looks as if he's having a great time. Maybe I should do a line, she thinks. That's the trouble with cocaine. It's really unbearable being around people who are doing it when you're not. It's like being a dog surrounded by wolves.

He gestures expansively at the open-plan room. No doors to cut off noise, nothing soft to soak it up. It looks like hell. Scattered with discarded glasses and ashtrays, shoes on their sides, empty bottles under furniture. The kitchen table, that great slab of polished cherry wood, is a mess of half-empty plates and half-drained wine glasses. I'll be clearing this lot up tomorrow, she thinks. What a weekend. He complains about no nanny, but I knew when he said he didn't want a house-keeper because we wanted our privacy that it would end up like this.

'We wouldn't have dared to get out of bed when we'd been put in it when I was little,' says Imogen. She has a lot of opinions about child-raising for someone who's never actually done it.

'That explains a lot,' Claire says sarkily. She just can't stop herself. Really: Imogen's either forgotten everything about being a child or she's been abused into this rigid set of rules that had her threatening to take away a three-year-old's nuggets if it didn't eat its peas this afternoon.

Imogen doesn't respond. Perhaps she hasn't heard her. Her

husband is, after all, making as much noise as a fire engine. 'I see Jimmy and Linda's children understand the rules, at least,' she says.

'Ah, we've got a technique,' says Jimmy, and waves his joint in the air like a conductor's baton.

'What about the garden?' ventures Claire. The French doors are all open, in an attempt to air the place, get some sea breeze through the muggy atmosphere. She'd like to be out there. In the cool, on one of those sofas under the gazebo. Maybe I'll just go anyway, she thinks. It's not as though anyone's acknowledged I'm here for the past hour. Even Maria doesn't really bother talking to me any more. I'm yesterday's woman. No longer interesting now I'm not Sean's princess.

'Is there somewhere to plug the alarms in, in the garden?' asks Imogen, looking up for a sharp moment from the lines of cocaine lined up on the island countertop. Such things you find out. She looks like such a matron on the ten o'clock news, following sternly along behind her boastful husband, but she's hoovering up the drugs like a Frankfurt whore.

Claire sighs. The alarms are lined up side by side next to the stove: one for Gavila, one for Jackson. There is no Orizio alarm. 'We don't need one,' said Linda, smugly, as they were plugging them in. 'They won't wake up. We've got them trained.' Claire puts an ear to her own alarm, hears her children snuffling in the dark above her. They'll be up at dawn, whatever time the adults get to bed. She feels weary to the bones just at the thought of it.

'No,' she says, and resigns herself to a long night under the glare of the halogen spots. Linda is one of those designers who think that the point of lighting is to show up every flaw in the paintwork, every speck of dust. It's not a restful room.

*

The fish pie so carefully thought about and transported from London in a cool-box has gone largely uneaten because Charlie Clutterbuck has brought cocaine enough that the dealers of north Kennington must have been able to take the weekend off on the profits.

Claire hates Charlie Clutterbuck. If she'd met him before she had been in too deep to back out, she might have thought twice about Sean purely on the basis of the company he kept. There are lots of Sean's friends she doesn't like much, but Charlie is the worst of all: a walking stereotype of Tory manhood. High red in the face, the teeth whitened till they look like dentures, a lock of oily hair detached from the slicked-back whole and flopping over the forehead, the booming voice drowning out everything around him, the spiky wife laughing that boys-will-be-boys laugh whenever he sweeps another group of people into a heap and dismisses them. We've had Lefties and Suburbanites and Poofs and Oiks already: words he would never use in his many handrubbing vox pops on *Newsnight* but ones he's happy to scatter about when he thinks the doors are closed. It's only a matter of time before we're on to the Coons and the Towelheads, she thinks. Only a matter of time.

The lads are discussing business. More specifically, planning law, and how it impedes Sean's march towards global domination. 'Well, I can tell you this for nothing,' says Charlie, 'English Heritage will be having its wings clipped pronto when the election's over. Bloody lefty busybodies.'

'Tell you another thing,' says Sean. 'This Special Scientific Interest malarkey. I've lost literally years across my portfolio. Bloody bat-breeding sites and special sand lizards.'

Robert Gavila, partner at the law firm of Kendall, Wright and Macy, school governor, stalwart of the Wandsworth Conservatives, leans over the kitchen island and fills his nose. Stands upright at the speed of sound, licks his finger and scoops what's left on to his gums. 'Ahhhhh!' he declares.

'I just think it's an outrage,' says Sean, 'that Tesco seem to get superstores waved through on a daily basis and I can't stick a garage on to a house just because it's Elizabethan.'

'Here,' says Jimmy. 'Have any of you lot ever tried sniffing vodka?'

Claire stopped drinking at eight p.m., when she realised that she and Simone were the only sober people in the house. Someone's got to be responsible, she thinks. Simone has retreated to the annexe with the laptop and a DVD of *Love, Actually*, so it's basically me. I wouldn't trust any of these people not to drop one of the babies down the stairs.

She studies her guests, one by one. The four men, three of them pudgy from their love of chateaubriand, the doctor thin in that way that suggests that forgetting-to-eat nights are a familiar concept. Jimmy's skin is pinky-grey and he has a mop of black curls in which tufts of white show his age. He laughs at everything, but the laughter has a mirthless edge. He's not really taking in anything anyone's saying, she thinks. Just laughing because he needs to show the world he's having a good time. That Linda will be moving on at some point, she thinks. She's ambitious, the way I was, back when I was a fool. Keeping her figure despite the children because she wants to keep her options open, and practising her flirtation with everybody else's husbands.

And what husbands! Kings of the world, full to the brim with self-congratulation. Hair that was once fair and is now mostly gone, tufts of wire in their ears. They come from the sort of background that insulates them from ever thinking that their good fortune might have an element of luck in it. 'I've worked *hard* to get where I am,' they would say, to a man, if anyone suggested it, and indeed, they *have* all worked hard. They've all put in their late nights and their early mornings, done the kow-towing and the ruthless defeat of their enemies. And yet, and yet. Privilege rarely knows it's privileged. Sean is constantly bemoaning his tax bills and never seems to remember that you only pay tax on money you've received.

Charlie has suddenly got interested in the fish pie, and is eating it from the dish with a spoon, going back in for more without a thought for hygiene. He'd probably be eating it with his fingers if the spoon weren't there, she thinks. I'll have to think twice about giving the leftovers to the kids tomorrow. I bet he drinks milk straight from the carton and puts it back in the fridge, too.

Claire is used to being the sober one in the room among people who are wasted. Back in the day, it was because of the calorie content, and men never notice if you're drunk or sober, once they're gone themselves; they just assume that you're whatever they are. Sean was quite drunk when she met him at the Gavilas' Christmas party five years ago. She's wished for some time that she'd left him there.

She goes out to the gazebo with a glass of Montrachet. Kicks off her shoes and curls up on a sofa and tries to tune out the sounds of singing from indoors. The men have moved on to whisky and rugby songs have followed. This wasn't what I had in mind, she thinks. When I met him he couldn't do enough to impress me with his sophistication. It was all Paris Ritz and private dining rooms, though those were mostly about Heather's friends not spotting us, I suppose. And now I'm married to a fifty-year-old yob who eats with his mouth open. Be careful what you wish for, she thinks, and lets out a small sarcastic laugh, because it might well come true. I wanted money and I wanted position, and, when I saw that Sean had both, I wanted him. It serves me right, really, because he wasn't mine to have. And suddenly I'm just another woman who stole someone's husband, and nobody ever really forgives you for that, whatever they say.

She sips her wine. It's quite exquisite on the tongue. There are good things, she thinks. I must remember the good things. The cars and the houses and the guilt diamonds, and the never having to poison my liver with cheap wine again. And my girls will never want for anything. God knows, the amount of money he pours into Milly and India, the alimony that goes on and on, the school fees, the skiing trips, the bloody riding lessons, my own will never go short even if he trades me in. Maybe it would be better if he *did* trade me in. Then I could sit in the quiet and drink my wine and never have to listen to him moan about his haemorrhoids again.

She hears her name being bellowed through the open door. 'What?' she calls.

An upstairs window at Seagulls, the genteelly dilapidated pebbledashed semi on the other side of the fence, is slammed pointedly shut. They must love us, she thinks. Six months of contractors and now this.

'Twins are awake!' shouts Sean.

For a second she considers telling him to go and sort them out, and then she sighs. The state he's in, he'll probably drop Ruby on her head on that hard tiled floor. She puts her glass regretfully down on the table and uncurls from her comfortable nest.

'Coming!' she calls.

'God almighty,' says Charlie. 'Do they never fucking sleep?'

'That's our godchildren you're talking about, Charlie,' slurs Imogen.

'Yes, but they're meant to go to sleep! It's grown-up time now!'

'Grown-up time?' enquires Claire. Charlie is splayed out on a dining chair like a scarecrow, legs straight as broom handles, shirt stained with wine and whisky and fish pie and cigar ash, wiry grey curls creeping out around his open buttons. Robert and Maria are snogging like teenagers on a sofa. Jimmy is lying face-up on the sheepskin rug, yet another joint scattering burny flakes on to the ruined hairs beneath him. Linda is doing a dance – some cross between Bollywood and stripper – and her husband is staring at the narrow waist and bulging buttocks in her bandage dress like a Bedouin staring at a water hole. Imogen bounces Coco on her chest. She's fallen back asleep, worn out by the constant up-and-down the night has entailed, and her head flops loosely on her shoulder. Imogen flashes Claire the sort of you-see? look that makes her want to start laying about her with the fire tongs. You see? She goes to sleep for *me*. You see? I *never* have trouble getting them to eat their peas. I don't know what the fuss is about. Childcare is *easy*.

'I suppose it's two o'clock,' says Maria. 'We should probably turn in anyway.'

'I just . . . ' mumbles Charlie. 'Oi!'

He looks up at Linda, wobbles on his chair when he sees her breasts swaying in the night-time breeze.

'What?' She twirls, puts her hands above her head like a ballerina, kicks one hip out to the side.

'How come your lot haven't been down?'

'Zopiclone,' she says.

'Zopiclone?'

'Zopiclone.'

'Marvellous stuff,' croaks Jimmy, from the carpet. 'I love being a doctor.'

135

Chapter Sixteen

I wake with a start in the dark. Someone is creeping along the corridor outside my room. I hear a door open, a voice whisper, a reply, and a dim light goes on. Burglars, I think. I've got burglars. And then I remember where I am and realise that it's Claire and Ruby, getting up before daybreak like some crazy cultists. I grope for my phone on the tea chest and see that it's seven-thirty. Living the boho life in the big city, you forget that day starts late, in the winter, as well as ending early.

I lie in the dark and listen to them move about, hear water run in the bathroom, their feet tread off towards the stairs. A couple of minutes later I hear the front door close. They must have gone out to do the chores. I hope so. They can't have gone off and left me, can they? I creep up the bed, taking the duvet with me, and peep out through the curtains. The window is covered with condensation, but through a small patch I wipe with my hand I see them trudging by torchlight across the yard towards the feed shed in their wellingtons, coat hoods up against the bitter air. I don't understand the country. I can't imagine why animals need feeding in the dark. Would they thrive less if they waited a bit? Does the food lose its goodness? I crawl back down the bed. It's already cold to the touch where the duvet has come with me. I go back to sleep.

When I wake again it's daylight and the phone tells me it's nine o'clock. I bound from bed and hurry into clothes, strip off my bedclothes and, after thinking about it a bit, leave them folded on top of the bed. I never know whether people would prefer your dirty laundry cluttering up their living space. It seems so ostentatious to take them down, as though you're expecting congratulations for a quite basic bit of manners. I don't bother to brush my teeth. It took hours for the tap to run warm last night and I suspect I'm late already.

They're at their places at the kitchen table eating toast and honey. Claire jumps up when I come in, puts the kettle on the Aga. 'I didn't know whether to wake you,' she says, 'but I thought best not. I know you city people like to sleep late.'

Late? Jesus. This is practically bedtime where I come from. 'Sorry,' I say. Late people always have to apologise to early people: it's the rules.

'Mint tea?'

I consider asking if she has coffee, but I already know the answer. 'No, thanks. A glass of water would be great.'

She shrugs, takes the kettle off again and fills me a glass. I sit down. There's one of those see-through cereal boxes filled with something that mostly consists of oats, and a jug of milk. I'm light-headed from sleeplessness, and starving hungry as I always am after a bout of insomnia. I reach for it.

'Home-made muesli,' says Claire approvingly, 'and goat's milk, fresh this morning. There's apple juice in the fridge if you want to sweeten it.'

It's too late now. I can't put it back down without being rude. I pour a dessertspoonful into a bowl and slosh strong-smelling white stuff on to it. It's still warm. And not because it's cooling down after being pasteurised, I'll warrant. 'You must need more than that!' she says. 'You've got a long journey ahead of you!'

Funny how people who live on sawdust always want to fill you up. My stomach growls for a bacon sandwich. Blossom probably didn't go for bacon. There's salt in bacon. 'I'm saving room for some of that lovely toast,' I say. 'Is it your own honey?'

'No. Sort of. There's a beekeeper who puts his hives in the wildflower meadow for a month in the spring. He pays us with product. And of course, they do a lovely job of pollinating the vegetables.'

'Of course,' I say. 'How clever.'

I stir the cereal around and take a little on the end of my spoon. It doesn't seem to have soaked the milk up at all. I put it into my mouth and close my lips over it. God damn, I need to go to the dentist. Longevity shot up worldwide when they invented white bread; people got to keep their teeth. The milk tastes a bit funky, but it's not as bad as people say. The cereal, though. It coats the roof of my mouth, scrapes between my tongue and gums, doesn't seem to give under my molars at all. I catch Ruby looking at me. There's a twinkle of amusement in her eye. I gulp it down. 'Lovely,' I say, meeting her eye and not looking away. 'I bet it's really healthy.'

'Fantastic for the heart,' says Claire. 'The commercial stuff is loaded with sugar.'

'Absolutely,' I reply. Take another teaspoonful and gnaw. In the modern world, 'home-made' means 'nobody would buy it twice'.

The toast is much better. The bread is firm and nutty and full of seeds and the honey is . . . well, honey. It still feels weird, though, eating breakfast without caffeine. It gives one a glimpse of what the dawn must have been like in the Middle Ages, and not in a good way.

'What time do you think you ought to be off?' asks Claire.

'Tennish? It's quite a drive.'

'Sure.' She turns to Ruby. 'Have you packed?'

'Pretty much.'

'What does that mean?'

'Mostly,' says Ruby. 'It means mostly.'

Claire sighs the sigh of parents of teens the world over. 'Well, you'd better go and finish, then. And get out of those old jeans. I'm not having people think I don't look after you.'

Ruby's head wobbles, and she licks honey off her fingers, one by one. 'What should I pack for the funeral?'

'Something black,' I say. Sean would want all the bells and whistles, I know that.

'And some tights without any holes in them,' says Claire, 'and some shoes that don't make you look like Bela Lugosi.'

She turns to me as Ruby lollops away. 'You will look after her, won't you?'

'I'll do my best, Claire.' How can I promise? People make promises so lightly. I don't want to be one of those people who make promises and break them.

'Because she looks all right, I know, but she's really not. She's pulled herself together because you're here, but I doubt she'll be able to keep it up. She's only fifteen. And those people . . . '

The sentence drifts away to nothing. I think back to Dad's friends: bluff, boastful, snobbish Charlie Clutterbuck; that sharp-faced Imogen, who never gave you a moment's attention if she didn't think you were useful, or if her husband was ignoring you. All those glad-handers and hangers-on, and the men who laugh too loudly in restaurants, the women whose faces can no longer move, odd weirdos like Jimmy Orizio leering blearily down your top from the sidelines; Simone . . .

'Robert and Maria will be there,' I remind her.

Claire wrinkles her nose as if she's smelled ammonia. 'Oh, God, those two.'

'I thought they'd stayed in touch?'

'Well, what was I meant to do? They were the only godparents who showed the remotest interest. All the others, all *those people*' – the words come from her mouth as though she's spitting them – 'couldn't have got themselves further away. Once I'd cut myself loose. But there wasn't a single person from then still in our lives. Not a single grown-up she'd known since she was little. She'd lost everything. What was I meant to do? Leave her with one single present under the tree at Christmas?'

'They always seemed okay to me.'

'Relatively,' she says. 'Relatively.'

'Yeah, maybe,' I say. 'At least they're not psychopaths.'

'I guess. Small mercies.'

I think about it. 'Claire,' I ask, 'what happened to *your* friends from before?'

You know, it's only just occurred to me. I know nothing about Claire from before she met my father. Their house was always full, they were always on their way out to dinner or drinks or some reception thing, but it was always *his* friends. All those people who didn't bother to keep up with my mum, who just carried on as normal as though the wives were just a bit of background scenery, providers of food and clean bed linen like an elevated housekeeper. They were all there, all the time, and with Linda too. It's as though marriage to my father came with a no-baggage clause.

Claire sighs again. 'You know what? I've asked myself that over and over again. I mean it, it's not like I didn't *have* any. I

140

don't really know what happened. But your father was so – full on, you know? He filled up every little corner and somehow there was never the time for my friends, or they wouldn't fit with the people he wanted to see, or he would turn up at the last minute with a helicopter and a booking at the Paris Ritz, and reminding him that we'd got something set up already would upset him so much, like I didn't love him enough.'

I nod. Nothing got in the way of Sean Jackson's whims, not ever. The weekend when Coco disappeared was just one of dozens where he 'forgot' about our access visits. We always blamed Claire, of course. Wouldn't you?

'I was blind, and stupid,' she says. 'He said his whole life had started when he met me, and I believed him. He said we should both be as though nothing had come before us, and I thought that sounded like romance, even though somehow he never actually acted on his own words. And you know . . . most people don't like it if you turn back up years later being needy when you've not had time for their lives in between,' she continues. 'They tend to take it badly, especially after . . . you know . . . I'd been in the papers so much. But there have been some. People who just came back without my asking. Tiberius. I hadn't seen him since I was twenty-three and he didn't seem to care at all. But there aren't many, no.'

And you were too scared to make more, I think. I get it. Once you've been public property you're never really sure of other people again. There were a couple of girls in my school year who were suddenly all over me when I went back after that summer holiday and all the rest of them were giving me the cold shoulder. Their gleeful curiosity, their sugary sympathy, was worse than all the awkward silences put together. India and I both failed our exams that year. Indy didn't go up to university until she was twenty.

'I—' says Claire, 'please keep an eye on her, that's all. People seem to assume that she's robust because of the way she looks, but she's vulnerable. She really is.'

'I get it,' I say.

'Can you – can I give you her medications? I just . . . You know. Responsible adult and all that?'

'Medications?'

'It's okay,' she says. 'It's mostly supplements. A multivitamin and fish oil and ginseng and goji berries.'

I feel my eyebrows start to rise and my eyes begin to roll, and hurriedly suppress it. It's her thing. It's how she shows her care. Let her have that. She's not the monster you knew back then.

'And an antidepressant,' she says, and blushes scarlet. Shame burns off her from across the table. All that care, all that control, and still my kid's fucked up. I have failed, and now I have to share it with the kid I fucked up before.

I keep my voice even, endeavour to hide my surprise. 'Oh, poor love,' I say. 'What's she taking?'

'Sertraline. It's a serotonin adjuster. It's not a cosh. She's not psychotic or anything. She just has a chemical imbalance.'

She's beginning to sound defensive. I throw her a bone. 'I took that for a while. It's good stuff.'

Claire gives me a funny look. Part relief, part – guilt? Really?

'Life is a tough old bugger.' I'm not there yet with, you know, patting her hand or anything, but a bit of kindness never did any harm. 'Whatever gets you through.'

'I'm sorry,' she says, trying to meet my eye. 'I guess I must have played a part in that.'

I brush the remark away. I'm not so evolved that I can go from years of contempt to forgiveness overnight.

*

142

Ruby clomps back down the stairs with a bag on her shoulder. She's changed into cobweb-patterned tights, one of those tube skirts in a giant houndstooth check and a striped matelot shirt with an off-the-shoulder sloppy joe over the top. It's all very eighties. She carries a pair of battered boots with three-inch heels. No fear of being taller than the boys for our Ruby. I kind of admire her for that.

'Right,' she says.

'Have you got your inhaler?' asks Claire.

'Yes.'

'Blue one *and* brown one?'

'Yes.'

'Rescue Remedy?'

'Yes.'

'Antihistamines?'

'Yes.'

'Eumovate?'

'Yes, Mum,' she says in that 'that's enough' voice. She must be tired of thinking about her allergies, if that list is anything to go by.

'I'm sorry,' says Claire. 'I can't help worrying.'

'I'll be fine, Mama,' she says. 'I promise.'

'You've got your phone and your charger?'

She has her back turned, and allows herself an eye roll. 'Yes.'

'And you'll call me, won't you? Let me know how you're getting on? Every day? I'll come and get you if you need me to, you know that, don't you?' Claire's brow is furrowed with worry. 'I'm so sorry I can't come. I wish I could. But I just can't. You do understand, don't you, darling?'

Ruby turns round and flings her arms around her mother, envelops her small body in the bounty of her bosom. 'It's all right, Mummy,' she says. 'It's okay. I'll be fine. Really. Please don't worry.'

After a few seconds I realise that Claire is crying. Ruby holds her, strokes her hair, soothes her like an infant. 'It'll be okay. You will be okay. Don't be scared. You'll be fine. You'll be okay. I'll be home soon. Don't be scared.'

We load the car up and set off not long behind schedule. Ruby winds the window down and waves a hand until we round the corner. I watch Claire in the rear-view, standing in the yard, her cardi wrapped tight around her. She cuts a solitary figure, frail and lonely. After all these years of hating her, now I feel sorry for her.

Ruby gets out to open the gate, latches it behind her, settles back in her seat and plugs in her seatbelt.

'I'll need to stop for petrol soon,' I warn her.

'And coffee, I should think,' she replies.

I smile. 'How did you guess?'

'Not rocket science,' says Ruby. 'If we can hold on till we get past Arundel there's one that has a Macky D's, as well.'

Aha.

'Okay,' I say. 'Well, it'll be time for elevenses by then, I should think.'

'And in the meantime' – she turns and leans her back against the door and stares at the side of my face – 'you can tell me what really happened to my sister.'

Chapter Seventeen

2004 | Friday | Sean

The builders start up. His head is wrapped in a pillow to keep out the horror of the daylight, but it can't prevent the sound of a pneumatic drill from penetrating the barrier. Claire groans beside him, curls into herself like a foetus. 'For God's sake,' she mumbles. 'What the hell time is it?'

He rolls over and finds his watch. 'Jesus wept,' he says, 'it's six-thirty!'

He sits up and swings his legs over the side of the bed. His brain has come loose inside his skull. It sloshes forward and back a couple of times before it settles. I'm still drunk, he thinks. How much did I drink last night? Jesus.

'Tell them to fuck off,' says Claire.

'I'm going,' he mutters. 'Keep your hair on.'

He's in his boxers and the shirt he was wearing last night. He has some faint memory of hopping around the bedroom pulling his jeans off, laughing like a hyena while she glared at him from the bed. Is it all women, he wonders, or is it just my luck, that every time I marry one she turns from party girl to prude in under

145

two years? She used to love to party with me. Stayed up all night and laughed at all my jokes, and she was always up for a fuck. If there's one thing I remember about last night, it's the sight of her face all puckered up like a cat's arse every time I opened another bottle. It's my birthday weekend, for God's sake. Don't I deserve to have some fun on my birthday weekend?

Over in the corner, on their inflatable mattress, the twins start to stir and Ruby starts up a grizzle. Oh, God, that's the last thing I need, he thinks. If they start crying the whole day will start and she'll be whining because I'm not helping her get their breakfast. For God's sake, it was her who wanted them in the first place.

He stands up. Wobbles. Looks for a clean shirt.

On the living-room floor, Jimmy has wrapped himself in the sheepskin and lies there snoring open-mouthed, a thread of drool attaching his face to the scatter cushion someone has slipped under his head. Sean makes a mental note: get him up before the children appear. And damn. That was an opportunity to sneak off for a bit of Linda-time, right there, though I suppose with all these kids around any opportunities will be short-lived things. I might see if I can request she stay down with me for a couple of nights to supervise the final touches, make sure the house is ready for sale. I know for sure Claire won't want to stay one minute longer than she has to, and we can put the drunk on a train.

Another beautiful morning. High blue sky, golden sunshine, clouds of dust and the roar of machinery across the garden fence. I'll have to get the contract cleaners in again before we go on the market, he thinks as he slips on his deck shoes and steps out on to the patio. Oh, well. Probably needed to get them in anyway. Jimmy and Charlie are both constitutionally incapable of sitting anywhere for more than five minutes without leaving some evidence of their presence behind. And the kids. There are jammy handprints all the way along the kitchen wall, three feet up. Might even need the painters back.

Builders. Strange, noisy creatures. He thought when he was young that it was a British class thing, but every construction site he's come across anywhere in the world – Dubai, Hong Kong, even the smiling Thais – has been filled with men who can communicate only at a roar. The Poles, it seems, are no different. Their fuck-offs and their oi-mates have more consonants and fewer vowels, but otherwise they might have come from some finishing school run by Barratt Homes.

He picks his way past the crane and stamps up the steps that run up the side of the bank. The digger is on the crest, ladling sandy soil – more like soily sand, down here – into the back of a dump truck. Four men stand by the wheels in hard hats, shouting at each other over the grinding of gears. He's impressed by how fit all these Poles are who've been flooding in since the gates were opened. Not a belly or a butt-crack between them beneath those hi-vis jackets. On his own build there was a fork-lift driver who had to literally lift his stomach up to get behind the wheel. Didn't stop him commenting on every teenage girl to pass along the road, though. He was glad they'd gone by the time his daughters turned up. No guarantee that these good Catholic boys are any better, but somehow he feels less bothered when the ogling isn't coming from someone who must be cultivating galloping fungal infections down his low-slung trousers.

He marches up to them and shouts, 'Excuse me!'

They don't hear him the first time. He adjusts the volume. 'OI! EXCUSE ME!'

Four pairs of eyes swivel to look. 'Foreman!' he shouts. 'Which one of you's the foreman?'

The men stare at him blankly. Of course. None of them has

bothered to learn the language before they set off across Europe to be here on the first of May, when Poland joined the Schengen system. 'Boss!' he yells. 'I need to speak to the boss!'

They look none the wiser. But one of them bangs on the door of the digger and shouts '*Janusz! e dupkiem z pokoju obok jest z powrotem!*' and the engine cuts out. I don't know if I'm getting the boss, he thinks, but I guess they're at least getting me the anglophone.

The door opens and the man he spoke to yesterday emerges. 'Hello, mister,' he says, and climbs down. Shouts a few words to one of his team, who climbs up into the cab and picks up where he left off. Multi-skilled, thinks Sean. I must get me a few of those. Can't stand watching men sitting around drinking tea while the plasterer's in, on my dollar.

'It's six-thirty in the morning!' he shouts, nonetheless. Sean has never had a problem holding two ideas in his head at one time.

There are big patches of early-morning sweat beneath Janusz's arms. Sean is sweating too. That last armagnac he had is seeping undigested from his pores and he has a raging, queasy thirst. I bet he can smell it, he thinks. But I don't care. It doesn't matter if I have a hangover or not; this is completely out of order.

'Yes, sorry, mister,' says Janusz. 'We got a deadline here.'

He's trying it on, the way they all do. There's not a builder on the planet who doesn't know the local noise by-laws and ignores them anyway.

'You know and I know you're not allowed to start with heavy machinery until eight-thirty,' he shouts. 'Shut it down!'

Janusz flips both hands out in the air. 'We're only doing our jobs, mister,' he shouts.

Sean invokes all the patrician gods who raised him up to his pedestal. Stares the man full in the eye with magisterial dignity and shouts, 'Tough!'

Janusz shouts something up at the man in the cab, and the engine stops.

'Listen,' says Janusz, 'we're running late.'

'Not my problem.'

'But it's part your fault, mister. If your trucks hadn't been blocking our trucks we would have got this pool in by now.'

'Not my problem, again,' he says. 'You stop until you're allowed to start or I'm calling the council. Want to see how delayed you'll be then?'

Janusz calls something to his men and they all take their hats off. Each one, as he does so, blows upwards from a pouting lower lip. Obviously some sort of commentary on the development, but Sean is immune to workman commentary. He's been telling site staff what to do for well over two decades.

'Right,' he says. He's starting to feel shaky now. This is going to be a long, long day.

As he retreats down the bank he hears a burst of laughter behind him. He knows they're talking about him, but he ignores it. Two more hours' sleep, he's bought them all, at least. Maybe if he gets an Alka-Seltzer and a couple of pints of water inside him the moment he gets back to the house, the worst of his suffering will have passed by the time the engines start again. He doubts it, though. This one feels as though it might be set in for the day. Thank God my birthday's not until tomorrow, he thinks. Claire may have been pissed off at the prospect of the extra night, but the first night of the holidays is always a big one and nobody's fit for anything the next day.

Two skinny figures, legs like storks', hurry along the road in the sunlight. Each one carries a pair of high-heeled shoes in her hands. Someone's had an even bigger night out than I have, he thinks; if that's not the walk of shame, I've lost my eye. And then he sees that the two figures are his daughters, and he stops dead.

'Where have you two been?' he asks. No one, he suddenly remembers, went to check whether they'd come home at any point during the night. Simone, no trouble at all as ever, simply stayed in the annexe with her book and her snacks. At least, he thinks, I suppose she did. None of us would know, in all honesty.

The girls' eyes flick towards each other and back again. 'We got up and went for a walk,' says India. 'It's such a lovely day.'

I could do without this, he thinks, swaying in the sunlight. Is it too much to ask, that I just have a jolly weekend without other people lobbing spanners into the works? 'You got dressed up in last night's clothes and smeared make-up halfway down your cheeks to go for a walk down to the chain ferry?'

'You're always on at us about making more effort,' says Milly. She's so damn sassy that there are moments when he wants to slap her. 'I'd've thought you'd be pleased.'

'Don't give me that,' he says. 'You've been out all night, haven't you?'

'What?' asks Milly. 'You *think*, or you *know*?'

Being wrong-footed makes him angry. What sounds like a ribald comment tumbles down from the bank behind him and is followed by a couple of laughs. Oh, go back to your *kielbasa*, he thinks, irritably. It's got nothing to do with you.

'Right, well, you're both grounded.'

The girls' heads turn and they look at each other. They burst out laughing. 'You're hilarious!' says India. 'That's the best one *ever*!'

Sean is dumbfounded. Feels his life slipping away between his fingertips. When did his daughters stop respecting him? And why has he only just noticed?

'He'll probably stop our pocket money next,' says Milly, in her performance voice.

'Oh, yes?' India waves jazz hands of imitation terror. Then drops them to her side with abrupt contempt. 'Mind you, I guess he'd have to give us some first . . . '

'Oh, yeah,' says Milly. 'I forgot about that.'

'You're old enough for Saturday jobs,' he says.

'Ooh!' replies India. 'Does that mean I have your permission to drop the court-ordered access visits and get a job instead?'

'Yes,' says Milly. 'They do rather get in the way of regular employment, don't they?'

'Still,' says India, 'as long as you're happy with your new family, that's all that counts, eh?'

'He'd better. He'd be terribly lonely otherwise,' says Milly, 'given how he doesn't even remember we're coming half the time.'

Sean feels as if he's been hit by a tornado. 'Listen,' he tries, 'while you're in my house, you live by my rules, okay?'

'Great!' says Milly, and marches past him towards the house. 'I'll open the brandy, Indy. You fetch the dope.'

Chapter Eighteen

I should have asked. Goddammit, I should have asked. Or Claire should have warned me, at least, if she's been keeping stuff back for so long. Let me in on the party line. Or maybe that's it. Maybe she's been waiting for someone else to have to do it, all these years.

'What do you know?' I ask, cautiously.

'What I've been told. And I know it's bullshit. If she'd died in a swimming pool accident there wouldn't have been journalists swarming all over the place when Dad died. And it's not the first time. They were here a couple of years ago, and they were here when I was eight, and I worked out ages ago that that must have been the fifth and tenth anniversaries. So yeah. I call bullshit. We're not famous people. I know Dad's rich, but that by itself isn't enough to make them interested. Jammy people's kids drown in swimming pools far more often than poor people's, it's a fact, because rich people have more swimming pools for them to drown in, but people don't keep asking about it for years after they have.'

Oh, boy. 'Tell me what they told you,' I say, playing for time. Stupid, stupid people. They didn't really think they could keep this from her forever, did they? And now I'm stuck not only with telling her, but telling her by default that her parents are liars. I mean. She was going to work it out sometime this weekend. Surely Claire saw *that* one coming?

She's not daft. She knows what I'm doing, but she plays along. 'I had a twin sister. Her name was Coco. She drowned in a swimming pool when we were little, when we were on holiday. That's all I know. I don't remember it. You'd have thought I'd remember some of it, wouldn't you? I mean, if we were on holiday I must have been there too, right? I barely remember her. If it weren't for that . . . *shrine* that Mum keeps in the living room I probably wouldn't remember her at all, really.'

'Oh,' I say.

'No,' she says, 'you don't get any more thinking time. Just tell me.'

Smart. She's been saving this up to catch me on the hop because she thinks that if I have time to get my story straight I won't tell her the truth. She's probably right.

'And you've never tried to find out? Looked it up on the internet? Watched items about it on TV?'

'Yeah,' she says, 'I always wondered why we didn't have a TV. I mean, I know she home-schools me and that and home schoolers are notoriously nutso, but I just thought it was about protecting me from all the rubbish. And, you know, porn and that. The internet's nothing but porn, isn't it?'

'It's got other stuff as well,' I say, and then I bite my lip when I realise she's been playing me. 'Oh,' I say again.

'We've had smartphones since before I was born, Grandma,' she says. 'And she's so dumb about it all that she never noticed what sort of upgrades I was getting on Dad's business account.'

153

'Oh,' I say again. 'So why did you pretend you didn't know?'

'I wanted to see if you'd toe the party line.'

And I haven't even had coffee yet.

'I might well have done if I knew what it was,' I say. 'I've not exactly been besties with your mum, you know? We've not been having long confabs in the wee small hours.'

'So what happened?' she asks again. Persistent, like her father.

'I wasn't there, Ruby. I can't tell you anything other than what I was told myself.'

'Which was?'

'Short version? Same as the one you know. Same as the one in the papers you've been reading. She disappeared.'

Ruby's jaw snaps shut. Whatever answer she's been expecting, it wasn't that one. I think she's been persuading herself these past few weeks that if she caught me on the hop she could force some admission out of me that the combined might of Fleet Street has failed to do. I know. I know how she feels. The whole thing stinks like old fish, but they've all stuck to the same story for the past twelve years and unless one of them cracks then I'm going to know no more than anybody else.

We reach the village, drive up past the shop towards the main road. A woman is pruning an already neat box hedge with a pair of oversized shears. She turns to stare at us as we go by. Ruby clamps a cheery grin to her face and waves as we pass. Recognising her, the woman waves back and returns to her chore. They don't miss a trick in this village. It's more secure than Wandsworth Prison.

As soon as we pass, her smile disappears and she turns to me again. 'What do you mean, disappeared? What happened?'

If we knew that, Ruby, we would have found her, wouldn't we?

'Look,' I tell her, 'I can only tell you what I know. I wasn't

154

there. I was there that weekend, and I know who else was there, but India and I had left ages before it happened. That afternoon on the beach you remember? With the jellyfish? That was that weekend. It must have been Thursday afternoon, because we were gone by Friday, and Coco didn't even disappear till Sunday night, Monday morning. We weren't getting on with Dad, and he'd forgotten we were even meant to be there, and we couldn't stand those people. I never could. That bloody Charlie Clutter-buck makes me want to throw up. So we went home. And don't think it's not crossed my mind that if we'd stayed we might have stopped it happening. I've thought it over and over. You were nice little kids. I actually liked you both, whatever I thought about your mum and my dad and the bloody awful mess they'd created. You didn't deserve that. Coco didn't deserve that.'

Ruby is quiet for a moment as she digests my words and then she says, 'So what happened?' again, very calmly, very firmly. I swear, the kid could get a job with the Stasi.

I take a breath and slow down. Try to order my thoughts so I can tell her in some sort of rational order. If she's been Googling the whole sorry mess, there's very little I can add, apart from working out which of the conspiracy theories she's soaked up with the facts.

'It's not like I don't blame them,' I say. 'But not your mum. I've got plenty of reasons for feeling sour towards her, but not for that. She'd left too, because Dad was being so unreasonable. And I'm not, like, all *Daily Mail* about it, either. I don't see why she shouldn't have left her kids in the charge of their father. But they were all drinking like fish all weekend. I don't suppose they'd have heard a bomb go off once they were asleep, let alone someone creeping around downstairs.'

Ruby just sits there and stares silently.

155

'I . . . ' I say, and dry up. We reach the main road and I get to concentrate on feeling my way out into the traffic for a moment.

'Just tell me,' she says, once we're bowling along the outside lane.

'I don't know what you want me to tell you,' I say. 'There's not some . . . back room where we've been keeping the whole story. She disappeared from the bedroom you were sharing in the middle of the night. No one ever found her, or any sign of her.'

'That's nice,' says Ruby. 'It clearly had a major impact on your life, then.'

'No, I . . . ' She's right, of course. It's not fair to leave it like that. Ruby is probably the person most affected by it all, in the end, even more than her mother, and she knows nothing.

'Okay,' she says, 'then tell me it in your own words and I'll see.'

See what? I take my eyes off the road to look at her for a moment. She is calm and dead, dead serious. Okay, I think. It's not like I'm going to be able to change the subject. I sigh and start from the beginning.

'Well, it was Dad's fiftieth birthday. Have you heard of a place called Sandbanks? It's in Poole Harbour.'

'Yeah, yeah,' she says. She clearly wants me to get on to the good stuff, but I'm not going to, not just like that. If I'm going to tell everything I know, she needs to hear what she's asked for: the story in my words.

'Fair enough. It's a bit of a tabloid favourite, because it suddenly became the most expensive per-square-foot property in the country sometime in the 1990s. There's no obvious reason. It's a suburban sandspit that cuts almost all the way across the harbour, with a chain ferry at the end, going over to Purbeck. It used to be the sort of place accountants retired to, and there was a

156

run-down hotel with the sort of sandy beach they market for family holidays. Then suddenly all these IT millionaires started buying up there and the whole market went wild. So Dad started doing quick-turnover refurbs down there. He was making a quarter, half a million in profit off each one. He was wallowing in easy dough like a milk bath.'

Ruby grunts. She clearly doesn't think a history of the British property market is going to get her very far.

'I'm telling you because it's why we were there, Ruby. And there rather than, you know, the South of France. I don't suppose the papers got on to that; they were too wrapped up in the whole Millionaires' Row angle. He had just finished a refurb and it was going on the market the following week, and it was the most deluxe conversion he'd ever done, so he decided he might as well make use of the facilities he'd paid for and have his birthday weekend down there.'

'Poole Harbour's Bournemouth, isn't it? It's not exactly Dad, is it?'

'No. Exactly. All honesty? I think he wanted to pretend he was a teenager again, and it's so much easier to do that if you don't have customs officials to get past.'

She thinks about this for a moment. 'So you're saying they were taking drugs?'

'You wanted to know, Ruby.'

She looks disgusted, the way only a teenager can do at the thought of someone of mature years doing rock-star stuff. Gawd. The whole Simone thing must be even more gruesome for her than it is for me. Primal trauma is one thing, but the old goat with a woman who is a couple of years shy of being legally able to be his granddaughter? Especially when that woman is Simone. I was as sick as a dog for weeks when I found out.

'Yes. What can I say? Yes. I think they were probably doing

cocaine, but they were certainly smoking dope. You can't really miss the smell of that stuff.'

'So I hear,' she says, archly. I ignore her.

'And they were drinking and gorging and shouting at each other the way grown-ups do when they're tying one on. I've no idea why they brought the kids, really. If they wanted to behave like kids themselves they should have made arrangements. But they didn't, and your ma had fallen out with your nanny, so they had no one but us and Simone to do the donkey work. And then, obviously, just Simone. There was this horrible staircase Linda had put in to appeal to the yuppies. It was all hardened glass and sharp edges and gaping handrails, and you two were going through a phase of wandering, so after the first night they decided to put you in the maid's room on the ground floor to sleep. They thought you'd be safer there.'

'The Law of Unintended Consequences,' says Ruby.

'I hadn't thought of it that way. Don't be angry with your mum, Ruby. She's had the whole world blaming her, and I don't suppose there's been a day gone by when she hasn't blamed herself.'

Ruby is silent. She folds her arms and stares through the windscreen at the unfurling road ahead. It's going to be a long drive.

Chapter Nineteen

2004 | Friday | Simone

She hears them coming from the other side of the garden, from her sun-lounger by the pool. The girls' voices shrill, defensive, Sean's fruity tenor booming across the still air. The building machinery, which threw her from her sleep half an hour ago, has come to a standstill and every word of their row rings across the neighbourhood.

'Fuck you, Daddy!' shouts India. 'Just – fuck you!'

'You can't speak to me like that! You *cannot* speak to your elders like that! My God, I'm ashamed to have brought you up!'

Milly's voice: 'Well, isn't it lucky you *didn't*, then? Perhaps you'll do a better job with the next lot, eh?'

'Oh, for God's sake!'

Simone sits slowly forward and cranes round the edge of her seat to watch. Milly and India, still in last night's clothes – no surprise to Simone, given that she has had the annexe to herself for the entire night – stand with their backs to her, clenched fists dug deep into their waists like fishwives. Sean has both sets of fingers buried deep in his thick hair to show his frustration.

'Are you two going to bear a grudge forever? Really?'

'Yes,' says Milly. 'If you want an honest answer, yes, why not?'

'That's the thing you're always saying to us,' says India. 'If you didn't want to deal with the consequences, you shouldn't have made the choices, should you?'

'I have done everything in my power,' he says, 'to make sure you weren't affected. I'm sorry Mummy and I couldn't get along, but you can't punish me for it forever.'

India thrusts a sardonic laugh in his face. 'Everything in your power? You think? My God, you didn't even remember we were coming down this weekend, Daddy!'

Simone sees him blush to the roots of his hair. For a moment, he looks as though he might actually admit to being at fault, then he draws himself up and says, 'Nonsense.'

I must remember that, thinks Simone. Alpha males like Sean can never apologise. It's just not in them. You just have to live with that, if that's the sort of man you want.

'I'd just been expecting you to call and let me know when you were coming, not just pitch up and climb over the fence without telling anyone. Anything could have happened.'

'Bollocks,' says India. 'My God, you don't half talk some bollocks, old man. Oh, and we climbed *through* the fence, not over it. Your security's not what you think it is.'

Milly shakes her head. 'I suppose once you get into the habit of lying,' she says, 'it becomes second nature.'

She turns to her sister and Simone watches a wave of that weird psychic communication you see happening between siblings cross between them. 'He probably actually believes it,' she says. 'Now, anyway. It probably took him an hour or so, but now he's rewritten it in his head so he looks good.'

'Is that something the *therapist* I lay out a hundred quid a week for told you?' asks Sean. 'I can see my money's being well spent.'

'Oh, piss off,' says Milly. 'If you didn't want us to have to see a therapist you should have tried not buggering off at the first opportunity.'

He gasps. Then looks suddenly, spitefully triumphant. 'Oh, Milly,' he says, 'trust me, it wasn't the first opportunity.'

All three Jacksons fall horribly silent. Did he really say that? thinks Simone. It can't have been what he meant. Sean would never deliberately hurt someone's feelings like that.

Milly turns away and her face is a picture of devastation. She starts to walk towards the annexe, stiff-backed, and her sister takes two swift steps to catch up with her.

'No, look,' says Sean, 'I didn't mean it like that. Come on, girls—'

'Oh, can it, Dad,' says India, and slams the annexe door.

He stands in the sunlight for a few seconds, staring after them. Right now, he looks every year of his age, and not in a good way. Simone has always liked mature men, ever since she can remember. She likes their strength, their authority, their confidence. She's never seen the virtues of the spotty youths who hang around the girls at her school, with their gangling, gropy hands and their way of dropping into some weak imitation of Rasta speak when they're feeling insecure. But right now she can see the old man Sean will become, and just briefly it frightens her. I wonder if I should show myself? she wonders. He looks as though he could do with someone to talk to. But, before she can decide, he turns and walks slowly back to the house, his head bowed and his shoulders slumped.

She leaves it a few minutes, then she goes into the annexe herself. Curiosity drives her, and a tiny twinge of glee. The Jackson girls have always been snarky with her, enjoyed finding opportunities to mock. She can't help but be tempted to relish their upset.

They're packing.

'Hello!' she says. 'What are you doing?'

India whirls round, surprised by her entrance as though she'd forgotten that she was even there. 'We're going,' she says. 'You can have this place to yourself.'

Simone apes a look of astonishment. 'But why? You've only just got here.'

'Mind your own beeswax,' says Milly, and they turn back to their bags, throwing clothes unfolded in through the zippered tops with vengeful energy. She can't stop herself from letting her thoughts out, though, even though Simone is standing there. They start to talk to each other as though she is invisible.

'He can't talk to us like that,' she says. 'I can't believe he thinks it's okay to talk to us like that.'

'He knows it isn't,' says India. 'Stupid old bastard. Typical. He knows perfectly well it's not okay, but he does it anyway. I'm done. That's bloody *it*.'

'If he thinks I'm coming for another of his stupid access visits he can think again,' says Milly. 'He can stick it up his arse.'

India plonks herself on to her mattress and dials Directory Enquiries on her mobile. 'A minicab company in Bournemouth, please,' she says. 'Oh, I don't have a pen. Can you put me through?'

She looks up at her sister. 'It's okay, Mills,' she says. 'It's not like we didn't know what he was like.'

Milly sighs, and her face starts to crumple. Then she shakes her head like a dog in the rain. 'Yeah,' she says. 'Sod him.'

'Hi,' says India. 'We'd like a car to pick up in Sandbanks and take us to the station, please. Yes. Soon as possible.'

Simone watches them stalk away to the front drive, and goes back to her sun-lounger. The grown-ups will be needing her help soon. It's gearing up to be a lovely day.

Chapter Twenty

Her mood turns to anger at the service station outside Arundel. I get into the queue for coffee and Big Macs, and she goes off to the loo, and when she comes back there are two vertical lines on the bridge of her nose and her cheeks are flaming. She stomps across the concourse and parents dive upon their children to remove them from her path.

The chairs are fixed to the tables at a distance designed to discourage lingering, and the gap is too narrow for her to fling herself into it. She manages a slide, nonetheless, that communicates the violence of her emotions.

'I got you a Big Mac and fries and a vanilla shake,' I say, propitiatingly.

She refuses to look at me. Peels open her burger and devours it in three disgusted bites. Chews like a wolf devouring a helpless lamb and sucks on her shake so hard she goes purple with the effort. Eventually I see the shudder that accompanies brain freeze, and she slams the drink down on to her tray. Then she peels off the lid and starts dunking the fries in the remainder. God. The things people think up.

'She fucking lied to me,' she says.

Thanks, Claire. Leave it to me to talk your daughter round, why don't you? After all, we've always been so close.

I sugar my quadruple espresso and take a draught. It's luke-warm, and the grind has been horribly burnt by overheated steam, but it's coffee. Another one of these and I'll make it to lunchtime, hopefully. I long for a cigarette. It's been almost six-teen hours. These people have no idea.

'They all fucking lied to me,' she says. 'No wonder she's been keeping me at home like a freak, pretending she was doing it for my benefit. What was the point? I mean, what was the fucking point? Did they really think I wouldn't find out? I'm not going to stay at home *forever*.'

She's like one of those princesses in a fairytale. Kept away from the world because the King didn't want her to come across a prick. Or something.

'I think it's more complicated than that,' I venture.

'I don't want to hear it,' she says.

'She loves you very much.'

'Oh, *please*.'

She returns to her fries, feeding them one by one by one into her mouth like paper into a shredder, and I concede defeat for the time being. Sip my coffee and wait for whatever's coming next. Ruby is not the weeping willow I'd been imagining on my way down to collect her. I'd been thinking that I would be an angel of mercy, glowing in my own virtue as I coaxed confidences, dabbed tears, draped consoling arms round shaking shoulders. Amazons don't seem to qualify for the same levels of sympathy accorded to dainty people. They're meant to *do* the comforting, not seek it. Looks like Ruby's learned her lessons well.

164

'It's all a big bloody lie,' she says. 'When I get home I'm tearing that bloody shrine down wholesale. D'you know what it's like, having to look at that every single day? She's mawkish about it. It's all Coco, Coco, Coco, and me keeping my mouth shut because . . . I don't know what. I don't even know why. She's lying to me and I'm going out of my way to protect her from it. I've not had a single birthday that's just mine. Not one single one in twelve years that didn't end up with her blubbing over the cake. And every summer's spoiled because I know she's going to go into mourning again, and I thought . . . oh, *fuck*. At least I used to think it was because she was dead. Now I just look at her and think, why? Why are you lying to me?'

Yeah, I think, actually it's worse than that. Claire's been waiting for a child who'll never come home, and telling this facile lie because a bit of her knows that she never will. I can't imagine anything worse than that. I always wondered how Sean managed to live with it so well. I guess men are just different. I can see why she would tell this stupid lie to Ruby when she was too little to grasp the complexities, but that time is long past and now they're trapped, both of them. All those things the general public in its infinite wisdom have had to say about her mother: and Ruby has had no one to ask. I need to calm her down before they speak again. If Claire finds out that Ruby has known it all, all this time, all by herself in the Coco museum, she will want to die. I would. I would have wanted to die every day since she vanished.

'I'm sorry, Ruby,' I say.

'What are *you* sorry about?' she asks, suspiciously. 'What did *you* do?'

'Not fair. You know sorry doesn't always mean that.'

'Oh, right, so it's *sympathy*. Lucky old me.'

She reaches the end of her snack, crumples up the cardboard holder and throws it on to the tray. Glares at me as she sticks the straw back into the top of her milkshake and drinks. 'So you still haven't told me what happened,' she says. 'Your version. Not anyone else's.'

'Okay. But we're going to have to do this outside. I need a cigarette.'

We take our drinks out into the car park and sit on a hump of pine-needle-covered bare earth as I roll a smoke. I've seen a lot of the world's glamorous places in the course of my habit. 'When they came to get you for breakfast on Monday morning, you were fast asleep in the bed and Coco was gone,' I tell her.

'Just like that?'

'There was a hole in the fence. Indy and I found it on Thursday afternoon when Dad left us hanging around on the street, and we let ourselves in and had a swim. It had probably been there all summer. Even by the sea, people can't resist the lure of an unguarded swimming pool. I should think half the teenagers in the area knew it was there. And the lock on the patio door was broken. No fingerprints. Well, no fingerprints apart from all the people who'd been there all weekend, and the cleaners and the builders and the craftspeople, but they were all ticked off the list one by one and after that there was nothing. No DNA, no traces of anything you wouldn't expect. It was like . . . like she'd vanished into thin air.'

'And I didn't wake up?'

I shake my head. Light my cigarette and drink my coffee and, just briefly, all is well with the world.

'Where was everybody? I don't understand. How could they not have heard anything? If someone broke in they'd have made a hell of a noise, surely?'

'I don't know, Ruby. It's possible the lock was already broken. No one remembers if it was actually locked when they arrived.

166

If you didn't try it before you turned the key you'd probably just think you were locking it and unlocking it when actually nothing was happening at all.'

'And there wasn't anybody else sleeping downstairs?'

'There was a baby alarm,' I say.

'And they didn't hear anything?'

God, it sounds awful. It is awful. They deserved every bit of the what-sort-of-people coverage they got in the papers. What sort of people do something like that? I bet he took a sleeping pill, too, though he's never admitted it. He didn't hear the baby alarm because he was snoring off a weekend of red wine and God knows what else.

'It was just Dad. Your mum went home on Saturday night – well, more like very early Sunday morning. I think they had a row, though the official story was that she had always been going to go because she had to get on with recruiting a new nanny first thing Monday.'

'So she left me with those people?'

'She left you with your father. That's really not that unusual, Ruby. You're sounding like the papers now.'

'The papers have a point,' she says, sulkily.

I can't be cross with her. It's not as though it's not been said over and over by people who had no link at all with any of it. If everyone who ever bought the *Mirror* has a right to an opinion, then God knows Ruby has one.

'You know what? You had a lovely weekend. Lovely. Ice cream and seashells and sandcastles and paddling and all the things kids really love. We all went to the beach. You remember that, right? The jellyfish? And it was like that all weekend. You had a brilliant time. You need to remember that. Coco and you were really happy on your last weekend together. You need to remember that.'

'I don't,' says Ruby. 'I don't remember. I don't remember anything. I don't even remember her, really. Not at all. I see her photo every single day, but I don't remember what she felt like.'

She looks suddenly, horribly miserable.

'I wish I did,' she says.

Chapter Twenty-One

2004 | Friday | Claire

'Sean, I really don't know about this. It just doesn't seem right.'

'Oh, God,' says Sean, and lays his end of the mattress down in preparation for a fight. 'Here we go again.'

'But I—'

His face suffuses with red as it always does when he senses a thwarting coming on. She will never get used to it, this change in the charming man who couldn't find a fault in her. But of course, she never thwarted him before she married him. 'Yes, you, you, you. It's always about you, isn't it? Do you ever think that there might be other people in the world?'

Same old story. When Sean feels as though he might not be going to get his way, the accusations come tumbling out. You're so selfish. You never think about what *I* might want, do you? You're ruining my life. You pretended to be someone completely different. I would never have married you if I'd known what you were really like.

'But Sean,' she protests feebly, 'they're just little kids!'

Their disagreements always go the same way. He wants something, and, if she points out the disadvantages of that thing, he reverts immediately to infancy. A giant toddler kicking and screaming I-hate-yous at Nasty Mummy. Over the years she has retreated from battle, taken to avoiding conflict if she can manage it, but her frustration leaks out in passive aggression all the time. She hears her own hurt little stiff voice saying, 'Oh, do what you want, you always do,' and despises herself. Passive aggression is still aggression, after all. Just the dishonest version.

'Oh, of course,' says Sean. 'All those years at medical school are as *nothing* in the face of your three years' experience as a *mother*. Do you think Jimmy would give them to his own kids if it was dangerous? Seriously?'

I don't think he'd even consider the possibility that it might be, she thinks. Nothing I've seen of Jimmy Orizio makes me confident that he considers any possibilities too closely. He didn't even get off the sofa till lunchtime, he was so hung over. Just lay there with last night's drool dried out in his three-day stubble. The kids must have thought one of those War Memorial drunks had got in in the night.

Sean picks up the mattress again and starts walking forward. 'Perhaps,' he says, 'you might have thought about maintaining a better relationship with your staff, if you didn't want us to have to get creative about how we were going to handle all these children.'

She can't stop herself. 'Perhaps,' she replies, 'if you could manage to maintain a relationship with your *last* lot of children we wouldn't be having to do this now.'

Sean rolls his eyes until the pupils disappear. 'Oh, God, there we go,' he says, and jerks on the mattress so that it drags through her hands and she feels a nail split. Oh, fuck you, Sean, she thinks. You'll be on about how I'm letting myself go if I don't go and waste half my Saturday getting that sorted out in time for your precious dinner, because you'll have a tantrum if I don't.

'Ow,' she says. 'You just broke my nail.'

He ignores her. 'You really are a piece of work, you know that? You'll just pick on anything if you know it'll hurt me.' Plaintive little boy again. What must his mother have been like? He says his father was a monster but he barely even mentions her. She probably only existed to supply whatever the menfolk wanted. I know the arseholes say you should see what a woman's mother looks like before you decide to marry her, but if I had my time over again I'd make it a rule to do exactly the same thing about men. Their attitude to their mothers says everything about their attitude to women in general. If their mother looks downtrodden, run for the hills.

They manoeuvre the mattress out through the patio doors and into the sunshine. Claire has seen very little of the sunshine today. She's spent all of it clearing up the debris from last night and making a ceaseless round of bacon sandwiches for the adults and cheesy pasta with peas for the children. No one even bothered to observe mealtimes. Just drifted in and out from the shrieks of laughter by the swimming pool and said 'Ooh, yes, how lovely' as she got the pan off the draining rack once again. Jimmy and Linda have almost reached the annexe with the mattresses from their own room. Imogen Clutterbuck stands in the doorway with a gaggle of infants round her knees.

'And are we really going to leave them with just Simone in charge?' Claire asks.

'She says she's happy to,' says Sean. 'I mean, sure, if you want to stay home instead, I'm sure she wouldn't mind. And at least I'd get a bit of peace and quiet without nagging, I suppose.'

Oh, that's so unfair. But she thinks about it and she thinks, yes, okay, at least I won't have to watch you dribble wine down your chin. He's booked at the café on the other side of the chain ferry. For a few blissful hours they won't even be on the same piece of *land*. 'Okay,' she says. 'Sure. Yes. Thank you. Good suggestion. I think that might make sense, don't you? You know, leaving an adult in charge the first time we drug our children?'

He stops again, turns and glares at her. 'It's not drugging them. God, how you exaggerate.'

'Well what would you call it?'

'What Jimmy calls it,' he says. 'They're medications, not drugs. Look, he's been doing it for years and nothing's happened to *his* kids, has it? It's fine. It's absolutely fine. If you can't trust a doctor to get this stuff right, who *can* you trust?'

The air mattresses have been arranged and the bedclothes tucked in on top. Joaquin, as the eldest, is to get Milly's bed, and Tiggy, who's six, the sofa-bed that had been assigned to India. The fact that the older girls didn't sleep in them means that no one is demanding the linens be changed, at least. Coco and Ruby will share one mattress, Inigo and Fred the second. Simone's bed has been prissily made and tidied, her suitcase repacked and slid beneath. She's not a teenager, thinks Claire, she's an automaton. I suppose growing up with parents whose careers are dedicated to keeping other people's shenanigans out of the public eye would make you quite paranoid about your privacy, though.

Simone, Maria and Imogen are herding the children in the kitchen, filling their tummies with chipolatas and mashed potato in preparation for their zopiclone chaser. The men have retired to the gazebo with a bottle of champagne. The scent of Sean's cigar drifts over the evening air. I'm glad I won't be going with them, Claire thinks. He'll be so much happier with that besotted girl hanging on his every word than he would be with me worrying about my babies. I may not have the strength of character to stop them doing this, but at least I can be there if something goes wrong.

She closes the door to keep out the cigar smoke and goes up to the house.

Tiggy, sitting with her elbows on the glass dining table, is being difficult about her carrots. 'Hate them,' she says. 'Horrible, horrible, horrible carrots.' Fred, Tiggy's four-year-old parrot, repeats the words while banging the handle of his fork on the table. 'Hobewel hobewel hobewal cawwots,' he says. He hasn't yet learned to pronounce his Rs, and all those Ws make him sound like Christopher Robin.

She can't help but sympathise. Linda's a terrible cook. She's boiled the vegetables till they're tasteless mush, and dumped them on the plate with no accompaniment – no butter, no oil – to make them more appetising. I hated carrots too, when I was a kid, thinks Claire. Funny, that. You'd have thought anything sugary would go down kids' gullets like Haribo. The others are pushing theirs around their plates, too, but Tiggy is the only one to actually voice her distaste. She's the eldest of the Orizio children, and with that comes a level of dominance that suggests that she's used to making her own decisions, even at the age of six.

Even when she isn't, thinks Claire. I don't suppose she gets much choice about sleeping, for a start. She checks her watch. It's past seven o'clock and the table is booked for half-past eight. If they're going to get them knocked out and settled enough for the diners to make the ferry, they need to step up the pace a bit.

'Tell you what,' she says brightly, looking at her daughters' faces as they contemplate their own plates, 'as it's the holidays, why don't we say everyone gets to not finish one thing on their plate? We need to leave room for ice cream, don't we?'

Six pairs of eyes swivel to look at her with undisguised relief. They nod enthusiastically. Joaquin, lofty in his status as the only seven-year-old, doesn't bother to look at her, but even he raises a nod.

'You shouldn't do that,' says Imogen reprovingly. 'You're teaching them to think they can be fussy eaters without consequences.'

Claire curls her lip at her. 'Okay, chop chop!' she says. 'Last one to finish is a banana!'

Pretending to look for the ice cream, she goes over to Linda at the kitchen island. She's already dressed herself for the evening, tight bodycon dress so white she suspects it's been treated with some chemical designed to make it glow under ultraviolet light, platinum necklace-bracelet-earring set – Jimmy's obviously not handing out his uppers and downers as a non-profit work of charity – and clear Perspex mules that show off every bone in her very bony feet. The dress leaves nothing to the imagination, and Claire notes with a twinge of satisfaction that despite the obvious gym habit – she's a teaky sort of brown and her face is starting to get lined from pulling faces on the weights machines – Linda still has saddlebags at the tops of her thighs. He'll start criticising those soon enough, she thinks spitefully, don't think he won't, for she knows, not that anyone has told her, that Linda is fucking her husband. Linda is too sugary-sweet to her, though they have barely met before last night, for it to be anything else, and last night Sean brought Linda a glass of chilled Chardonnay when they arrived without asking what it was she wanted.

Linda has a blister pack of pills and a small blue pill-cutter out on the countertop, and is carefully cutting each pill in half, then half again. A quarter of an adult dose for my three-year-olds? she thinks. You have to be kidding.

'We don't have to do this, you know,' she says in a low voice. 'I'm going to be with them. How about we just say we have, and not?'

'Chill, babe,' says Linda. 'We do this all the time, seriously. It's fine.'

'But one of those knocks me sideways, and I weigh nine stone.'

'That's because it works, love.'

Don't patronise me, she thinks, you bitch. Just because your pet cuckold's a doctor doesn't mean you're one.

'There's a massive margin of error,' Linda carries on. 'It would take six or seven whole pills before they got anywhere near danger. Seriously. Jimmy wouldn't do it if he thought it was dangerous.'

'But . . . I don't think the twins weigh much more than two stone. They're little for their age. Can't we give them something else?'

Linda shrugs. 'Like what?'

'I don't know. Calpol?'

Linda laughs, a nasty laugh. Starts lining up the quarter pills in a row, puts the remaining piece back into one of the blisters and puts the blister pack and the cutter into the top drawer of the island, with the cutlery. 'Mustn't forget those on Monday,' she says, and winks. 'They'll give any potential buyers a thrill! Honestly. Calpol. My lot would still be bouncing off the ceilings at ten o'clock.'

'But they're kids. You *know* you're not supposed to give kids adult medicines. It's all over the packs, for God's sake.'

Again, the laugh. 'Oh, Claire,' she says, 'you crack me up. Those warnings are for *stupid* people.'

Imogen gets out seven little bowls and seven teaspoons, puts two scoops of vanilla in each bowl and pours golden syrup over the top. 'They love this,' she declares. 'The cold turns the syrup into toffee. Much cheaper than Ben & Jerry's.'

'Sprinkles,' says Simone. 'I loved sprinkles when I was little.'

'Don't tell me you've forgotten the sprinkles, Linda?' says Maria. 'I thought this house came equipped?' and they all laugh. Claire's head snaps round on her neck and she looks at Maria, searches for a sign that it was just a casual remark. *They know*, she thinks. *They all know. That's why none of them can be bothered with me, this weekend. They all know I'm on my way out and this one has already taken my place, in their minds. I'm a laughing stock behind my back. They're probably cock-a-hoop that they're free from me, for dinner.*

Imogen carries the bowls over to the table, click click click in her professional-wifey heels. She has hair that's as stiff as a board from the chemicals that strain it into perimenopausal curls, and wears a shirt dress with snaffle bits all over it. Her jewellery is gold, of course; quiet classy gold with only the five-carat sapphire (a sapphire! Of course! Even her jewellery is Tory blue!) on her ring finger for bling. 'So!' she cries, 'Who's for ice cream?'

Linda sways over behind her, the pills in her hand. 'Vitamins first, Imo,' she says. 'You know the rules! Everyone gets vitamins at the seaside!'

The children look away from the hypnotic sweetness and gaze up into her face. 'We don't want you getting tired for tomorrow, do we?' she says. 'Come on, everybody. Just a little vitamin, one each, build you up so you've got lots of energy! Down in one and then it's pudding!'

She looks around the women. Maria is in her signature scarlet, a halter-neck dress that shows off her magnificent cleavage, nipped in at the waist for Mediterranean drama, A-line skirt with a flounce at the knee. Simone has followed suit, wears a matching dress two sizes smaller, in a pale blue that shows off her ivory skin. And make-up. She's wearing full make-up, as though she were going to a party, not a hamburger joint on the beach.

They gather over the table like a flock of harpies, bending sweetly over the children as they feed them soporifics and help them wash them down with sips of water. Ruffle their hair, kiss the tops of their heads, congratulate them on their co-operation. Tiggy doesn't want to take hers – she's going through the 'no' phase – but the threat of having to watch her mother eat her ice cream for her soon undoes her resolve. And then it's done. The bowls land on the table and the eating begins.

I can't bear it, thinks Claire. I'm a terrible mother. I should be able to stand up to them all, not let them bully me like this for their own convenience. If the girls found out about this when they were grown-ups they would never forgive me.

'You know what?' she declares, 'I've changed my mind. I think I will come to dinner after all.'

The women turn and stare. 'Oh,' says Imogen. 'Well who's going to keep an eye on the children, then?'

'Simone offered. Didn't you, Simone? You won't mind, will you? After all, it *is* my *husband's* birthday weekend.' She fixes Linda full in the eye. 'I wouldn't want him to be lonely without me,' she says.

She runs upstairs to change, pulls on her Chanel sundress and Stuart Weitzman heels that will be hell on the sandy path from the ferry to the café. Sprays her hair with glosser and twists it into a Grecian updo with the help of a blonde plait on a clip, tendrils curling down her long, smooth neck the way he used to love. He used to say she reminded him of a swan with her graceful throat, gliding through life as though it were limpid water. I shan't wear jewellery tonight, she thinks. I'll let Linda look flashy and vulgar and old among the seaside young and the boatyard customers who generally hang about that café. As a last thought she kicks off the silly shoes and dons a pair of ballet pumps instead. She'll save the diamonds he gave her on their wedding day for tomorrow night, just to remind him.

Back in the kitchen, the pills are starting to work. Simone perches dejectedly on one of the high stools, hands between her thighs, one shoe dangling from a toe. I'm sorry, Claire thinks. It's not your fault. You've got caught up in grown-up stuff and you deserve better than that. But this is my life, and my marriage, and I'm damned if I'm going to let my feeling sorry for you allow me to be humiliated in my own home. I've allowed myself to be bullied into an act of profound immorality. It has to be for *something*.

The children at the table are silent. Mouths have started to fall open and shoulders to slump, and Inigo has laid his head on one outstretched arm. Fred yawns, and, one after the other, the yawn passes through the group like a Mexican wave.

'You look gorgeous,' says Maria, and her tone is kind, the way you'd speak to an awkward teenager facing their first dance. Fuck you, thinks Claire. Too late to pretend to be my friend now.

'Bedtime!' she says, brightly. Tiggy opens her mouth to protest, but the thought, whatever it was, slips away before it can become words. She goes to the patio door, calls out across the evening light. 'Gents? The children are ready for bed! A hand here?'

'Coming!' calls a voice from the gazebo. She turns back and looks at her daughters. Coco's eyes drift closed and she jerks in her seat, as though she's dreamt that she was falling off.

Chapter Twenty-Two

2004 | Friday | Sean

He excuses himself and goes down to the annexe to see how they're getting on. The others are cheerful, carefree, and nobody, not even Claire, seems particularly concerned to check, so he does it himself. It's been a strained evening. The café, with its view over the silver water to the darkening hump of Brownsea Island, has smartened itself up since his youth, replaced the old menu of microwave pasties and cottage pie with a wider range of fish and shellfish and tiramisu, but the company has been uncomfortable.

He still doesn't understand why Claire, so obstructive all day, suddenly decided to come with them after all her high and mighty concern for her children. So, instead of getting to flirt with his mistress while her common-law husband drank himself comatose on Jack Daniel's and Coke, he had to endure her sparring with his dowdy little wife like Davis and Crawford across the checked gingham tablecloth. And now Claire's sticking by Linda's side like a remora and the chances of his getting a bit of alone time with her are zero. He fancies a cigar and a sit, and this is as good an excuse as any.

The blinds and shutters are closed across the annexe windows but dim light leaks out through the slats. He taps on the door and hears movement inside. A shadow falls across the glass and Simone opens up.

'Oh, hello,' she murmurs. 'You're back. Did you have a good time?'

'It was fine,' he says, 'though obviously you were missed. I brought you a glass of fizz and a slice of the awesome chocolate cake they're doing down there now.'

'Oh.' Simone blushes to the roots of her hair, as though he's surprised her with diamonds. Ah, young girls, he thinks, so thrilled by even the littlest presents. I wish my two were like this. They don't seem to appreciate anything at all.

'Thank you,' she stammers, and her eyelashes beat against her cheeks like moths. 'That's so kind.'

'Nonsense,' he says. 'It's the least I could do when you've been so generous. How have they been?'

'Oh—' For a moment it looks as though she's forgotten the children altogether. She glances over her shoulder and pushes the door open so he can see six small bodies still and silent on their mattress beds, medieval church memorials carved from stone. The room smells of farts and sun lotion. 'They've been fine. Not a peep all night.'

'Splendid,' he says, 'splendid. And how have you been?'

She beams. 'I've been fine. I read my book and watched some videos on YouTube.' A pair of earbuds hangs around her neck and she twiddles one at him to illustrate how she managed to do so silently.

'Haven't you eaten?'

'I grabbed a sandwich,' she says, 'but I didn't want to leave them for too long, in case one of them woke up.'

'Very conscientious. I'm sure it's not necessary, though. Have any of them stirred at all?'

'Not a peep.'

He feels a rush of hail-fellow generosity. 'Well, come out and have some fresh air with your cake,' he tells her. 'I was going to go and have a sit in the gazebo for a bit, if you'd like to join me?'

Simone practically shivers with pleasure. 'Of course,' she says. 'Thank you.'

It's lovely and peaceful out here. The sound of voices drifts to them from the kitchen, at much the same level as the background shush of the sea. It's a perfect night, the land still warm from the day, the breeze low and gentle. Simone sits placidly beside him, doesn't nag, doesn't compete for his attention, emanates contentment as she sips her champagne. The cake is in a container with a plastic fork included and she pops it open, takes a taste, sighs with pleasure.

'Good?' he asks, and lights his cigar as she nods. Lays his spare arm along the sofa back and crosses one leg over the other. Despite his trying evening, Sean feels filled with bonhomie and the joy of life. If only, he thinks, all interactions with women could be this easy. Something happens to them as they mature. They can't seem to stop themselves from turning bitter. If only they could stay sixteen forever – legal, unlike Simone, but still sweet and malleable and grateful for attention.

'Would you like a taste?'

'No, no,' he says, 'I ate my fill at dinner. You enjoy yourself.'

Simone takes two more bites then pushes the container regretfully away. Sips her champagne and remarks on how nice it is.

'Surely that's not all you're going to eat?' he asks.

'It's lovely,' says Simone, 'but it's very rich.'

'You're not worried about your figure, are you?' he teases.

'No, no,' says Simone, but she looks embarrassed in the half-light. Perhaps she's just trying to look un-greedy; perhaps it's a real worry.

'You've got a lovely figure,' he says, gallantly. Drinks his whisky and adds, 'I bet you've got a stack of boys trailing in your wake like ducklings.'

Her hair drops across her face as she looks down at the table. 'Not really,' she says.

'Oh, come,' he teases. 'Pretty girl like you?'

She looks back up at him. 'Boys my age are so immature,' she says. 'I prefer men.'

The words hang between them on the night air. In the distance, Charlie Clutterbuck's mature and fruity laugh clangs through the open door. In the pebbledashed semi over the fence, a window slams down pointedly. The fusty old queen who lives there has been complaining about noise pollution all summer, and his resentment clearly continues to burn. Well, good luck with that, thinks Sean. I don't suppose the people who can afford the three mil to buy this place will be wanting to spend their summers tending their hydrangeas in brown cardigans.

He checks his watch and realises that it's midnight.

'By gum,' he says, 'it's my birthday!'

'Oh!' says Simone, and wriggles in her seat. 'Oh, happy birthday!' She raises her glass and they clink and drink.

'And what a lovely way to go into it,' he tells her. 'Couldn't have asked for better company.'

'I hope you have a lovely year,' she says. 'I hope it's the best year ever.'

He heaves a grunting sigh. 'Not much chance of that, I'm afraid.' He's quite drunk, he realises, and careless with his confidences. But then, *because* he is drunk, he realises that he doesn't care. It'll all come out in the wash soon anyway. What's a fifteen-year-old going to do?

'I don't know if you've noticed,' he says, 'but Claire and I aren't getting on.'

Simone tucks her hair behind her ear and goes back to her cake. 'Yes,' she says, 'I couldn't help noticing. She's not very nice to you, is she?'

'Oh, thank God,' he says, and sits up, pleased to have found a sympathetic ear. 'Someone who believes me! You have no idea how difficult it is being a man. Everyone seems to want to blame us when things go wrong.'

'It's so unfair,' she says. 'Dad and Maria have to deal with that all the time, with the papers. Dad says it's the worst thing of all, because everyone believes women when they sell their stories, but if men do it they're cads.'

'Exactly,' he says.

'She shouldn't talk to you the way she does,' says Simone. 'It's not respectful.'

'She wasn't like that when I met her,' he says. 'Sometimes I think she's mad.'

Simone appears to consider this possibility. 'I don't know if I should say anything,' she says. 'She's your wife.'

'It's okay,' Sean feels a momentary twinge of guilt. 'I'm sorry. I shouldn't have involved you.'

'It's okay.' She rushes to reassure him. 'It's not like I'm going to say anything. And I – I started it. I shouldn't have said anything. It's not my business. It's just . . . '

He waits.

'If I were your wife,' she says, in a little voice that falters as it goes, 'I would never talk to you the way she does. You're so . . . and she doesn't seem to appreciate it at all.'

'I work like a dog,' he tells her, 'so she can have everything she wants, and she just seems to resent me.'

'You work so hard,' she echoes. Then, 'Why don't you split up?'

Sean takes another hit of whisky, sucks his cigar. She watches him in silence. She's so lovely, he thinks. So soft and gentle and kind. If I had my life over again . . .

'It's not that easy,' he says. 'A divorce . . . it's a hard thing. You see how India and Milly are with me. Their mother's poisoned them against me, because that's what happens, with divorces. The mother gets the kids and the father gets frozen out. I couldn't bear that, not a second time. The twins adore me right now. I'm not going to watch them turn sulky on me the way the girls have. If it weren't for the twins, it would be different. If they'd not been born. But we've got them now, and we're tied together for life because of it. Even if we did split up. It's just not so easy, once you have kids. I could never let them go.'

He feels smug in his own virtue. I am a good father, he tells himself. India and Milly might not see it, but I'm a good father.

'Besides,' he says, 'what hope would there be for them, if they went with her? She'd ruin them. You've seen her. She's as crazy as a cut snake.'

A flash memory. Sitting on a bench on the Thames Embankment with Claire, saying the same thing about Heather. Is that it? he asks himself. Do all women just go mad after a while? All the ones in my life seem to. They adore me at first but after a while they just turn bitter. My wives, my girlfriends. It's not fair. It's obviously got something to do with my choice of women. Maria Gavila's not like that, and Charlie Clutterbuck's been married nineteen years and he's a complete arse.

'Anyway,' he says, 'it's my birthday. Let's not talk about that. We're meant to be celebrating. Here.' He picks up the plastic fork, spears a bit of cake on to it and holds it out towards her mouth. 'Have some cake.'

'I can't!' she protests, and he notices that her pupils are huge.

'Of course you can,' he says, and moves the morsel closer.

Simone parts her pretty lips and allows herself to be fed.

Chapter Twenty-Three

It comes on to rain at Yeovil. Thick, blustery West Country rain that brings a dark sky which won't lighten now until morning. Two in the afternoon, and all the cars turn on their headlights. I hate January. Every mile or so, a gust picks the car up and slams it down again about a foot to the right. We stop talking. I need what's left of my brain to get us there alive.

An hour later and dusk takes over from storm clouds, and we're creeping through narrow lanes where white fingerpost signs loom up and point in random directions. We come to a crossroads where all four fingers point to Barnstaple and the satnav tells us that we are in the middle of a field. Ruby stirs from her misery coma and peers through the window.

'I remember this,' she says. 'You go right here.'

I go right. The road narrows: a single track between hedged banks that rise up and cut off the last of the daylight. Huge trees knit naked branches together above us and form a ghostly winter tunnel. I can't imagine Sean down here. I know it's where he grew up, but his tastes always ran to white corniches and blazing sunlight; to sea that, as he said, you could swim in, and terrace restaurants where the whole passing population could see that you were drinking champagne. Every two hundred yards the bank breaks to give a passing place-cum-field entrance, but not a light shows in the darkness. No suburban creep out here. I guess he came back to big-face his childhood, to be the one who did well. Whether anyone who knew him then is still here to see it is anybody's guess.

A car comes up behind us in the dark. Something much bigger than us, with LED headlights that blaze like a thousand tiny suns. I flip my mirror to dim him, and he thunders closer. Sits hard on my tail and roars his engine. Ruby looks over her shoulder. 'Oh, look,' she says, 'an arsehole.'

'Yep,' I reply. Try to focus on the road ahead, but those lights are illuminating our interior with a ghastly lunatic glow. It feels like being followed by a dragon. Despite myself I feel my speed creep up until I am as afraid of what might come up in front of us as I am of being rear-ended.

Another signpost looms through the dark. Orford, it says. The rivers out here have single-syllable names, a sure sign of ancient habitation. These roads once ran along the tops of bleak grazing pastures, through otherwise impenetrable forest. It's thousands of years that have made these banks, as the tracks sank deeper and deeper into the earth. Nobody built them up; they wore them away.

'Here,' says Ruby. 'Turn right.'

I touch my brakes and put on my blinker, and the car behind comes inches from ramming us. He stands on his horn. And yes, I know it's a man driving. Who wouldn't? God, these bloody people: they buy a big car and suddenly they own the road. He drops back and I turn. He turns with us.

'Bugger,' I say.

'Maybe we should let him pass,' says Ruby.

'Yes,' I reply, and slow down to look for a passing spot. Again he surges up my backside, roars his engine. I put a hand up to shade my rear-view; the light is so dazzling I can barely see the road ahead.

A break in the bank appears on the left and I pull in. The car veers round us and accelerates. I glimpse a woman in the passenger seat, rock-hard blonde hair, staring ahead as though we don't exist. Then vicious red brake lights dazzle us as he reaches the next corner and they disappear. A Mercedes. Of course a Mercedes. They're the worst drivers in the world, the Merc people. Well, maybe apart from the Audi scum.

'Christ on a bike,' I say.

'Arsewipe,' says Ruby. 'I hope he gets a puncture.'

Then, 'I think it's soon,' she adds. 'A few more corners, on the left. There's a sign.'

I'm feeling a little rattled. I trickle along at twenty miles an hour as I wait for my heartbeat to slow. Three more corners and the sign appears in the gloom. Discreet and yet not, face-on to the road in green and gold livery colours like one of those CHILDREN CROSSING signs they use to advertise prep schools.

BLACKHEATH HOUSE

PRIVATE

There are high metal gates across the drive, the sort you usually see on footballers' houses, and two cars pulled up in front of them. One is the Mercedes. From the other, two men in parkas are emerging to walk towards the driver.

'Those are journalists,' says Ruby. It's not rocket science. No one wears a bulky coat with lots of pockets while sitting in a car unless they're planning to get out in a hurry.

There's no one else around. The narrow grey lane turns a

corner a hundred yards away in each direction, following the estate wall. The Mercedes driver opens his door and steps down on to the driveway. It's Charlie Clutterbuck. I might have guessed. He makes a move towards the intercom, but the hacks are upon him. One carries a camera and the other wields a spiral-bound pad and some sort of recording device.

'Hell,' I say, 'we're going to be here forever. If there's one thing that man loves, it's the sound of his own voice.'

Charlie glances in our direction, waves a hand at us. I wind my window down to listen. ' . . . know you've only got your job to do . . . ' His voice, rich and stuffed as steak and kidney pudding, booms out over the darkening air.

The passenger door opens and Imogen steps out. In my headlights, I can see that she has not so much aged, over the last decade, as *set*. The hair, which occasionally moved in the breeze on Sandbanks, looks as if it's been encased in plastic, and the skin looks shiny and smooth. She wears a Chanel suit – I guess it might be a knock-off these days, now Charlie's lost his parliamentary wage and the non-executive directorships that went along with it – and black patent shoes whose sensible heels can just about cope with the worn tarmac. Crosses the drive and slips her hand into her husband's. They stand in the cars' glare and pull solemn faces while the photographer tsk, tsk, tsks with his shutter.

Well, that'll be nice for them, I think, their photo in the paper again after all this time. I press the horn ever so gently and they jump at the beep, as though they had been unaware that there were people waiting behind them.

'I recognise that man,' Ruby says.

'I should think you do. Charlie Clutterbuck. Former MP and professional bombast. D'you remember? He defected to the Nazis and lost his deposit. That gargoyle in the passenger seat is his wife, Imogen. I knew she looked familiar. I'll go. Don't worry. Stay put and keep the window up.'

Imogen lets go of Charlie's hand and presses the buzzer on the intercom while he booms about loyal friends and fifty years' acquaintance and glares balefully towards us. The journalists look our way too then bend their heads together, conferring. Ask something of Charlie in lowered voices and he nods curtly, self-important to the last. The gate starts to slide open. The Clutterbucks return to their car and I put myself into gear to get into line behind them. 'Bung that scarf up over your head,' I tell my half-sister. We might just get through the welcoming committee unscathed.

She slowly comes to life, plugs in the belt and drapes her scarf Meryl Streep-style over her head. The Merc drives forward and I creep along behind. The photographer lunges forward and fires off a few shots, but I suspect that most of them will be ruined by the reflection of the flash in the windows. The Merc passes through the gates and its tail-lights go on. He stops, dead, two feet into Blackheath.

'No,' I say. 'No no no no *fuck*.' Lean on the horn to tell him to move on. No response. He's deliberately blocked me. I slap the top of the steering wheel as I watch the gates slide closed. The brake lights go off and the Merc disappears into the darkness ahead.

'Why did he do that?' asks Ruby. 'Why? Why would you do that?'

'Because he's a shit. Because he's always been a shit,' I say. And now he's a desperate shit, and they are the worst of all.

'Stay here,' I say. 'You're fifteen, they can't actually take your photo, but I'm not having them all over you.'

Ruby is frozen with her hand on the door handle. She's only just encountered this world where one is the centre of attention whether one likes it or not. Whatever her motives, Claire has done her job well and Ruby has no idea of her own notoriety. More people should understand what a gift it is, growing up thinking you're a nobody.

I get out. The air is rich with the scent of damp soil and the banked-up verges are covered in moss. A clump of snowdrops bravely raises its heads in white and green among the tree-shadowed gloom. Dad's been dead for long enough that he won't have seen the leaf tips come up. Soon it will be crocus time. And I bet these woods are awash with bluebells in the spring. I feel another pang. I have no idea – will never know, now – if he cared at all for nature beyond how it could be harnessed to make his properties more saleable, but it feels weird to think that he will never see them again.

The photographer raises his camera and starts shooting. Tsk, tsk, tsk, tsk, tsk goes the shutter. I walk steadily to the intercom, pretend that they're not there.

'Camilla?' calls the journalist with the notebook. 'I'm sorry about your dad, Camilla.' Bloody psychopaths. All sympathy when they think it'll get them something.

I ignore them. Press the button on the intercom and wait, staring at it with a feigned fascination. 'We were just wondering if there was any news? Funeral's on Monday, right? How's the family doing? How's your stepmother? Is that Ruby in the car? How's she doing? She must be heartbroken. Has she said any-thing?'

The camera goes tsk, tsk, tsk, tsk, tsk again as I press the button once more. It's a strange thing, how deep our training to smile goes whenever there's a camera about. I have to concentrate with all my might to keep my face straight. It's all I need, a picture of me grinning over my father's coffin on the front of the *Daily Snark*.

'Have you seen Claire? How's she doing? Is she upset?'

I cast him a baleful look. Tsk, tsk, tsk, tsk, tsk goes the camera. 'You seem to be very keen on people being upset,' I say. 'What's that all about?'

Always answer questions with questions. Sean taught me that long ago. Sometimes passive aggression really is the best defence.

He's not abashed. 'Just doing my job, Camilla,' he says. 'They stayed on good terms, didn't they? That's quite impressive, given all the stuff that happened. What do you think happened to Coco?'

'My sister, you mean? You want me to gossip about one family tragedy in the middle of another one? Are you mad?'

'Are you staying for the funeral? Will there be a lot of people, do you think? Have you any idea who? Your dad knew a lot of important people, didn't he? Do you think the rumours about how he died will put them off coming?'

'Wow,' I say. 'Did you really ask that?'

Finally, finally, the intercom clatters to life. 'Blackheath?'

'Camilla Jackson,' I say.

'Oh,' says the voice. 'The Clutterbucks have literally just been through. Didn't you see them?'

'Yes,' I say, 'I saw them.'

'Oh,' says the voice. I don't recognise it. But then, there've not been many words to go on. The lock clunks and the gates start to slide open. I walk back to the car as calmly as I can while my tiny mob jog alongside me, pointing the lens into my face and pumping out questions. They know they've only got a few seconds left to raise a reaction from me before I'm out of reach. Journalists are like vampires. They can only come in if you invite them.

Ruby sits on, her mouth half open, her braces glinting silver in the dim light. I swing into the driver's seat, close the door. 'Seat belt on. They love it when you break the law.'

'Ruby!' shouts the hack. 'How are you feeling? I'm sorry about your dad . . . '

The drive curves through the trees and cuts off all view of the house from the road. Great splats of water drop on to the wind-screen from the bare branches above and black leaves line the banks on either side of the track. There's moss between the tyre tracks. Lichen-covered stones mark out the boundary between grass and tarmac to stop vehicles from pulling off onto the soft ground. We come to a passing place and pull in. I'm still shaking from the encounter; God knows what Ruby is thinking. I put a hand on her arm.

'Are you okay?'

She slowly unwinds the scarf and drops it in her lap. 'I think so. Are they going to be like that at the funeral?'

'I hope not.' It'll be like being picketed by the Westboro Baptists.

'What was that all about?' I see that she's shaking slightly.

'Oh, God, they're journalists. It's not really *about* anything as such. They do it in their sleep. It's why they have such a high divorce rate.'

'No, I mean the Clutterbucks.'

'How many swear words do you know, Ruby?'

'About eighteen, I should say.'

'Okay. Well basically all of those. Narcissistic Personality Disorder.'

'Oh, arse.'

'You know about that?'

'Once again, Milly, I didn't grow up in a box. I love me a good personality disorder.'

'Me too!' I say. 'Don't say it's a family thing! I keep a DSM-IV on my bedside table!'

'You're kidding! I've got a DSM-V!'

We look at each other and I feel a little shift of the atmosphere in the car. We respect each other that little bit more. Who'd have thought, after all these years apart? We have something – something concrete – in common. We both love a psycho.

'Shall we do a sweepstake for this weekend?' I ask.

'Oh, good plan,' she says. 'That church is going to be swimming in issues.' Then she thinks of the church and why we'll be there, and abruptly shuts up.

I put the car back into gear and we trickle on round another corner. And there's Sean Jackson's final achievement: Blackheath House. A country house turned, with his ineffable eye, into a country house hotel. A Queen Anne house that looks spray-blasted and painted and pointed, the roof tiles in perfect rows and the balustrade along the first-floor platform where the front door lets out replaced at an expense that normally belongs in the Hollywood hills. It's as old as the trees around it, this house, but Sean has stripped it of its antiquity and made it horribly, painfully perfect. Even if I'd not known whose house it was, I would have recognised his hand the moment I saw it. Everything gleams, the way it does at Disneyland.

A collection of cars sits on the gravel sweep below the front door. Two Mercedes, a Bentley and a Range Rover, and a V-reg Ford Fiesta with the front wing bashed in, scattered like Tonka toys discarded by a careless child. The Clutterbucks are by their big shiny car, which I notice has rental plates – keeping up appearances as they come back to the country – unloading a huge, ugly bouquet of flowers from the back seat.

I pull in at the edge of a swath of lawn that has either been kept with love for four hundred years or was laid last autumn. I'd hazard the second. We step out. The house is silent. No one has come out to see us arrive, to enfold us in the family bosom.

I march over to Charlie. 'What the hell was that about?'

He feigns a jump of surprise, as though he hasn't noticed me approach. It must be a politician thing; I'm sure I've seen Boris and Dave and even John Prescott pull the same pantomime. You're insignificant, it says, you matter so little I'm surprised you're even addressing me; but it does so in a way that you can't pin on them, because the surprise, you never know, might be genuine.

'Excuse me?'

Imogen stands back by the suitcases, her eyes running up and down my body, working out if I'm worth acknowledging. She was always like that. Only ever spoke to me when I was in my father's company. After all, back in those days I didn't even have a vote to offer. Can't think why I didn't realise it before, but she's a big old Dependent, is Imogen. Can't do a thing without the Great God Charlie's approval. That's why they've stayed married so long, of course. Only a big old Dependent would see life with Charlie Clutterbuck as preferable to life in a gutter.

'Oh, come on, Charlie. Don't pretend you did it by accident. Why the hell did you block me like that? What was that all about?'

He considers me. 'And you are . . . ?'

And suddenly I realise that he doesn't know who I am. These adults who loomed so large in our own lives – you forget how little you figured in theirs. In our self-awareness, our stew of emotions, it never occurred to us that to Charlie and Imogen, and the rest of them, I suppose, we were little more than blobs. Accessories of the adults in our lives. Not people at all. Ruby has got out of the car and is shuffling awkwardly on the gravel. He probably has no idea who she is either. We're just little people in a little car, probably the help.

'Milly,' I say. 'I'm Milly Jackson. And that's Ruby. The daughters? Remember us?'

Charlie jumps into action. 'Why, Milly, my dear! You've changed. And Ruby! How *are* you? My dears, I just want to say how sorry I am.'

'For your loss,' says Imogen.

' . . . for your loss. Your father was a great man. One of my lifelong friends, as you know.'

Oh, shut up, you pompous prick. 'We'd be better if you'd not blocked us out to run the gamut like that. I can't believe you did that. What were you thinking?'

'I . . . ' He can't think of anything that doesn't reflect badly on him. I'm surprised at my own boldness. We weren't brought up to talk to the adults as equals. Even a couple of years ago I would have been calling him Mr Clutterbuck. He's developed a very high colour over the years. His face looks purple and I can see broken veins all up the side of his nose, even in the gloom.

A voice calls from the porch. 'Hello! What are you doing down there in the cold? You must all be dying for a drink.'

We all turn and see Maria Gavila in the open front door, big dramatic hair and a soft red jersey dress. She's wrapped a shawl around her shoulders and hugs herself as she speaks.

Ruby bursts into tears.

Chapter Twenty-Four

2004 | Saturday | Simone

An outbreak of shouting outside, then the engine stops and the activity at Seawings falls silent. The women all look up the way you look up when a car backfires in the street.

'Ahh,' says Maria. 'It's like banging your head against a brick wall, isn't it? So lovely when you stop.'

The others laugh. Everybody loves Maria, even when she's spouting banalities. She shines empathy through every pore. Simone still remembers the delight she felt when her father found someone so warm and open-armed to marry when she was five. Maria made her feel special. It was a number of years before she realised that this is how Maria makes everybody feel. Every day. It's not her personality, it's her job.

Maria makes her living by selling stories to the press, or by diverting the press's attention from stories their subjects don't want to get out by selling other, lesser clients down the river. Mostly former clients. People don't realise, when they take on someone like Maria to raise their profile, that once she's raised that profile, made you someone the papers want to know about, you'll need to keep paying forever. The warm, empathetic air is there to gull you into spilling the beans, to soften you up for the inevitable 'if I'm going to represent you, I need to know everything. I can't keep those skeletons in the closet if I don't know they're there.' And woe betide you if you should ever fall out. To a business like Maria's, a new client is just an ex-client you haven't betrayed yet. Nowadays, when an ancient scandal about a long-retired boy-band member breaks in the Sunday papers, Simone's first thought is to wonder which of Maria's current clients has been caught taking part in a spit-roast.

But she admires her, at the same time. You have to feel respect for someone who can keep in touch with the first wife and stay cordial with the second. Maria and Linda are laughing as they cut up melon and grapes for the kids' breakfasts, joking about something to do with swimsuits. Linda is wearing a bikini, though it's not yet nine and no one's been near the pool. She wears a little shortie white kaftan on top, with a gilt chain belt draped on the tops of her hips, but it's see-through enough that it might as well not be there. On her feet are white slingbacks. Claire, strapping the twins into their high chairs, looks sourly at her. You can see why. To Simone she looks like the height of sophistication, as if she's stepped out on to the deck of a yacht at Cap Ferrat. Even though she has an old woman's body, she's at least made an effort to maintain it, even after three children.

Claire has never really got her figure back after the twins, and they're three years old now. Her stomach is still loose under her dress; she'll never wear a bikini again. The sight makes Simone melancholy. I would never let myself go like that, she thinks. I would exercise and exercise until my stomach was as hard as Linda's. Poor Sean, condemned to that for the rest of his life. No wonder he's vulnerable. Some women have no idea how lucky they are.

Maria catches her eye, and winks. Sucks her into her circle of warmth again. I'm on *your* side, the wink says. Simone smiles sweetly back at her. She has learnt at the feet of the best.

The children are still dopey. Only Joaquin was awake when the women came into the annexe to let them out, and even he was relatively easy, just sitting on his bed, staring at flies, rather than bouncing off the ceiling as he normally would have been. Inigo yawns and stretches over his cereal bowl. Though she had no pill herself last night, Simone knows exactly how he feels. She feels loose-limbed and languid this morning, as though she's been dipped in honey, entranced by her own burgeoning power. He would have been mine, she thinks, if he weren't such an honourable man. I could feel it between us, electric attraction, as he fed me that cake. I never knew something so simple could be so mesmerising.

'And that's another thing,' says Linda, proudly. 'No tantrums in the morning, either. Honestly, I'd give it to them every day if it weren't illegal.'

'When we get into power,' says Imogen, the 'we' presumably being her husband's party, 'we're going to dial back all these controls. Health and Safety is completely out of control. We're in danger of bringing up a complete generation of wimps.'

'And then who would we send to war?' asks Claire. 'Just imagine.'

Imogen doesn't hear the edge to her voice, though everyone else does. Simone has noticed this about the political wives who have drifted through their house while her parents covered up some peccadillo, some minor expenses irregularity: that the only humour they're prepared to acknowledge is the good-sport charity water-balloon kind. Imogen wouldn't spot irony if it got up and slapped her in the face.

'Well, you know,' she says, 'it *will* affect the economy. A certain attrition rate among young men does act as a check on population growth. And, of course, no pensions.' She beams. 'So nice to be somewhere where one can say these things,' she says. 'One has to mind one's Ps and Qs so much when one's dealing with the electorate. The Blairs have them so wound up about prejudice that they'll get offended at the drop of a hat.'

Claire bites her lip and pours orange juice into the collection of sippy cups. Puts two in front of her daughters and strokes their warm, silky heads. Coco leans back against her and she puts an arm round her shoulders, presses her closer in. Simone watches, feels a twist of envy. It's not fair. Why was I born so late?

'But surely,' says Linda, 'the cost of all the injured ones must cancel that out?'

'Not really,' says Imogen. 'They're not going to be starting so many bar fights if they're on crutches, are they?'

A little silence follows this statement, then there's a small explosion of laughter. 'Oh, Imogen,' says Linda, 'you're hilarious.'

'What?' asks Imogen. 'I'm only telling the truth. You just have to look at the statistics to see it makes sense.'

You really are the stupidest woman I've ever met, thinks Simone, and I've met the Spice Girls. No wonder your awful husband married you. You're exactly the way he thinks women are.

A sound in the garden, and the men, one by one, troop in through the patio door. Apart from Jimmy, they're dressed as one in Home Counties seaside casual: baggy shorts in Madras check, button-down cotton shirts, and, because the sun's only just started burning the dew off the grass, V-necked jumpers for warmth. Jimmy wears jeans and a faded Nirvana tour T-shirt from 1992. He looks as though he plays in a tribute act that tours caravan sites. They look pleased with themselves, as though they have won a great victory.

'Well done,' says Maria. 'What did you say?'

'Well,' says Sean, 'in the end I let money speak for me. What's the point of being a millionaire if you can't buy what you want, eh?'

'How much?'

'A grand,' he says, casually, as though he's talking chump change. 'Half now and the rest if they hold off till noon tomorrow.'

'They tried to claim they had a contractual deadline of tonight and they'd start paying penalties after that,' says her father, 'but I asked them if they really thought anyone would be over to check before the bank holiday was done, and they didn't have an answer to that.'

'I said I'd pay the penalty as well,' says Sean. 'I wanted to keep them off till Monday, but they're catching a boat back to Poland tomorrow night, so . . .'

'Oh, well *done*,' says Maria. 'You're my heroes.'

'Of course,' says Charlie, 'I asked them if their paperwork was in order. They came right back with the Freedom of Movement Act. Bloody EU. This country's going to be swarming with Eastern Europeans by the end of the decade, mark my words.'

'And then we'll have our brickies up in arms about their taking our jobs,' says Imogen. 'Should've thought about that before they got themselves unionised up to the hilt.' The average British builder, in her eyes, is a Labour voter. She'd be far more worried if the Czechs were heading for the Square Mile.

'Any coffee on the go?' asks Jimmy. 'I feel like something died in my mouth.'

'Maybe you could try brushing your teeth occasionally,' says

Linda, and doesn't look at him. He laughs and gives her the finger. Simone is sensitive enough to atmosphere to feel the tiny frisson that runs round the room. She's beginning to understand that banter is one of those things that unhappy couples use to cover up their loathing when they're in public. Linda and Jimmy, Sean and Claire: barbs flying between them wrapped in bare-toothed grins, and nobody, she sees now, is fooled by it. Her father and Maria never, ever talk to each other like that. But then, she's never seen them disagree, either. They're like a well-oiled machine, each thought, each emotion moving in such harmony that they can finish each other's sentences, the common goal so implicitly understood that it never needs to be discussed. Move ourselves forward. Move our children forward. Get what we want. Never make enemies.

'Eat up,' says Linda in a general address, 'and we can go to the beach.'

'I'm not going anywhere,' says Jimmy. 'If we've paid a grand to get peace and quiet at the pool, I'm damn well staying at the pool.'

'We?' asks Linda, eyes innocently widened. 'Where did *we* get a grand from?'

Jimmy's eyes narrow and he walks over to the espresso machine. Starts slamming it about, lifting lids and peering in, jiggling the coffee scoop. 'Here,' says Simone, crossing the kitchen to join him. 'Let me.'

'Ah, lovely.' A hand lands on the back of her neck, makes her shudder. 'At least there's *someone* in this house who'll give an old man a hand.'

She wriggles out from under the touch. Jimmy smells sour. Chemicals leaking out through his skin, she supposes, and the fact that he's not been near the shower since he got here. He's probably relying on the swimming pool for his baths. She makes a mental note not to go in there again.

Linda picks up her coffee cup. 'Well, I'm going to try out that jacuzzi,' she says. 'Are you ladies okay finishing up the breakfast? I'll load the dishwasher when I get out.'

'Ah,' says Sean, and starts to fall in step behind her swaying hips, 'jacuzzi sounds just the ticket.'

'You enjoy yourself,' says Maria. 'We'll finish up here and take the littlies down to the beach.'

'No,' says Claire, abruptly, 'sorry, Sean, but I need to go and get this nail sorted out. The one you broke yesterday, with the mattress? You'll have to look after the twins till I get back.'

Simone goes over to the island to look for a spoon to measure the coffee with. In the drawer are last night's pills, left there by Linda. Stupid place to put them, she thinks. At least three of those kids are tall enough to get in there. She tucks them underneath the cutlery holder, where they'll be out of sight but still accessible for later, selects a spoon and goes back to the coffee machine.

'Oh,' says Sean.

'Perhaps they'd like to go in the jacuzzi with you and Linda?' Claire says, ever so sweetly, and holds his eye until he harrumphs and looks away. 'Wouldn't that be fun? They'd love that. Wouldn't you love that, girls? Lovely hot bath with bubbles? And time with your Daddy?'

The twins don't look impressed by the suggestion, but they're barely awake.

'Can't you do it later?' he asks. 'Or take them with you?'

'Sorry,' she says. 'I'm going to have to just park up in town and walk around till I find somewhere.'

'Why don't you Google it on your phone?' asks Simone.

'You can do that?' says Imogen. 'Whatever next?'

202

'Yes, look.' She picks up Claire's phone and finds the internet browser. 'See? And here's Google. You can Google manicurists in Bournemouth.'

'Well, I never,' says Claire, though she looks sick. 'I'd heard you could do this on the new phones but I never imagined mine was one of those.'

'Oh, for God's sake,' says Sean, impatiently, 'do you never look at these things? Of course I got you an internet phone. The whole office has one.'

'I did think it was quite chunky. My last one was so little and neat. And all those little letters. It did seem pretty silly, just for sending texts. But how do I pay? Am I going to get some horrendous bill?'

'It's on your plan. Jesus. Women! Don't you read *anything*?'

'It's a *phone*, Sean,' she says in that little hurt voice of hers. 'I know how to work a *phone*.'

'I don't believe in the internet,' says Imogen.

'It's the wave of the future, Imogen,' says Maria. 'All the papers are putting themselves online. Charlie's got a website. Didn't you know?'

Imogen looks startled, as though someone's just told her her husband has a part-time job as a stripper. 'Well, I'll have to see about that,' she says.

'Oy oy,' says Charlie, 'old lady on the warpath. Up to my arse in alligators before long.'

'Anyway,' says Claire, 'it's beside the point. I'll have to go into town and find the place and find a parking space and get to wherever we're going from it with a pushchair and they really get fed up if you've got two three-year-olds in tow in those shops. They're never exactly over-blessed with space. It's no good, Sean. You're the one who *minds* if my nails are a mess. Do you want me showing you up at dinner?'

'No,' says Sean, sulkily.

'I know!' says Simone. She's been eyeing the jacuzzi hopefully since they arrived. She rather fancies the idea of a long morning wallowing among the jets. 'Why don't we take *all* the kids to the jacuzzi? It'll be fun!'

She sees an odd little look pass between Sean and Linda. Joaquin leaps to his feet, suddenly awake, and punches the air. 'Yay!' he shouts. 'Jacuzzi party!'

Chapter Twenty-Five

'Oh, my poor little girl!'

Maria trots down the steps in her elegant heels and enfolds Ruby in a long, hard hug. 'I should think you're exhausted,' she says. 'How are you, darling?'

Ruby lets out a sob and then a bleat, like a lost lamb. Her shoulders are shaking and I well up with guilt. It should be so easy. If Maria can do it, why on earth can't I? All the kid needs is a hug and to be told it'll be all right.

The Clusterfucks shuffle about on the gravel for a few seconds, looking awkward. I must remember to tell Ruby about the nickname later. It'll cheer her up.

'We brought flowers,' says Imogen, in some sort of bid for acknowledgement. Maria nods and takes them with one hand, never relaxing the arm that holds my sister's shoulders. Big, white, waxy hothouse lilies. I thought people didn't bring flowers to funerals any more? I'm sure I saw 'No Flowers' in the announcement in *The Times*. The Clusterfucks mill about for a moment, clearly surprised that they're not at the front of the priority list for greetings, then they start to walk towards the house. 'Robert's indoors, presumably?' calls Charlie over his shoulder.

'Yes,' answers Maria. 'They're in the drawing room.' She turns back into the hug. 'Oh, Ruby, I'm so sorry. Your darling dad. I know how much you loved him.'

I see Ruby's shoulders stiffen in her embrace, then she relaxes into it. She's not going to argue. Because that's the thing with dads like ours. They may be crap at the job, but they're your only father. I feel a wave of misery for myself. God, life is complicated. They're always going on about families and unconditional love, but they've no idea how complicated that is. How complicated those feelings are. What close bedfellows love and hate make.

After half a minute, Maria lets Ruby go, strokes her face and squeezes her hand. Then she opens her arms to me and, despite myself, I find myself accepting a hug in my turn. I always liked Maria. Of Dad's friends, she was the only one who showed any real warmth. She was the only one who treated us as though we were human beings, asked us questions about ourselves, offered us drinks and ice creams, laughed at our jokes. She taught us how to play Pinochle one rainy Tuscan holiday when I was eight and India ten, before Mum and Dad split up but not before they had started disappearing out of the house, hissing muttered swear words at each other under their breaths. Card games became a lifeline for us after that. I could still rip your eyes out playing Spit to this day.

'Oh, girls,' she says, 'what a terrible way to see each other again.'

She lets me go and picks up Ruby's bag. Holds a hand out for mine, but I shake my head. 'Come into the house. There's tea on the go somewhere. I bet you could kill for a slice of cake.'

'How's Simone?' I ask. Not because I care, but because I know it's manners.

'She's . . . ' Maria's brow furrows. 'Oh, lord. I guess she's as you would expect her to be. She's doing her best. Come in. Everyone's here now, I think. We'll get you a cup of tea and get you settled. And I suppose I'd better see what the Clutterbucks want. I knew they were coming down early, but I didn't think we were going to be hosting them five minutes after they got here. Still. It's clearly that sort of day.'

She reaches out her spare hand and squeezes Ruby's again. 'How are you doing, sweetheart?'

Ruby wipes her face with her sleeve. 'I'm okay,' she says, in a little voice that says the opposite.

'Oh, darlings. Such a terribly sad time. He adored you both. You do know that, don't you? Nothing made him happier than his beautiful daughters.'

Ruby lets out another sob as I pick my jaw off the floor. And this is how death works. I remember Gerry Adams and Martin McGuinness sucking down great gulps of crocodile tears for the press after Ian Paisley died. You don't get to say what you really think when death is in the air, at least until the body is in the ground and the canapés are cleared away.

'I loved him too,' says Ruby, and stops at the foot of the steps. Puts her face in her hands and starts to cry. We stand either side of her, a hand on each arm, and murmur those pointless words . . . oh, darling, oh, sweetie. I'm sorry, I'm so sorry. He knew you loved him, he did. You couldn't have been a better daughter.

In the hall I hear Charlie Clutterbuck's bellowing laugh. It's always set my teeth on edge, but now it sounds like a deliberate insult. A man's voice says something in response and they both laugh again. Robert? No. Robert has always known how to behave, whatever the circumstances. He and Maria, always present, always doing the right thing: Maria the vibrant, emotional one, Robert always there and quiet and thoughtful, making decisions so other people don't have to. They were amazing after the Coco thing; amazing. Supporting everyone, propping Claire up when she was on the point of collapse, speaking for the family, helping Indy and me know what to do when the press descended with their questions. I still find it hard to believe that these people are the same ones who produced Soppy Simone. So there are more people in the house. Joaquin, I suppose. He's her half-brother, after all. And staff. There must be staff. I can't imagine she's been running a house like this all on her own.

Behind the door – perfectly stripped and painted a neutral black – I'm immersed immediately in the Sean-ness of it all. Blackheath may be three hundred years old, but it's identical, really, to every one of the houses we grew up in. Dressed for sale, not for life, even though this was to be his forever house. For this was Sean's peculiar talent: restoring something perfectly while sucking out its very soul. English Heritage will have swarmed all over the restoration while it was being done. Blackheath must be at least Grade II listed, and once you're listed you can't move for regulations. They will have watched with baleful bureaucratic eyes, checking plaster mixes and tiles and window frames to make sure that the snow globe of Olde Englande remained intact. And they will have come away unable to complain, but still come away with heavy hearts. Walls, floor, wood and cornices are all perfect, as though the original builders had tipped their caps and accepted their gallons of ale only a few minutes ago. It looks, of course, a way it has never looked in its entire history. It's a Disney mansion, an Astor refurb with underfloor heating and fabulous water pressure.

And he's been to the warehouse. I can't think who else has

picked out the sale-room ancestors who adorn the smooth white walls, the French-polished side tables, the elegant bergère sofa that waits by the umbrella stand for no one to sit on, now that Linda's dead, head smashed in like an eggshell at the bottom of a flight of marble footballers' stairs. Simone? Did she adapt herself so thoroughly to his ways and his tastes even before they got together that she was able to simply step into her predecessor's shoes? The Gavilas found the body, of course. One of those weird coincidences, coming in to look at the place for a client. Was there some kind of freaky personality swap, like in a horror movie? The essence of Linda being sucked vampire-like into the child bride from her last breath? Is that how she managed to be so ripe and ready and perfect in every way? Because she's not just herself, she's both of them?

The entrance hall widens fifteen feet up into a central lobby from which the staircase rises. In the middle, a marble pedestal table I remember from my childhood, and, dead-centre on that, the urn that always sat there. It is filled with dead tulips. It's like one of those gloomy Dutch still lifes; all that's missing is the shot corpse of a piebald rabbit. Instead, the table is piled carelessly with more bouquets, wilting foliage rotting in their cellophane.

'I must cancel the order,' says Maria, quietly, and drops the Clutterbucks' offering on to the top of the heap. 'The florists keep sending them, once every three days, but she's just not up to doing the necessary.'

'I can imagine,' I say. I make a note to get rid of them when I find out where the bins are. It seems odd that no one else has thought of that.

Another burst of laughter from the drawing room. 'Who's here?' I ask.

'Oh, Jimmy Orizio, I'm afraid,' says Maria. 'He turned up

this morning and we could hardly turn him away. He's not well, I'm afraid.'

I lower my voice. 'Good God. I'm amazed he's still alive.'

A dry laugh. 'Just about.'

'I had no idea they were still in touch.'

'Your father was better at keeping up with the old friends than you give him credit for,' she says, reprovingly.

I can't help myself. 'Oh, so it's just his kids he dropped, then?' She gives me the 'don't' look.

'What's happened to him? When did he get out of prison?'

'Who went to prison?' booms Ruby.

I put my finger to my lips. 'Jimmy Orizio. The man in there with Charlie Clutterbuck. He was Linda's ex. Tiggy and Inigo and Fred's father. Don't you remember him?'

'Oh,' says Ruby, and she's ameliorated her tone to match ours. I'm not sure if she's ever thought about Tiggy and Inigo and Fred having a father. They were probably just there, in her mind. And even then not very much. They went to live with Linda's parents pretty soon after she hooked up with Dad. Surprise surprise. 'And what was he in prison for?'

'He was a doctor. A private doctor on Harley Street. Slimming drugs and painkillers and that.'

'Oh,' she says again.

I don't think she's getting it. 'Speed and opiates,' I whisper, though God knows why we're keeping the information from the man who knows best what that information is, 'for those who could afford his fees.'

'Vicodin,' says Maria. 'He was convicted for misprescribing Vicodin. He used to go on tour with bands and somebody died.'

'They called him Doctor Death,' I say. 'The papers.'

'He got six years,' says Maria. 'Out in less than four, though. And of course he got struck off.'

210

'When did he get out?'

'Best part of four years ago, I think.'

'What's he been living on?'

I see her eyes flick to the right. 'I think your father's been helping him out, actually.'

'Really?'

'Yes.'

'Is there no end to my father's munificence?'

An odd look. Maybe I've gone too far. It's difficult, changing the habit of a decade just because you're not supposed to speak ill of the dead. 'Anyway,' she says, 'it explains why he's here. Your dad had more of an effect on other people's lives than perhaps you think.'

The drawing-room door opens and Robert emerges. Barely changed in all this time; just a touch more distinguished grey at the temples and a couple of manly crow's feet around the eyes. He's always had a touch of the Clooneys about him, Robert. Was always going to be one of those men who improved with age, like his wife. I know they must both have had procedures, to be so unchanged, but both of them have had the sense to keep it subtle, to age well rather than trying to stop ageing altogether.

'Hello!' he says, and closes the door. Comes over and kisses Ruby on the cheek, squeezes her shoulder. 'How are you?' he asks, solicitously.

'I'm okay,' she says.

'I'm so sorry,' he says.

'It's not your fault,' she replies.

He turns to me. Holds out a hand for a moment, then steps forward and kisses me on the cheek. He smells of sandalwood and woodsmoke. They must have lit the fire in there. 'Camilla,' he says. 'It's been a long time.'

211

'Yes,' I say.

'I'm so sorry for your loss.'

'Yours too,' I say. After all, he's seen a lot more of Sean over the years than I have.

'You must both be terribly tired after your journey.'

'No,' I say, 'I'm fine.'

'I'm okay,' says Ruby, and stares around her at her father's last home.

'I wasn't expecting the Clutterbucks,' says Maria. 'I thought they were staying in a hotel?'

'Don't worry, they are. But they rang earlier and got wind of the fact that Jimmy had turned up. Thought they'd come and check him out.'

'Oh, God,' says Maria. 'Does Simone know?'

'Yes. She's insisting they stay for dinner.'

'Great,' she says, and some little message passes between them.

'I'll keep them all out of the way till then. Imogen says she'll drive.'

'Okay,' says Maria. 'Really – we don't need a houseful, though. They need to go to their hotel.'

'Don't worry. He's going on about having a "bit of business" to do in the local constituency. I don't think they'll be here too much.'

'Good. I really think we should just be family, Robert. Until the funeral.'

'Jimmy doesn't have anywhere to go.'

'Yes. Jimmy. Okay. We need to keep an eye on Jimmy.'

'It's what Sean would have wanted,' he says, and another little message passes between them. I'm surprised, I must say. I never exactly got the impression that they were intimates even before Dad waltzed off with Jimmy's woman.

'Anyway!' says Maria, turning back to us. 'Come through to the kitchen. I know Simone will want to see you.'

My final stepmother is seated at the kitchen table, smiling like a robot, peeling sprouts. A fearfully good-looking dark-haired young man I take to be Joaquin stands by the kitchen sink, as though frozen in place, and a little girl in pink dungarees sits on an alphabet mat on the floor, waving a wooden brick. The side nearest me has a picture of a duckie, and squashed beneath her fingers is a horsie. I remember having the same set of blocks when I was little. Not as new, though.

Another half sister, the one I've never met. Emily? I think. No, Emma. My God, am I really having to question myself as to whether I've got her name right? Am I really so self-absorbed?

I smile at them all and turn to Simone. Soppy Simone, Moaner, the Constant Nymph, her straight hair drooping like the *Mona* bloody *Lisa*'s into a watermelon cleavage. I almost reel back, the surprise is so huge. When I last saw her – what, five years or so ago? – she was one of those creepily thin girls, always pulling down the cuffs of their tops to hide the fact that their skin is blue. She looks like she's doubled her body-weight. She's bursting out of her dark blue dress, all breasts and tummy and a bum that pushes her whole body away from the chair-back. The only thing that's left that's thin is the hair. Linda piled the pounds on, as well – there were all sorts of mean-spirited gibes about how she'd compromised her balance with her *embonpoint* and that was why she'd fallen down those stairs – and Claire, and my mum is three dress sizes smaller now than she was when we were young. I used to think it was something to do with relationships, but she's not put it back on since she got with Barney.

Simone looks up as I come in and treats me to one of her

watery smiles. 'Sprouts,' she says, and points her little knife at a sack of the things. 'For dinner. I thought I'd get ahead. They always take so much longer than you think they will.'

'It's cutting the little crosses in the bottoms,' I say. 'That always seems to double up the time.'

She simpers. 'You father loves the little crosses in the bottoms,' she says. I suppress a shudder, at the evidence of the intimacy between them. I can't help it. India and I remember her when she was seven, following Dad around like a spaniel puppy. I still can't believe that they ever had an adult relationship.

Her face falls and she corrects herself. 'Loved,' she says, and freezes for a moment. 'He loved them.'

I sit down. Reach out a hand to touch her arm but she jerks it away as though she thinks I'm going to grab it. 'Must get on,' she says, and the robot smile comes back. 'We've nine to dinner.'

'Can I do anything?' I ask.

'No,' she says, firmly. 'It's all under control, if people would just stop fussing. Do you remember my brother Joaquin?'

'Joe,' corrects the young man. Steps forward and offers me a hand to shake. He must be nineteen by now. No more slugs and collecting spit in a bottle for him. Ruby stares at him, transfixed. No, no, I think. No, you can't get a crush on him. It would be . . . incest? Horrible, anyway. Our families are dreadfully intertwined as it is, the generations overlapping, the godparents and the best friends and the half-siblings and the horrible history. My mum is Simone's godmother. How creepy is that?

'I remember you,' says Ruby to Joe. 'You're the boy with the stick, aren't you?'

Joe blinks. 'Possibly,' he says. 'I don't know.'

'You were always hitting things with sticks,' she says.

'Oh. Yes.' He laughs, then looks guilty and glances at his sister. 'I think I did go through a phase of hitting things.'

'You sure did,' I say. 'You got the backs of my legs several times.'

He grins. 'I remember you, though. Your every third word was "bugger" and Mum started saying, "Who do you think you are – Milly Jackson?" every time I swore.'

'Which was a lot, I should think.'

'Yes. Your name's engraved on my brain.'

'I remember,' says Ruby. 'Your mum took us down to the café on the beach and you taught me about dunking fries in ice cream. You were nice, even with the sticks. I still do that, you know. Chocolate milkshake from McDonald's.'

'Oh,' I say. 'You prefer chocolate? Sorry.'

'That's okay. How were you to know?'

'I thought everybody preferred vanilla.'

'Your father didn't,' jokes Maria, then her shoulders go up to her ears as she sees the look on everybody's faces. I've never seen her slip up, ever. Maria has an ear for atmosphere that's second to none. She must be terribly out of kilter. God, she's known Dad twenty years or something. It's all of us, in our ways. We're all bereaved.

'Did I?' asks Joe. 'Oh, yes! I remember! How funny. All these years I've thought that was Coco.'

People say Coco's name without that little hesitation that used to accompany it, these days, even to her closest family, I've noticed. So much time has passed that in most people's minds she's no longer a tragedy, just a memory. A bad memory, a sad memory, but not one they expect to set other people off.

'No, it was me.'

'Really? Everyone was calling you Coco.'

Ruby rolls her eyes. 'Yeah. No one could tell us apart. They were always muddling us up.'

'Hunh,' says Joe. 'Well, I never.'

'How was your trip?' interrupts Simone, socially, as though we've just come for the weekend. 'It's a lovely drive, isn't it?'

The sprouts are halfway up the walls of the cauldron that sits by her left breast, a pile of stalks and outer leaves spilling over the edge of the newspaper she's laid out to take them. There must be enough there to feed us all twice over, but she rips open another string bag of the things with her knife. Ruby comes and attempts to kiss her cheek. Again with the ducking, the jerking away.

'Let me do some of those,' says Ruby.

Simone freezes, like a robot whose processor has hung. She's always done things like this, too. You would come round corners and she'd be standing there stock-still, her face frozen and her eyes empty, and you'd have an eerie feeling that if no one had come along she'd just have carried on standing there, like Hayley Joel Osment, until the Ice Age. And then she would reboot as you passed across her field of vision and the listless smile would reappear, the drippy hair would drop down over her eyes and she'd say hello. I remember getting a weird feeling, when I was about ten, on the last family holiday with the Gavilas before my godfather forgot I existed, that Soppy Simone was just a shell. That if you cracked her open there would be nothing at all inside: or some primeval worm—

'I wouldn't dream of it,' she says again, jerking suddenly into life. 'I want you to relax while you're here. I'm sure you're exhausted after your trip.'

I look at her. She's repeating lines, I think. It's the sort of thing she's heard someone's granny say, and she's stored it up for when she had a house of her own.

I have a horrible flash image of her and my father having sex in the big old four-poster bed his great-grandparents had sex in, the one he's carted from house to house like a trophy. The old man and his little doll, mechanically bending herself about to

216

please him, doing whatever he commanded with the same emotionless humility with which she brought him his tea. *Old fisshe and yong flesshe wolde I have fein.* Planting his seed in her because it's what you do with wives.

I suddenly want out. Not just out of this kitchen but out of the house, out of Devon – out of Europe if I can manage it. Out of my family, away from all this history, away from funerals and loss and having to find the right words when I don't even know what the right *feelings* are. I want to be curled up in bed in the dark. I want to be at a club in Camden Town with a brain full of pills. I want to be on a mountaintop in Wales. I wish I were in Bali, on some black sand beach pretending that none of us exists. Poor Child Bride. From Echo to *The Merchant's Tale* to Andromache in a few short years.

The door opens with a bang and Imogen appears, a silver ice bucket dangling from her elbow by its handle. She's picked the lilies up from the trash-pile in the hall and cradles them as though they are a precious child. Cocks her head to one side like a chicken and fixes Simone with a smile of ghastly sympathy.

'Simone,' she says. 'My dear.'

Simone glances up, then returns to her sprouts as though the greeting had never happened. Imogen looks wrong-footed for a second, then clicks her way across the quarry tiles, lays the lilies down on the kitchen table. 'We didn't know what to bring,' she says, 'but we couldn't come empty-handed.'

'How lovely,' says Maria, though she's seen them already. 'Lilies. Look, Simone!' she continues, in a tone better suited to talking to Emma. 'Imogen's brought you some lovely lilies!'

'How very kind,' says Simone, automatically, and barely affords them a glance.

'I'll put them in a vase,' says Imogen, and starts opening cupboards, one by one. Joe pushes himself off his perch and goes into the scullery. Returns with a giant Kilner jar that must once have held a whole goose confit.

'Will this do?'

'No vases?'

'The vases are all full,' says Simone.

'Never mind,' says Imogen. She fills the jar with water and cuts off the cellophane. A few dabs of yellow pollen drop on to the table. Simone pushes her chair back, goes to the sink and wets a sponge. Wipes it up, returns to her seat.

'There,' says Imogen brightly, and slides the jar into the middle of the table. 'That looks better, doesn't it?'

Ruby makes a polite murmuring noise, but nobody else responds.

'Thank you so much for having us to dinner,' says Imogen. 'It's terribly kind.'

'Yes, well,' says Simone. 'Sean would hate it if I let you go hungry. Or thirsty.'

Imogen looks a little uncomfortable. 'Talking of which,' she says, 'the ice bucket seems to have run out. Would you mind if I filled it?'

Simone gets to her feet again. Opens the freezer and pulls out a rubber ice tray. Starts to pop the cubes out, one by one, into the bucket.

'No, no, let me do that,' says Imogen, suddenly embarrassed. She's trying, I suppose. Very trying. She reaches out to take the tray from my stepmother's hands. 'You've got quite enough to do as it is.'

Simone rounds on her suddenly, her teeth bared. 'Leave it!' she snaps.

Imogen takes a step back. 'I was just—'

'Well, don't!' says Simone. 'It's my house and you're my guests.'

'But I . . . '

Simone purses her lips and Imogen falls silent. Waits as enough ice to sink a ship pops piece by piece into the bucket and the lid is slammed firmly on. 'Thank you,' she says, humbly.

'Dinner's at eight,' says Simone.

Imogen totters from the room, puts a hand on the door-frame as she goes, as if to steady herself.

'Simone . . . ' says Maria, then subsides as her stepdaughter's eyes flash in her direction. We all stand for a few seconds as Imogen's footsteps recede. Then Simone lifts the lilies from the jar, carries them, dripping, over to the giant chrome bin tucked by the back door, shoves them in and puts the lid on with a clang. Stalks back to her seat at the table and picks up her knife once more.

A smile affixes itself to her pale face. 'I hope you like lamb!' she says to Ruby. 'I've got a leg of lamb for you all!'

Chapter Twenty-Six

2004 | Saturday | Claire

'Are you really wearing that?'

He stands in the doorway and his eyes flick up and down her body, come to rest on her stomach.

'What's wrong with it?'

Sean sighs and looks away. 'Never mind. I guess silver's just very . . . unforgiving, that's all. If that's what you want to wear, wear it.'

And never mind my feelings in the matter, says the unspoken addendum. She looks at herself in the dressing-table mirror. She had thought that it looked great in the shop, when she was standing up, but now, sitting down, she sees that even with the Magic Pants there's a little bulge between her navel and her crotch. He wanted her to get a caesarituck when the twins were born, the way they do in Hollywood, and he's never forgiven her refusal. Maybe I should have, she thinks. Even after three years and frenzied Pilates my stomach still looks . . . deflated. And I knew going into it that I was marrying a man who had issues about women's bodies and any faults they might have. All those sneering jokes about Heather and her saddlebags and the way her tits had sagged; I should have realised that all that stuff doesn't just vanish because it's you. God, the way women are trained to compete with each other! When will we learn that all it leads to is the destruction of all of us? He's exploiting it in Linda now, and I've only myself to blame.

She gets up and pulls from the wardrobe the long black Grecian-style dress she brings everywhere, as back-up for these increasingly frequent moments. She's worn it several times before, which in his eyes will be a fault in itself, but it will have to do; the thing about being hypercritical, she thinks, is that you always end up disappointed no matter what anybody does. The dress has floaty panels of gauze that cover every sin. There's more and more black in what she wears each year. When she met him, she delighted in colour, enjoyed throwing together the contrasts and even the clashing, enjoyed standing out, got secret pleasure from the thought of Heather's wardrobe of taupe and beige and grey. And now the same colours dominate her own. It's a way to disappear, she thinks. Right now, Linda is Oz and I'm Kansas.

She drags the silver dress off over her head and hurls it into a corner. No point taking care of it now; she will never wear it. His eyes do the flick, flick, flick again as he sneers at the controlwear beneath. She hates wearing it. Hates the heat, the constriction, the way it digs into tender flesh, the struggles to get it back on again in tiny toilet cubicles. I should have just had the op, she thinks. I didn't want to because I thought it would be bad for the babies, being born early just to assuage my husband's vanity, but it was totally not worth it, for the grief I've lived with ever since. She pulls on the black dress, turns to confront him.

'Better?'

He purses his lips and says nothing. Clever, she thinks, glaring at his back as he leaves the room. You're so clever. You always know when to stop talking, so I'm still angry when I go out in public but you can pull the whole what-did-I-do? injured-innocent act for everyone else's benefit.

She picks up her bag and her shoes and follows him downstairs, fixing on her platinum bangle as she goes. The diamonds she brought for the occasion are inappropriate now that so much of her décolletage is covered, but she has nothing else to wear. The stairs are a death trap in shoes. Even in bare feet, her soles giving her some traction, she hangs on to the banister as though it were an amulet. It's no time at all until someone dies coming off these, she thinks. And only Sean would put a hard stone floor at the bottom of them.

Linda is wearing sky blue. Blue lace, just enough scraps of it to bypass obscenity laws, held together by pale blue net that tightly wraps the rest of her body. The dress stops at the top of her thighs. Charlie Clutterbuck's eyes are bulging out on stalks. She's rifling in the cutlery drawer while the children eat strawberries and ice cream. Well, almost all the kids. Ruby is missing, and so is Maria. Claire goes over to her elder daughter, strokes her hair back from her forehead and plants a kiss on her crown. I must remind myself of this, she thinks. At least that's one good thing that's come out of this disastrous union with Sean. We made good babies.

'Where's Ruby?'

'Oh, that's Coco, is it?' asks Linda. 'I still don't know how you tell them apart.'

You could try looking, thinks Claire. But then you'd have to tear your eyes off my husband, I guess.

'Coco's hair parts on the left,' says Simone, 'and Ruby's parts on the right. That's right, isn't it? R for Ruby? And the bracelets.

Same thing. That's why Dad and Maria gave them to them, wasn't it?'

'It wasn't the intention, but yes.' Simone is a smart cookie. Observant. Claire doubts that her own stepdaughters have worked that out yet. She's dressed for the evening in a gold tapestry shift dress that's far too old for her and slightly too large, and Claire realises that she's borrowed one of her stepmother's dresses to come to the restaurant too.

'She threw up, I'm afraid,' says Imogen. 'Maria's taken her to the loo.'

'Oh, dear,' says Claire. 'I hope she's not going down with something. She's been pretty quiet today. I thought it was just . . . you know . . . last night.'

'Oh, we had a lovely time in the jacuzzi while you were out,' says Simone, brightly, 'and she seemed to enjoy herself down on the beach.'

'Probably just overexcitement and too much ice cream,' says Imogen. 'She gave them *more* ice cream at the beach, you know. You'll need to put them all on diets when they get home.'

Claire laughs, then stops. 'Oh. You're serious. Really?'

'Obesity is going to be one of the big political hot potatoes soon,' says Imogen, looking down her nose. 'We can hardly lecture the great unwashed about their dreadful diets and be carting a bunch of porkers around ourselves, can we?'

How does that work with the War on Drugs, then? wonders Claire. The last time Imogen's husband was on *Question Time* he was advocating life sentences for dealers, and you could practically see the powder marks beneath his nose. She keeps the thought to herself. 'I hadn't been planning on lecturing anyone,' she says.

'Still,' says Imogen. 'You'll be wanting to keep an eye on their weight, all the same.'

'They're three years old.'

'Well, you know what they say about obesity starting young.'

'Do they look obese?'

'Goodness,' says Imogen, 'I wasn't *criticising*. I was just *saying*.'

'Well, don't,' says Claire. 'Just don't.'

'Nope,' says Linda. 'Can't find them. He must have taken them back, the stupid sod.'

She stalks over to the door in her four-inch heels and bellows out into the garden. 'Jimmy! Where's your bag of tricks?'

Silence. '*Jimmy!*'

'Crikey,' says Sean. 'If the lighthouse ever breaks down, the coastguard could use you to warn shipping.'

Jimmy slopes up the garden, shirt flapping over teak-brown skin. He's been topping up his already dramatic tan all day. Started drinking at eleven, too, with a quick vodka 'to straighten him out', and his gait is far from direct. His poodle curls are wet and cling to his head. He's clearly been in the pool again while the women fed his children. There's not a man in this house who's prepared to put in his time, thinks Claire. It's like the 1970s.

'What?'

'Where's your bag of tricks?'

'Over by the fireplace.'

Claire feels a prickle at the back of her neck. 'Really? Six children in the house and you just left it lying around?'

'Chill, sistah,' says Jimmy in his nauseating Mockney. 'It's got a lock on it.'

He wobbles across the room and fetches his briefcase from down behind the sofa. Opens it on the island counter like M showing Bond his latest gadgets. 'There you go, *madame*. One strip of zopiclone, at your command.'

Linda snatches them from him and starts popping the pills from their foil.

'And may I say' – he plants a groping hand on her lace-clad buttock – 'that you're looking especially tasty this evening?'

Linda swats him away, doesn't even look at him. He shrugs, as though this is the normal course of his day. 'Anybody want anything else, while I've got it open? Any aches and pains? Low mood? Little blue pill for the birthday boy?'

Everyone ignores him. No doubt they'll be changing their minds once they get back from the restaurant, but there's something about formal dress that seems to steer people towards alcohol. 'No?' He looks around with swimmy blue eyes. 'Okay, well, just a little Oxy for your poor old doctor's aching back and away we go.'

He taps a capsule out from a brown bottle, swallows it and washes it down with vodka. Smiles around the room triumphantly.

Maria comes back from the loo, leading Ruby by the hand. She's stripped her down to her bathing suit, and throws her little pink dress into the washing machine. Ruby is pale, with a greenish tinge.

'Oh, lord.' Claire goes down on her knees in front of her daughter, feels her forehead. It's hot. Not burning hot, but certainly warmer than it should be. 'Are you feeling sick, darling?'

'My tummy hurts,' says Ruby.

'I hope you're not going down with something.'

The corners of Ruby's mouth curl down and her eyes fill with tears. 'I threw up,' she announces.

'Oh, I know,' says Claire, and wraps her in her arms. Ruby is unresponsive. Just stands in the hug and tolerates it.

'Nothing a good night's sleep won't sort out,' says Linda, wielding the pill-cutter.

Claire sits back. Holds her daughter's shoulders between her hands as she stares at Linda in astonishment. 'No! No way! I'm not giving her that stuff if she's ill. I'm sorry, but I'm just not.'

Sean erupts. 'Oh, great! Here we bloody go again!'

She looks around, and all the others are giving her The Look. There we go, Claire Jackson, pouring cold water on the fun as usual. There's not one person who looks as though they might support her. They're all *his* friends. Even the ones like Maria who pretend to be Claire's as well. In the end they all follow the money. And their own pleasures. Even Imogen doesn't seem to have an opinion to offer on her lousy mothering skills, in this instance.

'Oh, look, I'll stay home,' she offers.

'No!' Sean is so close to shouting that she glances at the door. She suddenly has a horrible feeling that the entire neighbourhood is listening as they argue about whether or not to drug their children. 'Oh, you'd bloody *love* that, wouldn't you? Princess Claire the martyr, spoiling the evening by making all the rest of us look bad. You're so . . . ugh!'

'Sean! Come on! Ruby's under the weather. I can't just go off and leave her!'

'Oh, yes,' he snarls bitterly. '*Your* child. For God's sake, she's just got a twenty-four-hour bug. She gets them all the time. I don't know why you're suddenly coming over all Mum of the Year tonight.'

Because I'm not usually feeding her narcotics.

She gulps. I knew it. I *knew* it. He's jealous of them. He can act the loving daddy when it makes a point, but he's been in a sulk since they were born because he's no longer my only priority.

'You just—' he cries, '—you're just always spoiling *everything*! It's my birthday! My birthday! My fiftieth birthday! I'll never have another! I've gone to God knows how much trouble, let alone how much expense, to organise this dinner and you can bet your arse I won't get out of paying your share at this sort of notice. It's so typical of you. Throwing spanners in the works when *anything* is about *me* having a good time. Well, you can fuck off, Claire. I'm sick of it.'

'Sean, I just . . . I'm not trying to . . . I just . . . I don't . . . '

Seven pairs of eyes boring into her, six enjoying the marital drama. Absolute silence as they face each other. 'It was fine,' says Sean. 'You know how you went on about it last night and it was just bloody *fine*, despite all your best efforts. Jimmy's a doctor, for God's sake. He knows what he's doing. What, you've got a medical degree, all of a sudden?'

'But we won't be *here*!' she wails.

Linda has finished the cutting. She goes round the kitchen table as Sean rants, giving the littlies their 'special vitamins', one by one by one. Coco opens her mouth, lets her pop hers on to her tongue, swallows it down with a swig of orange juice. So wonderfully co-operative, my little girls, Claire thinks. They'll do anything if you're nice to them. He should want them there, on his big day.

'You just . . . you spoil everything,' he finishes. 'Whatever. Don't come. I don't care. Seriously, Claire, I'm done with caring.'

He turns away from her in disgust and storms out to the gazebo.

Charlie and Robert follow him, and, after helping himself to another vodka, Jimmy follows. Claire kneels on the floor by her daughter and strokes her hair with a thumb as she stares after her husband. It's over, she thinks. I think that was me getting my marching orders.

Maria is the first to speak. 'I really think you're worrying too much,' she says. 'Nothing happened last night, did it? It'll be just the same. They won't be able to get out of the annexe, even if they do wake up.'

'But Simone was there last night,' says Claire. 'Don't you see? They weren't alone.'

'I'll tell you what,' suggests Imogen, 'why don't we take it in turns? Someone can go back every half-hour and check on them. How about that? It's only a five-minute walk. We can just pop up and check on them between courses. It'll be fine.'

'But I . . . ' she begins, but she realises the fight has gone out of her. If I don't go, she thinks, it really will be over. I can feel how pleased that bitch is feeling from over here. A horrible, horrible woman. She goes on holiday with my kids but still she's ready to steal their father.

'Okay,' she says. 'Have it your way.'

Chapter Twenty-Seven

Time hasn't been kind to Jimmy Orizio. When I was a teenager, I thought he was the only cool one of Dad's lot, though I didn't really understand where he fitted in until Linda jumped over the wall. He always seemed so carefree and cheerful, in the afternoons and evenings, anyway, and he dressed like a rock star, and he'd kept off the couple of stone that success had put on my father and his other friends, and weight is a huge thing in a teenager's eyes. It's only now I'm older, and a few of the lovely teenagers I knew back then have gone to Little Baby Jesus because they didn't know when to stop, that I can see what he must have looked like to them.

I didn't know he was still part of their gang. I'd assumed he'd been dropped the way my mother was dropped, and Claire was dropped, once their function was exhausted.

Twelve years on he looks like a medical specimen in a pickle jar. Were it not for the mop of curly hair – grey now, but the curls still intact, something he no doubt puts down to not having washed it in thirty years – I doubt I would have recognised him at all. He's concurrently skinny and swollen: the face puffy and lined, the skin yellowy-white, like something you find if you kick a log over in a wood, knobs sticking through the shoulders of his Metallica T-shirt and a little belly that looks as hard as stone against the straining waistband of his skinny jeans. Jimmy Orizio is a poster boy for liver damage.

He and Charlie have been drinking in there for three hours now. The sound of their monologues wafted through the house as Ruby, Joe and I laid the table and threw away the flowers and did what we could without Simone fighting us off. She's cooked a leg of lamb, insisted on filling the dining room with every piece of silver, crystal and china in the house. Joe is lighting candles. Ruby is upstairs, putting her little sister to bed.

'Oy oy,' Jimmy says, as I come into the drawing room. Imogen and Robert have joined them and are drinking champagne as though there's something to celebrate. 'I thought you said she'd done away with the staff?'

'That's Milly,' says Imogen, who hadn't remembered me herself. 'Don't you recognise her?'

'Who?'

'Mila,' I say. I don't know why I'm bothering, really. It's what families do with you, isn't it? Put you in a box and never let you out of it. 'Sean's daughter. I remember *you*, Jimmy.'

'But she's only a kid still, isn't she?' Jimmy looks suspicious for a moment, then merely confused, through his vodka. His drawl has become more pronounced over the years, climbed so far up his nose he can barely manage a glottal. Weird how drugs will do that. Something to do with the septum, I suppose.

'I'm one of the older ones,' I say.

'There were older ones?' Faded blue eyes swim around the room.

Shit. Yes, of course. There you go again, thinking that just because you noticed people they will have noticed you too. 'Yes,' I say. 'We met several times, actually.'

Jimmy waves his glass in the air. 'Oh, well,' he says, 'the old memory's not what it was.' He takes a drink, tacks a 'sorry for your loss' on to the end as an afterthought.

'Thank you,' I say. 'I just came through to say that dinner's ready.'

'How's Simone?' he asks, and again it seems like a latter-day brain-fart rather than an actual question.

'Not great,' says Robert. 'I'm not sure if it's completely sunk in yet. We're all a bit worried about her.'

'Oh, well,' says Jimmy, and waves his glass once again. 'All that lovely money must help, eh?'

I hear a universal intake of breath. 'Right,' says Robert, 'let's go and eat, shall we?'

Simone sits at the foot of the table, that shocking smile still fixed gaily to her lips. 'Come, come,' she says. 'Sit. Eat.' Was this how she used to greet people at their dinner table before she was a widow? I can't imagine the girl I knew doing anything other than gawp at them through her hair. So much has changed while I wasn't looking.

The place at the head, where my father used to bask in his glory, has been left unlaid, empty. We fill the table from the bottom end, as though everyone is unwilling somehow to sit near the empty space, until eventually what would once have been the honoured guests' seats are filled by the two drinkers. Robert and Maria have seated themselves either side of their daughter, with Imogen next to Robert and Joe next to Maria. I haver for a second, and Ruby dives in between Joe and Jimmy. You snooze, you lose, says her look. I'm surprised she doesn't actually make an L sign with her fingers. I seat myself in the deepest circle of hell, sandwiched between two Clusterfucks. Of course they're all too grand to sit next to their partners. That sort of behaviour is reserved for the non-commissioned officers.

Jimmy has brought his glass of vodka through from the drawing room. No need, for Charlie has been down in the cellar helping himself to Sean's Crozes-Hermitage and a couple of bottles of Austrian Gewürtz for the ladies. He circles the table, dispensing the dead man's hospitality, then puts a fresh bottle on a coaster in front of him and settles down. Jimmy drains his vodka, with a clatter of ice.

'By the way,' he announces, 'we're out of tonic.'

Ruby turns to him. 'There are loads of shops in Appledore,' she says. 'I'm sure Simone would be delighted if you made a trip tomorrow.'

'Well, that's fine,' says Jimmy, 'but I find myself temporarily out of funds. Temporarily I *hope*.'

He looks down the table at Robert, who ignores him. 'How's your mother, Milly?' he asks me instead.

'Mila,' I correct. 'She's good. She's living in Sutherland.'

'Sutherland?'

'It's in Scotland,' I say.

He flips an eyebrow and gives me a smile. 'I know. I was just wondering what took her there.'

'It's where she comes from.'

'Really?' He looks astonished. 'She didn't *sound* Scottish.'

Doesn't, Robert. Just because you couldn't be bothered with her, it doesn't mean she no longer exists. 'You'd be surprised by how many Scots don't. And even the ones that *do* don't all sound like they're from Glasgow. Anyway, she took over my grandmother's house when she died and that's where she is.'

'Is she . . . doing anything with herself?'

'Tourism,' I say. Which is Scots code these days for 'land-owner'. I'm amazed how little anyone asked my mother about her background over the years they knew her, given that Dad's entire fortune comes from money she brought with her.

'Ah,' he says, and loses interest, which is generally the point.

'God, darling, you never listen to anything, do you?' says Maria. 'How's Barney?'

'He's great. They're great.'

'Any sign of them getting married?'

'I don't think so,' I say. 'I think she went off the idea of . . . ' And I find myself stalling. Simone's smile is trained on me and I can see all sorts of stuff going on behind those empty eyes. Four wives. The much-married have no idea how complicated they make life for their descendants. 'No,' I finish.

'And how about your mum, Ruby?' asks Robert.

'Fine,' says Ruby, 'she's fine. She grows things.'

'Still in Sussex?'

'Yep.' She helps herself to a couple of spoonfuls of couscous, studded with dates and prunes and apricots. It's madness. If I were Simone I would be lying in bed waiting for other people to bring me soup, not cooking banquets for selfish people. Ruby offers the dish to Jimmy. He peers at it.

'What's that?'

'Couscous.'

'Isn't that for lesbians?'

'I don't suppose Simone's turned *that* quickly,' says Charlie, and cackles at his own wit. Nobody else joins in. They just look at him until he stops and fills his mouth with Crozes-Hermitage. Jimmy scoops a heap of couscous on to his plate, doesn't take the dish to pass it on though Ruby sits there holding it, blinking at him. Eventually, she turns and offers it to Joe. 'Couscous?'

'Why, thank you,' he says, and helps himself. 'I'll pass it on, shall I?'

'That would be nice,' she says. 'I gather that's how it's done, isn't it?'

Gawd. There are few things more self-righteous than a teenager who's caught an adult out at table manners. But I remember the frustration at mealtimes with Sean, waiting as dishes piled up at his left hand until someone got up and moved them on. Some people just aren't made to notice the rest of the world. Interesting how all his best male friends were cut from the same cloth. Charlie Clutterbuck didn't even bother to leave the drawing room to say hello; just left it to his clumsy wife. Though I don't think narcissism is Jimmy's primary driver. I must look up substance-related disorders when I get home.

'Mint sauce?' asks Imogen vaguely, like a duchess reprimanding the staff.

'Oh,' says Simone, and pushes her seat back. 'I'll go and make some.'

'Oh, no, no, no, no, no,' says Imogen; a phrase that almost invariably means yes. 'Sit down, Simone, do. This is all perfect.'

'No,' snaps Simone. 'I won't have people saying I can't make a simple meal. While I'm out there I'll see if I can't find some *lesbians* with potatoes, shall I?'

'I wasn't—'

'Don't worry.' Simone's lips draw back from her teeth and Imogen looks slightly afraid. 'I'll get your mint sauce.'

She flounces from the room. Imogen draws breath, but Charlie puts a hand on her arm and she pipes down. Maria gets up and follows her stepdaughter. 'Don't,' she says from the door as I put my napkin down. 'Leave it with me.' I do as I'm told.

'I didn't . . . ' begins Imogen. 'Oh, dear, I'm sorry. I didn't mean to—'

'It's okay,' says Robert. 'She's upset.' Imogen gives him a look of liquid admiration, as though he's just declared world peace.

Jimmy starts scooping couscous from his plate into his mouth with a fork. 'Looks like *someone*'s not handling things too well,' he says, and a few pale grains fly from between his lips and sully the bleached white tablecloth.

'Really?' Robert sits back in his chair and glares at him. 'How did you expect her to be?'

Jimmy shrugs.

'Look,' says Robert, 'I know it's a lot to ask, but would you all mind trying not to wind my daughter up? Seriously, Jimmy. Do you have no empathy at all?'

'My empathy's a bit short at the moment,' says Jimmy, and doesn't pause in his shovelling. 'Along with my funds. I've got worries of my own.'

Robert blinks. 'I've told you, Jimmy. This is not the time or the place. I'll discuss it with you tomorrow. I'm sure Sean wouldn't have wanted you to go short.'

'You bet he wouldn't,' says Jimmy. Drains his glass and helps himself from Charlie's bottle. There's a chill over the table. Charlie and Imogen are staring at him like frightened children. Ruby and Joe frown, look confused. 'He knew how desperate other people can get.'

'Please, Jimmy,' says Robert. 'Just shut up, will you? I don't want any of this nonsense in front of my daughter, do you understand?'

'She's not here.'

'Nonetheless. It's not appropriate. Not at all. Let's just try to have a civilised dinner, shall we?'

Jimmy snorts. 'Right,' he says. 'Cause Simone's such an innocent.'

'She's deeply upset,' says Robert. 'Her husband is dead.'

Jimmy snorts again. 'Yeah. Funny old way to go, too.'

'Oh, Jimmy,' says Imogen, 'shut *up*. Do you really not care that two of his daughters are sitting here?'

He shrugs. 'I don't suppose they've exactly been missing the *Sun on Sunday*, have they? Well? Have you?'

Ruby goes red. Damn that smartphone.

'Shut up, Jimmy,' I say. 'It's his funeral on Monday.'

'Mmm,' he says. 'Lovely to see such loyalty, I must say. Sweet. Good old family secrets, eh? Always best when you keep them to themselves.'

A silence as thick as mud has fallen on the room. He looks at each of us in turn. Waves the fork in the air. 'Anyway, hypocrisy aside, I'm just reminding you, Robert,' he says, 'money can make people desperate. Or lack of it, anyway. Sean didn't seem to have trouble understanding that.'

That's a threat. Of some sort. I look round the table. It's plain to see that everyone recognises it for what it is. Even Ruby. She's staring at her plate, but she's not eating.

He goes back to his food. 'I'm pretty much brassic,' he says. 'Guess if I don't find a way to sort it out I'll have to start looking around for other ways to make a living.'

'Like get a job?' asks Joe, and his tone is no longer teasing.

'Oh, very droll, sonny,' says Jimmy. 'And what are you doing to make a living?'

'He's at university,' says Robert.

'Well, good for you,' says Jimmy. 'You come back to me when you're my age and see how smug you are then.'

Noises in the hall. I see the whites of Robert's eyes. 'If you don't shut up, right now, and behave yourself,' he hisses, 'I can guarantee you that there will be nothing, ever. Do you understand?'

Jimmy shrugs again. He has quite the talent for shrugging, with those bony shoulders.

Simone and Maria come back in. Maria is carrying a silver gravy boat. She puts it down in front of Imogen and gives her her sweetest smile, one that tells her how perfectly she understands her discomfort and would do whatever she could to relieve it. God, I like Maria. I can't help it. She's a true mensch. Imogen thanks her humbly and spoons some mint sauce on to the side of her half-emptied plate. 'Delicious,' she says. 'Just perfect. Thank you so much.'

Simone ignores her. She has a cardboard box in her hands. It once held a Dualit toaster, I notice. Of course. Nothing but top-end in this house. She comes over to Ruby and puts it down on the table beside her. Between her and Joe, I notice, not Jimmy. Doesn't trust him not to steal whatever's in it, I think.

'There's some stuff in here you might want to look at,' she says.

'What is it?' Ruby stirs her food around some more. Nobody seems to have much of an appetite, apart from Charlie and Jimmy, who would eat through the zombie apocalypse. Perhaps I could send them up to Claire's to clear some of those dining-room shelves.

'It's your father's jewellery.'

'Jewellery?'

She looks impatient. 'Oh, whatever you call it. I don't know. Watches and cufflinks and stuff. Things made of metal that men wear. You need to go through it and take the stuff you want. I'm sure there are things in there you'll find *interesting*.'

Ruby looks uncertain. 'Don't you want them, Simone? I mean, I'd love . . . you know, something. A keepsake. But they're yours.'

Simone's face hardens. Some resentment, some rage bubbling under that I don't really understand. Or maybe I do. The humiliation must be appalling. 'No,' she says. 'Not this stuff. There's plenty more, from when he was with me. This is the stuff from before. Take it. It'll only go to the charity shop otherwise.'

Ruby doesn't hear the underlying message. 'But surely Emma would like . . . I mean, when she's older?'

'No,' says Simone. 'Not this.'

'I—'

'Whatever,' says Simone. 'I just thought you might like them, that's all. Go through them tomorrow and take what you want.'

'Okay,' says Ruby. 'Sure.' Then, humbly, 'Just me, or me and Mila?'

'Mila?' Simone frowns.

'Me,' I say. 'She means me.' I'm touched that Ruby has taken my name on board, but I can see it's going to cause all sorts of complications. I'll always be Milly to these people.

'Oh,' she says. 'Yes, of course. And you must pick out some stuff for India too, of course. Yes. Anyway. I don't want them. Just take them, will you?'

'Thank you,' I say. I'll talk to Ruby later. Might be best if we take the lot and keep some stuff back for Emma. If we even know her when we're old. God, I'll be forty by the time she's Ruby's age.

Simone sits down. Starts to eat, mechanically and silently, ploughing through her cold food without any apparent enjoyment. She's set the tone for the evening now. She and Jimmy between them. I don't think anyone wants to say anything much, in case they set someone off. If I were the Clutterbucks, I'd be longing to get to that hotel.

Jimmy finishes scooping up his couscous and pushes his plate away.

'Anyway,' he says, 'how about a toast to absent friends?'

Everyone looks at him, silently.

Chapter Twenty-Eight

2004 | Saturday | Simone

There's a level of determination to their high spirits. The row between Sean and Claire has made them step up their game, show the world – show the party-pooper – what having a Good Time looks like. The women are leading the pack, giggling and glittering and flirting as though life itself were at stake. And Claire sits at the foot of the table, all hurt dignity and single-word responses and the oh-very-funny two-hit chuckle when someone addresses her directly. Her eyes are perpetually on her husband, the way a cat watches a bird in a cage.

Poor man, thinks Simone. And on his birthday, as well. She really is a pill. He's put on this magnificent spread for us, and she's doing her best to spoil it. She's not even made much effort with her clothes. Everyone else has dressed in their best, but she looks as though she's fished that frock from the back of the wardrobe and accessorised with her eyes closed.

She's heard of meals like this, but this is the first she's ever attended. Sean has booked the entire terrace of the Canard Doré and it feels as though they have the whole harbour-front to themselves. Longing eyes gaze at their luxurious unused space through the smoked-glass doors that lie between them and the air-conditioned interior, but no one else will get a sea breeze tonight. Her menu card tells her that they are on the third course of nine, but the *amuse-gueules* in between have been as sumptuous as the main events. A little pot of caviar each, two fat, buttery oysters with horseradish on the side to make them squirm, a *nid d'escargot*, which proved to be a *vol au vent* filled with garlicky snails (she wasn't so sure about this, but the adults wolfed it down with relish so she followed suit; the point, of course, being to reward their host's largesse with pantomime enjoyment), followed by a shot glass of an exquisite sweet-yet-savoury basil ice cream to clean the palate. Now she's looking at an oblong of slate on which four slices of jewel-coloured sashimi rest next to a tiny spire of something green, three perfect pea shoots, a little china cup of sake and a pair of elegant gilt-plated chopsticks.

In her gold shift dress and her peep-toe sandals, an array of borrowed bangles on her wrist and seed pearls dropping from her ears, Simone feels more sophisticated, more adult, than she has ever felt before. And Sean has honoured her with the seat at his left hand, Linda Innes to his right. She glows with pride at the compliment, even though he is giving most of his attention to the older woman. It's not that surprising. His manners are exquisite, and of course he has to make Linda feel wanted. Simone can see nothing to dread about the state of adulthood. A few more years to gather conversation and learn the skills, and she will be a butterfly.

Claire pushes her chair back and stands up. 'I'm going to go and check,' she announces.

The conversation dies back and they all look at her. Among

these glittering beings, she looks self-consciously dowdy in her cover-all dress. It's deliberate, thinks Simone. A deliberate humiliation for her husband, showing him how little she values him. She doesn't deserve him. She doesn't deserve the things she has.

'If you must,' says Sean.

'It's been over an hour. We said every half-hour.'

'Let us know if the house has burnt down.' He picks up his chopsticks and turns his attention away. Claire looks confused for a moment, as though she'd hoped for more of a response. 'Well what with Ruby being *ill*,' she says, then picks up her bag and her shawl and leaves. They all wait as she crosses the terrace, lets herself in through the sliding door and pulls it closed.

'Phew,' says Charlie. 'We can start having fun now.'

The table explodes with laughter.

'Happy birthday, Seanie!' cries Charlie Clutterbuck, and the guests laugh again and clink their glasses together.

'Oh, good,' says Sean. 'I was beginning to think no one had noticed.'

I noticed, thinks Simone. Oh, Sean, darling, I noticed. Only an idiot would fail to spot how badly she treats you.

'I think it won't be long before our Seanie gets his marching orders,' says Jimmy, and everybody stops laughing with a gulp. Imogen chokes on her champagne, needs a slap on the back from Robert. He's completely tone-deaf, thinks Simone. Then Sean raises his glass once more and clinks with him. 'Bring it on,' he says. 'Though I don't hold out much hope. She has some qualms about the girls. Doesn't want to leave them without a father or something.'

'Or *something*,' repeats Linda, sarcastically.

'Besides,' says Sean, 'it's not like she won't be insisting I do access visits every five minutes, like Heather does.'

Oh, thinks Simone, it really is like that. Poor Sean. I suppose he *has* to give them children. It's part of marriage, isn't it? People seem to have children without even thinking about it, and then the children become blackmail, to make them stay.

'I know,' says Imogen, oblivious, 'children are awfully resilient. It's not as if Indy and Milly have suffered much, is it?'

'Oh, I don't know,' says Sean, magnanimously. He always wants to be fair, Simone thinks. Always tries to see the other person's view. 'I'm sure they have their grievances.'

'We all do,' says Imogen. 'Time to grow up, frankly.'

'Poor little sods, dealing with the pony shortage,' says Charlie, and everyone laughs again.

'Not much grazing for ponies in Maida Vale,' Simone ventures, and is rewarded with another burst of laughter and a clap on the back from Charlie Clutterbuck that makes her very skeleton rattle.

Maria smears a dot of green stuff on a lump of something that's a pale creamy yellow and pops it into her mouth with her chopsticks. Closes her eyes as she chews, swallows. 'My God, you've pulled out all the stops tonight, darling,' she says. 'What is this?'

'That was sea urchin,' he says. 'The others are carp, otoro and a nice fat scallop. I tried to get hold of a fugu, but finding a chef who will prepare it is pretty much impossible outside Japan.'

'What? No larks' tongues?' asks Jimmy.

'Fugu?' asks Simone.

'Puffer fish. One wrong slice and it's—' He draws his chopsticks across his throat, dramatically.

'My God. Have you ever eaten it?'

'No,' he says, sadly. 'I'd hoped tonight would be the night.'

'Aw. Poor Seanie's yet to lose his fugunity,' says Jimmy, but no one laughs this time.

'And where on earth did you get hold of carp?'

He hoots with laughter, picks up his sake and swallows it down. 'Bought it live from a koi dealer in Wilmslow. Didn't tell him what it was going to be used for.'

Charlie bellows. 'You're incorrigible!'

'It's all fish at the end of the day, isn't it? I couldn't exactly get it flown in from Kyoto and still have it fresh enough, could I?'

Sushi. She's seen it through windows, but no one's ever taken her, yet, not even to one of those conveyor-belt places. Gavila family outings tend to be constructed around Joaquin's tastes, and she can imagine the gagging sounds if someone tried to feed him raw fish. She feels slightly nervous about it herself, but everyone around her is smacking their lips over the stuff as though it were sweeties. And after all, she's eaten two oysters today, and if she can manage snails she can manage this too.

Sean glances at her slate. 'Go on,' he says, 'try it. It's a great delicacy.'

So are hundred-year-old eggs, she thinks. And duck web.

'My first sushi,' she says, in a low voice.

'Sashimi,' he corrects. 'I can guarantee it won't be your last.'

He reaches across with his own chopsticks and smears a little of the green stuff on to what looks to her like a piece of tuna. 'Wasabi,' he informs her. 'The real thing, not that fake stuff you buy in tubes.' He picks up the morsel and holds it in front of her mouth. 'Take.'

She takes it whole into her mouth, imitates Maria by closing her eyes as she tastes. The pungent wasabi fills her nose, makes her want to sneeze, makes tears spring up behind her closed eyelids. She almost spits it out, then – boom! – the pain passes and her senses are consumed by the glorious fatty richness, velvet and cream together, not as fishy as she'd expected, not salty, as she imagined a sea-fish would be. Exquisite.

She opens her eyes. He is watching her, a half-smile playing

243

on his lips. So is the rest of the table. She's made uneasy by the expression on Jimmy's face: a sort of greed combined with amusement. She ignores him. He's creepy. Creepy and drunk. She flutters her eyelashes at Sean the way she's seen Linda do. 'Delicious,' she says. 'My God, that's wonderful. I had no idea.'

His smile widens. She glances up the table and sees her father watching them. His expression is unreadable, but she suspects that not everything it contains is good.

'Hurrah! A new experience for you!' says Sean, and turns abruptly to Linda. Before the older woman rearranges her features, Simone catches something speculative on them, a trace of annoyance. Is she jealous? she wonders. Of me? And she feels a tiny shiver of triumph run through her body.

They pick up their chopsticks and continue to eat.

The *amuse-gueule* this time isn't food at all. It's a tiny glass of *eau de vie* from, he says, the southwest of France, where the best foie gras comes from. The alcohol content is so ferocious it takes her breath away, makes her cough, and the grown-ups laugh at her consternation. She doesn't mind. The waiting staff haven't even blinked as they've served her her drinks. For the first time in her life she stands among the adults unchallenged.

A couple of minutes later, the alcohol hits her brain like a speeding train. She actually sways in her seat, grips the table-edge for fear that she is about to fall off. No one looks as though they've noticed, or have responded to the drink as she has, but an invisible hand has suddenly turned up the volume on the conversation.

The first wave passes, leaves her garrulous and smiling. Jimmy and Linda light cigarettes – Marlboro menthol – and Linda offers her one. She takes it.

'No.' Robert raises his voice from up the table. 'Absolutely not, Simone. No.'

'Oh, come on,' says Charlie. 'It's a party. What is this, the New Labour conference?'

'She's fifteen,' says Robert, and everyone cranes around at once to see if anyone from the restaurant has heard. But they're alone on the terrace. Indoors someone is pan-frying foie gras while someone else pours out nine glasses of Monbazillac to go with it.

'Typical lawyer,' sneers Jimmy Orizio. 'Always parading the letter of the law when it's in public.'

Linda reaches across her host and sparks up her lighter. Simone, delighted with the outrage she's caused in her father, sucks on the cigarette, suppresses the urge to cough then holds the thing in the air between index and third fingers the way Bette Davis does in the movies. She pouts a stream of smoke out into the warm seaside air. She can't claim that she's enjoying this particular experience all that much – it's making her head spin again – but tonight is clearly a night for rites of passage. It will all be different tomorrow, she thinks. Everything will have changed. She puts the filter to her lips again. It seems to have become damply cool against her skin.

'I can't say I much like the sight of a little girl smoking, myself,' says Sean, and the minimal pleasure is gone. She takes one more drag, just to show that she has a mind of her own, and then she stubs it out. Sits back in her chair, feeling slightly squashed, but then feels cheered by the rush of all the adult pleasures she's experienced tonight.

'This is the most fun time I've ever had,' she declares.

Another ripple of laughter. 'Plenty more to come,' says Sean. 'Don't worry. I envy you your youth.'

The foie gras arrives. Charlie leans over and helps himself to Claire's. One by one, the women take theirs off the slices of toasted brioche on which they sit, and push the bread aside.

'I suppose,' says Imogen, 'we should draw lots as to who's going to go next before Helicopter Mother comes back.'

Charlie groans. 'Do we have to?'

'Don't worry, Charlie,' says Maria. 'I don't suppose anyone's going to be asking *you* to go.'

'But really. It's so disruptive.'

'I know,' says Sean. 'What on earth possessed us to have them?'

'You know she'll just go herself if one of us doesn't,' says Imogen.

Charlie harrumphs. 'So? Look, if people want to impose their values on everybody else they need to understand that they won't be absolved of the consequences. If she wants to hover over them while they're asleep, let her.'

Simone sees her chance. 'I'll go!' she chirps.

'Wouldn't dream of it,' says Sean, and she feels warmed by his concern. 'You did far more than your fair share last night as it is.'

'Oh, but I don't mind. She'll miss this beautiful dinner.'

She's looked at what's coming up and seen that it's chateaubriand with truffles. After the next inter-course treat would be a fine time to duck out and earn her brownie points. It won't take that long to do what she needs to do, and the following course is only mangosteen sorbet. She doesn't much care for truffles and has no idea what a mangosteen is. She won't really miss it if she never finds out.

'Well,' says Sean, 'I daresay Claire won't suffer much if she misses a meal.'

Linda sniggers. From where she sits, Simone spots her plant-

246

ing a hand halfway up Sean's thigh. She glares at her. This is totally out of order, even she knows that. Sean doesn't seem to notice. He just reaches out and sups his wine like an emperor.

'Really,' she says, 'I don't mind. It would be a pleasure. My way of saying thank you for this amazing hospitality.'

Robert beams and Maria emits her usual warm approval. I'm a credit to you, she thinks. That's what you're thinking right now. Good. I like it when I'm approved of.

'Well, if you insist,' says Imogen. Linda has shown no sign of remembering – or caring, anyway – that three of the sleeping children are her own. She probably genuinely doesn't remember, half the time. They spend a lot of time at their grandparents' house in Godalming so their parents can pursue their itinerant careers. They're only here now because Granny wanted to go on a cruise. 'I can't say I'm going to fight you for the honour.'

Simone turns to Sean and gives it more with the eyelashes. 'Besides,' she says, playfully, 'you know I'd do anything for you, right?'

Sean laughs deep in his throat, mouth closed, and puts a hand on her shoulder. Strokes it fondly with his thumb, sending shivers down her spine. 'You really are a little miracle, aren't you?' he says.

Chapter Twenty-Nine

My phone wakes me at half-past eight. I think it's the alarm at first – I didn't have a smidge of a signal yesterday – but it's India. Cocktail time where she is, though all I hear is the rumble and the ding-ding-ding of a passing train. She's the only person who's rung me this weekend. Awkwardness? Or just the old out of sight, out of mind? Do I really have *no* friends who remember me when I'm not there?

'How's it going?' she asks. 'Oh, did I wake you?'

'Yes,' I say, and try to wipe the sleep fuzz from my brain.

'Sorry,' she says, though she doesn't sound it. She's so used to her six-thirty starts that it doesn't occur to her that other people might need to sleep. She will end her life far wealthier than I will, I can guarantee that. 'So how's it going?'

'Splendid. I had the great pleasure of sitting between the Clusterfucks last night.'

She shudders at me down the line. 'And how are the dear Clusterfucks?'

'Same, only more. Imogen's had herself laminated and Charlie's the colour of a beetroot. They've gone off to stay in some big-face hotel in Ilfracombe, if there is such a thing, thank God. I'm not sure how much I could take of his *bonhomie* at the moment.'

'He'll be next,' she says.

'Maybe not. You'll never guess who else stumbled in here yesterday. Only Jimmy Orizio.'

'Jimmy Orizio? He's not dead already?'

'Walking. Well, shambling. I keep expecting him to try to bite me.'

'And how's the Child Bride?'

'Weird.' I consider my answer. 'No. Even weirder.'

'Oh.'

'She's treating the whole thing like some sort of weekend hosting competition. With tantrums.'

'Oh.'

'Ruby and I and Joe were up till two a.m. washing up the wine glasses.'

'Joe?'

'Joaquin Gavila.'

'Wha-*keeeen*? What's he like these days? Still hitting things with sticks?'

'Doesn't seem to be. He's turned out a bit of a dreamboat, actually. Doe eyes and that. Ruby couldn't speak for about twenty minutes. I think the name-change seems to have made him more attractive.'

'And he washes up?'

'Yep. I know. Who'd have thought?'

'I should think there must have been a lot of wine glasses.'

'You would be right. How are you?'

'Okay,' she says, and sighs. 'Up and down. I'm quite surprised, actually. I ended up taking the day off on Thursday. I didn't know I had any tears left for Sean.'

'Me too! I had no idea!'

'But I wonder . . . '

'What?'

'What are we crying for? I mean, it's not like we'll miss him, exactly.'

I think. She's right. When I think of him, I only see him in my mind's eye with his cronies. A life force, certainly, grasping his pleasures with both hands and squeezing the juice from them, but I don't remember any of those dad things people talk about. Not since I was little, anyway. A bit of me has always assumed that all that stuff was a con invented by advertising agencies, like Mother's Day.

'I don't know.'

'I keep waking up in the night remembering all the crappy things he did. D'you remember the day he fucked off? And it turned out that all his stuff was already gone before he was, so he didn't have to come back and get it. Sneaking it all out bit by bit so she wouldn't notice.'

'Yes.' I remember Mum standing in front of his wardrobe, the drawers hanging open, empty. His study table, the surface swept clear but for a telephone sitting in the middle, his business line already disconnected.

'And he didn't say goodbye,' I say.

'No,' says India, and I hear her gulp back her emotions.

'Anyway,' she says. Back to business. 'How are you getting on with the eulogy?'

'Oh, God. Not good. It's awful how you realise you don't know someone else at all, really, when you have to speak about them in public.'

'Oh, I know. I had to do the professional eulogy for my boss last year and I realised that all I ever knew about him was this rather grey man who handed me files and gave opinions. Thank God for Google, that's all. I had to create a LinkedIn account just to find out what university he went to.'

'God, where *did* Dad go to university?'

'Really, Milly? *That* ignorant? Sheffield. Same as Robert.'

'Okay. And what do I do about the wives? I mean, two you can skate over, but four's straying into comedy, isn't it?'

'Well, Linda can be the tragedy Simone saved him from,' she says. 'So that's one down. And I don't suppose Mum or Claire are going to be there, are they?'

'Nup.'

'Well, the old fundamental incompatibilities will do with Ma. And Claire . . . oh, God, I suppose you can't avoid the Coco thing, can you? How's the Demon Spawn, by the way?'

And that's the thing about sisters. You've got all this stuff, these mutual memories, the common language, that only the two of you know. We couldn't be less alike, India and I, but we will always be bonded together because we are the only people who know what it was like.

'She's really sweet, actually. A big clomping thing, like a young shire horse.'

'Doesn't take after her mother, then?'

'Not so much. She's got our teeth. She's got exactly the same braces we had.'

'Oh, how funny. They must've been Dad's, then.'

'I guess so.' None of us really looks the way God intended, these days. In this world of plastic surgery and 'procedures' and orthodontics, you basically have no idea how your kids are going to turn out. The richer you are, the less of an idea you have, because the rich have more procedures at younger ages. The only way a man can be sure of what he's breeding with is

251

to pluck a peasant girl from a field when she's nine and keep her till she's old enough, a bit like they do in the Caliphate. And even then you need to make damn sure you've met the grand-mothers.

'And she looks as if she's been at the dressing-up box. I half expect her to turn up to the funeral in a pirate costume.'

'What are you going as?'

'Wednesday Addams.'

'Good choice.'

'Actually,' I sit up in bed. Another anonymous Jackson bed-room, cream walls, boutique hotel artwork designed neither to annoy nor to stimulate hung upon them, fabulous water pres-sure in the *en suite*. 'I should probably go. The Demon Spawn and I have to go through a box of trinkets and she's probably been up for hours.'

'Trinkets?'

'I don't know. Dad's bling, I think. Simone pretty much threw them at us last night. Says she doesn't want them.'

'Oh.'

'D'you want me to pick some stuff for you?'

A little pause. Then, slightly huskily, 'Yes. That would be nice. It's funny, isn't it? All those houses and there's not so much you'd think of as personal, is there?'

'No.'

'Something – yes, something would be good. It'll probably end up in a drawer somewhere, but . . . yes. Thanks. I'll try to call you on Monday. Have you spoken to Mum?'

'No.'

'Yeah. I don't suppose you like talking to her about Dad stuff any more than I do.'

'Divorce,' I say. 'It might be your easy way out, but it'll stay with your offspring for the rest of your life.'

'Too bloody right,' she says, and for the first time I hear an edge of a Kiwi twang in her voice. My sister's going native and she's never going to come home.

'I love you, Indy,' I say.

She sounds surprised. 'Yeah. Love you too, Shorty.'

I find Ruby in the garden, wandering slowly around the empty swimming pool. She's in polka dots today: white-on-black on her skirt and black-on-white on her jumper, grey and black striped tights and a bandana covered in bananas. Over the top, a Barbour and a pair of wellies borrowed from the back hall. Emma is with her, toddling back and forth across the lawn of the walled garden. It's still misty. The grass crunches with frost where I step, and I leave clear dark footmarks in my wake. It hardly seems to have even got light yet.

'Hi,' I say.

'Hi,' she says gloomily.

'Did you sleep?'

She shrugs. 'Those people. I just feel so bad for him.'

'What do you mean?'

'Just . . . looking back at your life and thinking that those were your friends.'

'Those aren't friends,' I say confidently. 'They're drinking buddies.' And then I think: God, what are yours, then, Camilla? When was the last time you spent any time around any of them without drinks in all your hands? And where were the people on your doorstep with the casseroles, or even the bottle of comforting whisky? The cards and letters? The phone calls? I like to think I've moved on from the way I grew up, but I need to sort myself out.

'We should go through that box,' I say.

She grimaces. 'I suppose so.'

Emma has found an earthworm in a newly turned rose bed. She squats down to watch it struggle to return to the frozen earth, chattering to herself.

'How old is she now?' I ask. I'm a bit ashamed that I don't know.

'I'm not sure. Just gone two, I think.'

I look at her properly for the first time. Try, unsuccessfully, to dredge up some family feeling. She's Sean's last hurrah, part of my family for the rest of my life whether I like it or not.

'Poor little sod,' I say.

'Does she look like anyone, to you?' asks Ruby.

I study her. Nut-brown hair – his first brunette – and fat little calves in her woolly tights. It looks as if she's going to be a mop-head, no sign of the poker-straight locks Simone has been cursed with. Of course, in the noughties we grudged Simone her good fortune as we obediently scalded our cheeks on straightening irons because Fashion Told Us To, but I like my no-point-in-trying Celtfro now. I'll never look sophisticated, but I'll never look older than I am, either. 'She has his hair.'

'Does she? I don't remember. There wasn't much of it left by the time I was old enough to notice.'

'Well, hopefully she'll keep hers. But otherwise, no, not much. Mind you, she's still a baby, really. No time to develop a nose, for a start. You two had little button mushrooms yourselves, at her age.'

She looks at me as if seeing me properly for the first time. 'Gosh. We have the same nose.'

'No shit, Sherlock.' I flash her a tentative grin. She grins back.

'Isn't that funny? I'd always thought it was mine.'

'No, it's Dad's.'

Emma pokes at the worm with a poky little sausage finger. It flips on the earth, rears up its middle like a snake and makes her leap back in surprise. She loses her balance, lands with a flumph on the lawn.

'Bugger,' she says, in a clear little voice.

We burst out laughing. 'Dad,' we say.

We return to the house via the back in the hope of finding someone to take the toddler. Maria says that there's a cleaning lady and a sort-of-nanny from the village who comes in every morning, and we hope that this means Sundays too. Simone wasn't keen on live-in staff. None of the wives was, apparently.

In the courtyard on the way, we come across a small knot of people. Simone, Robert, Joe, in front of the wheelie bins. There's a great bank of them – council spending at its best. A black one for waste, a green one for glass, a blue one for paper and a brown one that's simply marked 'recyclables'. Simone has the lid of the brown one open, and is dumping a pile of shirts inside. Joe sways silently behind her, his face almost hidden by the mound of suits he holds in his arms. Robert is pleading.

'Darling, please. Slow down. You don't have to do this now. You don't have to be in such a hurry.'

Simone is throwing the shirts in one by one, with a relish that seems surprising in a newly minted widow. She doesn't reply; just hurls and shoves and hurls and shoves. By her feet is a cardboard box filled with ties and brogues. Sean had his own last at Lobb. Each pair of those shoes was made to last a lifetime, though he had a new pair made at least once a year. Simone's lip is curled, as though there's a bad smell under her nose. She reaches back to her half-brother and starts to give the suits the same treatment.

'Seriously,' says Robert, 'there's thousands of pounds' worth of stuff there. Those shirts are Turnbull & Asser, most of them.'

'Good,' she says. 'I don't see why beggars should be excluded from wearing high-quality clothes.'

'Yes, but darling,' says Robert, 'they're *his* clothes! They're memories, as well. You don't have to keep everything, but they're still memories. And someone else might like them.'

'Not *my* memories,' says Simone. 'And that's why they're going in the recycling, not the trash. And who wants them, anyway? You?'

She spins on her heel and spits the last word at Joe. He blushes. I would guess that he would very much like a collection of Bond Street's finest. He must be starting work in a couple of years. But he just shakes his head and looks at the ground. Simone grabs another suit and shoves it, hanger and all, on top of the others. I hope he comes back in the night with a bin liner and takes as much as he can.

'Darling, *please*!' says Robert again. 'It's like you're throwing your husband away!'

She turns to face him, and that big old mechanical smile from last night's dinner is back. 'Don't be silly, Daddy. These are the clothes from *before*! Everything from *now* is safely upstairs. But these things don't belong here. They're not from *us*. They don't belong to this house.'

'So you're . . . '

'Yes,' she says. 'He couldn't do it, but I can. It was silly, holding on to all those things from before he was happy. Having them hanging around reminding him. I should have done it for him, I see that now. It's the very least I can do for him now. Only things from *us* in this house. This was our *home*.'

Oh, my God, I think, she's gone mad. We all stand around in awkward silence, unable to think of anything to say. There used to be photos of us in his study. I wonder if they're still there.

'I wouldn't mind a shirt,' says Ruby eventually, humbly.

Simone stares at her as though she's only just registered her presence. As though she'd wiped her from her database along with everything else that pre-dated their fine romance. 'Fine. Help yourself. Any particular one?'

'No. Just . . . something of his.'

Simone makes a strange little tut of disgust. Sweeps an arm, ballerina-style, towards the bin. 'Don't let me stand in your way.'

Ruby shuffles forward, leafs hurriedly through the pile of cloth and comes back with a blue-and-white-striped long-sleeve, the elbows worn thin. She clutches it against her chest like a blankey. Simone glares at her father. 'Happy?' she asks.

We take the box up to Ruby's bedroom. It doesn't seem right, somehow, to start sharing out the dead man's belongings downstairs. Especially under the nose of a man who's clearly nursing some financial grievance. Ruby has been put in the attic. At her age I would probably have felt slighted, treated like a parlourmaid, but as it is it's the most characterful room in the house, all beams and sloped ceilings and a wonderful view through the dormer over the treetops to the estuary. Appledore. Such a wonderful name for a town. Probably all pound shops and charity shops, like the rest of coastal England, of course.

Inside the box is a jumble. A tangle of chains and watch straps, as though it has all been thrown in by someone fleeing the advancing enemy. I can't imagine my fastidious father treating his precious gold like that. Simone must have bunched it all together while she was out of the room at dinner and hurled it in, the way she's done with his clothes.

'I think Simone's reached the anger stage,' says Ruby. I guess it's inevitable that she's read at least one book on the grief process, if she's already consulting the DSM on a habitual basis.

'Looks like it,' I say.

'I think I'm still in denial myself,' she says, and buries her face in the rescued shirt.

'Oh, Rubes.'

'It still smells of him,' she says, and passes it over. I take it reluctantly and give it a sniff, mostly to please her, and then I find myself breathing deeply. It's been washed since he last wore it, of course, but under the neutral scent of fabric conditioner he is still there. A faint, faint ghost of his custom-mixed cologne, heavy on the cedar and rich with citrus oils; the spice of once-warm skin; phantom Cohibas. And I'm back in the South of France, a little kid who's climbed over on to his lap to nod off as a long dinner progresses, bright moon-globes on the corniche, feeling safe and loved. What happened to us? God, he's been dead such a short time.

I give it back. I can't speak. Her pupils are huge as she meets my eyes. I up-end the box and the contents tumble on to the carpet.

There's a lot, and it's a mixed bag. Some of it must have come from his own parents, I realise: the cheap stuff, the worn-through gold-plated watch, the wedding rings. Well, maybe not all of those. He had amassed quite the collection of his own, after all. And a Rolex for each day of the week, enough cufflinks to carry him through two weeks in Dubai. A necklace with a single chip of purplish ruby in a golden heart. A christening mug, engraved. A couple of silver bonbon dishes. A gold hunter watch with his initials inside the lid.

A small gold bracelet.

'How do we go about this?' asks Ruby as I stare at it. 'Split them into types of thing, then choose?'

I clear my throat. 'Yes. Why not?'

It feels to me as though a spotlight has been switched on in the room and that it's trained on the subject of my gaze. Ruby seems

258

oblivious. She either hasn't noticed it yet or she doesn't know what it is, doesn't realise its significance. I stare and stare at it. It has to be. Ruby is wearing its twin on her right wrist. I remember now. It was how you told them apart. R for Ruby, Coco on the left. Given to them by Maria and Robert, each one a godparent, as christening gifts all those years ago, flexible metal and a sliding clasp so that they would grow with the wearer, and worn every day until she vanished.

But it vanished with her. I'm certain of it. That's what the story has always been. She was wearing it as she always did and the whole country – the whole world – was put on alert to find it. I remember it so well, on the Find Coco posters, on the TV screens, on the emails that came and came in those pre-Facebook days. No sharing, no retweeting, but still they think that a billion people have seen Maria's picture of Ruby's bracelet, blown up so you could see the engraving inside. Ruby's name, the twins' birthdate: 11.07.01. If it's the right one, it too will be engraved. I don't want to draw her attention by looking. Not now, not while I have no idea what to do. Because I have a sick feeling that, though she was far too small to remember it all, she will know what its presence must mean.

Ruby is working through the pile with her mother's punctilious efficiency. Watches here, cufflinks here, rings in a little Hobbit pile to the left, trinkets to the right, all the others – necklaces, chains, snaffle bracelets from the days before Sean reinvented himself as a country gentleman – in the middle. Her hand strays over the bracelet, stops. 'How funny,' she says.

I can barely speak. 'What?' I mutter.

She holds it up so it sits beside the one on her wrist. 'I've got one exactly like it.'

I unglue my tongue. 'Isn't that weird?' I say.

She doesn't look all that closely. Doesn't notice the inside. Lays it on the random pile. 'No use to me,' she says. 'Mine's at full stretch as it is. I'd never get it over my hand. Apparently I'd have to have it cut off if I ever needed an operation.'

I resist the temptation to snatch, but I see an opportunity. Ruby is much bigger than me, and I have my mother's small, elegant hands: useless for playing the piano but great for threading needles. I reach out for it, casually as I can. 'I wonder if I . . . ' I say, as though it's just an idle thought. I pull the clasp out till it's fully extended. Make my hand into a pincer and slide it on. It sticks at the joint at the base of my thumb. I push harder. It starts to hurt.

'Here,' says Ruby, and reaches under the bed into her suitcase. She produces a big bottle of Vaseline Intensive Care. 'She makes me take it everywhere. For my eczema.'

She flips the lid and squirts an obscene gush on to my hand, spreads it over my skin. As she pushes up my sleeve, she uncovers my most visible tattoo. I love them, but this is the only one that's not carefully placed where lawyers and interviewers and people's grandmothers won't be making snap judgements. It's a little line drawing of a pussycat, the first I ever had done. Just two curved lines in all, and two jade green eyes, on the tender underside of my forearm. I had it done when I was sixteen, and I never had another one done where India could see it and shout at me for being an idiot.

Ruby pauses and strokes it with a thumb. 'That's pretty,' she says. 'I'd love a tattoo.'

I'm still struggling to control my voice. Authoritative is easier, strangely. 'No, you wouldn't,' I say. 'It hurts like buggery and you're stuck with it for life.'

'You're not telling me you regret *this*?' She looks up into my eyes and sees me blush. 'Nah, thought not. Got any more?'

'Yes.'

'What?'

'I'll tell you when you're old enough to know.'

'Oh, God, don't tell me you've got a tribal armlet.'

'Who do you think I am? Robbie Williams?'

Ruby sighs. 'I probably won't be able to get one anyway,' she says. 'What with the eczema and everything. I'd probably end up with a lump of seeping pus.'

'You keep thinking that, baby,' I say. 'Even when you've been drinking.'

'So, go on. What else have you got?'

I consider for a bit. Decide to leave out the pubic stars. 'Not much. A curled-up pussycat on my shoulder and a *nil illegitimi hoc carborandum* on my hip. And there's one on my scalp. Three shooting stars.' They match the one on my mound of Venus, but she doesn't need to know that. 'But my days of shaving are well over. I'll probably never see those ones again unless I get cancer.'

'Gosh, you like getting them in places where it'll hurt,' she says. 'What does the Latin mean?'

'Look it up.'

She bends her head back towards the bracelet. 'Try now. Tuck your thumb in. Go on.'

I force my thumb joint that extra couple of millimetres further in and push again. It sticks, then slides and pops on to my wrist. The legend I know is there is safely pressed against my skin. I can look at it when I'm alone, verify its existence. Work out what the hell that existence means.

'There!' Ruby looks up, beaming.

'Well done! Top lube action!' I say, encouragingly.

'Now people will always be able to tell that we're sisters.'

I smile back at her, but it feels a pale and watery smile. 'Yay,' I say. 'Sisters.'

Chapter Thirty

2004 | Saturday | Claire

She has always been prone to stress headaches, and the stress of this weekend, and of four hours of gluttony and shouting, has produced a doozy. She can barely see for the pain and the party is showing no signs of slowing down. Jimmy produced a little bag of Ecstasy tablets for what he called a 'cheeky cheerer' while Simone was checking on the kids, and by the time she got back they were all as high as kites. Sean, of course, rolled his eyes, the way he does, when Claire declined to join in. Half an hour later he was pawing Linda and Simone in turn with a big goofy grin on his face and informing the table how much he loved each and every one of them. The only painkillers Jimmy had on his person were a mixed collection of opiates and, as it turns out, Health and Safety laws prohibit the restaurant from handing out things like aspirin or ibuprofen to customers because, well, Health and Safety, innit. Her head throbs and she's starting to get the dancing lights. If this doesn't turn into a migraine, she will be very lucky.

Now they're throwing shapes along the seafront while Linda shrieks out a painful version of 'Ride on Time' and lights go on in upstairs windows as they pass. Claire stumbles along fifty feet behind, the fireworks inside her skull impeding her progress, overlooked and glad of it. *I married a man and now I'm stuck with a twelve-year-old. Or is it me? Am I the odd one out? Even Robert Gavila is joining in, and dicking about with drugs would get him unlicensed in hours if the Law Society ever found out about it.*

They stop up ahead at the foot of a pontoon where a small collection of tenders is tied up, attached to dangling chains with bike locks and padlocks. She can hear giggling and laughing and 'ooh yes'es. She catches up. 'What's going on?'

'We're going to go for a nightcap on the *Gin O'Clock*.' Imogen points out to the deeper water, where a huge white gin palace bobs in the current among the quieter, lesser boats.

'Skinny-dipping!' cries Linda.

Sean jumps down into one of the tenders while Robert bends to unlock it, throws his arms out wide as it wobbles. 'Close one,' he says. 'Come on, ladies.'

Linda totters towards his out-held hand.

'No stilettos on boats, Linda,' says Maria. 'Come on. You'll go right through.'

'Oh,' says Linda. Puts a hand on Charlie's shoulder for balance and starts to fumble at the buckle on her ankle. 'Bloody hell, I'm all thumbs.'

'C'mere,' says Sean. She tittups over to the edge of the pontoon and stands above him, holds out a foot. *He's looking right up her dress*, thinks Claire. *I thought she at least must have a thong on under those scraps of lace, but evidently not. He used to love telling me to turn up to our dates without underwear. Once he sent me a fur coat – real fur, not fake; something that*

263

had been on the back of some ferret or another – and had me stand on the edge of Park Lane in it alone until he arrived in a limo and fucked me in the back seat while we drove round Marble Arch. He loves that stuff, the clandestine exhibitionist thing, at least until he marries you. I'm such a fool. I thought it was all sexy, just a kink so mild it was almost vanilla, but now I know it was all about power.

Sean starts to unbuckle the shoe. 'I'm going home,' she announces.

'Of course you are,' says Sean, and carries on staring at Linda Innes's vulva.

'I've got a blinding headache.'

'Well, there's a change,' says Sean, and Charlie Clutterbuck chortles, actually chortles. Claire is gripped by a wild, tooth-and-claw rage, almost hurls herself on the arrogant arsehole's face with her new red manicure. Crushes the urge down, as she always does, and stumbles off unwatched through the darkness and the flashbulbs in her head.

I hate him, I hate him. I thought until this weekend that I just disliked my husband, but now I know that I actively hate him. It's my own stupid fault, of course. I should have been able to work out that a man who treated his first wife the way he did wouldn't change just because it was me. God, women can be so stupid. All the evidence in front of our eyes and our own stupid vanity per-suades us that we're different, that we're The One. Feminists claim that romance novels twist women's expectations, but I think it's far worse than that. I think they simply reflect the perni-cious, self-sabotaging thing that's already there in us.

She kicks her shoes off as she walks up the drive, and carries them into the house. Leaves them on the island counter in a ges-ture of defiance because she knows it's one of the things he hates most of all in other people's behaviour. No one has bothered to

264

lock up. It's as though they think that Sandbanks is too posh to have burglars. She goes up to her room and finds the ibuprofen, washes four down with a glass of water at the bathroom basin. In the mirror she sees an angry woman with big black circles under her eyes. Thank God I stopped drinking after the first course, she thinks. The last thing I need on top of this is a hangover.

She's tempted to just crawl beneath the cool sheets on the king-size bed here and now, but maternal responsibility drives her back down the stairs and out to the annexe.

All is quiet inside, just the peaceful sound of six little bodies breathing, breathing, breathing. But it doesn't smell right. The warm air is thick with the acid smell of vomit. She flips on the light and finds that Ruby has at some point rolled over and thrown up all over her end of the air mattress. My God, she thinks, thank God she rolled over. I can't think we didn't at least think to put them in the recovery position. The poor little thing is still lying there, fast asleep in her own sick. Oh, God, I don't feel well enough for this. I'll throw up myself.

But she leaves the door open and takes a deep breath of night air before she forces herself to go and deal with it. She starts by lifting Coco off the sheet – she flops in her arms like a rag doll, but doesn't wake – and laying her back down on the flock surface of the mattress itself. It'll be hot, but she doesn't want to run the risk of waking any of them by doing more than she strictly has to. Then she sweeps the sheet, the pillow and Ruby into one big noxious bundle and carries them into the bathroom, gagging.

She unwinds her daughter from the bedclothes, throws them into the corner and places the child in the bath, gets down on her knees to strip off her pyjamas. There's another pair in her suitcase, at least; un-ironed and rolled in a ball, but clean. Ruby half wakes, groggy and barely there, and starts to grizzle. Her forehead is hot, her cheeks flushed. Hopefully just one of those twenty-four-hour bugs, she thinks. She's always getting them. My second twin, so much more vulnerable than her sister. She picks up every bug she passes, as though she is catching them for the two of them so Coco can go through life unscathed. No wonder Sean is so naked in his preference for Coco: she's so much less trouble.

'There, there, my darling,' she soothes. Her own nausea has worn off, the way it does. A couple of thousand nappy changes will alter your revulsion response forever. 'There there. Just sorting you out. I'll get you back to bed in a minute.'

She finds the Baby Bath, runs the shower lukewarm and hoses her daughter down. Ruby raises a starfish hand to fend the water off her face, but otherwise she doesn't resist. A lathering and another sluice, and all the yuk is washed away down the drain. She grabs one of the big white spa towels from the shelf and wraps her up. Rubs at her hair to get the worst of the wet out.

'My poor baby,' she says. 'Such bad luck, your silly tummy. You'll grow out of it one day, I'm sure.'

It's hard work getting a dozing child into clean pyjamas, but she's well practised. Once Ruby is clean and dressed, there's no sign that anything was ever wrong. Claire carries her back to the airbed, lays her down on her side and waits as the doze deepens, the breathing slows and she goes back to sleep. Claire kisses her girls on their foreheads, smooths their hair back, loves them once more, as she's always loved them.

'Night night, darlings,' she whispers. 'Sleep tight.'

Her daughters don't respond. Over by the window, Joaquin shifts in his sleep, mutters something about it being over there, falls quiet. She goes back to the bathroom and gathers up the soiled bedlinen to put in the washing machine with Ruby's dress from earlier. The pillow is ruined. No point trying to keep it. She can stuff it in the kitchen bin, which is big enough to hold a pig. She stands in the doorway for a moment and studies all the sleeping faces. Thank God they won't remember any of this, she thinks. I would be covered in shame if they ever knew. She turns off the light. Trudges back across the garden, checks that the swimming pool gate is latched, throws the bedclothes into the washing machine, turns it on and stumbles back up the stairs to fall, exhausted, into bed. She is asleep almost as soon as she is horizontal.

She wakes to dim daylight and the sound of laughter. Dawn has arrived but the sun has yet to lift itself over the trees, and the others are clearly home from the boat. She is begrimed by sleep, her mouth dry, eyes fuzzy. But the headache has gone, and with it her ability to sleep any more. She checks her watch. Nearly half-past four. Long past the time when anyone planning to take part in childcare in the morning should have gone to bed. I at least thought better of Maria than this, she thinks. But I suppose her kids are older now. She probably doesn't feel she should have to stay *compos mentis* to look after other people's toddlers, and why should she?

She won't sleep now. The party still going on downstairs will assure that. Though the pain has gone, her head still feels stuffed and she knows she will soon be having to make some decisions. She feels hemmed in and beaten down and angry. I need some exercise, she thinks. While the rest of them are busy drinking. It'll help me think. I'll do some lengths of that swimming pool. It'll be gorgeous at this time of day, with the sun coming up. There will be mist coming off the water and no one to bother me.

She gets up, pulls on her swimsuit and a sundress over the top, goes downstairs. The Gavilas and the Clutterbucks are spread out on the sofas, drinking tea. Well, the Gavilas and Imogen are drinking tea. Charlie is drinking Cognac from one of the over-sized snifters Linda has put in the cupboards to show off their storage capacity. Jimmy is asleep on the third sofa, snoring, covered in a rug. I don't suppose he'll ever make it as far as a bedroom, she thinks. I wonder when was the last time he did?

Robert sees her come down the stairs. 'Claire!' He calls. 'How are you feeling?'

'Better, thank you,' she says. She feels naked under their scrutiny, as though she's come down in the swimsuit alone.

'Where are you off to?'

'Thought I'd go for a swim to wake myself up.'

A short, sharp exchange of looks among them all. 'No, no! Stay!' says Imogen. 'Let me make you a cup of tea! How's your poor head? Still hurting?'

'No, thanks.' She doesn't want to spend any more time with these people. They're not her friends. 'I'm feeling a bit yuk, like I've not moved in centuries. Shouldn't you lot be in bed by now, anyway?'

'Why?' asks Charlie. 'What time is it?'

'Going on half-four.'

'Well, bugger me,' he says, 'doesn't time fly when you're having fun? How about a nightcap? Come on. A nice brandy to get the circulation going?'

She feels sick at the very thought. 'This is first thing in the morning to me, Charlie. Thanks, but I'm not so far gone I need a brandy to get me up. Maybe you should wake Jimmy up if you want someone to drink with.' She's passed the point where she can bother to be civil to the man. That laugh on the pontoon was the final straw.

'Well!' he harrumphs. 'Please yourself.'

Maria starts to get to her feet. 'Come on,' she says, 'a coffee to wake you up, perhaps?'

She holds up a hand. 'No, Maria. Thank you, but no. I don't want tea, I don't want coffee, I want a swim.' She knows they're trying to stall her. Wants to know what they're trying to stop her seeing.

'Oh, for God's sake,' says Charlie, 'let the silly bitch go. It's not like we owe her anything.'

'Thank you, Charlie,' she says. 'Always good to get things out in the open.'

'No, Claire—' Maria begins.

'Forget it,' she says, and walks out into the beautiful morning. She has a good idea what she's going to see when she gets to her destination, and her heart is pounding in her chest. Got to get it over with, she thinks. It's not like I don't *know* already, but if I catch him then he can't pretend any more that it's all my fault, tell me I'm mad while he lies and cheats and . . .

They're in the pool, humping on the steps in the shallow end. He's screwing her from behind, her skinny bottom rising in and out of the water with the rhythm of his thrusts. Eugh, is her first thought. My children will be wanting to play in that water tomorrow. Claire is barefoot, so they don't hear her approach. They've left the gate open so she makes no sound going through it. Stands by the sun-loungers and watches them for a minute before she speaks: Sean's shaven head bobbing back and forth, back and forth, the woman's buttocks smooth and brown without a single tan line. It's not *real* sex, she thinks. It's that performance sex he always liked: the sort that makes you wonder if he hasn't got a video camera secreted somewhere so he can watch himself later.

'You're going to have to change the water in that pool,' she says. 'I don't suppose anybody's going to want to swim in it now.'

He jumps like a pantomime villain, nearly loses his balance on the step and steadies himself by grabbing on to Linda's backside with both hands. 'Ow!' she cries; she was making too much noise of her own to notice Claire speaking. She twists round to give Sean a piece of her mind, sees her lover's wife and says, 'Oh.'

'Claire,' says Sean.

'What? Are you going to tell me it's not what it looks like? What? You're helping her find her contact lens? Giving her pipes a good cleaning?'

'I—' he says.

'Don't even *think* about it,' she says, and hears her voice rising. 'You have *nothing* to say to me right now. I've caught you bang to rights and there is *nothing* you can say.'

And she realises that there's nothing he wants to say. He has no interest in making amends, in sorting things out, in trying to find a way to make her stay.

'Fuck you, Sean,' she says, and realises that she's shouting. 'And fuck *you*, skank. You want him? You can have him. Don't think he'll want your kids too, though. He doesn't even want his *own*.'

She wheels and walks back to the house. They stay there in the pool, still plugged together, for all she knows. I can't go back in there, she thinks. It was bad enough when I knew that they knew. But now they know that I know, I can't bear the shame. The humiliation. The mistress turned wife turned cuckold in my turn.

But she has to go in, because she has nothing outside. She enters the room and feels all their eyes on her, raises her chin and looks straight ahead. 'Claire—' begins Maria, but she ignores the word. Walks past, gaze steady, her dignity strapped to her shoulders like armour. She mounts the stairs, one, two, three, four, five, the glass cold beneath her feet, the metal railing cold beneath her palm. I won't show it, she thinks. They won't see me cry. Not those people. Not ever.

In her bedroom she grabs her handbag, checks it for phone and house keys. Takes the car key from his bedside table, snatches up a cardigan from the back of the chair. What do I need? I need their stuff. I need Ruby's medicines and Coco's teddy bear and some way to carry them, when they're sleeping, when they're heavy, and I have to get out of here, I can't stay here, not with all these people, his cronies, his whore, looking at me and laughing. I can't. I can't do it. I have to get out. I have to go now. I can't go back out there, where they are, and get the girls. I don't want to look at them. I can't.

She walks back down the stairs again, poised and stately like a debutante entering a ball. They sit there, silent, and watch as she crosses the room once again. Linda has come indoors, and sits silently among them, for protection, she supposes. Of her husband there is no sign. Maria doesn't try to speak, this time. No one tries to speak. They are all on his side. They've practically forgotten her already.

Claire gives up on her children, goes down to the drive and opens the car. Gets in, starts to adjust the driving seat. The buttons are sticky, complicated; it takes her a couple of minutes to make it high enough, and close enough to the steering wheel, for her to be able to see out through the windscreen. Plenty of time for someone to come. Plenty of time, if he wants to, for him to beg her to stay.

She backs slowly out of the drive. The road is empty. The first ferry isn't until seven o'clock and no one on Sandbanks has anywhere to go, much, on a Sunday. She puts the car into gear and leaves. She doesn't start to cry until she reaches the Southampton ring road.

271

Chapter Thirty-One

'You'd better not be calling me to tell me you picked me out a watch.'

'Oh. Did I wake you up?'

'Revenge, I suppose,' she says drily.

'Sorry,' I say. 'But oh, God, Indy, I found something and I don't know what to do.'

'What?' she asks wearily. In our family I was always characterised as the dramatic one, and that's always the way everyone responds when I say something that fits the stereotype. I feel ever so slightly triumphant. I'm not *always* the drama, bitch. Sometimes I get to *bring* the drama.

'I found Coco's bracelet.'

'What?'

Now she's awake.

'In among Sean's things.'

'*What?* Are you sure?'

'No, I'm just saying it for effect. Of course I'm sure. It would be hard not to be. It's got her name etched on the inside.'

'Oh, God,' she says. I give her a moment. It took more than a moment for me to trust my own voice when I found it, after all.

'Oh, God,' she says again, 'that poor little girl.'

'I don't . . . what does it mean?'

'Come on, Mills. We know what it means.'

'Do we?'

'Yes,' she says. 'You know we do. It's not like it's turned up fallen down the back of a sofa. He's kept it a secret. He must have seen it practically every day, if it's in among stuff Simone just snatched up and threw into a box. There's no way he wouldn't have known he had it. Come on. If he'd found it later he would have said. He would have told someone. They had every amateur sleuth in Europe on the lookout for it. Don't you remember that time when Claire got hauled in by the cops in Alicante because someone spotted Ruby and didn't seem to notice who she was with? And that was years later. Literally years. He would have said something when he first found it. You know he would. But he didn't.'

'Oh, God, India. What do I do?'

'What do you want to do?'

'I don't know. I don't *know*.'

I look down at the bracelet on my wrist. I'm really wishing, now, that I hadn't let her force it over my hand. Hadn't let her turn it so quickly into a totem of our common blood. She'll notice if I take it off. But someone else is bound to notice if I keep it on. I can wear as many long sleeves as I like, but they'll roll up at some point.

'I think we shouldn't do anything right now,' she says. 'We need to think. It's a big old can of worms. And, just because it was in Dad's stuff, it doesn't mean Dad's the only person involved.'

'No. India?'

'Yes?'

'Do you think this means he did . . . something?'

'I don't know. I really don't. Look, if I were arguing this in court right now, I'd say that all it showed was that he wasn't telling the truth about one single thing. Not about everything, just about one thing.'

'Yes, but if you were opposing counsel you'd be saying that it threw every statement he'd ever made into question.'

'Well, haven't *you* been reading your Grisham?'

'You know perfectly well I only read the internet. You can learn all sorts of stuff off the telly, too. I could totally do the Heimlich manoeuvre, and I've never done a first aid course.'

'Whatever,' she says. 'Look, what I'm saying is that we have to think. Really. He's dead. We can't cross-examine him now.'

'But . . . '

'I know. But think what we'd be doing. Ruby's done a lot of confirming that everyone's been lying to her already over the last couple of days. Do you think it would make things better for her, finding out that the lie was even bigger?'

'Oh, God. I'm lying to her already. Oh, God, India, this fucking family does nothing but secrets. I'm sick of it. It's done so much damage.'

'That's fine,' she says. 'But this isn't just about *your* life, is it?'

'I know—'

'You know what the Buddha says about lying?'

'What the fuck do I care, India? I'm not in the market for a theology lesson right now.'

'No, listen,' she says. 'He says that, while you must strive to tell the truth, you must first ask yourself: is it kind and is it helpful?'

'And?'

'Who's it going to help, Milly? Ruby? Claire? Coco?'

'I—'

'This won't take anyone closer to knowing what happened, Milly. It'll just reopen old wounds and rub poison into them.'

God, she's right.

'But darling,' I say, 'there's also doing the right thing.'

'Yeah,' she says. 'But the right thing is more of a moveable feast than you're thinking, right now.'

I go downstairs, my head filled with thoughts, and find them driven away as I hit the hall. Simone sits on the bergère by the front door, rocking, Joe sitting beside her with a hand on her shoulder, while a shouting match plays out in the drawing room. A one-sided shouting match, for only Jimmy is shouting.

'I'm serious, Robert! You don't want to make an enemy of me!'

'Oh, please.' Robert sounds as I've never heard him before. The same modulated tones, but filled with contempt. It almost sounds as though he is actually laughing at Jimmy. 'You can't even remember what day it is.'

'I've been your whipping boy for too long.'

'Your troubles are entirely of your own creation, Jim. Nobody forced you to write dicky prescriptions.'

'Didn't mind taking a few yourself, though, did you?'

'I think you'd find that hard to prove.'

'I've got nothing,' shouts Jimmy. 'Nothing!'

Maria's voice. 'You haven't saved *anything*?'

I raise my eyebrows at Joe. Simone doesn't appear to have even registered my appearance. He gives me a look filled with conflicting messages. Help me: I don't know what to do. Go away, go away, we don't want you seeing this. I freeze. Stay, go: whatever I do, I do the wrong thing. I hover in the hall. Hard to just pretend it's not happening and go about my day.

Jimmy seems temporarily stumped by the question.

'Sean understood,' he says, after a pause, and he's no longer shouting. 'When you've got nothing, you've got nothing to lose.'

'Why, thank you, Bob Dylan.'

'Shut *up*, Robert!'

'Come on, Gavvers,' says Jimmy. 'It's not like he's not been keeping *Clutters* in electoral deposits all these years.'

'That's different,' says Robert. 'They were old friends.'

'Yeah,' says Jimmy. 'It's *loyalty* that's kept him shelling out all this time.'

'Both of you, calm down,' says Maria. 'Jimmy, which bit of "the estate's in probate" do you not understand? Simone can live off the money, but we can't start handing out wodges of cash to random non-family without HMRC asking questions. You're going to have to suck it up while Robert sorts the estate out. As it is there's a big issue with all the "gifts" he's handed out over the past seven years.'

'And in the meantime?'

'Cut back on pleasure spending?' suggests Robert, and the contempt is right back there in his voice.

'*You've* got plenty of money,' says Jimmy, meaningfully. 'I bet you've got a credit card or two, too. Just remember, Robert. You and Maria have as much to lose as anybody else.'

'Not so much,' says Robert.

'What's that supposed to mean?'

'I just have to say, Jimmy. Reputation management cuts both ways, you know.'

'Didn't notice you doing much to manage *my* reputation,' says Jimmy.

Robert heaves a heavy sigh. 'Yes. Look, we're good at what we do, but we can't work miracles. But trust me: there are any number of times you could have popped back up in the public eye.'

'Didn't want me to, *eh*?' says Jimmy, and there's some meaning to it that I don't understand.

'Listen,' says Robert, and suddenly the door closes in my face. A heavy, high-quality door that blocks sound as effectively as if it were made of lead.

I turn back to the others. 'Are you okay, Simone?'

She stops rocking and sits bolt upright. 'Good morning!' she says. 'How are you today?'

'I'm fine,' I say. 'Are you okay?'

'I'm marvellous,' she says. 'Just marvellous.'

She shrugs Joe's hand off her shoulder and stands up. 'Lunch!' she says. 'I've just got some charcuterie and some nice bread, if that's all right with you.'

'Yes, whatever,' I say. 'Can I help?'

'No,' she says. 'And soup. I must make some soup. Everybody likes soup. Those Brussels sprouts. And a pack of chestnuts. I'll make soup.'

I start to follow her down the corridor anyway, and she wheels on me. Her head darts forward like an attacking cobra. 'I said no! Don't any of you people listen?'

I recoil. 'Sorry,' I say.

'Right,' she says. 'You're just like your father, you know. You don't listen to anyone.'

Ooh, that's a low blow. I watch her stalk away towards the kitchen. Feel angry and diminished.

'You mustn't mind her,' says Joe. 'She's in a state.'

'Obviously,' I say, grimly.

'People take bereavement differently,' he says. 'We're doing our best.'

'Why's she so angry, though?'

Joe grimaces. 'Look, Mila,' he says, 'I don't want to speak ill of the dead, but wouldn't you be? She's all over the papers, and not in a good way. He couldn't have chosen a more humiliating way to go if he'd tried, could he?'

'It's not my fault,' I whine, and even as I say it I hear how I must sound. I look back at him and blush. 'Sorry. Sorry, Joe. That was pathetic. I'm ashamed of myself.'

His eyebrows flick up and he grins. 'Not so much like your father after all,' he says.

'What are they fighting about?'

'Um – Jimmy wants money. He seems to think he deserves it.'

'Ugh. Always a vulture when there's a funeral.'

'Seems like your dad's been keeping him ever since he got out of the jug,' he says. 'I don't suppose Simone's going to stand for any more of that.'

'Why on earth? *Why?*'

He shrugs. 'Guilt?'

'Why would he feel guilty?'

'I don't know. It does sound like his life unravelled rather after Linda left him.'

'Oh, bollocks,' I say. 'He was all over the place long before then. I'm not surprised she left him in the slightest. I mean, seriously: have you ever heard him speak without slurring?'

The door slams open and Jimmy plunges through it, sees us, glares and storms towards the staircase. Robert follows. 'Jimmy, come on! This is just . . . '

He sees the two of us standing there and pipes down. 'What are you doing?'

'Just wondering if we should be helping with lunch,' says Joe. He's fast on his feet, for a nineteen-year-old. I may not be my father's daughter, but he's sure as hell his mother's son. 'Where's Jimmy going?'

Robert rubs the back of his shaven skull. 'I'm very much hoping he's going to sulk in his room,' he says. Maria emerges behind him, composed as ever, but the pupils of her eyes have almost obliterated her irises.

A door bangs on the first floor and Jimmy reappears at the top of the stairs. He's pulled on the leather trench coat I remember him wearing in the 1990s, and carries a battered duffel bag. He's not shaved in days, and his sallow cheeks are thick with grey-black bristles. 'Oh, now, come on, Jimmy,' says Robert.

Jimmy ignores him. Throws the bag on to one shoulder and tramps down the stairs.

Robert stands and waits as he approaches and begins to pass. 'Jimmy, come on. It's the funeral Monday, for God's sake. Just stay. This is barking.'

'Oh, don't worry,' says Jimmy. 'I'll be at the funeral, for *sure*.'

'Well, why not just stay, then?'

'I'm not staying where I'm not wanted.' He sounds like a huffy matron in an Ealing comedy. When I was younger, I thought that growing up meant that you, you know, grew up. Even watching all the adults in my life throwing whoosh-dadas right in front of my face didn't change my mind. But Joe seems like the most in-control person here at the moment. Jimmy is like a sulky twelve-year-old who's had his football taken away, and Robert and Maria a pair of frazzled teachers, exasperated and ineffectual.

'And don't think I won't have a few things to say,' says Jimmy.

'Jimmy,' says Maria.

'You can't stop me, you know. It's a public occasion.'

Maria throws her hands in the air, diva-style. Clamps them to either side of her head, as though she's trying to block the row out altogether.

'But where will you sleep?' Robert sounds tired and bewildered.

'I'll find somewhere. It's not like it's the height of the tourist season, is it?'

'I thought you didn't have any money,' says Joe.

'Oh, shut *up*, Joaquin!' bellows Robert. 'Just shut *up*! Don't you have any idea of when's a good time to keep your bloody big mouth shut?'

Joe subsides; big eyes expressing hurt. Robert turns back to Jimmy, who's already at the front door, his hand on the handle. 'Look. You've got somewhere to stay here. It's far more comfortable than anywhere you're going to find at no notice, and your friends are here.'

Jimmy turns and laughs in his face. 'Friends? Don't make me laugh. None of you are friends. You're all just each other's prison guards, keeping an eye on each other.'

Chapter Thirty-Two

2004 | Sunday | Sean

They are all crammed into the doorway of the annexe. The men are silent – silent, at last – and the women are babbling. He hears Jimmy's name called over and over, Linda and Imogen crying it with hysterical desperation. Oh, God, he thinks, has he finally taken it all too far? I thought he was pickled; embalmed by his own intake, a low-rent Keith Richards destined to outlive the whole world, like a cockroach. But what's he doing in the annexe? When we slunk off he was sound asleep on a sofa, snoring.

He jogs the last few paces. 'What's going on? What's happened?'

They turn as one to look at him, Maria, Linda, Imogen, Charlie, and each of their faces has aged a million years. He sees four dead souls staring up at him from the pit of hell.

The earth stops. Jumps two feet to the left and almost tears his feet out from under him. 'What is it?' he asks, and feels as if he's been struck deaf, so quiet and far away is his voice.

No one answers. Sean pushes his way between them and his world comes crashing to an end.

Jimmy and Robert, suddenly sober, are on their knees by the mattress where his daughters lie. Simone is circling the room, feeling each child's wrist for a pulse. Ruby lies on her side, oblivious, her hair slightly damp as though she's had a shower in the night. No one pays attention to her, for the men are crouching over Coco. Robert pumps with the heel of one hand on her breastbone; Jimmy holds her head back and periodically covers her mouth with his own and breathes, breathes, breathes.

Sean has to put a hand on the doorframe to steady himself, for the strength has rushed from his legs. Linda tries to put a hand on his shoulder, sobbing, but he is filled with a sudden revulsion and sweeps the hand away with his own.

'What's happened?'

No one answers. They don't need to. They all know.

He stumbles forward, goes down on his knees beside his oldest friend.

'Coco,' he hears himself say. 'Coco?'

Her eyes are closed, as though she is still asleep. Her body bounces with each downward thrust of Robert's arm. One . . . two . . . three . . . four . . . five . . . breathe . . . and each time Jimmy breathes out he subconsciously inhales, willing the tiny chest to expand and slowly, slowly fall.

'Jimmy, do something!' cries Linda.

Shut up, shut up, shut *up*. Her voice sounds harsh in his ears, stripped of its wit and nuance, like some mindless seabird swooping down in pursuit of carrion.

'I *am* doing something, you silly bitch,' snaps Jimmy. 'Go and get my bag. Go on. Go!'

Linda stumbles off, weeping, into the beautiful dawn. From the dim interior he sees that the sun is up, now, the sanguine flush on the high, light clouds giving way to azure haze, and his new-laid lawn is emerald-green where the light touches and burns away the dew. He looks down at his other daughter, takes her wrist between his fingers. Her breath is shallow and she no

282

more responds to his presence than she has to that of the others, but her pulse is strong and even.

Coco is waxy white beneath the light suntan she's developed despite the fanatical slathering Claire has subjected them to over the summer. Her mouth is open, forced that way perhaps by Jimmy, and her pale pink tongue looks dry, like suede. He knows right down at a cellular level that she is gone. There's no one there now, he thinks. All the giggles, the tantrums, the cuddles, the broken sleep, the grazed knees, the tears and the smiles: what a waste. What a stupid, pointless waste. Abruptly he drops Ruby's hand back on to the mattress, disgusted by her survival. Coco was always the strong one. Why take the good one, and leave the faulty one behind?

Linda returns, Jimmy's briefcase horizontal between her outstretched hands like a butler's tray. Jimmy throws it open on the floor and Sean sees a cornucopia of pleasure drugs: little plastic bags, jumbled blister strips, a prescription pad, a zip-up canvas box with a white upright cross on the lid. FIRST AID, reads the legend below. What the hell? he thinks, as Jimmy picks it up. We don't need plasters and bandages and zinc ointment now. She's dying. My little girl is dying.

Inside the box: syringes, phials of some clear liquid, needles the size of biro refills.

'Oh, God,' says Imogen. 'Oh, God, oh, God, oh, God,' her tone and volume rising with each invocation.

'Fucksake, someone shut her up,' snaps Jimmy, and Maria, still calm, as she always is, but lily-white, puts a hand on Imogen's arm, firmly but kindly. Imogen clamps her hands over her mouth. Simone, who's checked her brother last of all, straightens up and watches. So calm, he thinks, like her stepmother. Nothing fazes her, even at her fragile age.

Jimmy prepares a syringe. 'You might want to look away,' he says. 'I'm going to try to start her heart, but it's not pretty.'

Sean nods, but keeps his eyes on the doctor's hands. Imogen lets out a little moan from behind her fingers and Jimmy looks fiercely in her direction. 'Seriously,' he says. 'If she can't keep quiet, you're going to have to get her out of here.' He fills the syringe from a phial, takes his time flicking it with a finger to make the bubbles rise. C'mon, c'mon, c'mon, thinks Sean, though he knows that a started heart will stop for good if Jimmy doesn't do what he's doing. But it seems to take forever. The seconds tick off in his head. C'mon. He waits, barely breathes, while Jimmy forces the plunger up until adrenaline arcs from the end of the needle. Such a tiny amount, he thinks. A tiny amount for a tiny body. Oh, God.

Jimmy turns his daughter on to her back, raises a fist and plunges the needle through her breastbone. A collective holding of breath while they wait for the scene they've seen a thousand times on television: the corpse, reanimated, bolt upright and gasping, eyes bugging and mouth wide open.

Nothing.

Coco bounces again, with the force of the blow, and her eyes fly open. For a second his heart skips as he thinks it's worked. But nothing. She lies on her back and stares glassily at the ceiling tiles.

Jimmy slumps back. Closes the eyes again. 'Shit,' he says. 'Oh, shit, I'm sorry.'

Silence.

Sean doesn't know what he feels. I should be crying, he thinks, but instead I'm numb. It's all over. Everything is over. My life, her life, all of our lives. We will never recover from this, none of us. Everything – we'll lose everything. Custody, jobs, reputations, liberty.

Maria's calm voice, businesslike, as though she's in the office, planning a campaign. 'We need to get the kids out of here,' she says, 'before they wake up.'

Chapter Thirty-Three

'I don't want to go back yet,' says Ruby.

It's not yet four, but the estuary is already deep in the final stages of dusk and lights are twinkling in Instow across the water.

'No,' I agree.

'I sort of don't want to go back *ever*.'

'I know what you mean.'

'It's weird, that house.'

'Yeah. The atmosphere's not great, is it?'

Ruby's nose is red with cold. We went to the supermarket in Bideford after lunch and we've been tasting the delights of Appledore ever since: around the tiny streets, out up Irsha Street to the lifeboat station and back. Contrary to my expectations, Appledore turns out to be beautiful. A maze of alleyways and ancient buildings: a smuggler's heaven with a hundred little boats tied up on the mud-flats. But real, somehow. Not preserved in amber, like Padstow. If we'd thought before, we could have taken a boat out to Lundy Island, but it somehow didn't seem right to be planning pleasure cruises in the house of grief.

'Nine point six per cent of the population has a personality disorder,' she says. 'It's interesting how they gather in clusters, isn't it?'

'Yeah.' So it's not just me, then.

'D'you think Dad had one?'

'Um. Yes, probably.'

'Narcissistic?'

'And antisocial,' I say. 'He was a bit of a psychopath, wasn't he?'

'Oh, thank God,' she says. 'I used to think it was me. It's funny how you always assume it's you, isn't it?'

'I think it's one of the ways you can tell you haven't got a personality disorder yourself, isn't it? But Sean's houses were always a bit weird. Like hotels. He didn't like a place to feel as though anyone lived there. But why did you think it was you?'

She snuffles. 'I don't know. I mean, maybe it was just the stepmother thing. Step-parents. I mean, it's a weird thing, isn't it? That's why there are so many of them in fairy stories.'

I think of Barney. He's never been weird with us. Took a while to get to know him, but then, he never pushed it. 'Dunno. My current stepfather's okay.'

'Mummy says that's why she never got married again. She doesn't want to inflict that on me from both sides.'

Hmm, I think, your mummy's being a bit economical with the truth there. It took mine a good decade before she could face the dating pool, but at least she was honest about why. Or is that a good thing? I don't know. I heard a hell of a lot of things I'd rather not have about my dad in the meantime. Is that what people mean when they go on about children being poisoned against their parents? Poison can be drip-fed, after all, like arsenic. It's not all cyanide.

'I don't know,' I say. 'Maybe it just reflects Dad's taste in women?'

A sideways glance. 'What was Mum like as a stepmother?'

This child is a bloody monster when it comes to questions. 'Honestly?'

'Yes.'

'Well, okay, then. Pretty crap, as it goes. She never exactly gave us the impression she was glad to have us around.'

'Oh,' she says, and looks sad.

'You did ask.'

So maybe it was Sean. Claire never gave any impression while I was at Downside of being the cold individual I knew when I was younger. Control issues, sure. Massive ones of those. But no coldness. None of the huffing in a corner I remember from her marriage to my dad. That's the thing with your psychopaths, isn't it? They're not always creeping around with knives in dark alleyways. Most of them kill you from the inside out.

'Thing is,' she says, 'I never really got the impression that he liked me much.' And her eyes fill with tears behind her glasses.

'Oh, Ruby.'

I put out a hand and squeeze hers. I can't say he ever gave us much of the same impression, once he'd moved on. Some men are good at that. The past is the past, *je ne regrette rien* and all the other self-help mantras. But we were older, at least. At least we had had a few years in which he wanted us around.

'I think,' she says, in a little voice, 'he always blamed me for not being Coco.'

'No,' I say. 'No, darling, of course he didn't.' and even while I'm saying it I'm wondering if I'm adding to the family lie bank again. Because I never talked to Dad about Coco, not once. Not about what he felt, not about what he thought; not even about what his theories were. It was a *verboten* subject. He seemed, when he wasn't on parade for Maria's campaign, to want to avoid talking about it at all. Plunged himself into a condo development for British expats in the Emirates and didn't resurface until Claire and Ruby were safely gone. And then it was Linda falling foul of her own choice of staircase, and mourning Linda, and then it was Simone, and now it's too late. I don't know. Guilty conscience? Wouldn't he have a guilty conscience anyway? Even if what happened to Coco had panned out the way he claimed?

'He never wanted to be alone in a room with me,' she says. 'Not ever. It was like the wives were under orders to never let him be alone with me. They even came in the car when he picked me up from the station. And I know he only ever saw me because Mummy made him. Once *she* stopped bothering, *he* did too.'

'When did she stop bothering?'

She thinks. 'Around when Emma was born, I guess. I only met her the once before today. I took a teddy up to St Mary's, Paddington, when she was born.'

'Oh, that's quite classic, isn't it?'

'I guess.'

We reach a bench that looks out over the Torridge. 'I could do with a cigarette,' I say, and sit down.

'So could I.' She sits beside me.

'Well, you're not having one.'

'Worth a try, eh?' She flashes me a little grin.

'Always worth a try. And when you're eighteen you might succeed.'

Gosh. Did I just say I'll still know you when you're eighteen? I think I did. Well, I never.

The bracelet is branding itself on to my skin under my jumper.

Do I tell her? Or do I carry on with the same old half-truths and keep the peace?

She plunges her hands up her sleeves like a muff and stares out at the water. The tide is in, and laps at the bank beneath the quay. 'It's nice here,' she says.

'It is. I had no idea.'

'I came down here a couple of times when I was staying. It's good around here, on a bike. I even went to Ilfracombe, one day.'

'Shame he couldn't hold off till the summer,' I say. 'Then we could've gone for a paddle.'

'Uh-uh.' She sniffs again. There's a lot of moisture in the air, though the rain has held off well. 'A lot of quicksand out there.'

'Really? Quicksand? Like in the cowboy movies?'

'Yep. Coastguard's always having to turn out to fish the tourists out, apparently.'

'Blimey.'

'I know.'

'Oh, well. I guess that's why it's still a town, not a collection of holiday homes.'

'Yeah,' she says. 'That and the shipyard, of course. Not too many Londoners wanting to send little Johnny out to build sandcastles unsupervised, and they hate it when people are actually *making* stuff in the countryside.'

The joke kicks some thought off in her and she goes quiet again. I smoke my fag and wait, and after a minute or so she says, 'Mila, what do *you* think happened?'

I don't need to ask what she's talking about. 'I don't know, Rubes. I honestly don't know.'

Even less so now.

'What you said before. About Mummy. All those conspiracy theorists on the internet. Why was everybody blaming her?'

'Human nature, my love. The general misogyny of group-think.'

Ruby frowns. She doubts me. Oh, little girl, you're growing up far too fast this weekend.

'If there's a cause, it has to *have* a cause. It's only logic, isn't it? And if there's a woman in the mix you can bet your backside she'll be the one to blame. Just think about the way they all danced in the streets when Thatcher died. When people get it into their heads that a woman is powerful her power becomes legendary, but never in a good way. Thatch ended up being some kind of all-powerful mistress of the dark arts rather than an ideologue with a talent for deafness.'

'But . . . it's women doing it, most of the time. It's all "Stacey's Mum" and "Little Angel".'

'Oh, Ruby. Hate to tell you this, but women can be the worst misogynists of all.'

'But *why*?' she wails.

'I don't know. Stockholm syndrome? Fear of change? Self-loathing? Getting in there first so the men don't turn it on them?'

'But she wasn't even *there*.' Her hands come out of her sleeves and she starts circling her thumbs. Glares down at them.

'Facts,' I say grandly, 'rarely get in the way of righteousness.'

I think about Claire. All alone facing the blame while her husband refused to even behave as though anything had happened. Dogshit through the letterbox and green-inked envelopes. I'm so ashamed of my own part in it all. It was so easy for me and India. A great big I-told-you-so that let us feel smugly that we'd been right all along. I remember her standing there at a press conference a few days after Coco had vanished, the rest of the Jackson Associates grouped together four feet away, literally distancing themselves as they realised who the company scapegoat was. Her face, prematurely lined and blank with fear

290

and heartbreak. And the die-cunt-die types on the comments sections, the shouters in the street, the as-a-mother-myself columnists earning their silver coins with their think-pieces, all agreeing the following day that she wasn't upset enough. You can't win, of course. If she'd cried until she burst, they'd have said she was acting.

Ruby stirs. I wonder if I can get away with lighting another cigarette while we're still sitting. There's nothing like restrictions to make you want to cram as much in between times as you can. My nicotine levels are seesawing like a seagull in a hurricane. Ah, dammit, I think, and light another.

'You know those boxes? In the hall?'

She's not talking about Blackheath. 'Yes.'

'They've been there ever since we moved in, you know. They were in storage before that, but when we moved in she brought them out and just left them there. And she never goes into them. Not ever.'

'Do you know what's in them?'

'Do you think I just power down when she goes out?'

Cheeky bint. 'So what's in them?'

'Everything,' she says. 'Her whole life, from before. All of it. Designer clothes and shoes and bags and perfume and face cream that's gone to wax and photo albums from before us and jewellery, all just chucked in together the way Simone did with Dad's stuff. Everything.'

'I don't suppose she has much use for them in your new life,' I venture.

She treats me to a snort of contempt. 'Oh, please. Why not just get rid of them, then? Throw them away? Sell them? Seriously: we could probably buy a house with what's in those boxes. Why's she still keeping them, making a mess of our whole house so we can't walk up the hall without turning sideways?'

291

'I guess she's just not there yet?'

'Where? Not where?'

My house is full of the same. The brain rewires itself wrong all the time. We moved so often when we were young, and all our stuff would get 'edited' when we did it, and it's left me constitutionally incapable of throwing anything away. In one of my many boxes is my teddy bear. I stopped using it when I was nine – I remember making a deliberate decision to stop – but throwing it away would feel like cutting out an internal organ. Someone else will do it, eventually, when my dead body is found eaten by cats. They'll pause with it in their hand, feel melancholy, then they'll stuff it into a black bag and my childhood will be gone at last.

'It's a holding pattern,' I tell her. The past put away, but still there, always there, to sabotage you.

'The photo albums are the worst,' she says. 'She had loads of friends once. There's all this stuff from when she was at university, and she's looking so happy. Surrounded by people, you know, boys, girls, people her own age, and they're all having fun and hugging and laughing and dressing up for parties, and it's almost unbearable.'

I hadn't even realised that Claire had gone to university. God, we were so absorbed by our own hurt it never occurred to us to ask her questions about herself. Besides, I never thought of the Wives as anything other than addenda to Sean, as though they only came into being when he turned his holy gaze upon them. And it probably suited him that way.

'And now she's sad all the time,' says Ruby, 'and no one comes to see us.'

My father knew what happened to Coco.

'Ruby,' I ask, 'do you think it would make a difference? If she knew? What happened?'

'Why?' She glances at me suspiciously. 'Do you know something?'

I back off, sharpish. 'No. No, nothing like that. Just a question. Just wondering.'

She turns away. She always turns away when she's going to say something that makes her uncomfortable. 'I fucking hate Coco for what she did to us,' she says, and starts to cry.

'Oh, Ruby,' I say. I think she takes it as a reproof, because she wraps her arms around herself as though she has a stomach ache. I put an arm round her shoulder, and she cries harder.

'It doesn't fucking *matter* what happened, does it? The damage is done now. Who *cares* if she's away with the gypsies or buried in an unmarked grave? It doesn't matter! The whole world hates us and my mum won't let me out of her sight and it's all her fault. She's just a – a fact. I don't even remember her, not really. She's a bit of history, a conspiracy theory like Princess Diana. I don't *want* to know. I don't *care*. I just wish people would stop bringing it up, or bringing it up by avoiding the subject, or asking me how my mother is as if I'd ever say *anything* other than that she's fine. I just hate it. I hate her. I can't even go to *school* because of Coco.'

I throw away my butt and finally wrap her in a hug. Smell her hair pressed against my face and realise that she smells like India. Smells like Sean. Smells like family. I wonder if Emma does too? Oh, my little sisters.

'It wasn't her fault, Ruby. I know it's unfair, but it wasn't her fault any more than it was yours.'

She raises her tear-streaked face. 'But what if it *was*? What if it was something I did?'

I put a thumb on to her cheek and wipe away the wet. Give her another squeeze. How do you explain the randomness of the universe to someone who's looking for comfort?

'I mean . . . ' Another sob catches in her throat. 'Why did he take her and not me?'

No answer to that. I hug her more and let her cry. Think about Claire and all her boxed-up finery, pretending to live but unable to let go of the past. What good will it do, raking it all up again, stirring the hornets' nest? Will she find it easier if she knows that someone who can no longer speak knew the answer to the riddle? Oh, God, oh, Sean, what did you do? Jimmy knows something. He couldn't have been making that clearer if he'd tried. And that means they *all* know something. What do I do?

Her breathing slows and she takes a great gopping snort through her blocked nose. Disentangles herself and sits back. But I give her a hand and she holds it.

'Sorry,' she says.

'Don't be. Better out than in, you know?'

'I guess,' she says. 'Never seems to feel like it, though.'

'No. I don't know why they say it, really. It's patently bullshit.'

'Just something to say, I guess,' she says, 'when someone's just made a spectacle of themselves.' She gives me a watery smile. 'Thanks, Mila.'

'Thanks for getting my name right.'

'Oh, I know! Why do they do that?'

'Have you noticed many signs of them listening to a single thing anyone else says? Come on.'

'Huh. No. Joe's nice, though.'

'He does seem to be. Won't break any mirrors, either.'

She doesn't respond to that. Thought so. Our Ruby has a bit of a Thing for the Gavila boy. Can't say I blame her. If this were London and I didn't know who he was and he walked into a bar, I'd be dragging him home and giving him the full Older Woman experience myself.

'They're all okay, actually,' she says. 'They're the only ones who aren't mad, really.'

'Even Simone?'

'Not fair. You can't tell, when she's such a mess.'

'Yeah. You're a better person than I am, Ruby. But I knew her when she was young, of course. We could never work out how she managed to be part of that family.'

She's quiet for a moment. 'I miss him, you know.'

'Yup.' I've been missing him all my life, it feels like.

'I know I shouldn't, but I do. Even though he was a crap dad. How fucked-up is that?'

'Yeah. Life's more complicated than that, though, isn't it? You can't love someone into being good and you can't stop loving them as if there's a switch inside. People have carried on loving far worse people than Sean Jackson. You've just got to live your way through it.'

'S'pose,' she says. 'Shit, I could do with a hot drink.'

'And I could do with a warming whisky. Want to go to the pub?'

'Am I allowed?'

'Jesus, your mother's not prepared you for *anything*, has she?'

'I told you,' she says.

We get up. 'All right, all right,' I tell her. 'People who don't listen to other people.'

There's a pub a hundred yards away; one of those foursquare Georgian things that hide a history of criminal endeavour beneath a veneer of respectability. I know, because it's called the Smuggler's Arms. We walk in silence arm-in-arm through the dark, the slosh of water to our left somehow comforting. And we push open the door to the saloon bar and find ourselves face to face with Jimmy Orizio.

Chapter Thirty-Four

2004 | Sunday | Maria

For Maria Gavila, every crisis is an opportunity to show her competence. It's been that way since she was a child. You grow up in the chaos of a family that's given up, living on an estate that's given up, in a city that's given up, and you have one of two choices: give up yourself, or become the one who refuses to give in. The one who gets out.

Already, she's making lists in her head. She itches to get to her Palm Pilot – no, no records: paper, it needs to be, and everything written one sheet at a time so no one who's looking for secrets can dredge them up from the lower sheets with some patience and a soft-lead pencil – and get the notes jotted down ready to tick off. Lists are Maria's life-blood. In a world where everything operates on a need-to-know basis, being in charge of the lists makes you God.

'Take Joaquin first,' she says. 'He's the heaviest, so he's the one most likely to wake up first.'

The others gawp. Maria is used to other people being behind the curve where reality is concerned. She and Robert have built up an entire fortune predicated on the fact that most people only consider the consequences of their actions after they've taken them and the consequences are making themselves apparent. Even while she was going along with the plan – weighed up the odds on it going wrong, found them so small she decided the convenience was worth the risk – her brain was going tick, tick, tick with contingencies. How to present as an accident if a trip to Casualty became a necessity, who to call for a charcoal flush. And this. This worst of all outcomes. So unlikely that it was only habit that had made her consider what she would do at all.

'Shouldn't we call an ambulance?' asks Imogen.

Jimmy, of course, is right there with her. They've had enough what-happens-on-tour-stays-on-tour rock-star messes to clean up in their time, from addictions to beatings to helicopter admissions to a private hospital most people on the outside think of as a psychiatric facility, for him to know exactly what is needed now. There's a reason why record companies hire Jimmy. He may spend most of his time out of his head, but he has an uncanny knack for snapping into sobriety when there's a mess to sort out. And this is a mess. An almighty, suppurating mess with a dead child in the middle, and it will bring them all down.

'She's dead, Imogen,' he says. 'There's nothing an ambulance can do.'

Sean gasps for air down on the floor. But he doesn't argue.

Maria knows this: that there is a window in time, when they've had a shock, in which people's brains hang, like computers overloaded by information, and they will stand there desperate for someone to tell them what to do. If someone doesn't step into the breach, chaos will ensue. Linda is close to starting up again with the gibbering, and if she does that it's only a matter of time before she attracts the attention of someone from the outside.

She kicks her shoes off. Though they make her taller and more authoritative, there are times when the practical is essential. 'Come inside,' she says, and holds open the door to show those on the threshold the way. Imogen glances back at the house as though she's considering making a run for it. 'Come on,' says Maria, all business. '*In.*'

Imogen obeys. She will never be a problem. She dresses to look formidable, but Imogen is one of life's followers. She would never tolerate that blustering fool of a husband if it were any other way. Charlie follows her, and stands in the corner like an overgrown schoolboy who's been given a telling-off. Robert drops his head and follows suit. This is how they work, the two of them, always have: Maria the one with the instant response, Robert the one who considers the case law and issues a cerebral solution. She's the speaker, of the two of them, the persuader, and he's ceded authority to her because it's her skills that are needed now.

Sean is sobbing. Big tears drop from the end of his nose on to the waxen face, but no one pays him heed. They're all looking at Linda, who hangs back on the gravel, her phone in her hand.

'Come inside, Linda,' says Maria. The seconds are ticking by in which she will have any influence at all. Once Linda goes off-piste, there will be no controlling the situation.

Simone crosses the room and kneels down beside Sean. Gives Linda a look that says, 'This is what *you* should be doing,' and lays a hand on his shoulder, forearm draped down his back. With her long hair she looks like a water-nymph in her nightie. She slept last night in the maid's room up at the house, at Sean's suggestion. As the annexe is next to the pool, they all know why now. She puts out her other hand and wraps it round his wrist. Sean sucks in a huge gasp of air and melts against her. She props him up as he sobs.

Linda steps inside. Maria closes the door.

'We need to talk,' she says.

'No,' says Linda. 'No, no, no, no.'

I wish I had a phone with me, too, thinks Maria. You always look as if you mean business if you're wielding a phone. Not that my phone would be much use to me now. There are any number of people who will clean up messes for a price in my address book, but even their fluid morality would be tested to the brink by these circumstances.

Everyone else is silent as the kids sleep on. She's not turned the light on – doesn't want to show them the scene in all its horrid detail, because she needs to be allaying emotion, not ramping it up – but dim morning light seeps through the slats in the shutters and shows their seven faces, white and grey. Sean and Simone look up at her from the floor. Jimmy has started circling the room checking pulses, as though he distrusts Simone to have done the job properly.

'Let's get something straight,' she says, and looks Linda straight in the eye as she says it. 'If we do what you want to do, we're fucked. Every single one of us.'

She chooses the swear word deliberately, enunciates it hard so that Linda jumps slightly when she says it. It's Linda she needs to get on side, and penetrating her self-absorption is a job of work. The others have taken in the gravity of their situation already, and stare at her as though she were a messiah come to save them all.

'Do you understand?'

'But—' says Linda.

'No. No buts. No one's going to look at this scene and say that it was an accident. We have six drugged children and one dead one. What do you think they're going to see, if you bring them here?'

A muscle works in Linda's jaw. She's thinking she can lay the blame on everybody else, thinks Maria. She still thinks she can somehow wriggle out of this scot-free.

'It was you who suggested it, Linda,' she says.

Linda is aghast. 'No, it wasn't. It wasn't!'

'Oh, it was,' says Maria, and lets the threat hang in the air.

'We were all there,' says Charlie. Never slow on the uptake where his own interests are concerned. He can see himself now, she thinks, the disgraced MP, no glory of Cabinet, no more non-executive directorships, not even, with a shady death attached forever to his back, fit for *I'm a Celebrity*.

'Yes,' says Imogen, picking it up. 'It was you all right. We would never have thought of it if you hadn't suggested it.'

Linda looks from face to face and her mouth falls open.

'You can't be serious. You *cannot* be serious. It's – you *can't*. She's not even cold yet, and you're . . . Sean!' She appeals to her lover and gets a shaken, shamed look in return. Sean feels emotions, certainly. But they're fleeting, compared with those of the normal run of people. There's no doubt he loved his daughter, but she's already receding into the past and turning into a problem to solve as her body cools.

'Because time is of the essence,' says Maria. 'I'm sorry.'

She's not surprised at her own coolness. She's always cool under pressure. She can take time to feel the emotions when the practical is dealt with. But often, dealing with the practical seems to deal with the emotions as well, and she feels nothing at all.

'I can't believe you. I can't believe you're this hard-hearted, Maria. Don't you understand? Don't you *get it*? Coco's dead. Little Coco. Your goddaughter. I thought I knew you, but I don't know you at all.'

No, you don't know me, thinks Maria. Robert is the only one who knows me. But you're not bringing us down by some sudden conversion into pretending you have principles. Drugging the kids so you can fuck the dead child's father? How do you think that's going to play in court?

'Let's get something straight, shall we?' she says. 'Every single person here is going to jail. No mitigating circumstances. No he's-been-punished-enough. People who do things like this go to prison. For a long time.'

Pour encourager les autres, she thinks. Even Sean is quiet, now, the tears long since dried up.

'Did you think it would just be Sean?' she presses on, staring Linda hard in the eye but knowing that her words will be sending shivers down the spines of everyone there. 'Well, it won't. Every person here has drugged a child or co-operated in it. That's prison, right there, and your kids in care. You think you'll get them back after you get out? Well, hello, Linda. They'll be caught up in the care system forever, and you know what that means.'

Linda starts to sob. Not the celebration you had in mind, thinks Maria, and seizes the advantage. 'And don't think you'll be able to go back to your lives when you get out. Charlie will be out of parliament, Jimmy and Robert will be struck off. I hope you've got some serious savings, Linda, because none of us will ever be earning again. I guess Sean will be all right. Though the whole company director thing gets trickier with a criminal record, let alone the ease of travel to foreign countries. And your social lives are over. How many charity galas are you going to get asked to now? Christ, we won't even be able to walk down the *street* with confidence, once the Great British Public's read all about it.'

It's Sean who speaks first. 'What do you suggest we do?' he asks.

Chapter Thirty-Five

He's propping up the bar and talking at the top of his reedy voice and he's surrounded by people he shouldn't be talking to. The men who were taking pictures outside the gate are there, and a hard-looking woman with a gammy eye and a tape recorder, and several other people who could be fascinated locals or could be more of the same. The pub is half empty. Or half full, depending how you look at it. Drinking time proper hasn't started yet, and there are pitiful few tourists in Devon at this time of year. No one is talking but Jimmy, and Jimmy is talking a lot.

' . . . they won't want coming out . . . ' he is saying as we come in. 'Oh, I could tell you a few stories. You're coming to the funeral, right? I would if I were you. I might have a few stories to tell, right there.'

'Why don't you tell them now, James?' asks a member of his audience.

Jimmy lifts a shaky finger and taps the side of his nose. 'I know I look like it,' he says from dry, flaky lips, 'but I wasn't born yesterday.'

I make a start at backing out, but Ruby is right behind me, and hasn't really taken in what's going on, and our feet get caught in each other's. And the confusion attracts his eye.

'Well, talk of the devil!' cries Jimmy. The whole pub turns to see who's there. This is probably the most exciting thing to happen in Appledore in January since the last hurricane. 'Come in, ladies, come in!'

We hover indecisively, but then I see recognition dawn on the faces of the press and realise that we've got a choice between brazening it out and being chased through the streets to the car park. I unwind my scarf and step into the saloon bar.

'Shut the door, love,' says the barman, and Ruby reluctantly obeys, looking like a rabbit in a snare but not screaming as loudly.

'How are you doing, Jimmy?' I ask in my most confident voice. 'You missed lunch.'

Jimmy cackles. 'I was in the mood for a liquid lunch, thanks. Gents, have you met Camilla and Ruby Jackson, aka *the daughters*?'

'Two of them,' I say, and the 'gentlemen' all regard us as though we're a pair of stray lapdancers.

'Can I get you a drink?' asks the man who shouted in my ear as I stood outside the gate on Thursday.

'No, thanks,' I say, and don't look at him as I say it. I'm longing for that whisky, down in one, but I guess it will have to wait, now. 'How are you, Jimmy? We've been looking for you for hours.'

'Getting there,' he says, meaningfully, and raises his pint glass to his face. 'Tell you what, gents. If you want a quote I'd start with them two.'

'We're all very upset,' I say smoothly, 'as is appropriate when we've just lost our father. Is this where you're staying, Jimmy?'

'Oh, that's a point. Got any rooms, John?'

The barman polishes a glass with ill-concealed disdain and doesn't respond.

'Got any rooms, John?'

'Oh. Sorry. Were you talking to me? Only my name's Terry. And no. We're all booked up.'

Jimmy tuts. 'Generic, innit?'

'Yeah,' says Terry, 'we don't actually do generic round these parts. People tend to think it's disrespectful.'

'Woooo!' cries Jimmy, and laughs. If it weren't for the sort of spending you get when the press are in a pub I suspect he'd have been out on his ear some time ago.

The woman with the gammy eye lights on Ruby. 'Are you the twin?' she asks. The twin. Nice. I can see how it must be, to have no legitimacy in your own right.

'Not any more,' says Ruby. She's quite composed for someone who's barely left the farm.

'Crikey,' says someone, 'they're going to have to redo the photofit.' And a couple of people laugh. She stiffens.

'Okay,' I say, 'we're out of here. Just wanted to check you were okay. Night, all!'

I usher my sister out of the door. 'Fuck,' I say, 'that was a close one.'

'My mum says it's rude to comment on people's physical appearance,' she says.

'Yes. That's why. Wanker.'

'I suppose he has a point,' she says. 'I'm not the moppet I once was.'

'No. You're lovely. I wouldn't like you half as much if you were some simpering bubblehead. Come on.'

We hurry along the quay to put some distance between us and the pub.

'What's he up to?' she asks. 'I thought he said he didn't have any money.'

'Oh, lord. People have different ideas of what "no money" means. As long as he's making other people buy him drinks, I should think he's fairly content right now.'

'But where will he sleep? That barman was lying about the room, wasn't he?'

'Wouldn't you?'

'Fair point.'

'He'll probably sleep in his car,' I say. 'I'd be surprised if he hasn't been doing that a fair bit lately, wouldn't you?'

'Ugh,' she says. 'No wonder he smells. Did he even have a bath, while he was at the house? He smells like dry rot. What was he going on about? About the funeral?'

'I don't know,' I say. 'He's full of shit, Ruby, I wouldn't let it worry you.'

So easy to say that, but I'm worried. They're all so damn shifty, shutting each other up and whispering in corners, hustling the Clutterbucks off to their hotel when they'd barely landed. Every one of them knows what happened, I think. Even Simone, and she's pretty much hollowed out inside. He wasn't a charitable man, my dad. He only ever did things that benefited other people if there was a banquet and an auction involved. Why would he have been keeping Jimmy all these years out of the goodness of his heart?

It takes five presses of the Blackheath buzzer before anyone answers. Then Joe's voice rattles out into the night air. 'Oh,' he says. 'Have you been there long?'

'A while.'

'Sorry,' he says, and buzzes us in.

The house is dark. Not even the light over the front door that greeted us when we first got here. Joe switches it on as we get the shopping out of the boot and stands at the top of the steps, waiting for us. 'Sorry about that,' he says.

'That's okay. Not your fault,' I say. 'Where is everybody?'

'Simone's in bed. The nanny's come and taken Emma up to the playroom. Everybody else is in the drawing room. Mr Clutterbuck's back.'

I'm a bit surprised to hear that. The buzzer is right by the front door and they must have heard it. But then, I think about the Clutterbucks and it doesn't surprise me any more.

Like a crab on a beach. Drawn by the scent of carrion. 'We've got some stuff,' I tell him. 'Bread and potatoes and milk and vegetables and that. And some cheese and charcuterie. I didn't get any meat, because I didn't know what to get. I can always go back tomorrow.'

'No, you're all right,' he says. 'The freezer's so full of meat you can barely shut it. All organic, of course, or shot by Sean.'

He remembers he's talking to the bereaved, gulps the words back and looks uncomfortable.

'He did love killing things,' I say. 'I guess it's how he exercised his inner psychopath.'

He smiles, relieved, and takes Ruby's bags. 'Thanks for these. I was trying to make a fish pie, and I was running low on spuds *and* milk.'

'Oh, great,' I say, 'a useful man.'

He grins. 'Anything to stop Simone from coming down and starting another production number. There's an entire suckling pig in that freezer. She needs to rest. She's exhausted. I don't think I'm very good at this sort of thing, though. I've had three goes at making béchamel and it just comes out as a series of lumps.'

The drawing-room door is closed. I can't hear voices from

behind it. Perhaps they just really didn't hear the buzzer. I'll have to go in and tell them about Jimmy. It's the last thing I want to do. I want to go upstairs and fling myself on my bed and think. Or not think. Not thinking would be a great luxury.

'I'll show you,' says Ruby. 'Can't have lumpy béchamel.'

'Great,' he says, and leads the way back to the kitchen. I hear them laugh as they turn the corner by the stairs. He's a cool drink of water, that boy. I wish I had my time over again. Maybe I wouldn't have turned out so cynical.

I take a breath and push the door open. A murmur of voices, cut short as the door opens.

'Hello, Milly!' says Maria in that false-bright tone that tells you you're interrupting. They're scattered across the sofas – period-appropriate sofas, Knowleses and chesterfields, covered in brocade as shiny as the day it was put on. If Simone sells up, the Elite Group could take it all wholesale, install a reception desk in the front hall and run it as a business from day one.

'Did you have a good time?' asks Robert.

'Yes, it was nice,' I say. 'Appledore is totally ceramic-cottage. We got some more vodka, and some tonic.' I hold up my shopping bag to show them.

'Oh, well done,' says Maria.

'Not much use for that now,' says Charlie. He's drinking armagnac, I notice; the Janneau bottle on a coaster on the side table, within arm's reach. Must have got through the VSOP, I guess.

'Oh, talking of which, we found Jimmy. He's propping up the bar at the Smuggler's Arms.'

'How predictable,' says Charlie.

'He's holding forth,' I say, 'and those hacks who were outside the front gate seem to have tracked him down.'

A frisson runs round the room. Yes, I think, you all know.

Know something, at least, that you don't want the rest of the world to be sharing.

'Oh,' says Maria.

Robert makes a weary grunt and starts pulling himself to his feet. 'The Smuggler's Arms, you say? Where's that?'

'On the quay in Appledore.'

'Of course it is,' says Maria. 'He's always liked a seafront boozer.'

'Seafront, town centre, suburbs. Frankly he's fine with all of them,' says Robert.

'So much for no money,' says Charlie.

'I don't think he's buying his own drinks.'

'When did he ever?'

'Okay,' says Robert. 'Well, I'll see what I can do. Charlie, come with?'

Charlie starts to haul himself from his seat. 'I don't know how much success you're going to have,' I say. 'He looks pretty dug in.'

He pulls the vodka bottle from the supermarket bag, cradles it against his hip. 'I'm sure this will help. And if there's one thing I do know, it's never too long before he pops out for a smoke. They haven't got a garden, have they?'

'Tables overlooking the water.'

'Okay,' he says, and they leave.

Chapter Thirty-Six

2004 | Sunday | Sean

The list is written. The women are scurrying about the house, putting children and their accoutrements back in bedrooms before they wake up, clearing the house of all signs that anything other than the most sedate of family weekends has been going on here. Empty bottles have been removed, one by one to mask the noise, from the recycling bins into cardboard boxes to take up to the big bins at the superstore along with Coco's mattress and pillow. The tops and tables will be scrubbed and polished until they look newly installed, the floors swept and washed, corners scoured for stray evidence. And meanwhile the men are going to dispose of the biggest evidence of all.

They don't speak. Not just because voices carry at six in the morning, but because they are all of them robbed of speech. They can't meet each other's eyes. Sean Jackson and Charlie Clutterbuck and Robert Gavila, walking silently together down the drive with their lifelong burden. Jimmy is asleep. Probably a good thing.

Sean is already rewriting his narrative in his head. Self-blame is not an emotion that lingers long in his psyche. It's not my fault, he thinks as he carries the body of his daughter in an old rubble bag that they have found stuffed against one of the walls of the floor-to-ceiling kitchen cupboards. If Claire had any self-control, if she weren't forever falling out with people, we would have had staff this weekend and none of this would have happened. What was I meant to do? I'd been planning for it for months, spent thousands of pounds. She was sabotaging my birthday and I was just trying to salvage the situation.

Coco weighs far more than she seemed to when she was wriggling and alive in his arms. He understands what they mean now by 'dead weight'. She moves and flops inside the bag like a marionette made of wood.

Sean's heart wrenches. Claire thinks I have no emotions, he thinks, but I do. I remember her puppy warmth, the clambering, the feel of her breath in my ear, the thud-thud-thud of her heartbeat. If anyone knew what I was doing now they would think I was as cold as ice, but I'm not. What would be gained by ruining fourteen lives more than they are already, just because of some notion that 'justice' makes things better? It's all spoiled already. Nothing will bring her back now.

Robert goes ahead as they reach the danger point where the drive joins the entrance to Harbour View and meets the road. There's still over half an hour before the ferry opens for its first trip of the day, but there could still be a queue building up. The people from the opposite end of life's spectrum, the people with whom he has nothing in common: the early-morning hikers, the dive-school runners with their Land Rovers filled with oxygen tanks, the Studland nudists ready for another day fiddling with themselves in the sand dunes behind the beach. All the people who think of the dawn as something you see when you get up, rather than the thing that prompts you to go to bed.

The road is empty. The whole of Poole must be sleeping off their bank holiday hangovers, making the most of the last weekend before retail starts the run-up to Christmas. Robert beckons with one hand and Sean and Charlie shuffle as fast as they can with their shared burden until they are under the cover of the locked digger. A single car drifts past in the local traffic lane, and they hold their breaths until it rounds the corner. The driver is drinking coffee; doesn't even glance in their direction as he passes by. Just a few more seconds of potential exposure and they will be inside Seawings' sheltering boundary.

They break for it, Coco bumping against their shins. He doesn't want to think about it. It's not his Coco any more. Now it's a practical problem that requires a practical solution. And practical solutions are what he's good at.

The garden of Seawings is in a state. Sandy mud churned up by tyres and boots, and those mysterious heaps of stones and painted wood and concrete that builders scatter about them wherever they go like cats marking their territory. The fibreglass shell that will become the swimming pool lies at the top of the bank beside six shoulder-high stacks of the paving stones that will border it once it's installed. Hard to believe that by tonight the whole place will be ready for the landscapers to come in and render it all green again, but he knows that the builders are booked on a late-night ferry from Portsmouth, and if there's one thing he's observed about this recent influx from the east it's that these Polish labourers are far more conscientious than their British counterparts. That man Janusz will magic an army of casuals out of the ether of the Polish support system to turn their hands to the final push if he's even slightly concerned that they won't make it, and his cash bribe will help make sure that he can manage it. Come noon, the grounds will be swarming with summer-tanned, ill-shaven men who will ignore every detail unrelated to the job in hand.

They hug the fence between Seawings and Harbour View as they make their way up the bank. That prune-mouthed old closet case at Seagulls will most likely be sleeping behind his firmly shuttered windows, but it's best to allow for the possibility that he might be lurking in there, keeping watch. They reach the top and glance around them. The only windows that overlook what will be the pool are the master-bedroom windows of Harbour View. There has been a lot of infill building on Sandbanks as its land value rose, but in this little enclave the suburban garden dreams of the original architects remain intact. They cross the mud to the ladder that sticks up above the hole's lip.

The hole is deep, and wet. The excavations have taken it below sea level. Water has seeped from the sandy soil and stands, brackish and uninviting, seven feet down.

'How deep do you think it is?' asks Charlie, his voice suppressed for the first time in his adult life.

'I guess we'll have to find out,' says Sean, and starts down the ladder.

They wait as he steps off the bottom rung and splashes in, knee-deep. The bag lies between their ankles, pitifully small for something so heavy. He paddles a few feet to survey the terrain. As foundations go, it is basic – really just a hole in the earth, the sand sucking wetly at his feet, little effort made even to demarcate between deep and shallow ends. He knows, having installed several of these in his time, that the shell will be lowered in with its drainage and pumps pretty much in place, ready to hook up to the filtration system that's already plumbed in under a manhole at the deep end. It doesn't need to be a carefully shaped hole. As long as it's deep enough for the pool to fit, that's all it needs to be. Rubble will fill it up and make a stable base. And weigh the body down.

We'll put her at the shallow end, he thinks. Away from the business end where the filters are. That way, even if something does go wrong and some nosy plumber has to burrow down into the pipework, he'll never reach far enough in to find anything. He wades back to the ladder. 'Okay,' he says, in a low voice. 'Pass her down.'

He's caught, for a moment, by the feminine pronoun. Stop, he thinks, just stop. You can't afford to think about it. It's not Coco, not your little girl; it's a package that needs disposing of. They'll probably be chucking half the rubble into here, and calling it hardcore.

'How deep is it?' asks Robert.

'A foot, eighteen inches?'

'Christ.'

Don't wig out on me now, Robert.

He can feel himself sinking into the sandy bottom. Shifts his feet and feels a suck. We need to be careful down here, he thinks. Need to keep moving, or we'll get stuck.

'Do we need ballast?' asks Robert.

He thinks. They'll need to take the bag away with them, give it to Imogen to put with the mattress and the pillow when she takes them up to the recycling bins at the big Asda in Bournemouth. Nothing that has been in touch with death can remain at Harbour View. If the police get suspicious, those sniffer dogs can scent a corpse at a thousand paces. It's a bog-standard carrier, as far as he knows, bought from a wholesaler along with a hundred others, but one can't be too careful. 'Probably,' he says, and reaches up for the bag. 'Maybe a couple of those paving stones? They should probably do it. See if you can find any broken ones.'

The two men take a handle each and start to lower the bag over the edge. Charlie groans with the effort, and Sean just has time to feel a tweak of contempt before he takes its full weight with stretched arms and finds himself staggering backwards. His feet go out from under him and he splashes backwards into the water, the bag on top of him, weighing him down.

Coco's hand slips out of the open mouth of the bag and slaps on to the surface of the water. He stares at it, breathless. She's wearing her bracelet. The sight of that, and the smallness of the fingers, the pale palm turned up towards the azure sky, makes tears fill his throat and hurt his eyes.

'Are you okay?' asks Robert.

It's a struggle to speak. Oh, my darling. My little darling. Best of all my children, I'm so sorry. 'Yes,' he replies. 'Go and get some spades, and a couple of those slabs. I'll be fine.'

He sits and looks at the hand while he's alone. Sean has never seen a dead body unprepared before today. He missed the deaths of both his parents – his father because it was a sudden, tidy heart attack, when he was up in Sheffield at university, his mother because he left the trip to Devon too late, just stayed those extra couple of hours to sign off on a deal to convert some warehouses in Shoreditch, and by the time he reached the hospital she was already laid out, clean and nice and peaceful on the side-ward bed, awaiting the grieving relatives. There's dirt under her finger-nails. How did that get there? he wonders, one of those stupid thoughts that wander through your mind when things are too much to bear. Did we not bathe them last night?

The bracelet looks horribly out of place down here in the gloom: too bright, too clean. He recalls putting it on her, the day they christened the twins at the smart church on Ludgate Hill, some favour Robert managed to pull in via a colleague in one of the Temples. He takes the little hand in his own and holds it. It's cold, unresponsive; still floppy because the air is warm and rigor has yet to set in. He strokes the palm with a thumb; traces the lifeline. It doesn't look particularly short. It runs all the way across to the outer pad. Suddenly there are tears pouring down his face. 'Oh, Coco,' he murmurs. 'Oh, my Coco.'

I can't bear it, he thinks. Nothing of her, no place to visit, no object to love. He touches the bracelet, lets it slide up the wrist. It's loose, and there's still give in the sliding catch. Can I take it? He thinks. It's something of her. If I keep it near me I can look, from time to time, remind myself that she was here, once.

It's a stupid thing to do, he knows it is. But Sean is overtaken by an unaccustomed flood of sentiment and the bracelet, at least in this moment, feels horribly important, as though it contains a part of his daughter's soul. He glances up at the sky above his head. If they look over the edge now, he thinks, I won't do it. But he can hear them some distance away, the rasp of stone on stone, and he carries on. Pulls the clasp to its full extent and slides the bracelet over the hand. It's small and surprisingly heavy in his own. Pure gold, he thinks. Nothing but the best from the Gavilas. He slips it into the breast pocket of his polo shirt and does up the button.

Chapter Thirty-Seven

I can't. I just can't.

I know nothing about my father. Even the things I *did* think I knew, I know no longer. And on Monday I have to stand up in front of a churchful of people and give an account of his life. I know what's expected of me. I've been to funerals where the dead person was far younger, far less high-achieving, than Sean – people who had done nothing at all with their life other than empty themselves out with drugs and drink till there was nothing left to sustain their bodies – but still the speaker made their life seem rich, their character full and lovable, the people left behind bereft yet glad that once they were there.

And all I have is a blank sheet of paper. Well, blank apart from the words 'Dad Eulogy' written at the top and the collection of spiky doodles that are all I have produced in two hours. Downstairs, the house is quiet, footsteps occasionally passing along corridors but otherwise nothing. There will be no dinner tonight. Joe's leaving the fish pie for people to help themselves and everyone has retired to separate rooms as though the thought of any more communal time is frightening.

What do I say? Robert's talking about the achievements: the houses built, the money made, the public face. I have to do the daughter. The happy family memories, the anecdotes that will make them laugh and cry. And my mind is blank. All I can think is this: *what was that bracelet doing there? What was it doing there?*

It's seven o'clock. Time moves on and on so fast and the funeral will be upon me before I'm done if I don't get it started now. I decide to try a list. India likes lists. She says they're the basis of all life. She says that no reasonable person can do any complicated task without them. Maybe she's right. I start. 'Things I know about my Dad,' I write, below the headline.

Five minutes later, the page looks like this:

He liked good wine.
He had four wives.
He moved house every six months.
He spent at least two weeks in Cap Ferrat every year.
Neither my mother nor Claire has ever been to Cap Ferrat again.
He once met Saddam Hussein. He did not call him indefatigable.
With the exception of Linda, each of his wives was considerably younger than the wife before had been when he married them.
He married for the first time at 32, for the second time at 44, for the third time at 52 and for the fourth time at 57.
His wives, when he married them, were 32, 27, 45 and 22.
His third wife was there the night his second marriage broke

up. His fourth wife found his third wife's dead body when she came to visit with her parents.

With the exception of my mother, the Gavilas introduced him to every one of his wives. Claire was a baby PR person, recently promoted from a PA, low down in their team and working her way up, when she met Sean at one of their Christmas parties. Linda was attached to Jimmy Orizio, who was attached to many of their clients. Simone was their daughter. A more suspicious person would think it was deliberate.

He smoked three fat cigars every day of his adult life.

None of us ever met our grandparents.

He voted LibDem, apart from in 1997 when he voted Conservative (Charlie probably doesn't know this).

He had five daughters. By the time he died, three were out of touch, one was missing presumed dead and the fifth was too young to have a choice in the matter.

I have the bracelet from the missing kid.

Fuck.

I have to have a change of scene. This is getting me nowhere. These bland surroundings, the could-be-anywhereness. Something new to look at might jog my mind. On the far side of the lawn, down by the swimming pool, I noticed a fussy little Roman temple when I was down with Ruby and Emma this morning, put up by some Devonshire squire who fancied himself a global traveller in the 1800s and barely restored by Sean. It's all moss and chipped marble; but sheltered from above and deliciously isolated. I won't be able to hear Charlie booming from there, won't even really be able to see the house from behind the trees. I grab a blanket and my notebook and go in search of a torch.

*

Cold. These near-the-sea places never really get that crisp cold you get further inland. The garden is dank and dripping, and wears that air of winter neglect, everything straggling and waiting for shears and binder twine to bring it back to order. The ground is slippery and the bushes look as though they're lying in wait, as I catch them with my torch beam. I almost turn back. But back is worse, in its way. It'll be fine when you're there, I tell myself. Once you've got your back to a pillar and you can see what's in front of you. Once your eyes have adjusted to the dark.

I'm so intent on keeping my footing that I don't notice that the folly isn't empty until I'm too close to turn back. Jump in shock when I see her at first, then realise who it is.

She's lying on a curved bench, wrapped in a blanket. Her hair has come loose, and tumbles in tangles down towards the leaf-strewn floor. She is so still that for a horrible moment I wonder if she's dead. I consider backing quietly away and fleeing back to the safety of the house. But no. I have to be bigger than all these feelings. I clear my throat and speak.

'Simone?'

She moves slowly, like an animal emerging from hibernation. Raises her head from the arm that's been supporting it and turns her face slowly to look at me. She's crying. A slow, thick wash of tears coats her cheeks, runs in rivulets down the side of her nose. She looks at me blankly, as though she doesn't know me; she's dazzled by the torch, of course, but there's more than that. She's gone from Echo to Andromache to First Mrs Rochester. I'm not sure if she even really registers that I am there.

I want to run. I want to run so fast. Go and find someone else to deal with this. Simone is nothing to do with me. She was his choice, his damage. I sit down carefully on the bench, keeping my movements slow as though she were a feral cat I didn't want to startle. 'Are you okay?' I ask. 'Is there anything I can do for you?'

She doesn't answer. Sits up on the bench and pulls her heels into her buttocks, wraps her arms round her shins and stares and stares.

'What are you doing here?' she asks, eventually, in her little-girl voice.

'I – I'm trying to write the eulogy and I thought . . . I'm having trouble. I thought maybe if I came away from the house . . . '

'Yes,' she says. 'What a sensible plan.'

Oh, lord.

'It's a beautiful house,' I say, experimentally.

'It was,' she says. 'It will be again. Once we get it back to ourselves, Emma and me. Once you've all finished and gone.'

I jolt. She's not balanced, Camilla. Don't take it personally. She doesn't know what she's saying. I had no idea my father could have produced such grief, but she's fairly much out of her mind.

'I can't be in there right now,' says Simone. 'It's like having my whole life sucked away.'

'Oh, love,' I say. 'I think I understand.'

'No, you don't.' Her voice hardens. 'If you understood, you wouldn't be here.'

'Wow,' I say. I can't stop myself: it's out of my mouth before I know it's there. But God, Simone, you're not the only person. 'He was my father,' I say.

Her tears have dried up. She wipes her puffy eyes with a corner of her blanket and looks at me the way a duchess looks at a salesman. 'Oh, come on,' she says. 'You didn't love him. None of you loved him. I was the only one who loved him properly. And he loved me.'

Another wow bubbles up, but I clamp my jaw over it. And all the other things I want to say. Like: didn't you notice the way he died, Simone? Does that look much like love?

'He was the best, best man,' she continues. 'And *none* of you could see that. I remember the way you used to talk to him, Camilla, don't think I don't. He was strong and brave and generous, and he did everything for you all, but all you could manage was sneering.'

Must not. I must not. 'I'm sorry you feel that way, Simone,' I say. 'I think it was a bit more complicated than that.'

'Not really,' she says. 'Poor Sean. I'm only glad he got to be loved the way he deserved, eventually.'

'So am I,' I say, because yes, obsessive possessiveness, and ignoring every inconvenient truth, might well have been exactly the sort of love that Sean deserved, in the end. It was the sort of love he specialised in giving, after all.

'It's freezing cold out here,' I venture. 'Do you think we should go in?'

'No,' she says. Then she ploughs on. 'He was the only person who ever loved me,' she says. 'He said he wished he'd waited all those years, you know. He said he felt like his whole life started when he met me.'

I'm sure I've heard this phrase before. Where? Claire? Yes, maybe Claire.

'You lot know nothing about love,' she says. 'Even Daddy and Maria don't really understand how big it was, that thing between us. And they'd do anything for me, just the way I would have done for him. Anything. And I did. I did everything for Sean. Everything. Nothing before me matters. Do you understand?'

And how's this going to help me get my eulogy done? Maybe you want to do it yourself? I'm sure everyone will want to hear about your great romance. 'Oh, Simone,' I say. 'I'm so sorry.'

'Oh, whatever,' she says. 'Anyway. We'll all just go through the motions, eh? You can pretend you cared and I can pretend I think you did, and once the funeral's done and dusted you can all go back to your little lives and leave me and Emma alone. We don't want you here, you know. We were happy when it was just the three of us, and Emma and I will be happy when you're gone.'

Chapter Thirty-Eight

2004 | Sunday | Ruby

'Where's Coco?'

Godmother Maria jumps in the air at the sound of her voice. 'Oh, hello, darling!' she says, her hand on her chest. 'You're awake, then?'

'I was sick,' says Ruby, proudly.

'Again?'

'No. When everyone was asleep. Mummy came and put me in the shower.'

'Oh, so *that's* what happened to that sheet.' She glances at the washing machine, going through the drying cycle quietly beneath the sink. 'Poor old you.'

'Where's Coco?'

'She went to the beach with Simone and Mrs Buttercup and Ms Innes and the other children. Joaquin's in the garden, though.'

'Oh,' says Ruby. She likes the beach and she doesn't much like Joaquin. He's too big and noisy.

'We didn't want to wake you up,' says Maria. 'You were sleeping so tight after your nasty night.'

'Oh,' says Ruby again, 'but I'm better now.'

Godmother Maria comes and squats in front of her, strokes her hair off her forehead with a finger. Grown-ups are always stroking her head, or patting it as if she's a dog. Ruby finds it annoying. She can't wait until she's big enough to do it to them.

'Do you know the funny thing?' she asks. 'I could have sworn she was you.'

Ruby giggles. The fact that people can't tell them apart has become a favourite game with her sister. Several times they have swapped their clothes and swapped their bracelets over and pretended to be each other, to see if anyone can tell. Mummy always can, even when they insist that they have the other's name, but they fool Daddy often. When they do it he calls them his Little Criminal Masterminds. She likes that. She doesn't know what it means, but it sounds better than Tiny Drunks, which is his other name for them. And far better than Go Away Daddy's Busy.

'She's playing the game,' she says proudly. 'Fooled you!'

Godmother Maria straightens up, her eyes all wide. 'Why, you clever little sausages! How long have you been doing that for?'

'Ages!'

'Goodness, aren't you naughty? But she had her bracelet on this hand' – she holds Ruby's right arm in the air to show her – 'and Godfather Robert and I got them for you specially so we could tell you apart.'

Ruby giggles, and shows her that she can slide the bracelet over the joint of her thumb.

'Well, I never!' cries Maria, impressed. 'You can still get them off! I thought you were much too much of a big girl now to do that!'

'No, we're still little,' Ruby tells her. 'We're the littlest ones of all.'

'Well, not quite the littlest. Inigo is littler than you, I think.'

'Yes,' says Ruby impatiently. 'We're bigger than *some* children, but we're the littlest *Jacksons*. My big sisters are grown-ups.'

'Almost grown-ups,' says Maria, with her lovely warm smile. 'Tell you what, shall we play the game too? It would be a shame if only Coco was playing it.'

'Daddy will be able to tell,' she says staunchly, though she knows it probably isn't true.

Maria slides the bracelet off her wrist and pops it on to the left one. 'Well, why don't we see?'

'Okay,' says Ruby, and laughs with delight. She's not had a grown-up join in the game before. Well, apart from Mummy, but she sometimes thinks Mummy's only doing it to annoy Daddy. She always goes 'You *see?*' in That Voice when he realises he's been fooled.

Godmother Maria gets her comb from her bag and combs the parting across so it's on the other side. Squats back to look at her handiwork and smiles.

'Coco!' she cries. 'There you are! I thought you'd gone to the beach!'

Ruby giggles with delight.

Joaquin comes in in swimming trunks while she's drinking her juice. His hair is wet and he carries the stick that seems to go with him everywhere, so he can hit things with it.

'Oh, God, Joaquin,' says Godmother Maria, 'you haven't been in the pool? Tell me you haven't been in the pool.'

'It's hot,' he protests.

'Oh, God, why can't you listen to *anything* anyone says? You *know* it's not safe to go in the pool by yourself. I couldn't bear it if we had—'

She breaks off mid-sentence and looks a bit green all of a sudden.

'Chill, Grandma,' says Joaquin, 'I'm a big boy now. And besides, Uncle Jimmy's out there on a sun-lounger.'

'Fat lot of good he'd be if you got into trouble,' she snorts.

Joaquin rolls his eyes and hits the door frame with his stick.

'And put that bloody thing outside,' she orders. 'No sticks in the house. You know the rules.'

The eyes roll again, but he hurls the stick out into the sunlight.

'God preserve me from disobedient children,' she says. 'Your sister was nothing like this.'

'Yeah, yeah, yeah. Simone's perfect, I know. Well, if I can't have any fun here, can I go to the beach?'

'*Please*,' she says. 'And no. I don't have time to take you. And Coco's feeling under the weather. It's too far for her.'

'God almighty,' says Joaquin, 'it's only the beach. What do you think I am? Five?'

'Seven. And they went to the one on the other side. I'd probably get arrested if I let a seven-year-old loose by himself on the chain ferry. And don't swear, Joaquin.'

'That's not swearing.'

'It's taking the Lord's name in vain, which is the same thing.'

'Ooh! Get you! Why aren't you at *church*, Grandma?'

Maria heaves a huge sigh. Ruby watches, fascinated, from her bar stool and pops mango chunks, one by one by one, between her lips. Mangoes are yum. She thinks they're her favourite. She doesn't understand big boys, though. Joaquin doesn't exactly scare her, but she and Coco avoid being alone with him. They're never quite sure what he might do.

Joaquin releases an ngggh of frustration.

'Tell you what,' says Maria, 'let Coco finish her breakfast and we'll pop to the café and get an ice cream.'

'Ooookay.' He sounds mildly mollified. Then, 'That one's Coco? I thought that one was Ruby.'

Ruby beams with delight. 'I'm Coco, stupid!' she cries, and waves her left wrist in the air.

There are lots of cars on the road outside the gate, all sitting in a line, like when they arrived. She feels sorry for all the children in them. They look hot and bored and their parents won't let them out into the lovely sunshine. Godmother Maria holds her hand as they follow the pavement and Joaquin runs ahead, whacking at bushes with his stick. Milly and India call him Whacking, which she thinks is very funny.

'How are you feeling today?' asks Maria. 'You're not feeling sick any more, are you?'

'No. I think I sicked it all up last night.'

'Good-oh. We wouldn't want you to miss Neptune's Kingdom this afternoon.'

'What's Neptune's Kingdom?'

'It's a big water park.'

'What's a water park?'

'You'll love it. Slides and rides and great big pools where you can go paddling.'

She feels herself glow with anticipation. Ruby loves water, far more than Coco does. She can almost swim already, throwing herself up and down the shallow end of the pool in her blow-up ring, flailing her arms, as Coco sits on the steps with her feet barely in the drink and flinches every time a drop from one of Ruby's splashes comes her way. 'Oooooh,' she says.

327

'Well, let's see how you cope with your ice cream,' she says. 'What sort of ice cream would you like?'

'Chocolate.'

'Is that what Coco would have? Cause you're Coco, remember.'

She ponders the subject reluctantly. She adores chocolate. Chocolate and fries, though she doesn't get to eat much of either.

'I bet Coco's having chocolate, if she's being you.'

'Yes,' she says sadly, 'the pink one, then.' She understands that if you're going to tell a lie you have to follow it all the way through.

Joaquin comes barrelling back up the pavement. 'Instead of ice cream,' he says, 'can I have chips?'

'Oh,' says Ruby, sadly again. She'd had no idea that chips were on offer. This early in the day she'd rather have a punnet of hot, salty, crunchy goodness than a soppy strawberry ice. 'I like chippies too,' she ventures.

'Tell you what,' says Maria, 'if you don't tell anyone, I'll let you share a portion of fries between you. How about that?'

Ruby lets go of her hand and claps her own together with pleasure.

'I spoil you,' says Maria, 'I really do.'

She feels very grown-up, out at a café without her sister or either of her parents. She hasn't even wondered where her mother is yet today, or her father. 'Where's Mummy?' she asks over the top of a dish of ice cream so pink it almost matches the naked back of the fat man drinking beer at the next-door table.

'Oh,' says Maria smoothly, 'she had to go back to London, sweetie. She realised she had something to do that she'd forgotten. But Daddy's still here. He'll take you both back up tomorrow.'

Ruby nods. She's a placid child, not prone to panic. If her mother has gone away, she will see her again. The thought of permanent loss has never crossed her mind.

Joaquin has picked a vivid green mint choc chip ice and is squeezing ketchup on to the lid of an open polystyrene package of fries. 'Now don't eat all of those yourself,' says Maria. 'You're sharing, remember?'

The eye-roll again, then he reaches out with a fry between his fingers and dips it into Ruby's ice cream.

'Hey!' she protests.

'Oi!' says Maria. 'You should ask before you do that.'

Joaquin puts the ice-creamy chip in his mouth. 'Sorry, Ruby. Can I dip my chips in your ice cream, *please?*'

'Yuk,' she says.

'Don't knock it till you've tried it, grasshopper,' he says.

'I'm not a grasshopper.'

He dips another chip. Puts it in his mouth with evident glee. Tries it with his own dessert and pulls a 'meh' face. 'Definitely better with strawberry.'

'Honestly, where do you learn these things?' asks Maria.

'Everybody knows about chips and ice cream.'

'Well, I don't.'

'Sorry,' he says. 'Everybody who's not a *million* years old.'

Ruby giggles. She's never heard a child cheeking its mother the way Joaquin cheeks his, but Maria doesn't seem to be taking it badly at all. She's still nervous of his big gangly body and his loud voice, but she admires him now. Joaquin is a risk-taker. He knows no fear. She takes a fry from the box and scoops up a lump of ice cream with it. Looks at it apprehensively – grown-ups are always telling her she will like foods, like spinach and peppers and broccoli, that turn out to be yuk – and screws up her courage to impress the big boy. Puts it in her mouth . . . and a whole world of culinary adventure explodes on her tongue. Up until now, everything she's tasted has been carefully divided on her plate. She has never even known that these things, these tastes and textures, *could* be combined, let alone that soft can make crispy better, that sweet goes so well with salt, that hot and cold taken together can expand the universe. It's horrid and beautiful, wrong and so, so right, all in one fleeting chew.

'Oh,' she says.

'Right?' says Joaquin.

'Oh,' she says.

'Don't tell me *you* like it too,' says Maria. 'God, kids. Can I get you to eat simple buttered peas? Of course I can't.'

She sips her black coffee and watches with a pained look as the two children dive back into creating their hideous snack.

'I had the weirdest dream last night,' says Joaquin. 'I dreamt all you grown-ups came into the room and you were making a great big hoo-ha. And someone was crying. And then when I woke up this morning I was in your room and I thought I'd been kidnapped for a minute.'

'Oh, yes,' says Maria, 'something went wrong with the plumbing in the annexe and the loo started overflowing. When Daddy came in to check on you there was an inch of water everywhere. We had to evacuate you or by the morning you would all have been floating to China.'

Joaquin bursts out laughing. 'No, we wouldn't, silly. We'd have bumped into the Isle of Wight first. Didn't I wake up?'

Maria lets out a hoot of laughter that sounds funny to Ruby. As if she's not really laughing at all, but screaming. But then it's just gone, again, and she's laughing once more. 'When have you *ever* woken up, Joaquin Gavila? I could let a bomb off next to you and you'd just turn over on to the other side. No, we carried you all, one by one, up to the house and Simone was up half the night mopping up, and you all slept right through the whole thing.'

'Freaky!'

'It was very late.'

'So who was crying?'

'Oh, that was Uncle Sean,' she says. 'Realising he wasn't going to be able to put the house up for sale till he'd fixed it. He's very emotional when it comes to money, is Uncle Sean.'

'Cry baby,' says Joaquin, and cackles disdainfully.

'Come on, you two. Finish up that disgusting mess. Coco's daddy will be wondering where you are,' says Maria.

Chapter Thirty-Nine

It's winter dawns like this that make him glad to be alive. When the tourists have slowed to a trickle and the estuary sands are empty, a million shades of red seeping through last night's clouds and the Atlantic still roaring out there to his left. Everyone warned him over and over again that the seaside was different out of season, that he'd find it grim, but it's the grimness that pulled him, always was. John was never a bucket-and-spade sort of person. Angry waters call to his Celtic soul in a way that sunloungers and palm trees never did.

Chip and Canasta run ahead across the sand, daring each other forward to celebrate the day. With their thick Collie coats and the shore full of flotsam, they love the winter too. No children falling over and blaming them, no family picnics or yappy lapdogs, the fishing boats all out until the tide comes in, or on chucks in the boatyard getting their annual overhaul, the rolling stretch of sand and all its tidal pools and secrets there for them alone. A gull swoops down on to a heap of something black – a great tree of weed ripped from its moorings and carried up the river mouth by the tide, some fishing net carelessly dropped from the back of a trawler – and the dogs step up their pace as one, barrel, barking, towards it until it flaps away with a resentful shriek. He doesn't bother to call them. They know better than to go into the water at this time of year, and they have the beach to themselves.

The wind is still high. He's wrapped up tight in his oilskin coat, flat cap clamped over his thinning hair and two layers of gloves to keep his hands from falling off, but his ears are starting to hurt. They have never been the same since that infection twenty years ago: drops in temperature, the pressure of an aeroplane cabin, background music are all nuisances now, his pockets never free of decongestants, but the remains of his Christmas cold is making them hurt actively. He stops and unwinds his scarf from around his neck, wraps it over the top of his head, hat and all, and ties it tight around his chin. I must look like a baboushka out on the Steppes, he thinks. Isn't it amazing how age and comfort will eventually erode away even the most deep-rooted of vanity?

Eight years on, and he still finds it hard to believe how much his life has changed. I was feeling so old in Vauxhall, he thinks. Trying to look as if I was enjoying the scene as the people got younger and younger around me and my body could no longer take the stimulants required to keep up. And here I am now, no more gym body, no more walks of shame. My twentysomething self would have reeled at the thought that I'd end up alone in the middle of nowhere one day, Chip and Canasta the loves of my life, but this is the happiest I've ever been. Appledore's a gossipy little place and getting through the visiting crowds is a pain in the season, but it's great to come out of the flat door in the morning and have your neighbours greet you, and I enjoy the pleasure on people's faces as they find just the *perfect* seaglass necklace, the most *wonderful* water-bleached wooden bail, the *loveliest* rusted coupler in the shop, and so what if they get it home to Basingstoke and wonder what on earth they were thinking?

The howl of wind and the rattle of rain in the eaves at night are always an enticing sound to him, because it means that in the morning the tide will have thrown more of his means of living up the river and on to the sand. He started off selling gaudy glass, trinkets and wind chimes and glinting waterfall mobiles to hang in the window – still does – but the discovery that the estuary is a trove of shipwreck jetsam, that after each storm its shifting sands will reveal something that has lain buried for a hundred, two hundred years, was a moment of pure exhilaration. It's actually better in here than it is out on the sands at Westward Ho!, perhaps because that beach is hardly ever deserted. People love a souvenir of someone else's disaster. The *Titanic* trade seems to get more enthusiastic with every cap-badge those submarines bring up. They'll slosh their holiday money about like drunken sailors if you can throw a few salty sea-dog tales into the mix when they start to finger a verdigris-coated capstan or a blunted whaling hook, and, if there's one thing the wild Atlantic coast has to offer, it's vivid yarns of mass drownings and miracle rescues by the hundred.

The dogs are feeling the morning. Of all the many gifts they have brought to his life, the greatest is the forgetting of age. Out here on the sand the three of them can shed the creep of the years, ignore the aches and the sadness, the fact that there is less time ahead now than there is behind, and simply be. Gentle Chip and snappy Canasta, racing each other in some imaginary hunt, tumbling over themselves in the rush to be first. Just the three of them and a container ship tossing in the far distance on the open sea. John inhales deeply, enjoys the salt pleasure of the sea air.

Head protected, he trudges on towards the edge of the river channel. He knows better than to stand still for any great length of time; though the sand is mostly firm, it has patches that suck liquidly, and a fair number of unwary people have had to be fished out by the coastguard as the waters rose above their chests. He finds a stick – just an ordinary stick, not skeletonised the way the tourists like them – and throws it overarm for Chip, who has trotted back to see what he's doing. The dogs race off in pursuit. For a moment he feels a wobble of fear when he thinks he might have thrown too hard, that they're going to plunge into the fast-flowing river, but it lands a few feet from the water's edge. Canasta, more sprightly and more competitive than kindly Chip, dives past her brother and snaps at it with her hard white teeth. She misses. Dog and stick somersault towards the water in a blur of black and white and flying sand and John holds his breath as he waits for them to land.

She hits, skids, enters the water with a mighty splash. 'Canasta!' he yells, pointlessly, above the wind. Should have done that before, he thinks. Not now. Not now she can't hear you. Not that she would have listened anyway. Bloody dog. So wrapped up in herself she doesn't listen to *anything*, and now I'm going to be one of those people you read about in the papers, drowned as they jumped in to save their dog from floodwater . . .

The wave recedes and Canasta bobs up like a cork, grinning around the stick. She struggles against the suck, then he sees her paws scrabble into the shifting ground, gain traction, pull her forward on to the sand. She bounds a few steps towards land, then stops to shake herself off. That's it, he thinks, that's enough for today. My blood pressure can't take any more of that.

'Come on, you silly bitch!' he calls. Always uses the appropriate noun when her recklessness gets too much. 'Come out of there!'

Chip has come back of his own accord and is sitting at his feet. He leans his chunky body against his leg and grins up at him with friendly, rolling eyes. John chucks him behind the ear, bends down and plants a kiss on his sweet white forehead. How two dogs can come from the same litter and be so different he will never know: Chip soft and gentle and loving, Canasta all bluster and barks.

The girl arrives and he takes the stick from her mouth while she growls and threatens, as she always does. He slings it through the air again, back towards the shoreline, and she races off in pursuit, showers of salt water flying off her. Chip trots sedately after. It lands by the pile of weeds he noticed earlier, and she snatches it up, then drops it and begins to bark. Look! she yells. Look what I've found! Come and see!

Chip lets out a sound that's somewhere between a sigh and a whimper, then falls into stride behind him, huffing, as John obeys orders. Sometimes the things Canasta barks about are indeed worth looking at. Chip, bored by his steady gait, races on ahead to his sister – and joins the barking.

Oh, God, thinks John, and steps up his pace. He reaches the dogs and feels a prickle of cold around his ears despite the scarf. What looked like another piece of marine discardings isn't that at all. It's a man, yellowish skin bloated by immersion in water, long black leather coat that must have contributed hugely to the speed at which his feet have sunk into the sand. He's buried up to the thighs, his eyes and mouth wide open in horror at the approach of the tide that has covered him. And, even in death, he clutches at the neck of a half-drunk bottle of vodka.

Chapter Forty

2004 | Sunday | Janusz Bieda

'Watch out, boss! Here comes trouble.'

Janusz looks in the direction of Tomasz's pointing finger and sees the man from next door stop at the foot of the drive. 'Fucking hell!' he shouts over the roar of the crane's engine, 'What now?'

'What time is it?'

'Twelve-fifteen. If he wants to complain, he's getting this right up his pipework.' He waves the giant wrench with which he's been coupling the flexible pipes attached to the pool liner's outlets to the filtration system, and the men laugh out loud. The atmosphere is cheerful on the site today, despite the heat. After ten days in which most of the crew allowed themselves to feel miserable with homesickness as the prospect of relieving it drew nearer, the fact that they have reached the home stretch has acted like a shot in the arm for them all. Everyone's joking as they throw themselves into scooping rubble into barrows to tip into the extra couple of feet they've dug out from the swimming pool hole, and the casuals he's called in for the day are keen to make a good impression and get on the full-time roster for the next project. Until one minute ago it was looking as though they were going to make their delayed deadline easily. But they can't afford any more delays, if that's what this man's bringing.

The man has one of his little twin daughters with him. They stand beside the tracks of the digger and watch the pool liner swing in the air above the hole, an army of labourers easing it carefully into position. Janusz signals to Gabriel, behind the controls of the crane, and hears the brake go on and the engine stop. A moan of disappointment goes up from the team. He walks over to the slope to greet them; switches to his English-speaking brain as he goes. He's close to bilingual now, even after just nine months, but he still has to concentrate when he switches from one to the other.

'It's afternoon,' he says, by way of greeting. He wants to make it clear from the off that he's not tolerating any more complaints. They've kept to their side of the bargain, but they can't give him any more.

'No, no,' says the man, and gives him a smile that makes him think fleetingly of vampires. For someone who's on holiday he looks exhausted, his rich-man's tan washed out in the bright sunlight. 'Not come to make a nuisance of myself, I promise.'

'Okay,' says Janusz suspiciously, and comes down the slope. Takes his hat off and gives the little girl a tentative smile. She stares for a moment then smiles back. Tiny white teeth and dimples, and the sort of baby-blonde hair that will be mousey by the time she's eight. 'Good afternoon,' he says to her, solemnly. She gives him the big eyes, and sidesteps in behind her father's legs. Suddenly he's missing his own four-year-old, Danuta, so badly it feels as though his heart is strained. She does the same thing when faced with strange adults. Only twenty-four more hours and I'll be with them, he thinks, and then we have a whole month of beautiful autumn days on the banks of the Vistula.

'We just came to say thank you,' says the man. 'We had such a lovely day yesterday, and a marvellous lie-in this morning, and we really appreciate it.'

'Okay,' says Janusz again. There has been no noise from his employers, as the men predicted, and it's looking as though he, Karol, Tomasz and Gabriel will be going home with a nice little tax-free bonus. 'You're welcome.'

'Coco has a present for you,' says the man. 'Come on, darling. Come out from there!'

The little girl steps unwillingly out from behind. Her father bends down and places a cardboard box into her hands. 'Go on, darling,' he says, 'give it to him.'

It's so large and so heavy that she has to hold it in both hands and clutch on tightly, for the fingers can't get a purchase on the corners. She walks forward. She's wearing a pretty little pink dress and jelly sandals with white socks. He smiles at the sight of them. Only a man, he thinks, would take a kid on to a building site in white socks. There are already a couple of brown stains where she has splashed into a passing puddle. 'Thank you,' she says, shyly, clearly reciting a pre-prepared speech, 'for letting Daddy have a happy birthday.'

He bends down and takes it from her before she drops it. It's whisky, in a presentation box.

'Knockando,' says Sean, '1973. A single malt from a good year. Thought you might enjoy something to remind you of England.'

'Thank you,' says Janusz, though he's pretty sure that the whisky comes from Scotland. He nods solemnly at the little girl. 'Thank you, Coco,' he says, 'that's very kind. Where's your sister?'

'They went to the beach without me,' she says mournfully. But then she brightens up. 'But I had chips.'

'That's good,' says Janusz. 'My little girl likes chips too. With mayonnaise. How do you like yours?'

'With ice cream,' she says, confidently. Janusz laughs and the father makes a sort of rumbling noise that he assumes is a sound of humour. 'Together?' he says.

'Yes,' she replies, firmly. 'Strawberry is best,' and he laughs again.

'So how's it all going?' the man asks. He's much friendlier today, the air of arrogance he carried when surrounded by his well-fed friends stripped away in the presence of the child. 'Think you'll make your deadline?'

Janusz nods. 'I think so. Pool's almost in now and the sealant's all mixed, so we should make it.'

'Well, thank you for delaying,' he says. 'It's greatly appreciated. When's your ferry again?'

'Last sailing. Eleven-thirty from Portsmouth.'

'And you're all packed up?'

'Yes. Everything's in the van and ready to go.'

'Terrific,' he says, then repeats the word. 'Long drive? Where are you going to?'

'Krakow. We all come from Krakow.'

'Ah,' he says. 'Nice.'

'You have been?'

He looks a little flustered. Janusz has noticed this about English people: that they can never simply admit to not knowing about something. 'No,' he says, 'but I hope to go, some day.'

Sure you do, thinks Janusz, and tosses his box in his hand. 'Well,' he says, 'thank you for this. But if we're going to get finished before dark we need to get on now.'

'Sure,' says the man. 'Sure. Listen: you guys seem to have done

340

a good job here. And you're clearly adaptable. You don't have a card, do you? Only, I employ construction people a lot, and frankly I'm not crazy about the ones I'm using at the moment.'

'A card? No, I'm sorry,' he says. 'But I have a mobile phone.'

'Great!' He gets out his own, a BlackBerry, the sort of phone owned by people who do a lot of business. 'Let's swap numbers. When are you coming back?'

Janusz reels his number off and Sean types it in. 'In a month, I hope.'

'Great. Let's speak then. What's your name, by the way?'

'Janusz Bieda.'

He sticks a hand out to shake. Better late than never. 'Sean Jackson,' he says. 'And this is Coco.'

He shakes Coco's hand too. His big hand goes halfway up to her elbow. 'Have a lovely day, Coco,' he says.

'I'm going to Neptune's Kingdom,' she confides. 'They have slides.'

'Oh, good,' he says, and makes a mental note to take Danuta to Park Wodny when he's at home. If this little one's old enough for water slides, then she must be too.

He carries his ill-gotten gains back up the slope and signals to Gabriel to carry on. Stashes the bottle in his work bag. He can break it out once they're on the ferry; it'll pass the time and save them money on the four-hour crossing to Le Havre. Funny, he thinks. You can never go by first impressions. If you'd asked me yesterday what Sean Jackson was like I would have said he was an arrogant wanker. I guess he was stressed. Everyone seems to be stressed these days. Especially in this country. You'd have thought that all that money would make them less stressed, but it doesn't seem that way.

The men get into position and the pool liner is gently guided into its final resting place.

Chapter Forty-One

Two solemn policemen. Sturdy country policemen with their hats under their arms, standing on the elegant doorstep as I open up, with that I'm-not-impressed look on their faces.

'Mrs Jackson?'

'I'm her stepdaughter.'

'Oh.' He looks at Ruby, who's lolloped along the corridor behind me, works out that if I'm a stepdaughter then she's certainly not a wife. 'Is Mr Jackson available?'

How funny. You think somehow that everybody knows this sort of thing. 'He's dead,' I say. 'He died three weeks ago.'

A visible ripple of discombobulation. However unimpressed by their surroundings, the police still don't expect people in houses like this to live with disaster. 'Oh,' he says. 'My condolences.'

'Thank you. Can I help you?' I ask. I don't know where anybody else is. I've been hiding in my room all morning, avoiding Simone. If I could I would have left. It's not as though she's not made it clear that it's what she'd like. But you don't. I've been a leaver all my life, a runner-away just like my father, and I have to see this out. At twenty-seven, I fear that I am finally becoming an adult.

'Is Mrs Jackson available?'

'We're getting ready for the funeral. I'm not sure where she is.'

'Oh,' he says again. 'Do you have any idea when she'll be home? We have a couple of questions we need to ask her.'

'If I had any idea where she was, I'd probably have a better idea of when she'll be home. Is there anything I can help you with?'

Simone's voice rings out from the hall behind me. 'It's okay, Milly. Thank you.'

I look round and see that Social Simone has returned with the daylight. When I left her in the dark last night, she looked like a ghost in a Japanese horror movie. Now she's made up and coiffed and dressed in one of those vaguely Moroccan draped-layer outfits that cost hundreds of pounds per piece on Sloane Street despite being made of viscose. Her hair is glossy and held up with a pair of chopsticks and her thin lips stand out against her pale skin in sophisticated scarlet.

She clicks along the corridor in sharp stiletto court shoes. She may be the same age as me, but she looks every inch the stepmother. 'Come in, gentlemen,' she says, with an efficient smile. Not a trace of the despair that filled her face last night, or the desperation that characterised her public dealings at that horrible first-night dinner. My God, I think. She's an accomplished little actress, isn't she? I wonder which one of those faces is real?

'How can I help you?'

He reels slightly, looks from stepmother to stepdaughter and back again, takes control of his manners. 'Mrs Jackson?'

'Yes.' She smiles again.

'Detective Constable Rice. This is Constable Summers. Can

we go somewhere a little more comfortable, Mrs Jackson? We could do with a word.'

'But of course! Come through to the kitchen! I'm sorry. I should have offered you a cup of tea!'

'No need. Thank you,' says the older of the two policemen, and we all trail her up the corridor.

Maria is at the kitchen table, buttering bread, Robert slicing tomatoes very very thinly with a giant chef's knife and scraping them into a pottery salad bowl. They see our visitors and jump to their feet. 'Oh!' says Maria. 'Sorry. I was making some sand-wiches for lunch. Shall I get out of your way?'

'Of course not, Maria,' says Simone, gaily. 'I'm sure there's nothing you can't say in front of my stepmother, is there?'

'I'm Mrs Jackson's father,' says Robert.

A little flicking of eyes. These wealthy types, it says. They must get so confused with all these stepmothers drifting about the place.

They lay their hats down on the table, neatly, side by side. 'I'm afraid we need to ask you a few questions, Mrs Jackson,' says Older Cop. Constable Summers is gazing around him at the stainless steel appliances, the stacks of bone china. I wonder if he's going to ask to use the loo, the way they do on cop shows. He looks about nineteen, and has sticky-out ears, but they don't age so quickly outside London.

'Fire ahead,' says Simone. 'Tea.'

'No, thank you. Just had one. Mrs Jackson, I'm sorry to say that there's been an incident down at Appledore. There's been a body found, caught in the mud in the estuary.'

'Oh, God,' says Maria, and looks concerned. 'How awful.'

'It looks as though the tide caught him. We don't know what he was doing on the sands, but there are patches of quicksand out there and you need to know what you're doing, especially in the dark. Tide was full around midnight last night. So I suppose he must have gone down there a few hours before then.'

'Oh, God,' says Maria, and sits back down. 'Poor man. What an awful way to go.'

Robert doesn't speak, but he lays his huge knife down in the sink. Runs his hands under the tap and dries them carefully on a tea-towel. I know where they're going with this. It's Jimmy who's been making crab food, it has to be.

He continues. 'We found some identification on him, and it identified him as a Dr James Orizio?'

'Oh, God,' says Maria again, and instantly starts to cry.

'I take it you knew him, then?'

'Yes,' she says. 'He's been staying with us. Until yesterday. But I think you probably know that, or you wouldn't be here, would you?'

'And you didn't miss him last night?'

'No. He left yesterday morning. We didn't know where he'd gone. Oh, God. Oh, poor Jimmy. Oh, poor man.' She pushes her chair back, goes and grabs a piece of kitchen towel and blows her nose. Dabs carefully under her eyes and throws it in the bin. So that's the mourning Jimmy Orizio gets at the end of his life. Thirty seconds of tears from the kindest-hearted person he knew.

Simone shows no emotion at all. 'We saw him in the afternoon,' offers Ruby. 'My sister and I. Down in Appledore. We went into the Smuggler's Arms after our walk and he was in there. Drinking.'

'Yes,' says DC Rice. 'We'd gathered that already.'

'My husband went to look for him in the evening,' says Maria.

The police turn to Robert. He clears his throat and speaks. 'I couldn't find him,' he says. 'We were worried when Milly and

Ruby came back and said they'd seen him, so I went down and looked, but he was nowhere about. I thought I should try, you know?'

'And what sort of time was this?'

'Sevenish, eightish? I wasn't really paying attention. It was before supper, though.'

I try to remember when he came back. I can't. But of course I was up in my room for most of the evening, then out in the garden with the Medusa.

'I looked for a while,' says Robert. 'I checked all the pubs in Appledore, as far as I know. I thought perhaps he'd gone on to Bideford, but that's far too large to even start, really. I didn't see his car.'

'He had a car?' DC Rice gets his notepad out and jots it down. 'I don't suppose you know the numberplate, do you?'

We all shake our heads. 'It's a Fiesta,' I say. 'Old, sort of greeny-blue, bashed-in front wheel well.'

He jots again. 'Right,' he says. 'And were you alone when you conducted this search?'

Robert shakes his head. 'No. I had another family friend with me. Charles Clutterbuck. The former member of parliament. He's staying at the Grand in Ilfracombe, if you want to verify.'

'He was a drunk, you know,' says Simone. 'Everyone was doing what they could, but in the end . . . '

'Yes.' He looks at us all speculatively. Another one who knows, I think. They've looked him up on their computers and worked out the connection. 'I'll make a note of that.'

'He was an old friend of my son-in-law's,' says Maria. 'He would be so upset.'

'I'm sorry,' says DC Rice. 'You could do without this, with all you're dealing with.'

'Yes,' she says. 'It's such a tragedy. Oh, poor Jimmy. I'm afraid we've all been half expecting to hear he was dead one day, but not like this. Oh, lord.'

'So,' he says, 'what time did he leave here?'

We all look at each other. 'Mid-morning, I think it was?' I say. 'Before lunch, anyway.'

'Any particular reason?'

The question sounds innocuous, but I know it isn't, really. Maria blinks a couple of times, then speaks. 'My fault, I'm afraid. I locked the wine cellar and he didn't like it.'

'Terry at the Smuggler's says that he was saying some pretty nasty things about you all,' he says. 'Sorry. I have to mention it.'

Maria looks at him. 'DC Rice, have you had much experience with people with substance abuse issues? I would imagine you have. Presumably you come across them quite a lot in the course of your work?'

He gives her a wry little smile. 'Once or twice.'

'Well, then,' she says.

'Sure,' he says.

'My son-in-law spent a dizzying number of thousands of pounds putting Jimmy through rehab,' she says. 'Several times. He was a good man. Loyal to his friends. But you know . . . sometimes . . . and alcoholics can be fantastically vicious when they're protecting their habits. I'm sure you know that, as well.'

'I do,' says DC Rice.

A pause.

'So . . . ' says Maria, all businesslike. 'Thank you for letting us know.'

'The other thing,' he says. 'Does he have a next of kin that you know of?'

And so it goes on. Tiggy and Inigo and Fred. More teenagers out in the hands of the world. 'He has three children,' I say. 'They live with their grandparents. Their mother died a few years ago, and, well . . . I don't think a custody hearing would have gone his way, you know?' I shrug. What can you say? The Jackson Associates are down to five. A pretty high attrition rate, even in people who lived as hard as they did.

The five of us walk them back to the front door, the Gavila charm switched on full-beam as they talk about the plans for the funeral, promise to contact them if we think of anything, discuss how they will be in touch with the Orizio children once their own travails are over. So sad, they all agree. Such a waste. I follow in their wake, admiring their grace, their composure, their wonderful teamwork. If only, I think as we stand in a row on the steps, Simone and Maria arm in arm as we wave the squad car off, if only my own family had had even a fifth of the unity the Gavilas have. Think how much easier life would have been: just simply, sweetly loving each other, the way they do.

Then the car disappears around the corner of the drive and Simone turns and slaps Maria full in the face.

Chapter Forty-Two

2004 | Sunday | Maria

Maria has something of an eidetic memory when it comes to lists. Once they're written, she can tick them off in her head as she goes along. She's left the original copy with the men, who lack this particular talent, but still, as she watches the suburbs of Bournemouth crawl past, she is ticking things off; seeing her handwriting in her mind's eye crossed through with black ball-point pen. Bottles (oh, God, so many bottles) to the recycling, tick. Jimmy's medication bag on to the *Gin O'Clock* as he refuses to part with it, tick. Annexe cleaned, scrubbed, bleached, dried, polished, scattered with Simone and Joaquin's belongings as though they have been there all weekend, tick. The men are in charge of breaking the lock on the sliding doors into the kitchen, of ensuring that the hole in the fence is large enough to fit a man and not just a teenage girl, of scrubbing every surface, every piece of grouting, every corner, to make sure they're clear of residues; I'll tick them off when I see it's done. Clear internet history, tick. Oh, God, I must check what they've all been doing online and get them to clear theirs as well. You're only as strong as your weakest link, and there are so many links to worry about.

She turns to Linda, next to her on the back seat of the Clutterbucks' people-carrier. Of course they have a people-carrier, though it's a rare day when it carries more than two people. Nothing less than a Chelsea tractor for the great parliamentarian. She's the weakest link of all, she thinks. She's the one I need to keep on side, the one we all need to keep an eye on. Ruby and Fred are playing some toddler game on the other side of her that involves slapping each other's hands and squealing, absorbed as only toddlers can be. Simone is in the front seat while Imogen drives, and Joaquin, Inigo and Tiggy are in a row, singing, badly, in the seat in front of them, and God help us if the police want to see how many seatbelts we're using.

'How are you doing?' she asks, quietly, though she doesn't think any young ears are listening.

In the daylight, Linda's tan looks patchy. She's one of those women who renew it every day, scrubbing off the old layer of skin with salt in the shower and leaving murky deposits for other people to clear up, but today she's neither bathed nor slathered, and the line around her jaw looks a bit like a clown mask.

'Awful,' she says. 'I feel awful.'

Yes, I know. You're more sensitive than the rest of us. All narcissists are. Only you can see the true horror, while the rest of us just swim in our murky soup of incomprehension.

'We all do, Linda.'

She imagines that somehow everyone will let her off because she's special. She's the one I need to work on. The rest of them understand how much trouble each of them, personally, is in. Linda's such a goose she thinks the trouble is all about everybody else. I might have to get Sean to keep her on side, she thinks. I know he tires of them quickly, these women, but Linda might have to end up as a fixture for a bit. He might even have to come up with another wedding ring, what with spouses not having to testify and that. Just for a while. We can sort something out for the long run.

'None of you seem to realise,' says Linda, 'how serious this is.'

Again with the special. Maria is well used to handling narcissists. In her line of work they're ten a penny. But you can make anyone do anything as long as you give them what they need. Imogen needs to be told how brilliant her husband is, how every sacrifice she makes is for the greater good. Simone likes to be told what to do. Jimmy just needs to know that his supplies won't be cut off. Someone like Linda? Praise her specialness and threaten her status. Easy.

She allows her eyes to well up. A skill she learned early in the day. Nothing flatters a narcissist more than receiving the empathy they never give. 'You're so right,' she says. 'You always get it when other people don't, don't you?'

You really can't overdo the flattery, with a narcissist. Linda's shoulders expand with satisfaction. Maria puts a hand on her arm. Squeezes. 'You're so strong,' she says.

'I don't feel strong right now.'

'We all depend on your strength.'

She leaves it a few beats, then, 'Have you thought?' she asks, 'what you'd do with the kids?'

Linda blinks. 'Do with them?'

'If you go to prison. Would your parents be able to take them on full-time? Only, they're not young any more, are they? Do you think they'd cope?'

'What do you mean?'

'Well,' says Maria, 'if this doesn't work. If they find out. It won't look good. You know how it'll look, to other people?'

Always remind a narcissist how other people will see them. It's the thing they think about the most of all.

Linda blenches. 'But I didn't *do* anything.'

'They could,' she presses on. 'You understand that, don't you? If someone's indiscreet, if someone lets it out. Jimmy? Do you think he can keep his mouth shut?'

'Oh, Jimmy,' says Linda, and starts fiddling with her phone. 'Christ, no.'

'And you?'

'Why me?'

'We're all in this together, Linda,' says Maria. 'We can't go and get Coco back now. We have to go all the way with this. A united front. Because no one will believe you weren't involved. You know that, don't you?'

'Oh, God. This is *so* unfair.'

Maria says nothing; just leaves her words to sink in. Looks out of the window and starts ticking off the list again. Everything that's been in contact with the child is on the boat. Even those bedsheets that have been through the washing machine, that dress Ruby was sick on, that might have got contaminated. It can go into the water before we get to Brighton. Even cadaver dogs can't smell a corpse on something after it's spent a few days in the sea. Robert's going to pack up our family's stuff so we can take off once we get back from Neptune's Kingdom. Should I leave Linda down here? Can she stick to the plan? I have to trust her. We're all going to have to trust each other. In a lot of ways they're the easiest bunch I've ever worked with. The only person who's going to be shedding genuine tears over that poor little girl is her mother.

*

352

Neptune's Kingdom is swarming, but Gina at the office has done her job and their VIP tickets are waiting at the front gate along with the press manager's assistant and a photographer. The promise of a boy-band photoshoot in the spring, whoever the spring's boy-band turns out to be, will open a lot of doors. The women, silent and tense in the car, leap into character as soon as they step from it: Imogen the veteran of a thousand of her husband's pratfalls, Linda at last, it seems, grasping that her performance is important. Simone looks like a smug little cat, running with a child on each hand and hoisting them into the air the way the people who actually birthed them haven't been able to do in a decade. Maria feels a swell of pride at how well she's trained her. She's our daughter in every way, she thinks. Thank God it was her who was here, not the Jackson girls. Imagine trying to persuade Milly that she should keep this a secret.

She strolls forward to greet the PR, her best professional smile on her face. 'This is so good of you,' she says.

'Not at all!' says the PR, though she must be longing to get off home again and carry on with her barbecue or whatever it is you do to amuse yourself in Bournemouth on a bank holiday. 'A pleasure!'

She hands out their special gold wristbands. Puts them all on everyone's left wrist until she comes to Ruby. 'Ooh!' she says. 'You've already got one!'

Maria laughs, gaily. 'Yes! She's got a twin who wears one on her right wrist. I gave them to them so we could tell them apart. Haven't you, Coco?'

Ruby waves her arm in the air. 'I'm *Coco*!' she shouts. She's enjoying this game. More fun when Coco's there, but still she's delighted by how many people she's managing to fool. She's not reached an age where she's realised that not everyone knows who her family are yet.

'Well, welcome, Coco!' says the PR, and slips the wristband on to her other wrist. 'I hope you have a lovely day!'

They pose for a quick round of photos and go in. Change into swimsuits, and the littlies – even Tiggy, who's officially down to waterwings – get to pick out a new rubber ring each from the stall beside the wave pool. Tiggy picks out a pink pony with a streaming tail made of glitter. Fred and Inigo choose to wear Ninja Turtles. Ruby stares at the choice for a long time while the teenage shop assistant fiddles impatiently. She fingers a blue dolphin with eyes the size of saucers, then reluctantly selects a pink pony like Tiggy's.

'Are you sure, Coco?' asks Maria, loudly, so the assistant can hear the name.

'Yes,' says Ruby. 'Blue's Ruby's colour.'

'Oh, I don't suppose she'd mind. We could get one for her too, maybe? We should take her a present, for being under the weather.'

Ruby brightens. 'Yay!' she cries, and snatches up her dolphin.

'Okay, everybody,' cries Maria, handing over her black card so the purchase is registered at the till, and treating the CCTV camera to her largest, brightest smile, 'last one in the pool's a jellyfish!'

Robert calls at three o'clock. Maria is exhausted. They're all exhausted. Imogen fetched double espressos for all the women as they took it in turns to close their eyes on the concrete-bottomed sand-covered 'beach', and they've barely even scratched the surface of their exhaustion. Simone takes Joaquin and Tiggy off to the slides and Fred starts up a tantrum about not being allowed to go too. Linda, in her gold mesh bikini, grabs his arm so hard Maria is sure there will be fingertip bruises there later.

'Shaddap!' she yells into his four-year-old face. 'I don't want to hear it!'

A couple of Boden Catalogue women a few feet away give them a Mumsnet look. Linda spots it, snarls a 'What?' in their direction and they recoil. Christ, thinks Maria, it's probably a good thing those kids spend so much time at Granny's.

'Mummy's awfully tired, darling,' she says smoothly to Fred, and smiles at the targets of Linda's wrath, waggling her eyes in give-me-strength sympathy. 'Why don't you go and play with Coco? She's over there. Looks like she's going to play on the Sea Monster.'

Fred trots away, more than happy to get away from the raging gorgon they call his mother. 'Coco!' he calls across the crowded beach. 'Wait for me, Coco!'

Maria finally gets to answer the phone. 'Darling?'

'How's it going?'

'Fine,' she says, loudly, aware that the Boden mums are still watching them, still earwigging to see whether she remonstrates with Linda. 'We're having a wonderful time. How's Ruby doing?'

'Sean's crying,' he says. 'I don't know what to do.'

'Oh, poor darling,' she says. 'But they get like that when they're under the weather. Why don't you give her a drink and send her to bed for a little while? Poor Linda's got a terrible headache, too.'

'Oh, shit,' he says, understanding the code they worked out long ago for talking in front of strangers. 'Are you going to be able to get her under control?'

'Yes,' she says. 'Once she has a swim and thinks about things she'll feel better, I'm sure.'

'Okay,' he says. 'Well, let me know if I need to have a word, won't you?'

'Maybe later. Perhaps if Sean—'

'Claire's called a couple of times.'

Oh, Christ.

'I told her you were at the water park with the girls and she seemed to take that okay.'

'Okay, darling,' she says. 'Well, we'll just have to call her later. She wasn't sounding like she was going to come back, was she?'

'No. She sounded like she might be going to call a lawyer on Tuesday, frankly.'

'Oh,' says Maria. 'I'm sure she'll have bigger things to think about by then.'

Chapter Forty-Three

Maria's hand flies to her face where the slap has landed and she stares at her stepdaughter the way someone stares who's been petting a pussycat and has just been informed that it's a cougar.

Simone shows no sign of being disturbed by what she's done. In fact, she's smiling, that weird *Mona Lisa* smile I remember from way back. Dropping her head to look up at her stepmother through her hair, the way she does.

'Simone,' says Robert, and his voice is full of despair.

'Shut up,' says Simone. Her voice is calm, as though she's handing out orders to the cleaner.

Ruby lets out a breath beside me, and it's only then that I realise that I have been holding my own. I exhale, breathe sharply in. Simone's eyes swivel to take me in, but her face doesn't move.

'Don't you ever, ever speak for me again,' she says to Maria.

Maria stands there holding her cheek, her mouth half open.

'*Simone.*' Robert's voice comes out as a low moan.

'This is my house,' says Simone. 'You have no jurisdiction here. I don't need you to speak for me. I would appreciate it if you remembered your place.'

'I'm sorry,' says Maria, humbly. 'Simone, we were only trying to help.'

Her voice turns scornful. 'As if I need your help.'

'Simone—' Robert tries to begin but she snaps him silent with a raised hand. Have you ever seen a cobra about to strike? Something about her reminds me of that. Robert gulps and falls silent. He's scared of her, I think. My God, this family is just wall-to-wall secrets. Was Dad scared of her?

'I've never needed your help,' she says. 'You interfered and you interfered, but I never did. He was my husband, and this is my house. He was always going to be mine. I didn't need you interfering, persuading yourselves that you somehow *gave* him to me when he was always going to be mine. I didn't need you to do *anything*. Do you get it? You think you're so . . . clever . . . but you're not. You never controlled *anything*. It was all me. I did it all myself. You're just . . . ' – she curls her upper lip, as though she's smelling drains – 'you're just *bit* players.'

Ruby's face is scrunched up with confusion, her eyes flicking from person to person. The drawing-room door opens and Joe emerges, sees us all standing in the porch like an early American painting and freezes. Doesn't say anything, just watches.

'I'm sorry, Simone,' says Maria again. 'We've only ever wanted to look after you. Your father—'

'Shut up, shut *up*!'

Ruby, still kiddish, trying to be grown-up, puts her head on the block. 'Are you okay, Simone?'

Simone whips round, bares her fangs in my sister's face. 'What are you even *doing* here? You don't deserve to be here.'

Ruby recoils, goes pink. 'I – sorry – I . . . '

'Christ,' says Simone. 'Stupid little girl. He didn't want you. He couldn't even stand to be in a room with you. You don't even deserve to be *alive*.'

Ruby gasps. Turns on the heel of her Doc Marten workboot and runs off up the hall.

'Jesus!' I say. I start off after her, but Simone shoots a hand out, grabs my wrist. She's surprisingly strong; jerks me back so I feel my shoulder give. Digs bony fingers in around the bracelet.

'I'll go,' says Joe, and jogs towards the stairs as Ruby runs up them. Oh, God. Oh, my *God*. Oh, my little sister. I want to chase her up there, throw myself on her, smother her with love, tell her lies about how it will all be okay. What sort of person says something like that? Was she always this vicious?

And then it's my turn. The smile is back. She looks – God, she looks pleased with herself, as though she has some fantastic trump card that she's ready to play.

She plays it. Pushes back my sleeve and holds out my wrist so Robert and Maria can see. 'I see you've found it, then,' she says, and treats me to a smile of such cold sweetness that I can't suppress a shiver. 'Daddy, Maria – did you see that Milly's found Coco's bracelet? Why do you think she hasn't said anything to anybody? What do you think that *means*?'

Silence. I have a horrible, disturbing feeling that all three of them are as old as time, that I'm being watched by dragons, that calculations are being made and odds weighed up. The house and grounds suddenly feel terribly far away from anywhere else. I feel myself sway.

Then Maria bursts into tears. Puts a hand on the door jamb as if to support herself and turns her face to the sky. 'Oh, God, Simone,' she sobs, 'how could you? How *could* you?'

Simone laughs, a nasty, triumphant laugh, and walks off. Her footsteps click their way up her cold and lifeless corridor, but no one moves to follow.

'Darling,' says Robert, and goes to comfort his wife. He touches her on the shoulder, then enfolds her in an embrace. That's what I should be doing, for Ruby. And I find myself overwhelmed by a sense of loss because there's no one to do it for me, never has been, because I never learned how to hand out such comfort myself. Their daughter might be a crazy fuckup, but the Gavilas themselves are strong and united. And I envy and admire that in equal measure.

And I'm torn. I want to go and do the right thing by my little sister, to learn how to do the caring thing properly. But I'm so close, now, to finding out what Robert and Maria know. And it's clear that they *do* know more than something. A lock of hair drops loose from Maria's elegant chignon and covers her flaming cheek. Robert gently tidies it away behind her ear with the back of his knuckles. Such a tender gesture. They look into each other's eyes and he nods. Just twice; slowly and regretfully. Then they both turn to me and he speaks.

'I'm sorry,' he says. 'We've not been honest with you.'

I follow them into the drawing room and he closes the door behind him. 'Come and sit down, Milly,' he says.

'Mila,' I say, a feeble attempt to take some modicum of control back into my hands.

Maria perches on the edge of a sofa, takes the clip from her hair and puts it down on the coffee table. Shakes the hair loose, a waterfall of shiny chestnut. 'Mila,' she says. Her voice is soft and low and carries the burden of the ages. 'Yes, I'm sorry. We've not been listening to you, have we? I'm not surprised you want to be a different person. God knows we all do. There's not a person among us who wouldn't go back to the beginning of that weekend and do it all differently.'

I wait. They're going to tell me something that will break my heart, I know that.

'I think you must have guessed that what happened to Coco isn't the same as the public story,' says Robert.

I nod. Maria takes in a gulp of air and covers her face with her hands. 'Oh, God. Oh, God, Mila. We didn't mean any harm. We didn't mean it to come out like this. You have to understand. Everything we did, we did with her best interests at heart. We had to protect her. She was so little.'

Protect her? Didn't do a very good job of that, did you?

'And it was stupid,' says Robert. 'A rash, panic decision, and we've all regretted it every day since, but once it was done it was too late to change.'

'What?' I cry. 'Please! What? What are you telling me?'

Robert sits down beside his wife. I continue to stand; cling to the dominant position while they gaze up at me like supplicants seeking absolution. I stay over by the door, space between me and them, my exit route easily accessed if I need it. I no longer feel secure in this house, not that I ever really did. Even if you suspect that you've been lied to, confirming it still shakes your whole world.

'Her whole life would have been ruined,' says Maria, and another sob comes out with the words. 'She didn't know what she was doing. Claire would never have forgiven her. She could never have lived with it; it would have ruined her *whole life.*'

They *can't* be talking about Coco. They're talking like Fundies explaining why they burned their tainted daughter in her bed. 'Who? *Who are you talking about?*'

She tosses her hair off her face and looks me direct in the eye. 'Ruby! I'm talking about Ruby!'

I judder to a halt. 'Ruby?'

'It can't . . . oh, God, Mila. It was the worst moment of my life. Worse than – than *anything*.'

The strength goes out of my legs. I sink on to one of the hard ebony thrones that sit either side of the door. 'What happened?'

'She didn't mean to do it,' says Robert. 'God, of course she didn't mean to do it. She was three. She won't even have known what drowning was, really. She just thought – well, I can't say what she thought. She was just little.'

'They were sleeping in the downstairs room,' says Maria. 'It was boiling hot down there. We should have got a fan. All these things you think of after the event. If we'd got a fan, we should have checked the locks, *why* was the alarm not on? But I keep thinking: if they'd had a fan . . . I don't know. I was boiling. I woke up at four in the morning and the house was silent and I couldn't get back to sleep because it was just too *hot*. So I went downstairs, and I thought . . . I thought maybe if I had a swim and cooled down . . . it didn't even occur to me to look in their room. The door was half open, I remember that. But I thought, you know, that Sean must have left it that way to give them some air. And that damn door lock. I don't think any of us had realised it wasn't working. The key turned fine, you see. So I think, you know . . . everyone just thought when they went through it all weekend that someone else must have been through before. I didn't even think about it then. Just thought, oh God, someone must have forgotten to lock it, I must remember to do that when I come in.'

I stare at them both. They look broken. Robert seems to have shrunk inside his big-man suit, and Maria's face is streaked with mascara and eyeliner despite her attempts to quietly mop it up. It's a chilling sight: both of them naked before me, undone.

' . . . and she was by the pool,' she says. 'Sitting on a sun-lounger, wrapped in a towel, and Coco . . . oh, *God*.'

She starts to sob again. I go cold. Then hot, then cold again. Oh, God. 'What happened?'

'You remember how much she loved the water?' asks Robert. I nod. Having to shepherd her back from the sea that day in Poole Harbour, over and over; Coco always happy to just sit in the sand, but Ruby always wanting to go out there, to paddle just that bit deeper, wanting to wade, wanting to feel the little waves from the boats slosh up her chest, always in danger of taking herself out of her depth. I remember thinking that she was weeks off being able to swim. A water baby.

'She only wanted to swim,' says Maria. 'She didn't *mean* it. But Coco wouldn't go in. So she pushed her. No ring, no water-wings; nothing to help her keep afloat. She didn't even know what she'd done when I found them. She thought Coco had learned to swim under water, that she was at the bottom of the pool because . . . *oh* . . . '

Robert puts an arm round her.

'And we couldn't,' he says. 'We just couldn't. Your father was *destroyed*. And we thought, you know . . . the blame. Not just her, but him. They would probably have prosecuted him, even though none of it was . . . meant. And we looked at Ruby, and we thought, oh, poor kid, poor, poor little kid, she's so small. Imagine carrying that burden with you for the rest of your life. The child who killed her sister. And Claire. How was she going to live, knowing what had happened? Living with the daughter who'd killed her other daughter? You've seen her. She's fragile enough as it is . . . '

'It was a stupid thing to do,' says Maria. 'But we were in a mess. Everyone crying, and all these thoughts – the other kids, how we could explain. And Ruby. She was just sitting there, all smiles, thinking she'd been clever. She wanted to go back into the pool. When her dad came down. And he couldn't even *look* at her.'

'So you . . . '

I remember them. Stupid little puppy creatures, still half formed. Oh, God, poor little Coco. I have dreams, sometimes, in which I'm drowning. The breath, that last breath, getting bigger and hotter in my lungs as it fights to burst out, the struggle towards the surface. Would it be less bad, if you didn't know what it was? If you didn't really understand about death?

I realise that tears are pouring down my face. I think about Ruby, crying upstairs, enough of a burden as it is, being the surviving one. I can't do this. I can't tell her this.

'It was all such a rush,' says Robert. 'None of us was thinking straight.'

'You're saying you . . . disposed of the body?' The words sound vile. Like a police report read out on the news. Something gangsters do, or rapists, or men who don't want the expense and inconvenience of a divorce. Not us. Not people like us.

They both go silent. Both thinking about the things they've done, how it must look to the world.

'Yes,' says Robert, eventually.

I don't want to know. I don't want to know how they did it, what they've done. I think back to them all, that weekend: those glossy, handsome, confident people, so sure of their place in the world, so certain that their money and status had armoured them against everything.

'It was stupid,' says Maria. 'I know you think it was stupid. But we had to make a decision before the other children woke up. I think that was partly it. Just the thought of the other kids, all those little children, waking up to discover what death was. I know. We were half out of our minds and we did what we thought was best. We didn't want that poor little girl to have to grow up like that.'

I'm still in shock. Distant, somehow, from my thoughts. 'And you thought that this was . . . better?' I say, slowly.

'I suppose we did at the time,' says Robert. 'And then, once it was done, and the whole hunt snowballed and everyone was looking for her and the whole world was watching, it was too late to back out. What could we possibly say that would have ended without all of us in prison and Ruby labelled a killer forever, in front of the whole world?'

I shake my head. Crazy. It's crazy. 'But she didn't *mean* to . . . '

'I know. I know. I told you, we weren't thinking straight. And it would have been the same, for Claire. Every time she looked at her, that's what she'd have seen, and what sort of way is *that* to grow up?'

'I don't know what to do,' I say again. 'I don't know what to think.'

I can feel them both watching me, waiting. 'So Simone knows?'

'Simone was there.'

'And did you . . . did she help?'

Maria's eyes fill with tears again. 'Mila, we *all* helped. Once it had happened, once the whole thing had started, we *all* helped.'

'And no one tried to argue against it? Not one of you?'

'I know it's hard to believe,' says Robert, 'but you weren't there. And you know, when you're in a group, you just . . . '

'Whose idea was it?'

'Your father's,' they say, together, with a single voice.

'He was devastated,' says Robert. 'But all he could think about was what it would do to Ruby.'

'And to you,' says Maria. 'You were so young. He loved you all so much.'

Me?

I think. What *has* it done to me? Is it worse, now that I know the truth? Now that I know Ruby as an almost-adult, now I feel responsible for her, now I've come to like her? Now she's no longer an amorphous blob that represents my grievances, but a whole human being who weeps for other people and tells jokes to get through? Can I destroy everything she knows about herself, just for the sake of revealing the truth? Everything that Claire knows? If there's one thing I do know, it's that, despite their problems, those two love each other, demonstrate it, are at ease with it in a way that no one on my side of the family has ever managed. Can I really destroy that?

And Dad. To blame, all my adulthood, for everything. Keeping a secret that must have ripped him apart every day. In my head I've been calling him a psychopath, a narcissist, a borderline, and all that is turned on its head. The emotionless affect, the obsession with work, the constant search for control, the huge wheezing laugh that always somehow seemed that little bit empty . . . they're all different now, open to interpretation. Everything about the man is different, now I look at him through the prism of his despair.

'I don't know what to do,' I say, once more.

'You must do what you think is right,' says Maria. 'I'm so sorry that Simone has put this burden on you. If you can find it in your heart to forgive her . . . she's not thinking straight, Mila. She's so unwell.'

'I should find her,' says Robert.

She lays a hand on his forearm, strokes it with a thumb. Gazes at him with adoration. More people who love each other, whose lives I could destroy.

'Of course,' I say. 'I should go and find Ruby. I understand that Simone's not well, but Ruby's dreadfully upset.'

I don't know what to do. I really don't know what to do.

Chapter Forty-Four

2004 | Sunday | Sean

The Gavilas leave at half-past five. They had always been scheduled to leave this afternoon, and, despite being a couple of hours later than they'd intended they still hope to cover the seventy-five miles to Brighton before nightfall. The *Gin O'Clock* can easily manage thirty knots once they're past Cowes, and though the nights are shortening they'll still have dusk until well into the evening. The rest of the party breathe a sigh of relief as they trundle their cases off up the road to the harbour. Joaquin is undoubtedly the weakest link in the plan. Boys don't notice much the way girls do, it's true, but even he would have been likely to clock eventually that there was only one twin.

Public performance has drained the women of the last of their strength. The kids' supper is a silent affair of ham sandwiches and the remains of the watered-down orange juice, a handful of grapes each. The fridge is almost bare, but no one has much appetite anyway. Ruby is back to being Ruby, and

Coco is in bed already. It's very easy to fool children. They ask questions all the time, but they're really not interested in the world beyond themselves, are generally content with the simplest answers and a diversionary tactic. A bit like a lot of millionaires, he thinks.

'So,' says Imogen, as the last crust is torn off a quarter-sandwich and shoved to the side of the plate. 'You know what? As it's the last night of the holidays and you've all been in the pool all afternoon, I think we can miss bathtime tonight.'

A wail goes up. No bathtime means early bed; that much they have all taken in. And, though they're dropping on their feet, no child wants the day to end. Imogen waves her hand in the air. Sean is impressed by how composed she has been today, how efficient, once she understood what was needed. She has, he supposes, been running political gatherings, helping her husband pursue agendas, for nearly twenty years, and the single-mindedness shows. 'How about,' she says, 'we all line up on the sofas and I'll read us a story? How about that?'

'What story?' asks Tiggy, suspiciously.

Imogen holds up a book and they all eye it. Of the six of them, only Tiggy can read, and their skills haven't got much further than cats sitting on mats. No geniuses among them, thinks Sean, and thank God for that. My Coco was no genius, either. She would never have grown up to save the world, or lead it.

He feels a lurch and waits for it to pass. Already Coco is moving into the past, a tragedy that has happened. His powers of recovery have always been little short of miraculous, and he likes that about himself. Other people weep and wail for weeks, months, years, but Sean has always had his eyes on the future. It will be difficult, the next few months, he thinks, but I will get through. And Claire: Claire doesn't even know what's about to hit her. She still thinks that the worst that's happened in her world is losing her husband.

'Simone left it for you,' says Imogen, and holds up the dramatic cartoon cover for them all to see. 'Look! It's the new Harry Potter!'

There's an outbreak of oohs. Not one of them can have actually experienced Harry Potter, he thinks. It's a crowd delusion, this. They all want him because they see the older children going mad for him. They'll be bored stupid listening to something so much too old for them, but they will never, ever admit it until someone else does. 'And we can have hot chocolate,' says Imogen. 'How about that?'

Another ooh. Hot chocolate in high summer: they've never heard of such a thing. 'Go on,' says Imogen. 'Everybody go and get into your jammies, and by the time you've done that the chocolate will be ready. Biggies look after littlies, yes? Take care on the stairs!'

'Do we get our vitamins tonight?' asks Inigo Orizio.

'No,' says Linda. She's barely spoken since they came in, moving mechanically from sink to fridge to dishwasher to island to table, her eyes puffy and her expression grim. But she's got past her protests of the small hours; seems to have taken in that it's too late now, and she has no alternative but to go along. 'You're all better now. You don't need them. Just a little one for Ruby, because she was sick last night, but the rest of you are all sorted. Go on. Off you go. You stay here, Ruby. I'll go and get your pyjamas. We don't want to wake Coco up. First one back gets an extra marshmallow!'

The children run off, Ruby left sitting at the table.

'Imogen, do we have to?' Sean asks.

'Yes,' she says. 'We need her to sleep. I'm sorry.'

'But can't we . . . '

369

'Christ,' says Jimmy from the couch where he has been sitting staring silently into the dead fireplace. 'It's a herbal one. Not the same thing. You think I'm completely stupid?'

Sean doesn't answer. You said the dosage was safe, he thinks. Last night you were laughing at Claire for being unsure. But he's become strangely passive, this evening, as though the leadership has been sucked out of him. The pill is on Maria's list, so it must be taken.

'I'll need you to clear off there, Jimmy,' says Imogen. 'Make room for the littlies.'

Jimmy's head turns, and his face seems to follow seconds later. He has aged overnight, his skin grey and the flesh drooping. Sean could swear that the amount of grey in that slovenly stubble has increased. 'Where should I go?'

Imogen shakes her head wearily. 'I don't really care,' she says. 'I think Charlie's down in the gazebo. Why don't you go and sit there? In fact, all you men should clear out, really. Let us get them settled.'

Jimmy levers himself off the sofa and sways a little. He's even moving like an old man, thinks Sean. Did he not even keep a few of those drugs back for himself when he handed the case over to the Gavilas? He looks as if he has lumbago. He follows him out through the doors, into the early evening. Another beautiful night to come. The sky is almost entirely clear, just a couple of pinky wisps of cloud high up above their heads. Like yesterday, he thinks, only so not. This time yesterday we were halfway down the second bottle of fizz and a great night of pleasure stretched out in front of us. This time yesterday I was going up to see what Claire was going to inflict on us by way of clothing. This time yesterday, I was the king of the world.

His phone rings. He glances down at the display and sees that it's his wife. I can't, he thinks. I know Maria said I should, but this much I cannot do. She'll hear my voice and she'll know that something's wrong. And tomorrow she won't believe me. He sends the call away. She's rung six times today already. To pick a fight, or speak to the girls. Should have taken them with you, he thinks. If you'd taken them with you, this would never have happened. He's already wiped from his mind the fact that by the time Claire left, Coco was most likely already beyond saving. The human mind is miraculous in its defence of the ego.

Charlie sits on a sofa in the gazebo and stares into the air, much the same way Jimmy was doing in the kitchen. He looks up as they approach, and it's obvious from his expression that their arrival is unwelcome. All day, in moments of inaction, they have been avoiding each other: taking up positions where the others aren't, each filling his head with reasons why they, personally, are not responsible.

Sean and Jimmy sit down, each on his own separate sofa. On a normal day, Sean would be reaching into his pocket for his cigars, setting about the warming and the snipping and the ritual lighting. But this evening he feels desire for nothing. I'm dead inside, he thinks. Not even pleasure will help me. He sits, and drums his fingers on the armrest. Looks at the glass table top, freshly washed and wiped and polished. There's no sign at all, he thinks, that anything happened here. No sign of the fun we had.

'There must have been something wrong with her,' says Charlie. He speaks into the air, as though he's consulting the oracle. 'She must have had some condition or something.'

'Yes,' says Jimmy, his eyes unfocused. 'She had the same as all the others. It should have been fine.'

'If only,' says Sean, 'she weren't so paranoid. If she hadn't picked a fight with Emilia we would have had someone to look after them.'

371

'I did everything I could,' says Jimmy. 'You saw. Didn't you? The adrenaline did nothing.'

'It's not like we're the only people,' says Charlie. 'People are so fond of judging, but we're hardly the only ones, are we?'

'No,' says Jimmy. 'Doctors do it all the time. It's totally safe.'

'Normally,' says Sean. 'How was I to know? You're a doctor. You said it was safe. It's not my fault.'

'It was,' says Jimmy. 'It shouldn't have happened. There must have been something wrong with her.'

They sit on and ruminate on their misfortune as the evening deepens. Indoors, Imogen and Linda read the children to sleep, carry them to their beds, tuck them in, ready for the morning.

Chapter Forty-Five

'Oh, no,' says India. 'Oh, no, oh, no. Oh, those poor little girls. Oh, no, Milly.'

I've taken the phone down to the hotel garden while Ruby showers in our tiny bathroom. I'm weary to the bones. Ruby too. Though she slept at some point, her tears assuring it, I lay silently, staring at the dark.

'I can't tell her, can I?'

I'm not really asking advice. I know already that I can't.

'No,' says India. 'I don't see what that could possibly achieve.'

India was right, about the truth. Some truths will shatter worlds. Some secrets are best kept, though the keeping can eat you up. Ruby is a sweet young woman whose burdens are already heavy. How will smashing her life achieve anything other than some clumsy tabloid interpretation of justice?

I think of Coco, bones bleached at the bottom of the ocean, and the sadness is overwhelming. Nothing will bring her back. A rash decision put her there, but no one killed her. Not with wickedness involved. A broken door lock, curious minds, an adventure turned to disaster and the idiot decisions of minds in frenzy. And nothing will bring her back. She's gone for good.

India is crying at the other end of the phone. I've not witnessed her crying since she was thirteen. She doesn't cry. We don't cry. Jacksons are not weepers, but oh, the sadness. 'I should have come,' she says. 'I don't believe I thought it was okay not to. But I . . . oh, God, why didn't they tell us? I've been despising him all this time and I never really knew him. And Claire. Oh, poor Claire.'

'And poor Ruby.'

'She can't find out, Milly. She and Claire, she can't find out.'

'No,' I say. 'No, they can't. He took the right decision.'

'He did,' she says. 'Oh, Camilla. Is it too late for me to do something? Send flowers? Something?'

'I'll take some for you,' I say. 'If there's anything of him left, he'll know.'

Black tights, black slip, black dress. Black shoes for each of us, flat for the uneven ground in an English graveyard. A strange calm has settled over me. I half expected to wake in tears this morning, but it didn't happen. Instead, I got up in the dark and wrote my eulogy sitting on the floor of the bathroom while Ruby slept, because I know now who he was. He wasn't the monster I'd come to believe. Self-centred and thoughtless, but in the end everything he did since Coco was intended for good. It wasn't only Claire and Ruby who lost her that day: it was us as well. I never knew her, and that's my own fault. I can, at least, make sure that I have one sister in my life.

Ruby has put her hair into a single plait that rolls thickly down her back. Her dress is plain on the top, black crêpe, the skirt pleated down to the tops of her knees. She's obeyed her mother's admonishments and wears lace tights whose only holes are the ones woven into them. I've only just realised that she is short-sighted, as she's wearing a pair of heavy-framed glasses because she's afraid she'll cry her lenses out. And after my night's no-sleep in the hotel where we decamped last night after Simone's outburst, I am filled with that eerie calm that took me over the day I went to see his body three weeks ago. Really, only three weeks? It feels like years.

The church starts to fill half an hour before the service: a parade of expensive cars nose-to-tail along the verge all the way through the village, chauffeurs gathering under the unused lych-gate in their dark coats, banging their hands together in black leather gloves and waiting for their employers to disappear inside before they start smoking. The modern pieties: tobacco *verboten* in front of millionaires, but nobody cares about smoking in the sight of God.

Simone stands in the porch like a siren, smiling, her parents flanking her on either side. *Thank you so much for coming. So lovely to see you. So kind of you to come.* The scandals – not the old one, not the one surrounding his death – are clearly not enough to put the coterie of bankers, arms-dealers, politicians and their younger wives off coming to the party. They compose their faces gravely as they pass the pair of press photographers by the main gate, only to break into beaming smiles as they recognise each other among the graves. I glimpse the Clutter-bucks, glad-handing men whose quality suits declare them useful. I suppose once you're old enough, once you've been to enough of these, most funerals become social occasions. Places where you see people you haven't seen in years. And, because they're usually shorter than weddings, they're a lot more fun.

Ruby and Joe and I mill self-consciously among the grave-stones, handing out orders of service and smiling weakly at all the people who don't know who we are. It's Simone's occasion; we accept that. We are essentially the bit parts, lucky to be given a few lines. Emma is passed placidly from mother to grandparents as their arms tire, dressed in powder-blue and extracting coos of admiration as people pass by. I feel Ruby tremble beside me. I don't know what she expected. I know some people see a death in the family as an opportunity for attention, but I don't think that's either of us.

And then we're going in. That familiar smell of wood polish and candlewax, of cut flowers beginning to turn by having their feet in ancient oasis, the pootle-pootle-pootle of an organ played freestyle as everyone finds their seats. We walk to the front, and I feel a little stir among some of the people. *So that's the other family. How many were there? Is that all of them? Is that the twin?* And then we're sitting on the right, Simone and her family on the left, nothing between us and my father, safely wrapped in his panelled oak coffin. They make them out of banana leaves these days, and cardboard and even wool, but it was always going to be the oak of Olde England for Sean. There's one floral arrangement alone lying on the top: a small white bouquet. Everything's been done by Maria, efficient Maria, taking responsibility so no one else has to. Leaving Simone and Emma alone and stately in their grief.

And then the music changes, and we're singing 'Guide Me O Thou Great Redeemer', and my hand is shaking because I remember the big deal he'd make of the rugby, how he'd take a box and go with his buddies for a good singsong, and I'd forgotten that right up until this moment. So many things I don't remember, won't remember now because the cues will never be there. Ruby doesn't remember at all. She's singing out bravely, dabbing beneath her specs with one of the Kleenexes I slipped in her pocket before we left the hotel, but to her it's just a hymn. And then Charlie is booming out a piece of Christina Rossetti and some vicar I've never met before is talking about my dad and how he's in the bosom of Christ when God knows he's probably gone the other way, and I'm walking up the aisle to the lectern and the whole world has focused in on the wodge of paper I've got in my hand, and on not looking at anyone's faces, on keeping my voice clear and steady and on sounding, above all else, like a whole real person giving account of the man. I think of all the things I thought I would say yesterday, and the deep sea-change that's gone on within me and how all the anger I've carried with me all these years is pointless, useless, in the face of this loss. And I speak.

'I've been thinking so much about my father over these last days,' I say. 'How there were parts that only I knew, and parts that only each of us knew, how nobody ever really knows the whole of another person. But what I do know is this. Sean George Jackson loved us, in his own rough, vibrant way, and by that we are all uniquely blessed.'

Language is weird. I hear my voice as I speak, and I hear the responses – the laughs, the sighs, the holding of breath. But, inside my own head, these words I've written sound of nothing; make as much sense to me as the barking of a fox in the woodland. I hear syllables and consonants and mellifluous alliterations, but the sense has flown away. And then I reach the end and my face suddenly flames as the crowd swims back into focus, and I'm desperate to get down from there, get away from all those eyes. I force myself to fold the papers, step down slowly, give a small, loving bow to what's left of Dad, and walk back to Ruby. Sit for a moment as she gives me the British arm-rub of consolation, and then the tears come, howling out from wherever I've kept them imprisoned, breaking over my head like a wave, and I'm drowning. The organ starts up again, the congregation stands and Ruby and I stay there in our seat, bowed forward together, rocking. 'Dear Lord and Father of Mankind,' they sing, and I weep and weep and weep.

Chapter Forty-Six

2004 | Monday | Claire

She doesn't wake until ten o'clock; the first time she's slept this late, or this long, since the twins were born. When she looks at the clock she feels a second of panic at the oversleep, then she remembers. Relaxes her tensed muscles beneath her Egyptian cotton sheets, starfishes into the cool side of the king-size bed where he so rarely sleeps these days. Remembers again what has brought her here alone and tenses once more with rage and sadness. *What has happened to my life? Is it my fault? Did I bring this on myself?*

Of course I did, she thinks. I was plenty old enough when I met him to have no excuses for what I did. I know people like us like to throw around those tired old phrases. *We couldn't help ourselves. It was bigger than both of us. The heart wants what the heart wants.* But there is always – always – at least one moment when a choice is made.

I knew he was married from the moment I met him. Good God, Heather was even in the same room, looking harassed and frizzy-haired, but it didn't stop me. I just tamely handed over my business card and knew perfectly well what doing so meant. I could have stopped it before it even started, but I didn't. I made a decision at another person's expense, and I'm paying the price now. It serves me right. It serves me bloody well right. I remember several people saying it, the warning – *Claire, if he can do it to one wife he can do it to you* – but all I did was rid myself of my friends so I didn't have to see the adulteress reflected back at me in their eyes.

She checks her phone to see if he has returned her calls, though it's been sitting beside her all night and she's known since he didn't return the first one that he wouldn't. Sean likes to punish with indifference. If he feels slighted, he'll throw up a wall of silence around himself that is impossible to penetrate until he decides he's done enough. It's infuriating, frustrating; it fills her with rage and impotence.

And hang on. She sits up. What am I saying, *if he feels slighted*? Has he really trained me so totally that I'm forgetting that he's the one in the wrong?

I must make a list, she thinks. Take a leaf from Maria's book and start being organised. Make a list of all the things I must do once this bloody bank holiday is over. Get funds transferred into my bank account so he can't freeze me out. Find a lawyer. Change the freaking locks. Once he brings the girls home, he's out. He can go and live in one of his luxury condos. It's not like he has a shortage of them.

She gets up and makes a cup of coffee, takes it with her to the bath. The house is wonderfully silent, only the murmur of traffic out on the King's Road to remind her that there are other people at all. I won't be able to do this, of course, she thinks. Not for a while, till they're old enough for me to be able to leave them alone and close the door. I can bet that if it turns to war I'll be running the house, running the kids, without the help of staff.

Well, so what? Other people do it. It's not as though I grew up in this sort of luxury. I know how to work a hoover, cook a meal, mend a car. Only another year until they go off to school, and then I can get a job. Get a life. See if any of the people I used to know still want to know me. My God, I've been such a fool, making myself so dependent on him, letting him cut me off, one by one by one, from the people I knew before. I think he's a psychopath, really. That thing, where one by one the old people disappear from your life because he doesn't like them, or they've offended him, or you've become so unreliable from catering to his last-minute whims, it's a classic abuser tactic. He may never have hit me, but there's more to abuse than being a punchbag.

She longs to speak to them. Her little ones. Regrets leaving in the night without taking the time to sweep them up, but she was in such a state that all she could think of was getting out. Getting away from those people and their secret smirking. Humiliation can kill you as surely as sadness, she thinks. But I'm not taking it any more. Today's the day when I start my life again.

She slides beneath the water and holds her breath.

At eleven, hair wrapped in a towel and body wrapped in her oversized silk bathrobe, she goes downstairs to make more coffee. She's lost her appetite over the past twenty-four hours. Stirred some pasta round a bowl at ten last night and ended up throwing it in the bin. Which in itself is more like me, she thinks. I've been eating my misery for the last few years, but a crisis always makes me want to fast. No wonder I couldn't shed the baby weight, with the drip, drip, drip of gold-plated hopelessness falling on the back of my neck.

She looks around her kitchen. Sean's kitchen. Not a room she would ever have chosen for herself. He's done it all out in white, except for the black granite work surfaces that are an even greater hell to keep clean than the cupboard doors. No handles, anywhere. Press and slide, press and slide, a man's fantasy of living in a spaceship. And the garden she sees through the floor-length windows: paved side to side to save on weeding, a horrible formless Henry Moore knock-off in a pond of gravel in the centre, the only vegetation a pair of palm trees in gigantic pewter pots. Palm trees, for God's sake. We're in the middle of London. We need a paddling pool and a sandpit for the cats to crap in and beds where the girls can learn to grow tomatoes, not a fricking *palm tree*.

She rings again. No answer. My husband is a shit, she thinks. He's probably palmed them off on Linda to look after while he enjoys his last day. Well, I hope she enjoys them. It's the last she'll ever see of them.

The coffee is good, and strong; filter, the way she likes it, not the endless fuss and spraying steam from the overlarge, over-complicated espresso machine that looms on the work surface waiting to burn the grind. One of her fingernails has chipped in the rush to take her luggage from the car. Claire looks at it, holds her hand out to admire the damage. Smiles. And no more freaking manicures, she thinks. I'll find the nail scissors in a bit and cut them right off.

She goes to his study – takes a small, profound pleasure in invading his sacred space – and digs out a notepad from the bottom drawer of his desk. No time like the present, she thinks. I'll start my list now, in the sunshine in the garden. Once the girls get back there will be too much noise to concentrate. She pours herself another coffee and opens the door.

She's lost in thought till lunchtime. Planning, dreaming, thinking of all the good times ahead. I could sell this house, she thinks. Or he could buy me out. It all seemed so dream-come-true once upon a time, living in Chelsea, going to restaurants every night, swanning from shop to shop. Funny how your priorities change when you understand what these pathetic consumer dreams actually cost. A little house will do us somewhere. In the country, where the schools are nice and you know your neighbours. South, near the coast. But not near Brighton.

She is so absorbed that she almost doesn't notice the doorbell when it goes. Sean has, of course, installed a low, smooth electronic ring that won't disturb his peace and quiet when someone else always has to go. It's not until it goes again that she takes in that she'd heard it the first time. She stands up and re-ties her dressing gown. It can't be him, she thinks. No way he'd have got them up and out in time to get back to London for one o'clock. Won't be the postman, not on a bank holiday. Who is it?

She takes her time about walking up the stairs; half hopes that whoever it is will have got bored and left. And then she looks through the spyhole and sees two police, a man and a woman, their hats held in their hands and serious looks on their faces, and her world falls apart forever.

Chapter Forty-Seven

We leave straight after. We packed our bags last night and put them in the car before we set off for the funeral, and don't even bother to change back into civvies; just jump into the front and drive in our mourning weeds. Back at some hotel on the seafront in Ilfracombe, one that's been cleared of its character, Seanwise, to go with the Damien Hirsts, stout middle-aged men are spitting pastry as they laugh over Good Times Had and Good Times To Come, and Simone stands in the middle in her black satin muu-muu, smiling that smile until her face freezes. I don't know if I will ever see her again. Or Emma. I should try. Later. Further down the line when the shock has worn off and, perhaps, just perhaps, the frenzy of her bereavement has died back. I've already lost one sister, barely have contact with the other, nearly never found the third. I must try. Family matters, I understand that now. And God knows, Emma will need my help one day, if Simone doesn't get better.

We barely talk until we're almost back at Arundel. But it's a different sort of not-talking from on the way up. We've cried ourselves out for the time being, and an odd sense of peace has descended. Or perhaps it's exhaustion as much as peace. I've noticed that crying – really big, wild crying – can give you a sort of high. Endorphins, I guess. Or God's little joke.

But we have changed. Over the course of four days, my whole life has changed. In dying, in losing the control he'd exerted over his darkest secret, my father has renewed my life and given me a sister. The true story of Coco's fate has done nothing to change the way I've learned to feel about Ruby. All it's given me is a determination to protect her from it.

We try music for a bit, but west of the M25 my radio never seems to pick up anything other than Radio Two and phone-ins about incest. When we find that three stations back to back are playing Simply Red, I hit the off switch and she doesn't object. Just settles back, folds her arms and falls what seems like instantly asleep, her head against the window and her braces glinting in the light from the dying sun. Ruby, my little sister. I promise I'll look out for you. Take care and protect you. Because of you, I am becoming a better person.

And a tired one. A worn-out, wrung-out, fatherless child. My life will never be the same again. And though I know there will be bitter regrets about how I judged him, all the lost time and the wasted opportunities, I'm grateful that, in dying, he's given me at last the chance to love him. Life is a strange collage of greys. No wonder I've had such difficulty appreciating it, when all I've been looking for is black and white.

As soon as the road signs for Arundel get down into single digits, she pops awake, stretches, gives me the big eyes and says, 'Macky D's.' Interweaves her fingers in prayer position and looks at me like a starving puppy.

'My God,' I say. 'Are you psychic or something?'

'My last Big Mac till term starts,' she says.

'Term?'

'Oh, please. You don't think I let her make me do more school than any other teenager, do you?'

She waits. Sees the sign for the services come up and presses her knuckles to her chin. 'Pleease,' she says, 'pleasepleaseplease-please *please*.'

'Christ.' I put out my blinker and turn off the road towards the golden arches. I swear I'll never go near the place again, after just this one last time. Those fries must contain kiddy smack.

We take it in turns going to the loo and changing out of our funeral gear while the other one queues, and I give her my wallet when it's my go. When I come back out in jeans and tank top, she's already sitting at a table with the lid off her milkshake. 'I got chocolate this time,' she says. 'You should try it.'

'Never,' I say, 'in a million years.'

Ruby shrugs, and grins. 'You'll see. One of these days, when you least expect it.'

'Please. Hypnotist now, are you?'

She shrugs again and applies herself to dunking.

'Are you looking forward to seeing your mum?'

She nods, and eats.

'I'll bet she's missed you.'

'Of course she has.' She waggles her head. It's so amazing, the way a fifteen-year-old can vacillate from twentysomething to eight in the course of a few hours. 'She larves me.'

'Would you like to go to school, Rubes?'

'Oh, God, would I? I'm turning into the freak on the hill.'

'Well, I wouldn't go *quite* that far.'

'Yes, but,' she says.

'This weekend must help,' I say. 'You've been so amazing. I

don't think she could possibly think you wouldn't cope if she'd seen you.'

'Yeah, but she didn't, did she?'

I wrinkle my nose. 'I'll tell her,' I say. I'm staying the night at Downside. I'm so tired I think I'd be dangerous driving back to London tonight.

She grunts and eats another chip. 'Mila?'

'Yes?'

'Will you come back? To see me?'

'You want me to?'

Her hand stills. 'If you want to, yes.'

'Okay, then,' I say. 'I'll try and make some time in my busy schedule every now and then.'

'Fuck off,' she says. In a good way.

And so we go home. Through the dark, rain flickering in the headlights. Mills Barton is all shut up for the night, glinting light through paned windows so twee I want to stop and lob a brick. Ruby is sitting forward now, tense with anticipation, peering through the windscreen as though the trees will pass more quickly if she counts them off. 'D'you think she's been okay?' she asks.

'I'm sure she'll be glad to see you,' I reply. I mean, how do I know? I've seen enough madness this weekend that I'm not predicting anything. But you know – suddenly Claire seems the least unbalanced of the lot of them. I'm actually looking forward to seeing her. Who would have thought?

I pull up at the gate and she jumps out to open it. The rain is coming down full pelt now and she's got her head wrapped in her coat. Swings on the gate as I pass through then runs back, laughing. 'Welcome to the seaside!' she says. 'We get the best winds up here.'

And we trickle through the woods, come out the other side and, as our headlights hit the house, the door opens and light floods out on to the puddles in the drive. Roughage barrels forth, turns circles, dances in the spotlight; huge white teeth flash and his tongue lolls out to catch the rain. Ruby throws the door open and suddenly the car is full of wet dog and she's crying fit to burst, smothering his muzzle in kisses as he covers my upholstery in mud. And then there's Claire, standing in the porch, looking out at us, her big cardi wrapped tight around her body, and she's smiling.

Epilogue

2004 | Saturday | Simone

I'm a little miracle. He said it; he called me a little miracle. It's not in my imagination. He *notices* me.

She dances on air down the harbour road. This is the best night of my life, she thinks. I shall remember it forever. This wonderful dinner, and getting dressed up, and he sat me next to him because I'm special. He doesn't see it yet, still thinks I'm too young, but underneath, down where you *know*, he's already noticed. He said I was pretty. He said I was smart. He said I was a miracle . . .

The evening breeze caresses the bare skin on her arms, makes her shiver with pleasure. Everything is perfect. All of it. I see for certain that he doesn't love her. She's everything that is wrong in his life. Wonderful Sean Jackson, tied down by a vampire, having his joy sucked out just so she can feel that she's right.

Her confidence grown, she does what pleases her most, when she is alone: tests out how her own name sounds attached to his. Simone Jackson. Mrs Simone Jackson. Mrs Sean Jackson. I know I'm too young, still, but it's not just a dream. He notices me. He does. He *sees* me.

All is quiet at Harbour View, but the lights have been left blazing all over the house to make it look as though it is occupied. Simone makes a stop at the downstairs bathroom mirror, combs out her hair and smooths another drop of glosser on to make it shine. Linda has left a browny-pinky lipstick by the basin; Chanel, she sees from the label. She examines it, likes the colour, smears a little on her lips and sees them bloom fuller, darker, and is pleased. She spends a little time practising her poses. Drops her reflection into three-quarter angle so the hair falls across her eyes and looks up through it, curls the corners of her lips up coquettishly. He will see me, she thinks. He's seen me now, and when she's gone he'll see me again. More and more, until he doesn't remember what there was before me. They think that age gaps are wrong, but they don't know. It's not my fault I was born so late, nor his that he was born so early. Love is love is love, and my love will conquer all.

Time to see to the children. She gives herself one last smile and drops the lipstick into her little evening bag. Linda won't need it. It doesn't suit her the way it suits me. Then she goes to the kitchen and opens the drawer. The pills that Linda used tonight are still in their strip, lying in the fork compartment. She pops out a couple, to be sure, then lifts up the cutlery tray to find the ones she hid beneath. Yes, there they are. Small and white and pointed oval in their little blister pack.

Simone takes them over to the kettle, fetches a bowl and pops them, one by one, into it, crushes them with the handle of a fork. Puts six spoons of sugar in and dissolves it all in a little boiling water. Tastes it. The sugar is strong, but that is good. It masks the bitterness of the medicine. She dilutes the syrup down

389

to drinking consistency in a little glass, washes up the bowl and the fork, wipes down the countertop. Puts the blister pack into the bag with the lipstick. There's a bin on the front she can pop it into on the way back to the restaurant.

The annexe is warm with sleeping bodies. Simone tiptoes in, kneels down beside the Jackson twins. They're out for the count, top to toe and lying on their backs. She shakes Ruby by the arm first, then shakes her again. Her eyes roll and she begins to stir. Her forehead is warm and her hair is sticking to it. Never mind, thinks Simone. No need to worry now.

'Hello, darling,' she whispers. 'Mummy wanted me to give you your medicine.'

Ruby grizzles and tries to push her away. She lifts the little girl up to a sitting position, puts a hand behind her back. 'It's all right,' she soothes. 'Come on, darling, just a little drink.'

Ruby doesn't even open her eyes as the glass touches her lips; just lets the liquid into her mouth and gulps until half of it has gone. Curls straight back up and is asleep again the moment she does so.

She crawls up to the other end of the bed, wakes Coco. I'm sorry, she says, inside her head. Sorry, little girls. But you're making him so very, very unhappy. You won't even know about it. Just drift away and never wake up, and then he will be free. Nothing to tie him to her then. He said so. If it weren't for you . . .

Coco is easier. She doesn't even protest, just squeezes her eyes shut tighter as she takes the syrup into her mouth. Simone lays her back down and looks for a moment. Caresses her cheek, gently.

'Night night,' she whispers. 'Sleep tight.'

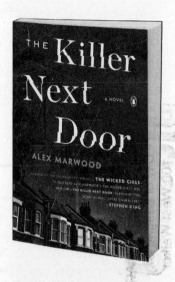

The Killer Next Door

Everyone who lives at 23 Beulah Grove has a secret. If they didn't, they wouldn't be renting rooms in a dodgy old building for cash. The six residents mostly keep to themselves, but one unbearably hot summer night, a terrible accident pushes them into an uneasy alliance. What they don't know is that one of them is a killer. He's already chosen his next victim, and he'll do anything to protect his secret. Marwood's tightly paced thriller will keep you up at night and make you ask yourself: just how well do you know your neighbors?

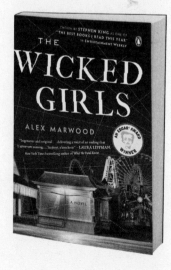

The Wicked Girls

On a summer morning in 1986, two eleven-year-old girls meet for the first time. By the end of the day, they will both be charged with murder. Twenty-five years later, journalist Kirsty Lindsay is reporting on a series of sickening attacks on young female tourists when her investigation leads her to interview carnival cleaner Amber Gordon. For Kirsty and Amber, it's the first time they've seen each other since that dark day so many years ago. Now with new, vastly different lives, will they really be able to keep their wicked secret hidden?

PENGUIN BOOKS